The King of Erotica
II:
The Crown

I am whut I am
I be whut I be
I be whut I see
I see whut I be;
I be whuteva,
whuteva makes me bleed
if I am to be phony,
then my ghetto becomes
Insolent Dreams:

BY DAPHAROAH69

Dapharoah69 Presents: The King of Erotica 2: The Crown

In case you were wondering:

This fiction novel is a creative work by Larry Wilson. The characters, incidents and dialogue is the product of my imagination. This work in no way reflects people I know or deal with. Any similarities to people, dead or alive, are purely coincidental.

—The author

The KING of Erotica II: The Crown ™

Published by T.K.O.E Publications
ISBN# 978-0-6151-5308-7

Cover Photo: by Steve Shires, Fort Lauderdale

Inside photos by Adriyel Todman (88 Entertainment) and Larry Wilson, Naranja, Florida 2007

First printing, 2007

Printed in the United States of America

When You
by Dapharoah69

When you look at me
you see beauty, sexiness
raunchiness.
When you touch me
You feel lust, passion,
pleasure and satisfaction.
When you kiss me you taste
ancient ruins
mistakenly camouflaged as
taste buds.

When you listen to me speak
you hear
Confidence!
Elegance!
Intelligence!
When I look in the mirror
I see a crooked smile
self-doubt and a painful past
when I touch myself
I feel alone, deserted
and misguided.
When I kiss my reflection
I taste air, emptiness
and the atmosphere.
When I hear myself speak
I hear echoes
reverberations
air, intoxications
and broken silence.

ALSO BY DAPHAROAH69

The KING of Erotica I: The Throne
The King of Erotica: Throne's Special Edition

PHAZE PUBLISHING EBOOK:

The Diary and the Strap

ANTHOLOGIES DAPHAROAH69 BEEN FEATURED IN:

Voices From Within (co-editor)
WSN 2007
Mocha Chocolate March 2008

MAGAZINES FEATURING DAPHAROAH69:

Body Positive Magazine May 2001
Voices From Within
Book Club

CLIK Magazine's 25 Most Eligible Bachelors in America, October 2007

ACKNOWLEDGEMENTS:

Everyone who got a copy of the *King of Erotica I: the Throne* I thank you so much. For *me* the book was a huge success. From South Africa, Brazil, London and Puerto Rico, to the U.S. people have purchased my book online and I appreciate the feed back and the love that has washed over me. I thank God for that.

This book is dedicated to the ghetto. To me the ghetto is a very beautiful place. I'm at home there. I'm content and I'm familiar. This is for the people who never picked up a book and read one. I urge you to try it. This is for my family, of course. Quincy Lathan, thanks for the love and support you've shown me. Damian Campbell. You inspire me, and thanks for having my back. Without you I would have never seen the flaws in writing, my growth or my emergence. I thank God for you. For Tamereka Cassimere. I love you so much. Thanks for always being there. Victoria and family, love ya'll, especially *you* Ashley. Matthew Anders; I love you very much. My sister Chandra McCray. I'm proud of you for finishing school. My brothers, ya'll are a goddamn trip sometimes, but I love you, wouldn't have it any other kind of way. My little brother Tyrone Payne. Congratulations on graduating high school. Another black man with a diploma. The world better watch out. Adi Todman, thanks for being there for me and always helping me out. Thanks for the bomb ass photo shoots and helping me capture my vision. For Jedi, Miss Danielle. Love you always my dear. For David Jackson, hope you didn't think I forgot about you, you've been there for me damn near more than anyone, and for that I love you. Darlene, C.J. and family love ya'll very much.

Without all of you I am nothing.
Dapharoah69. The King of Erotica

DAPHAROAH69

THE CROWN

To the strongest woman I know.
A woman who is my mother and father.
You may not think I appreciate you.
You may not think I respect you.
I am my own person. I am my own man.
You may not support everything I do.
Whatever I do may never be enough.
I don't care what people say about me.
I never have.
I'm glad I made mistakes. I'm glad I made bad decisions.
Taught me something. That I can grow.
That I'm far from perfect.
That I don't have to live up to no one's expectations but my damn own.
Friends have come. Friends have gone.

Friends have died. Family have come, gone and died.
But you're still here.
I am an author. A writer.
I have already changed lives with the very words
I write. I have won award after award.
But I do love you.
Always.
For all your hard work and struggles.
For all your tears and sacrifices.
For all your complaining and strife.
For everything you have gained and lost.
This book is a living testament
that out of the darkness comes
something greater.
Your son.
Writing his poor heart out.
And I thank you.
For everything.
Love you.
Larry.

I write to express myself,
and that's the only
impressing I'll
ever do—Larry the King of Erotica

THE KING OF EROTICA II: TABLE OF CONTENTS

SHORT STORIES

Author's Praise
the KING of Erotica
Part I:
The Throne

"If you are a fan of Erotic poetry and stories, look no further than Larry Wilson aka The King of Erotica and his latest book: *The King of Erotica: The Throne.* Each piece is crafty, sensual, sexy, passionate, and last but surely not least, creative. I especially enjoyed the poems 'Plagiarism.' And the short stories 'Rayne in the Bedroom,' and 'Purple Panties.' Larry goes deeper than merely describing a sexual scene to readers with the obvious endings and outcomes. In *The Throne,* you will see Erotica taken to a new level that is compassionate as well as sexually stimulating." ~Anthony Chavon Hanes, author of *An Abstract World Vol.2*

"*The King of Erotica: The Throne"* is a back flipping compilation of the known facts. You hunger for more when you read it. I love the way he touches on every source of subject matter. He's a poet of his own design. I've been touched by Mr. Wilson to release my words of wisdom and not hold back my artistic nature. His many titles can startle you as you're reading one thing and it ends in a whole different consequence. I can't wait until he releases many more books in the future. God Bless you Larry that you succeed in many of your success—Iona Gaines: Author of *Poetic Lyricist.*

I have a special place in my heart for authors who *aren't* afraid to write about those taboo subjects that make other writers *shudder*! I *admire* a person who writes without fear, pouring their heart and soul into their work without apology. When I begin a novel, a poem, or a short story, I am looking for something. I am searching for that special spark that calls out to me and makes me raise my eyebrows with admiration.

Larry Wilson, Jr., AKA the King of Erotica, sufficiently accomplished all of these things with his debut collection of short stories. In *The King of Erotica: the Throne*, Wilson took me through a flurry of emotions as I flipped through every single page of his beautifully put together book. I am in awe of his raw, uncut, in-your-face literature, and I applaud his confidence and dedication in bringing the audience what they came for—Naiomi Pitre: Author of *Broken Vows* and *In the Panty Drawer*. www.naiomipitre.4t.com

Larry C. Wilson, Jr. is hilariously blunt and descriptive in his writing. You'll fall head-first into the pages of his books and get consumed by his world. The mixture of steamy scenes and raw human emotion is enough to make you laugh, cry, and say 'Oh, no he didn't write that!'

all at the same time.

Reading Larry's work is an escape into a forbidden world you never knew existed, yet are pleased to have found. His erotic stories leave you thirsting for more while prompting you to reevaluate your standards and inhibitions. If you're open-minded, you'll appreciate every line that is written. If you're closed-minded, be prepared to unlock your mind as well as your heart.

I found it a struggle to close up *The KING of Erotica: the Throne* and do some writing of my own. Do not read his books in public. People were staring at me because I couldn't stop laughing and shaking my head with a smile on my face.

He's called *The KING of Erotica* for a reason. You will be left satisfied—Jenise M. Dew/Ccep: Author of *Vanity*: a collection of thoughts and emotions in poetic form.

Its very clear to everyone who's had the pleasure of reading Author King of Erotica...We definitely know that it's obvious to all that Larry Wilson has a way with words. His word flow will take ones mind to that inner love/freak you know those places we dare not always admit to others....See how much Larry will captivate the hearts and minds expressing his inner thoughts about how women need to be treated at all times!"

Watch out fellas...If you're not careful, Larry will school a brutha on how you need to treat your woman—J. Silas Green—Founder of Diversity Entertainment and Media Group, (Atlanta, Georgia)

STRAIGHT FROM THE FANS: ABOUT THE THRONE

When I find myself stressed and needing a release from reality I just pick up the book. Once I pick it up, I can't put it down. I get lost in the characters and it takes me to another place. Every detail is precise and you can actually visualize the characters.

The DL stories were eye opening to me because it appears to be a lot more common than I thought. Larry has an extraordinary imagination to come up with such captivating stories that grab you from the beginning to end. He puts his all into every story because of his description from A to Z. Larry Wilson is someone we MUST all look out for—Barbara, (Pembroke Pines, Florida).

What can I say but damn this book is hot! One of the best Erotic books out there. This book of short stories and poems are so visual the way he writes you see everything that's happening. You can really feel all the emotions and feelings that were involved with his very talented writings. This is a definite must have book—Sabby: Maple Heights, Ohio.

I was fortunate to come across a man of greatness in the world of Myspace blogs and books. This man is the King of Erotica, Larry Wilson. His blogs have consumed me and taken me to places that I may have never thought possible, but never imagined entering. I have been exposed to a world of erotic bliss that no one could have prepared better than the King himself. I have been challenged by the words that flow through the text. Tested by the scenarios that lay on the pages before me. Encouraged by the content of which I have read. It has been a rollercoaster ride of erotic ecstasy. Each time I read another story it enhances the inner most part of my erotic being. The book I read and read again. That is a true testament of how magnificent it is. The King touches women indeed and men as well. He is a complete package that should never be overlooked or ignored for he is great. It is a pleasure to be in the circle of talent known as Larry Wilson Jr. King of Erotica—Dean Smith (Life long fan and friend).

Often when individuals find something impressive, they begin expressing this with the phrase, 'words can not describe...' However, in this rare exception I can say, with full honesty, the words are clear and defined as to the brilliance in the work of Larry Wilson, Jr., the self-proclaimed King of Erotica. Do not be fooled by this show of confidence, for Wilson's work fully supplements this title he has given himself. The reader is guaranteed to find him/herself in complete awe at the vivid imagery of his work, as he confesses inner most thoughts, shares his deeply rooted fantasies, and pours his pain out through his pen and pad. His work does not leave you breathless; rather it provides one with a rhythmic flow of respiration, as each verse symbolizes his inhalation of life itself, and exhalation of perceptional visions as only a King could see it. I highly recommend his work, and there is great assurance that once readers examine this poetical prowess, they will do the same—R. J. Andrews, 'the Voice of Reason'

Larry Wilson is a breath of literary genius. He lives within his poetry and short stories. When you are able to feel his soul it can only from someone who has felt these emotions deeply and has the ability to use ink and paper to express it.

You are unable to wait till the next part or chapter to find how it ends, the words use to define the power of his poetry is limitless. Always leaves me thinking.

That is a true writer, when you can't wait day to day to see what else he has to offer—Me'Chelle Faulk-Moody (Beaumont, Texas)

EMAILS: THE GOLDEN MASK

God damn...now that is hot and makes me salivate for more...the best part is the imagery....considering that I used to live close to Dadeland Mall just makes this even more x-citing!—Rasta Puppy, (Trinidad).

Wow Larry I just sat here with my mouth wide open, whoa and now I will take a lil' trip to my bedroom and close the door!—German Chocolate, (Germany).

AND you remain the King of Erotica—Sweet Desiree, The UK (United Kingdom)

Continue to REIGN on YOUR throne....The King of Erotica you are....Talented and Amazing!!—God's Poetic Voice, (Florida)

EMAILS: PURPLE PANTIES.

Damn, that was a very deep, very realistic story, wonder if it has happened to you before? It almost sound like a memory, you kind of write better from a man point of view in what he said, but also how she felt when it happened. What it boils down to is that women do stupid things too, but usually we don't do them to hurt anybody, maybe just to calm the freak in us and know that we still sexy and desirable? Anyways, the story is real good and I would like to read some more, I coulda went reading on and on, so that means you know what u doing, you are a good writer, and when you talked about how she felt when she was all horny and wanted her man up in her, I knew *exactly* what you was talking about and how she felt, my God how do you know all these things about women? You must sit down and really study us? Either way you know what you talking about, I really liked your story, and it was also easy to read and easy to get into it fast, I couldn't stop once I started, keep it up baby boy you have skills!—Melanie. (Germany).

You have a great talent my friend and I know you have led an interesting life cause your words are so—in your face—What hit me the most was the

Pink because your favorite spot on your body is your pussy and pink reminds you of that and your favorite food is shrimp, grilled shrimp with extra Lawry's

Season Salt and Louisiana Hot Sauce, which is more for flavoring. And you are a Leo, you hate Valentines Day, your wear your bra one size too small cause you like the way your pretty titties look in it, you hate chocolate, you detest peanuts and your favorite entertainer is Patti Labelle.

This lets you know he is in this because of emotions whereas she just wants to fuck. How's that for real life. A lot of people think men are the only ones that just want to have sex--yet I've found nowadays men want home and heart more then women and I see you have also discovered that fact—Hope, (Houston, Texas).

It's sounds real; some can relate, You got me playing a movie in my head so I laugh, smile then got sad and surprise, that was deep....I love the fact that you'd know how a woman would react, I'm guessing that's why you have us all as your fans!!—Passionate Sweet: (Canada

Emails: The Strap

I love it! I was holding onto the edge of my seat praying that this didn't have some drastically crushing sad ending. It seemed too good to be true. I'm so glad everything worked out happily.

That really made my day, OMG thank you so much Larry. And I'm so glad to see you back!—Boss Lady. (Chicago, Illinois).

YES YES YES.....OMG! That was *so* hot! You're just fabulous! And a great talent! God has truly blessed you in the form of writing, never give up on your dream—Rodney Wifey, (Miami, Florida).

Damn... my ex-boyfriend was 11 inches.... and I didn't get any of it. We had to wait 'til we were married...Part of the reason why he's an Ex—Angel, (Texas).

Over 12,000 copies sold

Wind is like a soft
Finger, wiping
Away my tears as if I'm
Air, galloping like
Gentle white horses
Destroying storm clouds,
Taking the black,
Becoming one with them
And out comes the black stallions.
Yet I stab the clouds
when I reach for the sky
and they don't bleed.
Where's the blood?
Where's the pain?
—dapharoah69: Larry Wilson 2007

The S:O:U:L of a Woman

Let there be light,
and somehow darkness came about.
Let there be water,
and somehow ocean shores,
and heightened cliffs
brought about perilous drought.

Man couldn't do it alone,
so God dug into the earth,
removed several ribs
to create something so elegant,
so real and so pure
even Adam took one look at her and
his heart skipped a beat.
Meet the Woman,

elegant and sensual
witty and intellectual
outspoken and loving
When she's happy she's loyal and giving
when crossed, Hell hath no fury!
She will reluctantly take flames
And burn infernos
into obsolete ashes.
She has eyes that strike
appreciation from the masses,
she has a keen mind that have professors
rewriting lesson plans and rearranging
seating arrangement in classes,
she has a voice so soft and pure
out of blackness comes stellar vessels;
she has breathtaking curves
That got a lot of automakers fired
because they didn't rethink the motor vehicle.
Back in 1883 women were considered property,
They couldn't sue and be sued,
Men were the sole owners of American
Families
God sent Abigail Adams
who stood up and fought for women equality
so why should I demean women
just for my own sexual pleasures,
Because 50 Cent and selfish rappers
sell the unique souls
Of our beautiful women in music videos?

Many years ago to say that I loved women
would have never progressed in my mental;
because I had so much hate for them,
so much hate for myself
the sight of a woman excited
what was in my silk briefs
but in my mind my hate remained,
I was lost and confused,
my days didn't have a woman's touch,
I cried at night, tore up pictures of females in
my family
because I thought I would never miss women
that much
Hoes in the hood had me blind,
sluts had me open wide
drug abusers had me vexed,
single women with many babies
said they had it hard,
I rolled my eyes and went on about my merry
way,
not wanting to hear that mess.
But my body went through withdrawal
and my soul rejoiced the day my only sister was
born
God recreated the vehicle in my heart
when my nieces came about this earth
with innocence that needed protection,
so my stellar lesson is that I have
new found faith for my adoration and love

for the Soul of a Woman
and you all came along
changed my views
showed me love,
with all the lovely things you do,
you built my confidence
you accepted me for who I am,
you have reached out to me,
some even causing my cell phone to ring
well after the AM hours,
somewhere around three.
I am in love with Lady Gemini,
She is my chosen Queen.
I love you,
I love you all
and if men can't understand that,
I suggest you tap the missing spot
on your rib cage
and take it up with
God.

MAMA'S WOMB

Sometimes:
The butterfly
finds the cocoon
it left behind
several seasons ago
to try to recover
the serenity and the
security
it once had.
If only I could

shrink in size
return to my
Mama's Womb,
go through
a rebirth.
back to
a seed.
give daddy
back his ballot
labeled "absentee."
and let Mama's body
shed me in the form
of her monthly period.

WHAT IS AFRICA?

What is Africa, my words aren't nowhere near
the observations of Cullen Countee
what do I know?
I'm just the Erotic KING.
I don't quite know my "Heritage."
I don't think I'll ever know.
I've been stripped of my soul,
Right on down to the pelvic bone

In my life there are a series of gaps
Taught to me by racist teachers
About Africa,
Hide from Larry's eyes Queen Hatshepsut
Teach him about Queen Elizabeth
In class I forced myself to go numb
I didn't wanna learn about the bitch!
Confuse him about Pyramids
Make him study Napoleon.
Martin Luther King
Was only an "I Have a Dream" Speech!
African Warriors Superstars
were from my mind disbarred.
Hollywood doesn't know glamour
Africa's the Heart of Earth
of which my very essence
was finely chiseled before my birth.
No wonder I'm an enigma
As misinterpreted by the Zulu King Chaka
No wonder I resist tempests
Like Africa did to European rule
No wonder in school
My white teacher told me we were only slaves
And she pissed on my soul
By showing me and my angry black friends
Roots.
No wonder I don't understand myself,
who the *hell* am I?
Even history books are stark contradictions.

Leaving me wondering
am I fiction or non fiction
Professors *can't* get it right,
Archeologists tend to get it wrong,
You can't find two that *ever* agree.
Even Africans sold themselves to slavery.
Africa is now an embodiment of a whorish stripper
After her incongruous number,
A mass of sweat, all riches snatched,
new laws hatched
Warriors who don't consider us black
A land that don't want us back
A brain-mashing misinterpretation
Currently being taught and lectured
To young ignorant black kids
While they are still teaching us that *Lie*
A hero was that of Christopher Columbus,
I don't think so.
With a hundred different biases
now our mis-education.
Or lack there of.
There in the problem lies
Just ask J. A. Rogers.

GOULDS FOREVER

Barbra Streisand

Tonight, in class
Dis Caucasian lady got mad
Cuz dis niggah
didn't like Barbra Streisand!
On my face a spark didn't ignite
from the gentle hymns of
Frank Sinatra's talented plight.
But today I was criticized
Cuz at Hitler, Stalin, Bush
and the Confederate flag
I threw mentally sharp darts.

And now hangs the pictures of Harriet,
Sojourner, and Hatshepsut
That made her frown her face,
And seemingly want to barf.
Then I got personal,
Remembering the two white men
Who pissed on me in a Miami alley
when I was 14.
Because I kicked one of them for calling
My black skin a disease.
And I still stood up,
my heart broken in two
Keeping my head pointed towards God
and said, "Now, ya'll have a nice day."
I told dat Caucasian lady in my class
"Look, *what* has Barbra Streisand
done for a Niggah like *me*?"
When did the bitch hop in her flashy Rolls,
take a ride through the inner city
That shaped my masculinity
To get a look at our poverty?
The lady turned up her nose and tried to leave
And I said, "*Wait*! Miss High Society!
Don't ask me to have any sympathy
for the selfishly wealthy!
And don't *you* worry
some of my *own* black people
unfortunately fall into that category.
My grandmother died

after spending years cleaning
white people's toilets
back in the 60's and 70's.
Your kind watch us on TV
Being shamed sexually,
talked about haphazardly.
And when our great leaders die
they barely cover .00011 of the bottom
Left hand part of *USA Today*.
Its *not* about colors,
But you made it an issue with me.
You said blacks are always in the news
But Charles Manson and Jeffrey,
Who ate human bodies
Seem crazier than me.
So don't make me put my fist,
Up against your dimples.
And knock away them
Golden, shiny Shirley temples.
Bye, I got to go:
Go back to the hood
And deal with my own kind,
Trying to steal each other's shine,
And on you I will keep my eyes
Listening to some R&B,
Turning Barbra off my TV.

The Heiligenstadt Testament: The Vision of the King of Erotica

By Johnny B.
F.I.U. Student

My absolute favorite non-fiction book would be *The Life of Ludwig Van Beethoven*; the Bicentennial Edition 1770-1970. This isn't a book you just skim through in a day or two. No. This was a book you took your time to read. You dissected and became *one* with it. You *appreciated* it. That was until I read, in its entirety, *The King of Erotica: 1. The Throne.* I read about Beethoven a few times, getting from it the very passion dapharoah69 contains in the ink of his pen alone. His keyboard is fire! His body, passion! I have read this book through and through. Shocked at certain things, entertained, enraptured and eventually I was encroached inside his personified vision. He writes the very things people are scared to write; let alone talk about. He doesn't think on his peers' level. He is so beyond his years it's mind-boggling. How a young man who doesn't own his own home yet could possess such talent. He has the frankness of Tupac Shakur but throws a little James Baldwin and Langston Hughes in the blender, go a little deeper than Tupac, give Zane something other than erotic musings and you have a delicious drink. Dapharoah69. His thought process is simply divine. His smile is electrifying. He's a veteran of poetry, having studied Yeats, Shakespeare, Langston Hughes (his personal favorite) Maya Angelou, Imamu Amiri Baraka, and tons of others since the age of six, at the behest of his elementary school teacher. Miss Mike forced poetry on him. And for good reason. She was an angel sent to push him in that direction, because he had a voice. In the past he sat on his voice. Let others suppress his literary voice.

Now? He is screaming with it. Making people from the church he's come in contact with and ex lovers to certain family members shake. I had the pleasure of being invited to spend some time with the Erotic King, who is so much more than erotica. He's literature; he's pure talent sun-kissed with obvious scars of ghetto life. He bares scars inflicted on him from his older blood cousins, who he says "can kiss my ass if they don't like me or what I do. I'm so sick of them. I don't talk or go see half of them anyway and I haven't for years." He is a black man searching for a job. A black man who needed to be bilingual to get a job in Dade County, Florida. A black man who looked me dead in the eyes and said, "The hell if I learn Spanish! This is America! Goulds isn't *Spanish* so why the *fuck* should I have to learn their language? Why *should* I have to take a class? Half their asses can't even speak English, so how did *they* got a job? Bilingual my ass. Discrimination is more like it. To take a class would be to admit defeat. That they came and conquered and I'll be *damned* if they conquer me."

For some reason I shook when he said it, with enough fire in his eyes to burn an inferno to ashes. He meant every word.

Initially, when I got out of my beat-up Camry in his mother's front yard, I expected to meet an arrogantly intrusive man stuck on his looks and hell-bent on being one of Myspace's super bloggers, with enough popularity to raise the entertainment business's eyebrows. He has enough Most Popular Blogs to gain respect from other bloggers (currently he had 289 Top Ten Blogs).

He was a man on 467 different Top Friend Lists, most of those slots he was number one on the page or in the top five. His demographic is startling. Go to his comments section or the subscribers on his Blogs and you'll see straight men of all colors, gay women of all ages, old women young thugs, military personnel, university majors (I'm one), family, family friends, childhood friends, haters and enemies. They are all there. Zane subscribed to his blogs. Zane is arguably the biggest human being writing erotica at the moment. When I go through his subscribers and see her face I smile. He doesn't know the path he's on will lead to greatness. He still denies his talent. In fact he denounces it. I see other writers with books out subscribed to his stuff. They don't comment. But with traffic of two thousand plus views a day on his writing, reaching over

1,000,000 views to date and over 789,000 comments and equal that in kudos I tell him a simple roses are red, violets are blue poem don't warrant this type of attention. He brushes it off like its nothing. I like that about him. I witnessed the online drama. Larry has been controversial ever since his very first blog post a year or so ago. Called "Sexing the Greek Gods: Chaos." The blog that earned him the slow, gradual title of the King of Erotica. He talked about having sex with every Greek God in the fabled mythology. He has poured his feelings, sexuality and life over the wires, hoping people going through what he went through could a) relate and b) learn from his bad decisions. It paid off. This young man has seen so much hell that if it was me I would have went crazy and committed suicide a long time ago. He's still here. With stories to tell in the process.

Many denounce Myspace. But Myspace is the biggest thing on the internet since Janet Jackson's Wardrobe Malfunction, and quite frankly it's bigger than that.

Larry said, "I *loved* that Superbowl performance! Janet is a warrior. Justin, well, anyways. All that over a tit? I just don't get it." You could hear the love he has for Janet in his voice. But he was very warm, very open. He shook my hand firmly. The grip told me more about the man. He offered me something to drink, even gave me options. "What do you want, water, orange juice or soda? Personally, orange juice is the shit." I declined. I was pressed for time, and I was overly excited to be in his presence. *Why?* Don't even ask. I'm still trying to figure it out. Going through my brain were the words of Kari's interview, a friend of his who used him as a source for her college essay paper (he's the source of my paper as well), which she aced. Look at her subject matter. Who wouldn't have given her an A? She also blogged it for the King's readers on Myspace, and he's contemplating publishing it in his book the King of Erotica 2: The Crown, which, he says, "Is completed." The Blog made it to number 2 on the most popular list. Three thousand plus people read the interview. The feed back washed over him like a blessing.

I decided to take him to lunch. I treated. I asked him where he would like to go. He looked at me and said, "Peanut butter and jelly does me *just* fine, but fuck it let's do pizza."

Pizza it was. I had a light bill due and I was behind on my telephone bill but spending money for this enigmatic man to eat was a treat all in itself. He was also popular in his neighborhood of Naranja, Florida. Every time I exhaled somebody blew a horn at him, screaming out his name, zooming along Moody Drive in vehicles… "Heey Larry!" And "Sup, Niggah!" And "You better call me, Niggah!" And "Where's my damn book?"

He looked at me discreetly, with a sly smile. "Who needs a little black book when booty calls zoom by you every damn day? Constant reminders of successes and failures in the sack all up in your face. But it's all about my *fiancé*. I love her, I'd never hurt her. I'd die first."

The stern look on his face told me he was telling the truth. His temples twitched.

I just shook my head. He told me he and his family moved in the house on the corner of Moody Drive a year after Hurricane Andrew, 1992, basically wiped out Miami. This was his mother's first house. A dream fulfilled. He was only 15 years old in 1993. He told me back then life was no bigger than masturbation, chasing girls and Janet Jackson. He said 1993 was the *best* year of his life. I asked him why. He looked at me like I was stupid and said, "Are you kidding? The hands over Janet's tits picture on the Rolling stone magazine cover? Every Niggah in the hood had Janet pasted on the wall." He didn't want to get into it about the hurricane. In fact sadness befell his face that rendered me speechless.

When he got in my car, he called the "Batmobile," he snatched my keys, crank the ignition, said, "I'm driving, let me give you the grand tour de la Naranja, make your seat belt click like a cluck looking for a hit. And enjoy the ride." Very down to earth. I laughed so hard I chocked. Very humorous. I asked him had he thought about doing comedy. He pushed me playfully. "I'm sick of everyone asking me that. Either being a model or comedy, God shoot me." I left it alone. He switched on my radio without asking and looked at me, daring me to protest. I damn sure didn't. After going through the channels, he opened his book bag, pulled out a CD, put it in the player, already bobbing his head before the music started and said, "Well, I didn't hear no Janet so 'Get it Out me' will do just fine."

Get it out me, such a good song. And I wasn't a fan of Janet.

When we entered the bustling restaurant, not too far from Harris Field on Campbell Drive, he didn't utter a word and already the women and men eyed him pleasingly. They watched him with fascination. One short black woman tapped what looked like her sister and nodded at Larry. She licked her lips, eye fucking him. He didn't notice. A married man was playing with his young daughter. His wife graciously nodded at Larry. Larry smiled and minded his business, facing the cashier with a self-assuredness that all men his age should have. Calm and graceful.

"How many in your party?" the pretty, Cuban girl asked, with her black Cici's Pizza cap pulled low over her tired-looking eyes.

"Two," Larry said. He never volunteered information. He answered the question he was asked and left it at that.

After paying about 12 bucks for the meal, she worked up enough nerve and asked him for a kiss on the cheek. He obliged quietly. "Be careful," he joked. "My fiancé will have your ass, kissing all on me."

She sucked her teeth. "She doesn't want to see me."

Larry said, "You're *right*. She doesn't. Not with all this good loving she got." She was jealous instantly. He looked at me, slickly said, "I sunk her battleship," and we slapped palms. He was very playful when he wanted to be.

She told him he was beautiful. He dismissed her comment with the wave of his hands. "I'm ok, I am not no better than the next man."

She rolled her eyes and said, "*Boy*, if you don't know you're absolutely beautiful then I don't know what to say."

We got our plates and trays. But the minute he walked by the table, clad in a Superman T, his jeans sagging showing off his incredible bottom hidden behind red shorts, someone's husband waited a few seconds, discreetly glanced at his ass with a sly smile plastered on his face, winked at Larry and focused back on his wife as if he didn't know him. The silent passes further told me just how deep this DL bisexual life thing has really gotten.

When we ordered our food and sat down, he told me, "I know they're watching me. I don't even nod because all people want to do is *fuck* me, not get to know me and my Jergens Lotion bottle fucks me every goddamn night, without fear of pregnancies, HIV and those side effects I call STD's."

I never laughed so hard in my life. The Niggah was tough talking, bluntly up front, yet he had a very child-like aura about him that made the thugs want to protect him and the women want to hug and love him. Empty plates were on the table, as well as utensils.

Cici's Pizza offered a buffet of different pizza, and we were supposed to help ourselves but Larry wanted to read some poems before he ate. So he pulled out a small book from his backpack, he took everywhere with him. Cracked it open. A series of black faces were on the cover, the edges worn from the sands of time. Paul Laurence Dunbar. And others. He silently read a poem by the late Rita Dove. One of my personal favorites. As his eyes danced across the *Adolescence II* magnum opus, he frowned at certain points, taps his finger on the book, drum his fingers on the table, a finger on his temple like Malcolm X, then once he was done he says,

Although it was day, I was still raped
no one heard the wooden floor boards creek
but me and my insanity
I was of clay, molded into blasphemy.
My body was of Legos, built into clemency.
My sanity came into question,
Because I was only 6,
Robbed of my innocence,
You tore me down,
Rebuilt the church body,
Dusted my hips for prints
erased the evidence

manufactured my very essence
and after four years of hell,
being bound to iron bed railings
with leather belts
I prayed of Moses, of Egypt
closed my eyes and tried to will it loose
LET MY PEOPLE GO!
But my words were dressed in cloaks of ignorance
too weak to make it to God's ears,
so Satan became my devastatingly erroneous fear.
you set the butterflies free.
My bed seemed a zombie,
the very spot I was deflowered
Released seeds of pain sprouting towards
a misunderstanding
I wasn't born bisexual,
I was put together by the evilly masterful perpetrator
my bare window presents a darkened, muggy earth
with a termite-infested frame.
I remember the smell of rain,
beat at the roof like Vietnam
I feel as foreign as Guam
walking through Goulds
a complete fool
He leaves behind
a monstrous find
another breed of black man's anger
release it all,

burn anything you touch,
on your lips forever rest
the residue of an
ex step-father's deadly kiss

Freestyle it off the top of the brain in response to Adolescence. He said, defiantly, "Bet you she can't write *that*! How's *that* for some Adolescence?" I got from this that he was very competitive. I was all together perplexedly taken aback with both glee and jealousy, glee because another black man sat before me with a stellar I.Q. for words and word play and I was jealous because it took me days to write a poem and even *then* I only come up with four stupid lines. I rewound the small recorder and pressed "play," again in awe of the way he spoke, the way his lips formed certain words. You could hear the scratches, the pain, it was all there. He looked almost like a ghost. He sipped his Sprite in silence, tears falling down his face. Then abruptly, he smiled, brushing them away like Van Gogh's long lost paint brush. He studies me, head tilted east and says, "I wasn't crying, too much dust in the air, my allergies are kicking my ass."

The man had such a beautiful face. His composure, how he carried himself in public surprised me. I expected loud talking and laughing. He was an oil painting, sitting on his canvas with the skill of a trained interviewee. No one will encounter this poet/storyteller and walk away the same.

I ask him to recite a couple poems, not the whole thing but parts of it. And he sounds off like bullets.

He looked devilishly. "I wrote this for the president. Its called 'Uncle Sam.'"

Yea lemme tell ya' 'bout my
my Uncle Sam.
He
g'on save me from
this here hood.
I won't hear the gunshots anymore
when I try to sleep the
cries of broken homes
won't flow through my window.
Yep, he's the president
of the United States!
He live in a big ole
White House!
and the CIA
will protect my
family.
Yet why did he abandon me?

I was deeply impressed.

"I wrote that for black history month years ago. I never wrote it down. It's always in my head."

"How do you remember it?" I ask.

"Easy. I recite it a hundred times, after that its like a bad habit you try to break: you can't. I'm gonna recite the first poem I wrote. I was a kid. I was a lover of dictionaries I always tried to read them. And being that I hung around older people, my vocabulary was always more advanced then my peers. It's called Come. And do what you wish."

Please.
Come do what you wish.
Just provoke erotic thought.
Then. Please. Go.
Because every time your finger tips
caress my developing fine lines.
Takes another part of my soul.
Please. Come and do what you wish
then. Please. Go.
Because I'm scared.
And I'm only 6.

I was quiet for a minute. I told him he didn't

have to recite any more poems. I was trying my best not to feel what he just said, and the way he pieced together his words. I could see why many loved his spoken word poetry. He's amazing. He may not have taken lessons in counterpoint from Haydn, like Beethoven, he may not be as famous as James Brown and Shakespeare, but he surely received an angelic gift from God almighty that has become his blessing and his untimely curse that will give James and Shakespeare, lyrically, a run for their money. The emotion in his writing challenges your own life, he forces you into his world through sex, greater sex, incredibly greater, *sensationally* written sex, death, love, hate and turmoil and forces you into his realm and you become addicted by his stories. I have read his blogs on Myspace. All 567 of them. He has an amazing body of blogs that has touched people globally. I have listened to him on Blog Radio with Being John Sweet of the WSN Network. I have listened to his outstanding praise, "The phone lines are already *bloooowing* up for the King of Erotica." I listened to the callers. A woman from London. *Amazed* Larry. He couldn't believe he was talking to someone who was actually in London.

Another caller from Brazil called Larry

and told him of his impact on her life. He didn't even know Brazil had phones, he joked and everyone laughed. He spoke on being accused by J-Von and T-Max publishers of plagiarism. They put up a blog about him a while back, complete with his picture and all. The blog did the *opposite*; it made him 85 percent more popular than he already was. I told him my father is a lawyer and said he could still sue them for defamation of character and slander.

He frowned when I brought it up. "I got *love* for J-Von." I could still see the hurt and betrayal coloring his eyes, they were sad now. I could see them watering, he wiped it away and gave a quick smile. He seemed uncomfortable. "He *knows* me, inside and out. When I thought about suicide, I confided in him. I knew him before Myspace. Back during the Black Voices day on AOL. I saved every email he ever sent me; I used to read them for hope, for striving. Now I read them for revenge. He knows I got talent in erotica. He should have known!"

"I agree."

"As brothers you *never* let outsiders separate you from your brother, people will try. I looked up to him because I never had a big brother type role model. I was his biggest fan. I adored him. But outsiders brought out his true colors. I was supposed to have a future with T-Maxx. Or so he said. That was probably a lie as well. This is like the Literary American Idol. You *knew* Tamyra Gray had the voice to make it so you cut her out of the show and give it to Kelly Clarkson, J-Von is Kelly Clarkson. The company want J-Von to be the biggest thing on T-Maxx. But not for long. I'm too hungry, I want revenge. And I will get it. I can't believe that all blew up in my face. They deleted all my hard work off their site like I was worth a penny."

The smile died from my face. "Does that hurt you? And how deep does it hurt."

He folded his hands like a school boy, lowered his head and closed his eyes. "Hurts like hell. Loyalty is *everything* to me, once that is gone you don't have anything." He opened his eyes with vengeance seeping from his ears. "J-Von and the others involved remind me why some black people are a bucket of crabs. One makes it to the top, but you got a million pinchers trying to pull you back down. They want to be the Chiefs; no one wants to be the Indian taking dictation *from* the Chief. I hope he slept well at night, because I am destined to be great. And I am going to *die* trying. I got the soul of Scarface right now. The world is Mine. I want it. I am willing to do what it takes to get it."

"How is the book doing?"

"My best friend Legendary Deno told me don't focus on the numbers, it's about the art, the people who bought it who pass it on to others. I promote my book heavily. I go all out. I sold over a thousand copies of the Throne in a month and a half. Over a thousand sold, but more than a thousand people read it, because *those* thousand people have passed it on to friends, 'Hey, check out this cat Dapharoah, he off the chain.' That means a lot to me. And I'm only online. Soon I will be on Barnes and Noble and Amazon.com. I talked to local bookstores about getting my book. I put on my white suit with Italian blue collar and I shopped my book. Who else g'on do it? J-Von? They are *very* interested. I showed them the numbers. Numbers are talking. When I get my ISBN number, it will be on and popping then. My friends who have the book hype it up all over; people hit me up everyday about how they can get their hands on it. That's God, telling me I didn't need T-Maxx or J-Von. Anyone who wants to challenge me writing erotica or anything for that matter, bring it baby, because while you dust off your keyboard I'll be typing the last word of my story or poem a few seconds after. That's how fast it comes to me."

The passion in his voice, the willingness to stand behind his work made J-Von and everyone else who accused him of plagiarism without providing any proof look like childish liars. He spat a poem off the brain on the Blog Radio Show December of 2006. About going home to three things. Your conscious, the bed you made (that you have to lie in) and the mirror that made his enemies shake. I shook and I was a friend.

I was pretty sure his accusers listened because rumor had it that everyone from the Blogfather to J-Von listened to the show, which came on directly after their show ended. The difference was J-Von, Eros and B.F. Redd, a friend of Larry's, shared an hour on Blog Radio together. The King of Erotica had the entire next hour all to himself. He has star power and star quality all wrapped into a humble mix of personality. Rare for an author to have. People love this man, who tells it like it is. He stands behind his bisexuality, the love for his fiancé, a Texas girl who occupies the top slot on his Myspace page, a women he says has changed his life, gave him breath to breathe and wants to share a family with. He tells her everything, every aspect of his life his fiancé knows. "Can't nobody go to my girl and tell her shit I haven't already told her. I took their power away instantly." She doesn't judge him. She embraces him, loves him and adores him. She is what I call a real black woman.

I listened to him on the *Lamont Carey Show*, an author/actor who appeared in the sensational hit show *The Wire* and appeared on *Def Jam Poetry*. I watched the 6 Part Interview instructed by Adi of 88 Entertainment in his blogs a few weeks ago. They became very popular. He loves the ghetto. He finds it beautiful. When he said the words I rubbed my goatee and simply said, "This boy is history in the making and he has no clue." Even if he never sells books of Maya and Terry McMillan proportions, the books he's already sold worldwide and his blogging has captured the hearts of the 1,500 plus people subscribed to his blogs, people from all walks of life. Old housewives love him, young thugs look up to him, married women come to him for advice and he's never been married but what he suggests has always worked out.

Who would have thought the next great writer would have been residing and going through personal hell in Miami, Florida, in one of the Forgotten Cities called "Goulds?" No one. Not even natives of Goulds. Many hate him because he does in ten, maybe twenty minutes what take other writers a month and monstrous brainstorming to do: pump out quality work in no time. He writes his poetry in five minutes or less, sitting behind a keyboard, typing 89 WPM, you can damn near see the smoke from his glossy fingernails river dancing across those poor keys. He doesn't stop until he is done. He doesn't edit. "Because, every time you edit, you take *away* the poem's true intent, and by the time you're done cutting and erasing and adding, the poem is going to sound like another poem and not the one you intended to write. I don't care what they say about editing. Kiss my ass, do it my way and see the rewards."

He does a simple spell check, press print and viola, "Another King Masterpiece," he said with a clever, sly smile kept guardedly secret by his enchantingly beautiful eyes. In fact his eyes are his best features. While he goes off and does his thing, I am left; amazed, thinking about how he appeared to be in a trance when he typed his art.

He'd stare, unblinkingly, at the screen, the words sensually pouring through the cerebrum at break neck speed, and he creates! Of course I was cynical, always looking for flaws, but his stanzas, his metaphors are unlike anything I've ever seen. Take his poem "Ey:i's" (Eyes) for instance.

Some may think
my ey:i's are simple beings
that separate
light places from the dark.

others classify my eyes
as something that can decipher
shapes from colors.

Instantly, I am hooked. I wondered why he spelled eyes "ey (colon) i's. I read over the opening, searching for an answer. For his poetry have so many hidden meanings.

He touched on a lot of subjects, expertly weaving them together like ghetto braids emphasizing the beautiful face of what one would call a "Hood Rat."

stand on the platform of
my ey:I's
here, Eye'll help you
the bottom of your heels
stimulates my retinas
baby...grip my irises
for balance
and ride my pole
work it
'til you work my optic nerve
because my ciliary body
is so full of passion
a cacophony of obscenities
makes me smile,
coo, and sigh...

When I *read* this part, I was left in silence, with my mouth open. I printed it out and showed all my friends at F.I.U. when I first read this a few months or so ago. I didn't know Larry then. He was just another Myspace Profile Traffic Stop for me. Even they marveled at his use of the eyes by using the different parts of the human eye into one sexual fantasy. Retinas. Iris. Aqueous Humor. Optic Nerve. Ciliary Body. Simply stunning.

He has an absolutely mind-blowing body of poetry that will surely make you think, and surely make the rounds at universities upon his death. I remembered I hit him up and asked for his number. He gave it to me and we talked for months about everything. Felt like I knew him all my life. An undiscovered model, he has the height of a basketball player and the look of a movie star. His photos are captivating, forms of art in themselves. He's as photogenic as an airbrushed cover model. His eyes tell you a different, untold story of his life. The way he stares at a camera will stun you. The way he provocatively takes control of the very images of himself will amaze you. From the time I knew the King of Erotica, he has always done things his way. Passionately sensual. Unapologetically honest. I have never met a man, a black man with as much drive, ambition and talent that he possesses. He is a triple threat: model good looks, talented poet and breathtaking author. For The King of Erotica hasn't always been known as such. He was a product of the evils of the ghetto. At a very young age he was introduced to sex forcibly. Emotional and physical abuse from someone he trusted dearly. After being manufactured, he was released into the world a confused kid forced by certain family members to keep the abuse secret. It took a village to raise a child back in the 80s, and the very same village failed him. Fired up he began fighting back. Once meek and simply quiet, he became loud-mouthed and aggressive. He lost his virginity at ten years old by two older female cousins who tricked him into becoming their secretly well put together boy toy.

His life has been a series of gaps filled with the many voids so-called friends and so-called family had tried to fill with rumors and back biting. But the King is a warrior, he told me, because "Soldiers take orders from the element leaders and higher ups. I don't take orders."

So while we conclude this outing, he looks at me and said, "My treat, lets do a movie. The Hills Have Eyes Part 2 I heard rocks."

I looked at him and said, "Yea. Sure. I'm glad you're paying, because I gotta pay my light bill."

Johnny B. 3/15/2007
Florida International University

read with an open mind
and exxxtreme caution
Get something from it
Are you ready?
Turn the page

Booty-Do

INSTEAD OF PICKING UP A GUN WHEN ANGRY
PICK UP A PEN.
THE POSSIBILITIES ARE ENDLESS
PUSSIES CARRY AND BRANDISH GUNS
REAL MEN BRANDISH A GOOD BOOK

My name was Princess Webster. And I was having the time of my life at a party in sunny Florida City, Florida.

It took Ed a few weeks to convince me to go. I didn't like a crowd, and I liked being to myself. My business was *my* business and every time you met new people they wanted to *know* your business, especially down here in Florida City, the boondocks.

Against my better judgment, I remembered last week. I was helping my mean-ass Daddy clean his Chrysler 300M. He was buffing and waxing and I was using Windex to clean his windows on a perfect sunny day. I hated living on Lucy Street because black folks always got in your business without a care in the world. West Homestead Elementary School loomed about a hundred feet away from me.

Ed called my cell phone and told me he was having a party. I rolled my eyes.

"Are you coming?" he asked excitedly. He loved entertaining people. I loved entertaining myself.

I thought about it all of three seconds.

"*Nah*, Ed. Got things to do."

"Aw *come* on, Princess! You'll be the life of the party."

I cracked a smile. I appreciated the flattery. But my Daddy didn't. He glared at me and squirted some water from the hose in my face. The water was so cold I jumped out of my skin, dropping my phone. Now I was pissed. I gave him the middle finger. He stared at me, daring me to get lippy. I kept my mouth closed, picking up my phone. Couldn't live without it.

Getting myself back together, I said, "Ed. I don't know about coming to your party. I should go…maybe I shouldn't."

"Like I said. You'll be the life of the party."

"Ed. The shit talker."

"Nah, girl I'm the smooth operator."

"That's funny. I didn't know you looked like Sade."

"*Whatever.* Are you coming?"

I thought about it again, holding the phone to my ear with my shoulder, squirting window cleaner all over the windshield and wiping it off with Bounty paper towels, since they lasted longer.

"Yea. I'll go."

"Sweet, Princess. See you there."

"Just let me know what day. And call and remind me. How's Georgia doing?"

"She's out with her cousins. Cool Niggahs, too. They just moved to Miami. Well, they've been living here for a few months now. They're addicted to South Beach."

"Sorry ass beach. What is it about that crummy beach everybody loves so much?" I asked rhetorically. "Smells like piss half the time." I kissed through the phone. Daddy stood in my face and kissed my forehead. I squeezed his shoulder. I loved Daddy. "Bye, Ed."

"Talk to you later, Princess. And come to the party."

A couple weeks later, after postponing it several times, Ed had his party. He had a huge house off on Redland Road, about ten minutes from my house. So the two DJ's he hired for the festivities played their music as loud as they wanted, without the neighbors calling the police every five minutes, because his house sat on 8 acres of land, surrounded by monstrous trees and bushes. Creep paper, confetti, balloons everywhere, this was an adult party. Over 20. Free drinks for the ladies. Five bucks for the fellahs.

Since I knew the game plan I didn't drink at all. I had the same plastic red cup for two hours, holding the same ole beer. Looked like a prop in my hands. I remembered when a short, handsome black man with huge dread locks brought me the beer. I wasn't here ten minutes and already the jerk magnet on my body sent out invitations. He was too pushy, too direct. Every fifth word was "My Niggah." And his vocabulary made me sick to my stomach.

It had turned me off, so I accepted the beer (I could have gotten for free anyways, so he didn't do me a favor) and told him, as politely as I could, "*Look*. I came to party. Solo. That means *without* a man."

To my dismay, he called me a stuck-up bitch and walked off.

"Your Mama's a bitch!" I yelled behind him, tucking my chin back. He turned, grabbed his dick, wiggled it at me and stormed off. Very immature. He was too damn old to be doing junior high school shit.

Men wanted to get the ladies' drunk so they could fuck 'em every which way. I knew the play. I knew it all too well. I did it plenty of times. Getting drunk and then I come off my pussy like it's free. Now, if I wound up in *anybody's* bed I would *know* how I got there.

The party was in full swing. A blanket of lust and sensuality lay under such a glorious Miami, Florida moon. The air cool and crisp, a little wind, but nothing alarming. I got tired of carrying my red cup so I gulped the beer, tasted all right, tasted like Corona. I tossed the cup in the trash. The women looked nice tonight. A few lesbians, pretty women at that, tried to get with me but I got somewhere after telling them, "I don't do the same ocean water I came out of, you feel me?" They respected that. I had my gun in my purse if they wanted to get rowdy.

Ed, clinging to his wife Georgia, danced up to me. She kissed my cheek and I hugged them both. My very good friends. I knew them for ten years. My Dad was in the Marines with his father, they actually retired together. So we were damn near family.

"Enjoying yourself, girl?" Georgia asked me, her Asian/black ass pulling on her joint. She had red eyes, and could hardly stand up. I liked her Baby Phat pants suit; she was rocking it with some rhinestone stilettos. The accessories, the chain belt, the matching chain earrings, brought out her eyes.

I took her hand and cupped it lovingly,

she was like a sister. We have been through it all together. Two abortions, two heartbreaks and bad yeast infections forever tarnished our freaking resume. I was there for her when she first met Ed years ago. He was a different man then. He used to cheat on her, beat her and talk down to her. He was a prick and I tried to shoot him plenty of times. He used to hate women, yet he dated them like he loved them. He didn't even have respect for his own mother. Back then he was a big time gangster. He would shoot you in a heart beat. But once my father got a hold of him, and showed him a better way of treating women, he got his act together, married Georgia and never cheated or beat on her again. He needed a role model because his own father was too busy chasing skirts and putting his Mama through hell to be bothered with his seed. Bottom line Ed was big and all mighty, but he feared my father.

We withstood it all.

I brushed lint from his jacket sleeve. "I'm having fun," I said, noticing a tall guy trying to get his grind on with a white girl over by the pool. Beach balls were flying here and there, water splashing, half naked adults finding solace in their watery heaven. I shook my head. I hoped he was careful. That white girl, Pauline, was a robber. She'd rob his ass in a heartbeat, all while keeping it classy. She robbed so many men that she lost count after twenty.

Ed said, "Dance with me, girl." He took me by the arm.

I pat his shoulder. "*Nooo*, dance with your wife." I kissed his cheek, taking my arm back. Georgia nodded in appreciation. She *knew* that deep down Ed wanted to fuck me; all these men wanted some of my apple pie. "I'm going to peep the scene. See ya'll later. Its money to be made out there, girl!"

"Girl don't be tricking all through my house," she joked, kissing my cheek. We squeezed hands fondly, and then I went on my way.

The instant I turned around two men were in my face. I jumped out of my skin, patting my weave job. One took my hand.

"Hey, baby." Gold teeth, dirty shoes. Oversized coat. *Bitch let me go!*

The other grabbed my other hand. "Are you here with anybody?" His T-shirt was too small. Tight jeans, you could see the size of his nuts. Suddenly I didn't like Planter's anymore. He reminded me of a Shabba Ranks and Johnny Gill music video: out of air play. There was nothing slow and sexy about these men.

Before they could say anything else I danced to Khia's "Look Back at it." Shaking it like it just didn't stop. I pranced past them, snapping my fingers, released a "*Heeeeeey*!" as loud as I could, twirling my head and out into the sea of dancers I went; shaking my ass all over the place.

Everybody rushed out to dance, this was the jam! I was in a crowd of horny women, all shaking their asses, trying to get the men to notice. One fat girl, clad in tight pink patent leather, did the "Walk it out" dance, looking more like someone pulling a pink Now and Later candy from the pack and actually struggling with it.

I laughed to myself, went over to her, gave her a high five and said, "Girl, you doing that damn dance! And your hair is cute!"

She hugged me. "Girl, thank you."

Her hair looked like shit.

Thugs were everywhere. Lifting glasses of booze in the air, rocking back and forth, looking gangster. I loved it.

I smelled liquor and weed in the air, a dizzying cornucopia of aromas blending easily with different body fragrances, colognes and deodorant.

Feeling it, and feeling good, I pulled my dress up to my thighs and kicked off my heels. I was jamming. Throwing my weave like Britney Spears. Wait a minute. She was bald now.

It wasn't everyday I got to jam and have fun. Since I worked as an undercover prostitute, content on the money I made and not caring about people, I cut loose.

I didn't have to worry about ducking and dodging the police, even though five of Miami's Finest were my regulars.

But tonight was different.

I wasn't going to lure any prospects from Ed's party.

I wasn't going to disrespect his house. Most people didn't care, but I was a woman who respected her friends. I was damn thirsty.

That beer didn't do it for me. So I made a last minute decision to go take advantage of the free drinks. Why not? I lived for times like this, when you could just let go and live a little, not worry about problems or bills. Just forget your damn name, honestly. I was going to take full advantage of Ed and his party.

Putting back on my heels, I walked through the dancing crowd.

The marijuana and alcohol putting her on cloud 9, Georgia lovingly looked at Ed, kissing his lips. "Baby. The party is live and in charge, baby." She was happy, on top of the world. Happy to be married to an ex gang banger who now worked for FP&L, making honest money. She was a hair stylist, charging her clients as much as $200 for their hair styles.

He sipped his Heineken beer. "Yea, that's true, even though there are people here we didn't invite."

"Aww baby," said Georgia, licking the white residue from his cute nose. He loved when she did that, made him get a hard on. They lip-locked. "Let the people have fun." She tasted the cocaine in her mouth, which upset her because Ed told her he'd stopped, yet there was white residue on his nose.

Aggravated, because he just remembered he had a ton of bills to send off tomorrow, Ed replied, "Hell, I have been doing that all night." He held her tight, looking down into her pretty eyes, suppressing a smile. Felt like he could see Japan. His baby, his love. He could not live without her. He wished he could take back all the heart ache and grief he once brought to her life, but he chose to leave it where it was.

In the past. Where it was now buried.

Over by the bar, just in front of the back door, a short man asked the tall, gullible bartender for a small cup of Hennessy. Light ice. Top it off with Coke soda.

The Bartender looked him over. He got a bad vibe from him. He looked good, but he spelled trouble. "Sure, coming right up," said the bartender. Working for Ed, for some side cash on the side. His regular 9pm-5am job was on South Beach, at one of the popular clubs. The crowd here wasn't really his type of crowd, but when someone paid you $300 for five hours work, you jumped at it.

He poured the Hennessy in a red plastic cup, threw in four ice cubes, and topped it off with Coke soda. Handing it to the short guy, he said, "Five dollars, player."

The short guy handed him a ten. "Keep the change."

Sipping the drink, he cautiously turned, slowly walking over to one of the tables by the dark corner of the huge house. Sitting down, he cautiously looked around, making sure no one was watching him.

With the skill of a tight rope walker in the circus, he opened one of the small plastic bags he pulled from his left pocket, no bigger than the little bags the dope boys sold weed in, and he dumped the GHB into the drink.

Smiling sinisterly, he eyed one of the women, a short, Cuban woman, shaking it with some girl like there was no tomorrow.

Working up enough nerve, he tossed the small bag on the ground, used a dirty finger to stir the drink, making sure the date rape drug dissolved properly, and he snapped his fingers, dancing over to the fine woman. When she seen him she was instantly turned on.

Her body-clinging gold dress itching her skin, she reached out and shook his hand. She loved fine black men. "That drink for me?" she asked, grinding her ass all over his groin region.

Bingo! Free pussy tonight! "Yup." He handed it to her.

She had to use the bathroom. "Give me a

second, Papi. Be right back. Gotta pee."

"I'll be right there, Senorita," he said smoothly.

He could not keep his eyes off her huge breasts.

Her friend she was dancing with took his arm and said, "Dance with me 'til she gets back. You're cute, Papi."

Holding her ass, they danced the night away.

"Hey, Princess! What you getting from the bar?" I looked at my good friend. With her pretty self. Her name was Eli Rodriguez. I called her the Latino bombshell. Very sexy woman.

"I'm getting a Hennessy and Coke," I told her.

She waved her hands feverishly, thrusting her drink at me with a smile. "Here. You can have mine. I just got it not too long ago."

I accepted the drink, sipping it slowly. Yummy. Just right.

Eli, her hips moving to the playing salsa, told the bartender, with a voice of butter, "I'll just have bottled water. With no ice."

He couldn't take his eyes off of her.

"No problem, sexy," he told her, trying not to admire her amazing curves. Yet he had to look anyway, just in his nature.

And I felt their chemistry. She rubbed his hand. "And pour it in one of those red cups. *Thanks* Papi.

I felt good; sipping the drink opened me up.

Just what I needed. All that salsa music died away and the DJs were playing my cut. I didn't know who sung this jam, but I loved the beat.

Take it to the floor. Now drop, drop, drop bring it back now. Yes, I was feeling this dance song. Straight Hood!

It was when I bent over to touch my toes and shake, shake it, that a man got behind me, holding my ass, and smacking it. Whack. I loved it. I turned to face him. Huge diamond earrings. The most angelic face. Hazel eyes.

I ran my hands over his bare arms. I was being hypnotized by his presence. Never have I met a man who initially made me feel this way. He was dressed in Phat Farm gear. A hat angled on his head. Well-trimmed, smelled nice.

"And your *name*, Ma?" he asked, barely able to keep his eyes open.

I studied him.

"You're *not* from here, are you?" I asked him, noticing he was lit. Drunk and high.

He could barely look at me.

Eli sipped her water, making her way out of Ed's bathroom. She made sure she cleaned up behind herself. The house was packed with people, dancing and having a good time. Four Niggahs utilized the dining table for their noisy, cussing game of dominoes. Slamming the game pieces to the point where the table shook. She gyrated past the low-table, the dining room, and out the back door. She stopped and asked the bartender, "What is your name?"

He wanted to lie. But he decided against it. "Dan."

She went in for the kill. Sticking her breasts out. "You're cute. Can I get your number?"

Taking a sharpie marker from his pants, he gently pulled out her plump tit and scribbled his number just above the nipple. He then kissed it, sending electricity through her body. She just stared at him. "That's an erasable marker, so the more you sweat, the faster my number disappears."

"Really?"

He looked deep into her angelic eyes.

"Really. So I think you shouldn't dance that hard. By the time the song goes off, my number will vanish into this air."

She said, leaning over and giving him

some tongue.

"How about writing it on my pussy. And *eating* it off."

There was activity in his boxers. "I leave at about 3 a.m."

"I'll call you."

"I'll come find you."

"*Oooh*, a man coming to find *me*. I should feel so special, 'ey Papa?"

"…Whatever makes you happy, sexy lady. And your name is?"

"Oh, I'm Eli. *Cuban*, baby!"

"Looking forward to kicking it with you."

He looked past her and noticed the short man he served the Hennessy and Coke to staring at her with the most evil eyes.

He shuddered.

Not liking the feeling in his gut.

Eli took her friend by the arm and playfully pulled away from the fine black man she was getting her groove on with.

"Ok, girl I'm back, I'm cutting in." She killed the water, feeling the cold liquid trailing down her throat. "Shit, that hit the spot!" She handed her friend the cup, dancing to rapper 50 Cent's "Just a Little bit."

"Thanks for the drink," she told her new friend, kissing his cheek.

He studied her.

Yes. She drank all of it. Now all I need to do is get her to my SUV, and when she starts to fall asleep I can take her home and beat the pussy up. I can't believe how easy that was.

"Want another one?"

"No, I'm straight," said Eli with an attitude.

Before she could hug her new friend and kiss him, Dan took her by the arm and said, "Mind dancing with me?"

"*Oooh*, Dan! Yes! I thought you would never ask."

Dan looked at the little guy and said, "Yea, I'm cock blocking. She's mine, you lose. *Peace*, pimp."

And the little guy stormed out of the party, arms folded, cursing under his breath.

Goddamn! I don't get to have sex!

In a drunken stupor, he responded casually, "Nah. I'm from out of town."

I suddenly had an interest in him. "What's your name?"

Slurred speech. "Thomas."

"I'm Princess, nice to meet you playboy."

"Princess is a pretty…name…" He hugged me and almost fell over. I didn't know what to do. He was heavy, yet I used all my strength to hold him up. I decided not to leave him in this state. I helped him into Ed's house, past Niggahs kissing face with women, rubbing on their asses and all that. I helped him up the stairs. I was five feet 9; he was about five-eleven, maybe six feet tall. He was moaning piteously. Damn he was lit pretty badly.

Once we reached the top of the stairs, the coast was clear. Up stairs was off limits for partygoers anyways. I was family. The stipulation didn't apply to me.

I took him to the guest room and locked the door, helping him lay on the bed. I nearly dropped him on the floor. One of the heels of my shoe snapped off and ricochet off the TV. I just laughed, rubbing my forehead. Then it happened, a run up my stocking made me cuss under my breath. I shouldn't have worn panty hose anyways, that shit was played out like Vanilla Ice, the rapper.

Two huge framed pictures of Bob Marley hung above the head of the bed. Black carpet. Red furniture. Very deep neo-soul feel in this room. Huge plasma TV mounted in the wall, 70 inches of pure beauty. A huge fish tank. I loved fish tanks, every time I came in this room I just admired it, afraid to touch anything.

Showing off my sincere side, which I hardly shown to anyone, I took off his shirt and tossed it on the Lazy Boy. What an amazing chest. I looked him over, my eyes raking his body like Daddy rake leaves. Turning on the tube (ESPN, *figures*), I sat on the Lazy Boy and watched him writher all over the bed. He was rubbing his head, his eyes slammed shut. He said he had a head ache. I debated. Should I help him? No. Girl, *yes*! Do *something*. I didn't know him. We're strangers. No you're not. His name was Thomas. And he was the most beautiful black man you have *ever* seen! Rape him, girl! No, bitch! Girl, get that dick, shit its free! No its not, Chile. You crazy! Get on his dick and ride it reverse cowgirl style. I guess get a hat, too, 'ey? Shit, he's out of it! He won't remember it in the morning. No, girl I can't! Scary, bitch! You're just scary!

Against my better judgment, I took off his shoes. He had on crisp white socks. Feet smelled good. Like lavender powder. Taking off his socks I noticed the pretty feet. Very nice. I liked this, a man who took care of his body. His toe nails were a little long. I opened the night stand drawer and took out the toe nail clipper. I spent ten minutes giving his toes special treatment. I felt good doing it. Why not? I would rather be here then at the party.

Wanting to go the extra mile, I went into the bathroom, wet a wash cloth with warm water, turned it off, kicked off my heels, sat next to him and placed the folded rag on his forehead. I dabbed it all over his face, his chest, like I was dusting his skin for prints.

He smiled. The most gorgeous smile. "Oh, Ma. That feels good."

I kissed his cheek. "No problem."

I noticed the wedding ring on his finger. So he was married. My eyes racked his killer chest. Damn! And he had huge, gorgeous nipples. I rubbed his pecks, massaging him. Hell, men took advantage of women all the time. It was time for me to take advantage of a drunken man.

Get that dick, bitch!

Oh God, conscious, shut the fuck up!

You better get it, or I'ma give your ass plaguing migraines for the rest of your natural life.

I'll just make a doctor's appointment and swallow pills until they vanish, so do what you gotta do.

Damn, you a scary Ho!

I was getting sleepy, very drowsy. I tried to keep my eyes open but I couldn't. I was getting dizzy, my vision blurry. What was wrong with me? I felt good, though, my body tingled. I felt hands on me, the softest hands. They were on my face. A kiss. I was kissing Thomas. He dabbed the rag on my face. We tongue kissed again, his hands massaging my shoulders.

"Lay down, Ma," he said. "You tried to take care of me. And even though I'm fucked up, let me take care of you."

I felt safe. My panties were going down. I felt his tongue all over my pussy. Before you know it I was out for the count.

Ed was looking over Georgia silently. She wondered what he was thinking. Judging from the look on his face he was worried that someone was going to break something in his house. He was very anal about things like that. Last year someone broke his favorite statue. Some drunk happened to accidentally push it over while he chased ass all over the place and never replaced it. And thinking about it he smiled. Because Princess pieced it back together like it was never broken. Yea. He smiled bigger. He loved that girl…

Booty-Do Part II: Was it a Dream

Groggily, I awakened from a deep sleep when I heard my alarm clock. Sitting up, I looked around wildly, not knowing where I was. The clock read 9:56 a.m. I felt good, actually, the warm Miami sun shining through lacy curtains, making shapes on my body. And despite my body feeling relaxed, pleasantly relaxed, I couldn't quite shake the shade of wearifulness that had me on the verge of collapsing back into hibernation.

My weave job was fucked. Another $100 gone down the drain in one night. I swear sometimes I had to remind myself that money wasn't going to grow on trees any time soon.

Benevolent, I asked myself, "Where am I? That is not my clock." I felt weird, like I was trapped in a surreal world where nothing made sense.

Black carpet, big screen TV. Turned off. Bob Marley pictures on the wall.

Oh. I was in Georgia's guest room. I smiled then. I wondered where they were.

With the feeling of wanting to monkey around, I got out of bed, a terrible wringing in my head. Feeling vulnerable, my eyes were burning. I was butt naked with a nasty after taste in my mouth. I smacked my lips, narrowing my eyes for effect. Did I fuck or something? Because my body felt good and my pussy felt incredible! In fact my pussy has never felt this incredible in my life!

Racking my brain for answers, which was more of an empty tree trunk with echoes bouncing around haphazardly, I went into the bathroom and took a much-needed shower. Ed and Georgia always said I could make myself at home when I came over and I never had. I had every intention of doing so, I loved using my friends' houses to do my thing but I didn't want to overstay my welcome or seem selfish so I wound up taking my black, sexy ass home and crashing in my own bed, using my own shit. Well, goddamn, I meant Daddy's shit.

Again, I wondered where they were. I wondered how I got up in this room. I knew I had a good time at the party last night; I guzzled the beer like Kool-aid, and then the Hennessy and Coke didn't make matters any better. That's what did it, produced this conduit of problems seeping into every chamber of my body.

I felt good, the warm water falling all over me, snatching my uneasiness and spreading it all over my skin, waking me up even more. I just smiled, smiled really big, staring at the tile. I felt sensational, despite the lingering effects of the alcohol wearing off like an old pair of blue jeans. Just what I needed. I was so discombobulated I didn't even know what day it was. I knew I had to go to work at about 4 p.m. So I was safe for right now. I didn't jeopardize my job, even though I worked at Burger King in Naranja, Florida, on U.S.1, and 268th Street. I used that as a smokescreen to hide my real profession, prostitution.

I used Dove liquid soap and cleaned myself. I hated the smell of Dove, plus the liquid sometimes irritated my sensitive skin but I didn't feel like being dirty another moment and I damn sure didn't feel like getting out the tub and getting some more soap. Rubbing the sponge all over my breasts, I felt tingly. I felt alive, good. I was held spellbound by the horniness that catapulted from every opened pore on my body.

Attentive, I leaned against the light blue tiled wall, free of mildew, and started rubbing my wet opening, the pleasure shooting through me, my hair wet, now I had to get rid of this weave…

I shuddered as I slid the sponge over my pussy, carefully manipulating my clit…my legs drummed together as steam enveloped me, taking me up and out of the bathroom with the force of a powerful wind, producing powerfully breathtaking images of last night in my skull, causing them to explode in my brain, from some unknown force in my soul, something that tried to make me remember, wanted me to remember, needed me to…remember. I was floating, rising and falling like a feather, making loops around the sudden urgency to be touched, to be loved, to inevitably be fucked good, long and hard…

I saw a fine man, clad in Phat Farm gear. His face I could not make out, but he had the most incredible smile. His name was Thomas. He was taking off my panties…tasting the wetness, sucking my panties until they no longer smelled of good pussy…he tossed them, opening my legs, tasting the sliced peach, reminding me why I wished I was born in Georgia, so I could be called a "Georgia Peach," sweet to taste, sweet to the touch, sweet to all the human senses.

His "touch" was heaven, lifted my clouds and presented the Red Sea, which spilt open and revealed a man eager to have me, eager to love me, eager to pleasure me. Over rapturous waters I was the feather, again, rising, falling and floating towards the cliffs of desire. I smelled liquor on his breath, he was intoxicated. His "sight" tore into my soul, sliced my retinas in half, revealing my optic nerves which made the pulse in my thighs pop with jubilancy. His tongue and hands moved over me effortlessly. I was ungrateful, because I was too out of it to really get into it, but I felt my torso twirling like wind chimes.

His "smell" opened chambers in my heart and soul I never knew I had. I felt the wind of pleasure pick me up, turn me on my stomach, while his fabulous, baby smooth hands spread my ass cheeks apart, like God peeling away petals, telling a sick planet earth he loved it, he loved it not and his tongue dove into my hole with such abandon I felt like putting up no vacancy signs all over my body, just so he would never stop licking, slurping and tasting the chocolate…from my hole to my pussy he was tasting perfection, tasting what took Daddy ten minutes to release and took Mama another nine months to make.

My "hearing" increased, the instant he slid his passion deep into my soft place. Maybe his dick became the eager archeologist, roaming my tomb, searching for Nefertiti; trying to find out if she was buried in the Valley of the Kings, or in the trunk of the baobab trees. Unshapely, my promiscuity got the best of me, I saw myself, with Thomas tapping my pussy from the back, beautiful ass cheeks jiggling in that manly way, his back strong and firm, his hands planted firmly on the bubble of my ass, mounting the horse, feeding it the apples which lined the veins of his dick like grapes on vines, like intersections on road maps.

Like…the…uh, feather: rising, falling…then elegantly floating.

The sponge brought me sheer pleasure as

I felt my toes curl, nearly causing me to slip in the tub and break my head open…on my knees I was, humping the sponge, my buttocks jiggling like Jell-o…the water turning me into a seductive tsunami, of which I begin to rise and fall like Anne Rice Vampires, full of power, devoid of reason, homely and deformed, seekers of blood.

My eyes remained on the bed, Thomas lying on his back, guiding my throbbing pussy on his incredible dick. My tits bounced like Michael Jordan was trying to win Chicago Bulls the 6th Championship, such drive and skill with his tongue out.

It took a moment before I realized that Ed, Georgia's husband, was sitting on the toilet before me, naked, closing the bathroom door and locking it. He was sweaty, able and willing, jerking his juicy dick, his nuts jumping up and down like the House of Pain died for another hit.

I was stunned, but my sense of "taste" caused my tongue to grow a mind of its own, and I leaned over, my wet hair all over his muscled thighs, and I kissed the head of his passion while his eager hands inherited my head. Feeling like an eager slut, I took him deep into the contours of my mouth while Thomas, from last night, in my mind, brought me to orgasm. I shook and shivered in the tub, Ed rubbing my face, talking to me, loving me, telling me he'd been wanting me for years, that what we did would stay between me and him, that he loved how I worked the tongue, brought the dick the much needed joy it so wanted forever.

I came and I came, manipulating my pussy with the sponge, I moaned pleasantly, loving this freaky episode. He picked me up, sat me on the toilet, and he stuck his tongue so deep inside me, triggering my G-spot instantly, I rode his face, I had to pee. I told him, he sucked my clit while I took a piss. He took some of it and rubbed it over my nipples, suckling the right one, carefully biting it in a way that brought pleasure and not pain.

He sat on the floor and guided his throbbing member inside me, deep inside my pink walls, pulling back the 21 Century logo, from the movies, in my wide eyes, looking for the red carpet. We grinded on the floor, I took the Nike hat from his head, slanted it on my head and rode this good dick, but all I could see was Thomas. Loving me, wanting me and desiring me, and suddenly my body shut down. What was I doing?

Georgia was my homegurl. I couldn't fuck her man! I was a woman of assured probity, at least I thought so.

Girl. Oh, no! No! NO! Conscious, please, don't start. Yea, girl its me! Get the dick, get the dick GET THE DICK! Fuck Georgia, this was *not* about her. *Yes it was!* She's my best friend. Who was sitting on good dick and never offered to share it with you. Friends share. *Yes*, conscious. They do, but they don't share their significant others.

Fuck it I'm going to grind on Ed's dick until my pussy screams!

Deeply ashamed and simply unprepossessing, I hopped up, snatched a towel from the niche and ran into the bedroom, taking up my dress, my shoes. I couldn't breathe, I could still feel him inside me. I wanted and needed Ed back inside me, to replace Thomas, to beat the Niggah out of my system because I just admitted to myself that I love him, I love Thomas with all my heart. No I didn't. Girl, yes you did!

I'm just fucked up right now. Nothing was making sense. I had to go, I didn't know what was going on, and I didn't want to know. All I knew was that I didn't want to hurt my girl; I couldn't stay here and feed into this infidelity when my heart ached for a man I could hardly remember. I would probably never see again.

I started to cry, my insides opening so

wide I almost fell into myself, in search of myself, trying to *find* myself. It was just me, myself and I; we got each other until the end. Men weren't shit; well, Thomas was my soul mate, my angel.

He was perfect.

God, would I ever find him again?

Ed spun me into his face. God, he brought sexy back. The hell with singer Justin Timberpussy. Ed was so unlike the white boy. He grabbed both my tits with fire in his eyes, ready to say *fuck the world, yea I was doing the unthinkable*! The mood was right and I wanted her, his eyes told me. He didn't pull a "wardrobe malfunction," leaving singer Janet Jackson before the world, gripping her own tit.

I wanted him so damn bad. But should I go through with it?

"Where are you going? You can't run out on me, girl. I need you."

I would not meet his demanding gaze.

"What about Georgia? I can't do this to her."

He tried to turn on the Rico Suave charm. "Look, I *love* her, *you* love her, but I want you. I need you. Please, baby, make love to me."

"I can't! I just can't!"

"Just open yourself…uh, and let yourself be free."

"Ed, this is not *General Hospital.* And I said 'no.'"

He was pleading, wanting me, reaching out for me and I grabbed both his hands and pulled myself into his arms and when I realized it was the business woman in me, the prostitute who was all about money I told him, "Two hundred dollars and we can fuck all over this room. Georgia is my girl, but business is business."

He smiled victoriously, pulling me into his embrace. We kissed, rose on the tidal wave of lust together and crashing on the bed, wetting the ocean shores, building sand castles with tongues, fingers and whispering sweet nothings that didn't mean anything in each other's ears as he guided his rod into my green pastures and we spent an hour rewriting Psalms 23 all over the sheets, making me come over and over and over, while I dug my nails into his back and his hips quivered between my legs the same time his dick throbbed between the pink walls. "I'm gonna nut in this pussy," he promised and he exploded deep inside, grinding me to oblivion as my moans filled his ears, but wasn't powerful enough to fill the room and when he fell on top of me I hugged him, stroking his hair, kissing his lips, looking into his eyes.

"Where's my money?"

He produced his wallet and gave me five hundred dollars.

He was standing by the bed. I weakly stood up and yawned. "When can we do this again?"

I felt like shit. I just fucked Georgia's man and made him pay for it.

"Never, Ed. Georgia must never find out about this."

I was nervous, ready to run out of the room the minute the time was right. I tried putting on my clothes but he took them and threw them across the room, taking me into his arms, sucking on my neck, making me so weak in the knees the left one slammed into his nuts and he was on the floor, like a helpless lady bug, holding his sack, whimpering.

I snatched up my clothes and fled from the room. Stomping along the hallway, I accidentally knocked wedding photo off the wall. It fell on the floor, the glass shattering. Fuck the picture! I gotta get out of this house! I gotta get far, far, far away from this hellishly induced scene. Destroyed inside, I was running down the stairs, fumbling into my clothes, and hurriedly put on my heels. I was reminded that one of the heels was broken when I fell flat on my face, by the coffee table. Ouch! That hurt. On my feet I was, racing through the kitchen where I came to a screeching halt, quietly grabbing the island counter, inhaling deeply and holding my breath.

Georgia was on the phone. She was talking so loud, and the radio was going a mile a minute. I was shocked. She was home? Oh, God! What had I done to my girl? I wanted to cry, I was shaking all over. I hated to admit it, but Georgia could fight. The bitch was notorious for whipping so much ass Playboy might, just might call her for a job molding the ass it sold monthly across the U.S. and all over the newsstands.

She didn't see me. I was looking at her from behind, with the news of her potential separation from her husband drying in the form of his saliva all over my pussy, neck and nipples.

But I'd let it dry, because I'd die before I hurt my girl.

She turned down the radio. "When are you going to fix my sprinklers, John? And what is that smell, I have a really sensitive nose…" Georgia joked through the phone, her hand on her hip, stirring some black beans. The kitchen smelled like the Chef's quarters, made my stomach growl. Shit shit shit! She heard it. She froze, paralyzed. Oh, God what do I do? Think think think! Before she turned around I ducked, hiding behind the counter. "John, yea

I'm here. Thought I heard something, anyways you gonna come over and taste my black beans and my famous ribs…? What do you mean? Yes, I used my mama's recipe!"

I crawled to the opposite island counter, by the start of the living room and I carefully and quietly stood up and tip toed out of the kitchen and into the living room and I had never run to my car so fast in my life. Half naked, I hopped inside, and did 65 mph heading for my Daddy's house, crying the entire time.

In love with a man I'd never see again.

Thomas. And. Princess.

My sweet, sweet Thomas.

Georgia was opening the oven to check the status of her mouth-watering ribs when she thought to herself. She loved Princess like a sister, would do anything for her. They confided in each other, stuck up for each other. She trusted this woman with everything in her soul.

Her heart burst with joy at the very thought of Princess. The realest, illest woman she'd ever known. She was down to earth and cocky, was a hustler and knew how to get her money.

When she heard a strange noise she'd turned around and hadn't seen anything. She dismissed it as nothing. Then a familiar smell overcame her nostrils. She'd sniffed the air, smelling what…seemed…like Dove. Dove soap, yea. Dove. Had to be Dove. Dove was her favorite soap. She used it everyday for nine years plus. Ed hated Dove with a passion. She tried to get him to use Dove for years instead of that god-awful Zest soap but he was stubborn.

So she didn't sweat it, fuck it. But when she opened her counter to take out the salt, she looked in the small mirror hanging under the counter and froze when she saw Georgia crawling out of the kitchen.

She didn't know why, but something wasn't right.

And she intended to find out.

Humming the tune "Secret Lovers" in her head, she picked up the phone and called John back, her friend.

Stirring the beans, she realized she didn't like the feeling in her gut.

She tried to ignore it.

"I'm back. What were we saying now?" She held the phone to her ear with her shoulder. "Oh, yea you wanted the recipe for my mama's ribs. What? I'm cranky? I need a massage? Nah, my husband will do that. What does that got to do with ribs? His job is to make sure I'm ok not yours. Ok?" And she said more sternly, "I don't cheat on my husband and he would never cheat on me…"

And she believed that with everything in her.

Ed would never deceive her.

Never.

She could almost guarantee that.

Booty-Do: Part III: Kenny

A few days later Daddy and I nabbed a table at Applebee's restaurant by the super Wal-mart in Florida City.

I sat down and started flipping through the menu, on the verge of taking advantage of the two for one drink special. I wanted the strawberry daiquiri.

"Are you ok, baby?" Daddy asked, handsome in his suit. He had attended a real estate seminar hosted by a city slicker by the name of Bobby Taylor. I personally thought it was a get rich quick scheme Daddy fell for because he bought two books from the man. *How to milk Home buying and Investing in Real Estate.* Price tag? Fifty dollars per book! Could you say "Daddy you're a dumb ass?" I was like what the fuck? A hundred dollars for some bullshit he could have downloaded or looked up, for the price of running America Online once a month, without spending a penny. But Daddy always dreamed big.

"I'm ok, Daddy. What about you?"

His Fossil watch was nice. It had a black face and three little diamonds he liked. I paid $150 for it from Macy's at the Dadeland Mall, with an extra 20 percent off. In fact Daddy was dripping in diamonds, with his wrists and ear lobes getting the pleasurable frostbite it deserved from his only daughter.

I gazed at him. "I'm ok." I had so much on my mind. He opened the menu, carefully looked it over. I watched him. Very handsome man. If I was true and real with myself I'd admit that Daddy was fine. But I didn't look at my Daddy in such a whorishly incestuous way. I couldn't stop thinking about how I betrayed Georgia. Shit burned me up day and night. "I wonder what I'm going to drink tonight," I mumbled. Before I could say anything Daddy told me with a smile, "Strawberry daiquiri is your thing. Real men don't drink…fruity drinks, I want something with punch, some Batman shit Pow! Bang! Boom!"

We laughed easily, a few people at the opposite table looked over at us, laughing as well. Daddy was quite the comedian.

"I hear ya. You should just order a vodka."

As if on cue a tall, sensual looking blonde paused at our table, her work uniform crisp, with a few bills peeping from her pockets. She gave a smile and a warm, "Welcome to Applebee's. I'm Stacy, how may I help you two? Do you know what you'd like to drink?"

I looked at Daddy. He looked at me, grinning.

"I know what I want to order. I want a strawberry daiquiri, the two for one, and the appetizer entrée. I'm not that hungry. And Daddy will have the steak and shrimp dish and he would like to drink some Parrot Bay."

"Very good," Daddy said, taking my hand and kissing it. He always made me feel like a woman, letting me know if I met a man he better pamper me like Daddy and take my bullshit in stride like those racing horses. "But then again, you always order for me."

"Daddy, every time we come here we always order the same damn meal."

"The same darn meal, don't cuss at me young lady," he said sternly. "I'm your Daddy! I'm *not* your best damn friend."

"Best *darn* friend, Daddy, *don't* curse at me."

He gave a warm, defeated smirk; his eyes

lighting the entire restaurant. "Got you." Annie Lennox's "Sweet Dreams" came on the speakers. Daddy snapped his fingers, he loved this song. He extended his hand and I shook my head in the negative.

"I don't dance in public," I told him and he stood up, stuck his chest out, and snatched me from the chair, pulling me into his arms, and we did our little strut to the middle of the floor, just in front of the bar, having fun. I warmed up, it wasn't so bad, I just didn't want eyes on me. I didn't want to think about the fact that I was in love with a man I couldn't see and that I fucked Georgia's husband.

Amongst cheers and jeers, Daddy and I did our thing, wowing the crowd. My phone vibrated in my pocket. Taking it out, doing the salsa with Daddy, I looked at the caller I.D.

I decided not to answer it.

Why aren't you returning my calls? What is going on with you Princess? This is so unlike you. A bitch could be bleeding to death, I could be getting raped and you wouldn't know it because you're too busy for me.

Angry, Georgia, hanging up her cell phone, looked at Ed. He was managing the high octane precision of his brand new Mustang, 2006. His hands galloped over the steering wheel with the grace of a NASCAR driver;

maneuvering in and out of rush hour traffic.

He was perspiring. The AC wasn't doing much. "Damn it, I knew we should have taken the 836 West, instead of the 826."

She smirked. "I told you, but no, you don't listen."

He leaned over and quickly kissed her cheek, pretending she was Princess. "You didn't tell me anything…."

"Yes I did." She was defiant.

He glared at her. "Now is not the time to get smart. I'm trying to get us home."

Rolling her eyes, she sucked her teeth. "Why are you rushing home anyways?" she asked, taking off her Baby Phat jacket, a knock out in tight pink pants and matching pink blouse that left one shoulder bare and barely covered her amazing breasts. She was accessorized with bangles, leather belts and huge chandelier earrings that trapped the sunlight every time she looked around.

"Got things to do."

The only thing you're concerned about is your dick. Can't even stop whacking off three times a day and you got a wife. Her brows rose. "Such as?"

"You know…, uh…yea, I'm going to play ball with the boys."

Wrinkles on her forehead, deep in thought. "What boys? You haven't played ball in ages."

His cell phone vibrated. His heart racing, he ignored it.

Damn! What if it's Princess and she wants to give up some more of that good pussy? Goddamn it, why did I have to be stuck in traffic with my nagging wife?

She got mad. "Aren't you going to answer that?"

He looked down at it, then at her with a discreet smile. He tried to play it off. "It's nothing, probably a bill collector."

She grimaced noticeably. "But our bills are caught up. And since when did you start putting your phone on vibrate status?

"Since last night. I need a change, don't you agree?"

Her heart rate quickened. "This conversation isn't making any sense." Determined to find out what's going on with him, she took his phone and flipped it open and he flipped out, snatching it from her.

He said angrily, "Do I go through your phone?"

She was appalled, thrown by his reaction. "Well, no."

Fire in his eyes. "Good. This is my phone."

Something is not right about you! "But I pay

the bill."

"But you're my wife."

Damn. Defeated. *What is it?* "Ok, I respect your privacy."

"Good."

She remained quiet as two things went through her mind with the force of wrecking balls.

1). He never put his phone on vibrate and 2). He had been smelling like Dove soap ever since the day Princess crawled out of her kitchen. *What am I not seeing?* She didn't like the feeling in her gut. It was the same feeling she got the day she went in her guest bathroom and saw two things. Georgia's earring by the toilet.

And Ed's boxer briefs, soaked and wet.

Daddy and I were eating when he looked at me and said a few words that made me choke.

"When was the last time you talked to Georgia?"

Oh, God! The "G" word! Are you serious, Daddy? "Dad." I was coughing hard, my eyes watering. He handed me a glass of water. *Damn it, how could I betray Georgia? I should go and just be a woman and tell her I fucked her husband. Would she cut me or shoot me? Or both?* "I haven't spoken to her in days." I quickly took a heft swig, suddenly getting nervous. What made him think about her? And why were my hands trembling?

He was watching me, actually studying me. "You can't go two hours without talking to her." A beat of silence. "And now it's been days. Unusual, if you ask me. Are you and Georgia having problems?"

Yes. I fucked her man. And she didn't know it. "Nah. We cool, Daddy."

He used his butter knife and fork to cut up his meat. He looked like a private school veteran giving a class on etiquette.

"*Cool.* Is that what they say these days, 'cool'?"

I felt really uncomfortable. "Daddy, what's wrong?"

He dug into his pocket and produced my missing earring. I smiled, reaching out for it. "My fucking, I mean…" He glared at me sinisterly. "I mean my earring. Dad, where did you find it?"

"I didn't find it. Georgia did. By her toilet in her guest bathroom."

Grabbing my stomach, I jumped up to my feet, heading for the toilet.

I threw up the minute I laid eyes on it.

Two months had gone by since Ed and I had sex in his guest room. Two months of pure hell!

Nothing went right. I cried every night for Thomas, a man I was deeply in love with, a man that changed my soul in some unexplainable way. And to add insult to injury, my soul went through withdrawal, because I could never see him and didn't know where he went. I searched phone books, looking for Thomas and found over three thousand Thomas's, which depressed me even more. I didn't know a thing about him, his birthday, his last name nor where he was from. He could be from out of town for all I knew.

I could have asked Georgia, but I was scared of that house. Her husband would be there, and he would probably press me for pussy. I should tell her, like any real friend would do. But what if she didn't believe me? What if she blamed me? What if Ed turned it all around and told her I seduced him? At any rate, he really wasn't her husband if he's tip-toeing around on her. I was sure I wasn't the only woman he had sex with behind her back.

I did proposition him, turned my guilty pleasures into a business transaction. Then where would I be? Without a good friend, so I decided to just keep my distance. Plus she told me people were at the party who were *not* invited, so there went the notion of Georgia actually *knowing* Thomas. That house became garlic to the vampire in my heart, the blood-sucking, selfish bitch who sucked all on her husband's dick, a man I didn't want around me with a ten foot pole. I had lost respect for him, and I truly cared nothing for him. And if I had half a brain I'd admit that I lost respect for my damn self. I was just as much to blame as he was, truth be told. And the truth hurts because I couldn't even think straight right now.

Suffice it to say, Georgia found my earring, in her bathroom. Maybe I was overreacting. There was no way she'd figure out Ed and I fucked. And I doubted if he told her. Ed was loyal, especially when it came to things he wanted. So what she found my earring. Didn't prove she knew anything.

She has been calling me left and right and I always made up excuses as to why I couldn't come hang out with her. I had to work. I just got off work. I gotta do overtime. I gotta close tonight. I gotta open tomorrow. She took it all in stride. But there was only one problem.

I never stood her up before.

And Ed. God. This bitch has been calling me for months. On my cell I declined his call. When he came by the house I slipped out the back door before he could come and talk to me. I didn't want to tell my Daddy we had sex, because Daddy loved Georgia like a daughter, and I already knew what he would do to Ed's skull. Not to mention he'd have my head as well, because he raised me better than that. Daddy always taught me not to be a home wrecker, yet I wrecked so many homes with my prostitution that it was pathetic.

Right now I was still glowing from the good dick I was enjoying. Yes. It was back to the prostitution business, had money to make. A very fine, sexy man was tearing the pussy up, my hands became closed fists…I was punching his chest as he took my legs and put them behind the backs of his elbows and he grinded into me, moving with me. His hardened friend bringing me pleasure beyond this world, dick that took my mind off my problems, and I had a big problem, one I couldn't shake, even if I tried to. A problem that had me in denial. It was one of those problems I just didn't know what to do with; I didn't know *how* to handle it. One of those problems you hid from everyone in your life because you didn't know how they'd handle the news.

So I pushed it to the back of my mind when I looked at us fucking from the reflection of my bedroom mirror, loving the eighth wonder of the world. This sexy God and I. Bumping together. Kissing and hugging. Cursing and whispering. It was 8 a.m. to be exact. Kenny, 23 years old, from East Harlem (and just moved down south to Miami, never been here, well he been here for seven months) was a stone-cold freak and I was hoping that he became one of my regulars. Selling pussy was a business; just ask the porn industry and Hollywood. I was the type of prostitute that had a big clientele, I only messed with men who had money and drove flashy cars. They had to pay up front. Fifty dollars for head lasting twenty minutes. Yea, I kept a stop watch. A hundred dollars for an oral session lasting an hour. Anything beyond that we could talk about. To simply eat the cooch (my word for 'pussy') ranged from $50 to $150, depending on his cleanliness, looks and charm. Believe me…men paid out the ass just to eat my cooch. Nothing more and nothing less. Mainly chubby men who couldn't get it up or lacked the proper skills to pay the bills… To have sex in the cooch, a hundred dollars flat fee. Up to thirty minutes. To get the ass, two hundred dollars for thirty minutes. Anal sex was dangerous, so the fee was a little high. I supplied the condoms. Gotta protect my investment, which was my taut, voluptuous body. I followed my menu to the T, never deviating from it.

If my clients were good enough, I kept index cards with their information and stored the information in my palm pilot, a digital organizer given to me by Georgia for my birthday a couple years ago. I saw particular clients probably twice a week, and we kept it simple and discreet. We always met in my room. Daddy worked at a doctor's office, filing papers. Twelve to thirteen hour days. So he was hardly ever here. I had enough money to go out and get one of those expensive condos being built all over Dade County, but I decided to work from Daddy's house, and lay back and leave the driving to my pussy. I wasn't about to give these greedy, trying-to-take-over-Miami Cubans my goddamn hard-earned money. And I didn't give a shit if Castro didn't like it, either.

But Kenny! Lord, he had his way with me…using huge cucumbers and bananas to sex me…and sucked coconut juice off my pussy while I was on my period. I wouldn't tell him. I was selfish like that, couldn't help it. Money was money, and bill collector's still rung your goddamn phone while you were on your period so PMS became my motto and every time that day of the month came, I worked *three times* as hard. This was my "secret weapon," because we all knew men loved running and playing women like the Sweet 16 in college basketball soon to be the Elite 8, so being that men have run game on me before, getting a Niggah to go

Downtown and eat some sushi while Aunt Flow was in town made me laugh inside. You know, get' em before they get you.

Hell if he couldn't figure out coconut juice was white and not reddish white then that's on *him*. Kenny and I were doing all this fucking while my Daddy was fixing the shelf in the living room, dancing to some Sam Cooke. I could hear the wooden floors squeaking, Dad was heavy-footed. Twisting the Night Away. Now he was singing so loud he'd wake the dead, which didn't bother me at all because he was less susceptible to hearing Kenny's good dick hanging Head Shots on my pink walls. He had a late day, so Dad wouldn't be leaving for another hour or so. Normally, I'd wait for him to leave, because I hated disrespecting my Daddy, he was a good man; but I wanted Kenny with a passion, so we did the old school sneaking around thing.

Being the adventurous, rebellious woman I was, I took a chance. And with that in mind I think back to when I met him. Mr. Good Bar. Kenny.

I was just coming out of the Dadeland Mall, looking so hot to trot in the most expensive dress and high heeled pumps Macy's had to offer. Huge bangles on either wrist, six necklaces, off all sizes around my sweaty neck. A huge medallion resting on my titties. My hair was looking flawless.

I was getting in my Nissan Altima when I heard "Goddamn, girl you fine!" coming from behind me.

The silkiest, most smoky ghetto voice I'd ever heard.

Of course I blushed, quickly wiped the smile from my face and gave my famous mean scowl. A bitch like me had to play hard to get. Even though I was notorious for giving up the pussy to a fine ass man, when I saw a tall, sexy chocolate man approaching me, like a lion on a lioness before the actual beast penetration, clad in Gucci, I was wet. Goddamn it, now I got to change my panties. I was tired of changing panties five times a day. I hated my panties stuck to my cunt every time a fine man looked, breathed or winked at me. Maybe I should buy some Depends, put the diaper on before I put on my panties, so when I got wet, the diaper would get soaked and not my goddamn panties! I pay good money for my draws, $50 a pair from Victoria's Secret.

When he smiled, I looked him over. Cadillac Escalade behind him, another man in the passenger seat. He wasn't so pleasant. I rolled my eyes. He got bitchy, saying, with a whiny voice, "Kenny, she think she all that. Her name is probably Booty-Do."

Kenny held up his hand, not breaking away from my gaze. My mouth ajar, my hand on my neck, I looked past Kenny, sashayed up to the Escalade, and said, "Excuse me, my name is what?"

"Booty-Do. Your stomach sticks out further than your Booty-Do, bitch you ain't all that!"

I hated when people called me names my parents didn't name me. Infuriated, I jumped in the SUV and yanked the Niggah by his huge earrings and tried to snatch them out. So what my stomach stuck out further than my ass, I was pregnant, what did he expect? He reminded me that I had a problem, a problem that would change my life once nine months passed by. What would my father *think? Knowing I didn't have a clue where the Daddy was? Thomas disappeared off the face of the earth. He came into my life just to help me make the little angel in my womb.*

With that in mind I eyed this sack of shit inside the Cadillac. I wasn't scared to get grimy and dirty with these no-good men. They thought women couldn't fight, but I had a trick for this man today!

I was fuming. "Who you calling a bitch?"

Angrily, he slapped me across the face. My teeth bit down on my tongue. I winced. Damn that hurt. Fire in my eyes, I spat in his face, scratching his cheek. He opened the passenger side door, tried to jump out and I grabbed his huge chain and wrapped it around my hands and pulled the bitch like I was bucking an out-of-control horse.

"This bitch is crazy!" he said aguishly, wiggling, and flinging his arms wildly. Dadeland Mall security caught wind of the fiasco and flashing lights were headed our way.

Alarmed, Kenny grabbed me from the back, kicked his door closed, looked me dead in the eyes and said, "Damn, baby. I need a woman like you. Ready to fight like that? Calm down, Ma. He cool. That's my brother."

I was huffing and puffing, fixing my hair. I said, "So I take it your name is Kenny." I tried to calm down, I kept glaring at his pussy-of-a-brother.

He squeezed my left arm gently. "Yea. And your name is?"

I breathed in deep and got it together. I brushed off my outfit, making the transition back to being a lady in the streets. "Miss Webster. They call me Diamond." Diamond was my prostitute name.

He kissed my hand. His brother was cursing and making a huge scene. He acted just like a female. What real man you know fought pregnant women? Sad. People were starting to gather around, but up here on Kendall and 88th Street, where the mall was located, these people were the stuck up type. They had money. Drove fancy cars. And I didn't like the atmosphere up here. I was from further south. Florida City. I wasn't used to snobbish people sizing me up.

Security parked next to Kenny and I, and an out of shape white, Texan-looking white man got out, pulling up his pants, grabbing his walkie-talkie. He said, "What seems to be the problem over here?"

I looked at him and said, "Go about your business and stay out of mine."

Kenny pulled me behind him and said, curtly, "We're fine. Really. We were just leaving." He glared at his brother. "Weren't we?"

He remained quiet, rubbed his neck, got back in his brother's ride and closed the door. The next second he blasted rapper Young Jeezy "The Inspiration" so loud we couldn't hear ourselves talk.

I had to strain to hear Kenny. "He's mad. He just lost his wife and his job. So he isn't in a good mood." He looked at me a little more fixedly. "She left him because he called out another woman's name in his sleep, and was actually having sex with her in his dream. She couldn't deal with it, and she packed up and left him."

I felt sorry for him. No wonder he was acting crazy. Losing your woman and your job had to be doing a number on him.

"It's cool. Look…I'm on my way to a D.J. party in Richmond Heights," I told Kenny. "You got a number I can reach you?"

"I can do better. How about we tag along. We need a diversion."

I took his phone from his hip, put in my name and number.

"Ok, sounds like a plan. Follow me."

A few days later Kenny and I were in my father's house. Playing around with fire. Because if my ex-Marines Dad found us in here playing House he was going to shoot us both.

I loved playing around with the fear of being caught, living on the edge. So I had given Kenny specific instructions: Come to my bedroom window. Because the back of the house was shielded by huge oak and palm trees. And since you wanted to do something different bring some props with you. I was open to anything, within reason.

He followed orders. I loved when a man listened. There was a big difference between a man who listened and a man who listened when he wanted some pussy. When he crawled through my window and got naked and I laid eyes on his *Playgirl* Centerfold-type body, he politely gave me three hundred dollars to bounce in the cooch, eat my pussy, get some head, and we got right on down to good ole sex. I was glad he remembered I didn't have sex for free. Some men thought they were so damn fine that women would just waive the fees. Not me, honey.

I had told him about my services when we left the DJ Party. I was a tad bit uncomfortable. After getting to know each other a little better, we'd gone out to *Flannigan's* and grabbed a bite to eat. Georgia was on my mind the entire time. Yea, his whiny brother came along. He got his own table, refused to sit by me. I didn't give a shit.

I also told Kenny I turned tricks. I did what I had to do to make my money. He seemed amused, telling me he spent half of his paychecks at the strip club anyway.

And now pushing all of that to the back of my mind, I examined his dick, making sure he didn't have any bumps and scrapes. Looked good, of course. He was somewhat offended, but he remained quiet. Didn't care how he felt anyway, I was the star of this show.

I then did a rush job on his dick, trying to suck it as fast as I could so he could come as fast as he could and we could get on to doing something enjoyable. I didn't like giving head, not even with Georgia's husband. I guess part of me wanted Ed, too, which was why I sucked him up with the energy and desire that I did. I shook just thinking about it.

But Kenny was so happy somebody was sucking his dick he didn't care that my teeth kept making him jump and his blood run cold. I saw the anger in his eyes, but he swallowed his pride and savored the smoother moments I gave him with my mouth.

"Ouch, shit you *bit* me again, girl!" I loved his gentle voice.

I rolled my eyes, wishing he could be going down on me. "I didn't mean to."

He huffed and puffed. "Are you sure you know what you're doing?" He eyed me evilly.

A flick of the tongue on the bulging mushroom head of his passion. He smiled then. "Yea, I do. *Don't* talk shit." I just didn't want to give him head. He was *too* anxious.

He shook his head in the negative. "Don't bite my shit."

I bit it purposely and he yelped like a dog, trying to get away from me and I gripped his nature so hard he froze. "You *better* be happy…" I sucked on his nuts and his eyes rolled to the back of his head. Oh he loved that. "…Somebody is sucking you up."

He narrowed his eyes, kissing at me, admiringly rubbing my cheek. "Girl I got a lot of Hoes."

Is he calling me a Ho? "Then *why* are you here with *me*?" I got an attitude.

He smiled. Damn he was super *fione*! "Because I felt—*lick right there baby, yes suck my balls, God, yea*—sorry for…you."

Can you believe the nerve of this man? "Sorry for me?" I was wet. I didn't want romance. I just wanted to have a good time. And homeboy from New York had one of the prettiest dicks I'd ever seen! I never knew dick could be so pretty. They all looked so, I didn't know, little, big, or some-what all right. Dick, for me, was nothing but different shapes and sizes, and I never thought one could actually look appealing. Yet *his* penis was a light shade of caramel, blended with some Swiss Mocha. Slightly curved, thick and huge, about ten inches. Definitely a perfect ten on the old school scale.

I couldn't shake Thomas. The length of his dick. The way he felt. The way he looked at me, the way he appreciated me caring for him when he was *too* drunk to walk. The way he moved deep inside me, the was he became the human Van Gogh, the famous painter, and painted his magnum opus inside my womb with the skill of the Great Creator himself.

The night we made our baby.

My Dad walked to my room door and knocked. I was licking around Kenny's testicles. "*Yes*, Daddy?" He didn't stop my party.

"I'm on my way to work," he said, Kenny losing his erection, slightly.

He looked at me, whispering, "Are you crazy? Is the door locked?"

I sucked the head and got it back up, and he pushed the pillow on his face to shield his moaning.

Man, shut up! Be a man and stop being a pussy. "Love you, Daddy. Talk to you later."

"I can't get a hug?" he asked. Dad always hugged me before going to work, we were very close. Daddy never hurt me, always provided for me and my family.

I wrapped my breasts around Kenny's dick, spat on it, lubed it really good and tit fucked him. He went crazy, his legs trembling; he tossed the pillow and was whispering all kinds of bullshit in my ear. How he wanted to marry me. Yea, right! How he would die for me. He wanted me to be his bitch. Yea, I heard that before.

"Dad, I'm naked." Wasn't a lie, of course.

"I'll call later, baby, have a good day," he said, walking off, the floor squeaking like rats on cheese.

After Kenny came, silently I might add, he said it was his turn to please me. He ate me out slowly, expertly, talking to me, telling me how cleaned the pussy was, how good it tasted, that it was pretty and black on the outside, and a pretty pink on the inside…magnificently framed, like Renaissance art, by well-trimmed pubic hairs that reminded him of fettuccini. I came all on his tongue instantly; no one had ever praised the Cooch quite like he had. Were all New Yorkers this smooth, this in tune with tongue to pussy interaction?

His cell phone kept vibrating, getting on my nerves so I gave him a very cold stare and then said, while his head bobbed and weaved, "Your girl calling you?"

He laughed, sucking my clit. He spelled out his answer.

I. A-M. S-I-N-G-L-E.

Not believing him, because he was just too fine, probably had many bitches, I rolled my eyes, shivering, holding on to his head. My legs began drumming together as this man took me into orbit. I had some good head in my time, but never like this.

"Then why is your phone vibrating out of control."

His eyes sparkling, he spelled it out with his tongue again, all over my pussy.

P-R-O-B-A-B-L-Y M-Y B-R-O-T-H-E-R.

Probably his brother.

And with that in mind I picked up the cell phone, placed it on my left nipple and when it vibrated again, it sent tremors throughout my breast while I pulled the right tit up to my lips and begin suckling my right nipple until it got erect.

Kenny held my upper thighs, munching the Cooch, separating the walls, sliding a cucumber up in there, tearing me up sensually, driving me crazy.

I shuddered with glee. Then came the coconut juice, which was a treat. He'd peel bananas, fuck me with them, eat and feed them to me like a bird putting food in the baby bird's mouth.

A sharp pain shot through my abdomen and I knew it was Aunt Flow knocking, but I didn't care. I felt it.

More coconut juice on my pussy. I still couldn't believe my period still came on when I was pregnant.

I could feel my blood mixing with the milk. He didn't have a damn clue. So I didn't say anything, but when he tried to kiss me I faked a yawn.

On my breasts and vagina he made a salad with the offending vegetable and fruit, adding tomatoes and crisp lettuce he said he had in the ice box at his brother's house for about three days. He'd just gone grocery shopping when the Government gave him his food stamps on an American-flag-clad debit card. I loved the originality. But I was even more impressed that a man who drove a Cadillac Escalade, a $55,000 vehicle, paid off, was on government assistance.

Now we tongue kissed, I melted like butter on a flame into his skin. We rose and fell together, my hair plastered to my face. The humidity reached intense levels.

I was moaning uncontrollably as his huge bat tried to find the batting cage in my pussy. He dug and dug, like Osama Bin Laden was hiding deep in my cervix.

We kissed again; I wrapped my legs around such stern hips. He bounced off the pink walls, slip and sliding me into pure promiscuity. I felt like a silly fool, the way he dug me out. The way he'd look dead in my eyes and tell me "Do you like it?"

The look on my sweaty face told him "Yes!"

I would come a total of four times before

he exploded again, the finality of his Magnum condom capturing his fiery seeds all in one whop. He pushed his dick all the way inside me, paused, I could feel it pumping and throbbing, his body pressed against mine, the heat enveloping the both of us. His eyes fluttered closed. Then he rolled over, his amazingly chiseled body spent, and he then started gathering up his clothes, turned on my shower without permission, took a quick rinse off, using my wash cloth and soap. I didn't appreciate that at all. He looked peaceful.

Trapped in my own thoughts, thinking about his brother, I sat on the edge of my bed, smoking a cigarette, watching him. He tried not to look at me.

When he was done, he dried off, put on his gear, didn't as much as look at me. He didn't kiss me.

He hopped out my window, closed it and jumped in his Cadillac.

Why it hurt me I would never understand.

His phone vibrated. Oh, yea. Let me see if those hoes were trying to get at him.

Why I suddenly felt territorial was beyond me. Kenny was not my man.

I looked at the caller I.D.

When my eyes locked on the name flashing in the screen all the breath left my body.

I couldn't stop smiling. I couldn't think straight.

The name read:

Thomas.

BOOTY-DO PART IV: THE PHONE CALL

I stared at the phone.

Praying to God I was seeing things.

I opened Kenny's phone and started scrolling down, looking for Thomas's name. My heart was racing so fast I was about to hyperventilate, I couldn't think straight. All those days I was miserable, wondering where he was, what he was doing, was he healthy, dead or alive, all those days turning into even more miserable nights, when I cried myself to sleep, cursing and hating myself, the showers I took, trying to erase his scent, his lips, his tongue and his immaculate touch, and I couldn't because he was some unknown bodily sculpture and he chiseled hieroglyphics all over my body, symbols of Egyptian warriors engaging in various hand gestures, and I'd cling to my pillow, afraid of my own sheets and I'd tell myself, "God, why am I going through all this torment?"

I was a woman who lived by the mood, a woman who got into prostitution because men always made me feel beautiful, I used to listen to Too Short rap songs and he always preached "Don't fuck for free," the pornography business was a multi-billion dollar empire, Bill Clinton got his dick sucked in the Oval Office, Hollywood stars were always paying for it, look at Heidi Fleiss, Hollywood's ex-madam who got busted by the law. I worshipped her, so I started charging men when they wanted to have sex with me, getting deeper and deeper into it, becoming lost in it, telling myself that I'd do it for just one more day, one more hour, one more night only to fall back in it every time I thought about the money, every time I thought about my vanishing self-esteem, the love I claimed I had for myself and my body yet I didn't love myself or my body until I met Thomas.

And now I didn't want that life, I didn't want the money, yet I had clients, who came to see me on the regular, how do I stare a potential $2,500 a week in the face and turn it down? How did I turn down good dick? Good dick was just as addicting as crack, as a matter of fact it was a-dick-ting!

Yet wanting to be with Thomas overshadowed it all.

When I found it I clicked on it, there were pictures next to every name in his phone. When Thomas picture came up he was smiling.

Oh my God! The smile the smile *the smile THE SMILE!* Perfect match!

Dropping the phone in my lap I found my angel, the same man who slapped me at the mall, the same man who said my stomach stuck further than my booty do.

Before I could write down his number Kenny snatched his phone from my hands.

"Why are you looking through my phone?" Laser beams in his eyes make me shudder.

I tried to think of a lie, wiping tears from my eyes, sucking in sex-clad air. "I didn't look through your phone."

He tilted his head to the side and gave me the blandest look. Made me stir on the bed in an uncomfortable way. "Damn, *why* are you lying? I stood at your window watching."

"Let me ask you something. Do you happen to know what name your brother called out in his sleep?"

He stared at me, shaking his head. "You don't even like my brother. Why should I tell you? And why are you getting personal?"

He's the way to your man, girl keep it together. I can't lose Thomas again, I just can't! "*Calm* down, damn Kenny my Dad's here."

"You need your *own* crib; you're too grown to be living at home, sneaking men into your Daddy's house."

Ok, now I was getting offended. Just because the Niggah had good tongue and dick didn't give him the right to diss me in my own goddamn home! "And you need to get off welfare,"

"For your information, this card doesn't belong to me. It belongs to my bitch."

I knew it. I just knew it, he was a damn snake.

"So you do have another woman."

"Look, the game has never changed. Adam and Eve made the game, and it hasn't changed since then. Get a clue. I just wanted to fuck. Let's be real, girl I knew you were Diamond, every Niggah down here said they paid for that pussy, they talked about how good and tight it was, I just had to find out, and they never lied, its good as hell. But I paid you, so the transaction is complete. Nice meeting you and when you see me on the street make like you don't know me. Got that?"

"Fuck you, asshole! Who are you supposed to be?"

"At least I'm not a prostitute."

And before I could say anything he hopped out of my window and I tried like hell to forget he ever existed.

But I couldn't forget that his brother's name was Thomas.

His brother was my soul mate.

And I'd never see Kenny again.

I cried myself to sleep, telling God that if I couldn't have my baby and my man I would just die inside, it felt good, it felt right and I knew I was his missing rib.

Deep down he had to know his wife wasn't the one.

I was the one.

Maybe I was just crazy.

Quite honestly, I didn't know if I was coming or going.

And I didn't want to know, either.

My cell phone rang a few hours later.

Waking me from a deep sleep. Rubbing my stomach, giving my baby some love, Thomas's baby some real love, I looked at the clock with an exhausted smile on my face. It was after 3 p.m., I was about to be late for work. But I decided not to go, I didn't want to see people or be around people. I got out of bed and answered my cell; it vibrated on the night stand.

"Diamond."

It was Kenny. I got mad instantly.

"Hey, girl."

Calling me like everything is all right. When you had good pussy, they always called back. "What do you want?"

"I know we'll never see each other again, which is all good. But you asked me a question and I will answer it."

"What question would that be?" I couldn't keep the contempt from my voice. It made me shake with anger.

"I never understood it, but my brother said the woman he fell in love with never told him her name; not that he could remember."

I got quiet. My heart was racing. "*And*?"

"I don't know *why* I'm telling you this; my family prides itself on keeping family business between family."

"Yet you're on the phone with me."

"I know, shoot me. I can't even stand your ass, going through my goddamn phone. And I thought you were a cool broad."

"I don't have time for this."

"Well make time. I have something to tell you."

"That you're an asshole?"

"You know what…"

I was getting defensive. "What, jerk?"

"Well *listen*."

Listen to what."

"Diamond…"

"Maybe this wasn't such a good idea." I didn't like the sinking feeling in my gut.

"My brother called out for her in his sleep. He told me all he could ever think about was this woman, he doesn't remember her face or anything, he said he was drunk when they met, the same night she helped him up to the room because he was too drunk to walk…I talked to my sister-n-law, who is bitter over the entire thing, and she told me he called out for Princess Webster all night, and was actually making love to her in his sleep."

I didn't hear anything else because when he said my name I dropped the phone.

The line disconnected.

I grabbed my coat and ran out to my car, devastated.

Kenny's brother was my soul mate.

***

I have a white friend. Her name was Veronica Simms, a tall, gregariously ugly Ho who thought she knew it all. I called her a Ho because she called *herself* a Ho. And was proud of it. Simple as that.

Veronica and I did everything together, we shared our men, never talked behind each other's back, cooked for each other, talked all day on the phone and always had each other's backs. Worse case scenario, she acted black. She was like a black woman trapped in a white woman's body. She was bipolar, or so she said. I didn't think so, I knew what bipolar people did and said and she didn't fit the description.

I didn't consider myself a bitch because Ho's got paid and bitches got played. Bitches fucked for free, I was for a) rent and b) available for a limited time. I was a reliable prostitute, undercover of course because I still lived with my father, even though I was 21 years old and my Daddy would kill me.

My new prostitute name was Booty-Do. Because my stomach stuck out four inches further than my Booty Do. Well, actually I was punishing myself. Thomas called me that, the day we met, again. The day that would prove to change my life, because the man I have been searching for was right in my face, we were in a fight, cursing each other, causing security to come and try to calm things down. That was Satan keeping his rib from finding her home.

Now I was sick to my stomach.

Now I was very insecure about my body,

though I wasn't going to lie. I was *very* down on myself, whoring away while being pregnant with another man's child. Did I care about the safety of my child? STD's? HIV? Potential ailments that could erase my baby's bloodline before it developed and in the process destroy my own?

As a child I always had issues with my weight. I used to read Aesop's Rhymes to keep myself cool and calm growing up. I read Aesop every night before I went to bed. My parents were welfare-stricken during those times, before Dad joined the Marines, that got us out of poverty. So they couldn't afford much of anything, except food, and boy did I eat when I was mad, angry, happy or sad. My room I shared with my older brother, Big Scooter, who would die three years later from a hit and run driver who was never found. We were very close. And when he died I just withdrew into myself. The world was suddenly lonely and cold.

I used to have funky posters and stars ripped from magazines on my red and green colored walls. My bed was much too small for me. When I slept I always fell on the floor when I turned over. My clothes I outgrew two weeks after getting them. My feet always had corns because my shoes were too small. Nah, I just grew into them quicker than the average child. My hair barely grew. My Daddy called me a fat bitch who needed to stop eating. My Mama called me fat and ugly. They would do this for years. It would ruin my self esteem, it would be the reason I went out and got some dick.

To belong, to fit in and to feel special.

And on top of that I was black as tar. Blue-black my enemies called me. All the light-skinned, skinny-need-to-eat-bitches always talked about me. At face value I never showed my true worth. I never let them know they hurt my feelings and made me feel low. Hell, if my parents used to do it then why shouldn't I let everyone else?

Veronica and I used to work at an Auto Parts store in Homestead months ago. She was the only friend I had. She treated me good and always had good things to say about me. We've known each other since the eleventh grade, attending pissy-smelling Homestead Senior High School. Back then I was quiet and to myself, never thought I'd have a female friend. I didn't bother anyone, did my school work, lived for the Pep Rallies, and went home. That was until she waltzed into my Home Economics class trying to run shit. A white girl talking tougher than the black girls.

We kind of hit it off real big. Despite

trying to be bossy, she had a heart of gold. Very upbeat and outgoing. I was introverted and much of a homebody. She had just moved to Miami from Lebanon. I had never heard of Lebanon. She said that's where she was born, and where most of her family remained.

That became evident when, a few days ago, she came to my Dad's house, banging on the door, screaming at the top of her lungs, "Girl, turn on the TV! Conflict is erupting in Lebanon! I'm concerned about my family over there…"

I was thankful my Dad wasn't home. Despite his love for her, he would have cussed her out for banging on the door like the police.

Exhaling audibly, I opened the door for her, gave her the evil eye and invited her in.

"Girl, what are you talking about?"

Quiet and tears falling from her gray eyes, she turned on the TV and picked up the remote, turning up the volume. On the news a reporter, in Lebanon, was talking about the violence over there. My heart went out to Victoria. She hung onto the reporter's every word.

I told her to sit down. She didn't want to sit.

"Crying isn't going solve the problem, Victoria."

"I know. But I feel so empty inside. I wish all of my family were here and not just me."

I gave her a lingering look. "They *can't* come over?"

She sadly thought about it. "I don't know. Quite honestly I don't think they *want* to come over."

"Can't they get visas or passports or whatever that's called?"

"I'm pretty sure they can. Believe me I've spoken to them and practically begged them to come to the states to have a better life. But they are so stubborn."

"They're probably scared, girl. Moving and change isn't very pretty sometimes." I looked at her, hurt on my face. She was studying me. "Its not."

"Suddenly I don't think we're talking about my situation anymore. What's up, girl?"

I looked away from her. "Nothing."

She was concerned. "Is it the *baby*?"

I looked at her in shock. "*What* baby?" I tried to suck in my gut, but her eyes fell down on my womb so fast I held my breath.

She smiled. "The one you're carrying, we *all* know you're pregnant, girl."

I started to cry. "Oh, girl, I'm in love, I don't want to be a prostitute anymore, his name is Thomas and he's the most incredible man. He's my air, my soul mate, girl I will die without him."

And Veronica not only believed me she held me, because she knew, deep down, I never talked about any man the way I was praising Thomas.

I would never get to see him or be with him again. Because Kenny, the man with the key that led to him, was gone out of my life forever.

I had to call Georgia, I needed her right now.

While some women who faced the empty nest syndrome, a depressed state felt after their children grew up and left home, tried to cope and find new and exciting things to do with their lives, I felt the Lost Love Syndrome. Thinking about my lover Thomas made me feel whole. He gave me some good love, then he just up and left me, leaving me to fend for myself.

Feeling like an imbecile, it took me a little minute to gather my composure, and it took extra effort for me to tell Veronica not to tell my business to anyone. Georgia was on my mind. I needed to do something and fast. But I didn't know how to tell her. But I knew I had too.

Veronica's lips were like holes in the bottom of cups—couldn't hold juice, milk or water, got to tell everybody everything and the minute somebody wanted to whip her ass for running her big mouth, she wanted to dial my ten digits.

After telling Veronica I'd call her later, I went out to my car and attempted to call Georgia.

On second thought I hung up the phone.

I parked next to Georgia's Toyota Camry. Bad ass car. Deep dished rims. Killer stereo system. I wondered if Ed was home, I haven't been over here since the day after their hugely successful party.

When Ed did what he did, when *we* did what we did…I could *still* taste him on my lips, I could still see the sexy image that dangled like a carrot on a fishing hook before the library of my brain.

I shook the images away, and knocked on the door.

Georgia answered and embraced me, happily, when she saw me.

"Hey, girl! I have been trying to call you for *months*!"

"You have?" I knew she was, but I

thought she found out I had her man and she wanted to call me to set up a date when she could shoot me and I was too goddamn scared to find out so I kept my distance.

She stared at me. "Yes. You didn't see the missed calls on your cell?"

"I got a Metro PCS, the lowest cellie on the cell phone totem pole, Chile, you know how they do, mess everything up."

She knew I was lying. "Come in! And I been telling you, girl, I can put you on my Cingular plan so you can lose that Metro Piece of Shitty-ass phone."

I gripped my purse and walked inside, the cool AC hitting me in the face. "Girl, whatever, don't be talking about my phone."

I walked up the hallway, passing framed photos of her and Ed's family and made my way over to the lavish sofa. Georgia turned on the TV, looking dashing in vest with pleated mini skirt, huge earrings and flawless make up. Breathtakingly gorgeous, and she knew it. I could *never* be that pretty. The entertainment shelf had beautiful engravings of roses, beautifully polished to a shine. The low-table held four crystal bowls, with intricate carvings. Potpourri filled them to the brim. The three baccarat-crystal chandeliers were just dashingly breathtaking, made my Dad's house like an episode of Scooby-Do.

"So what brings you by after all these weeks, girl?"

I looked at Georgia, trying to keep the tears from my eyes. I lowered my head, and, alarmed, she rushed over from her chair and sat next to me, taking both my hands. I was shaking my head, I didn't want to be held or touched, I just wanted to be left alone.

She said, "Talk to me, girl. We been through hurricanes and tornadoes together, what is it?"

Say it, Princess, tell her you fucked Ed. Tell her you are just as messed up as he was for deceiving her.

"Is Ed here?"

"You want to talk *alone*, come on." She snatched me off the sofa, pulled me up the stairs, kicked open her bedroom door—and, to our surprise, Ed had his pants around his ankles, whacking off to a porno playing on the huge plasma TV. *Asian Bubble Butts Volume 2.*

Startled, he jumped up, pulling up his pants, frantically trying to explain himself.

Georgia was fuming and clearly embarrassed. "Get your nasty ass out the room so I can talk to my girl, God you men can't keep it in your pants for *nothing*, can you?"

He gave me a discreet look, zipping up his pants and flying out of the room, embarrassed and we were laughing.

"That husband of mine," she said to herself, closing the door. She pointed across the room. "Girl, have a seat on the sofa by my closet. And tell me what's wrong."

Before I could even lift my foot I blurted it out. "I'm in love, girl."

She laughed, waving her hands, "*Yea*, right! What's wrong, girlfriend?" she said, not hearing a word I just said.

I said it more cautiously. "I. Am. In. Love."

"With money, got that. *Houston*, we gonna have some big problems this bitch don't tell me what the hell is up with her."

With a huge smile I said, "I AM IN LOVEEEE!" and she fell silent, slowly sitting next to me, staring at the side of my face like I was Marvin the Martian. I tried to hold my smile, hold it, girl, hold it but I couldn't because the tears fell and I shuddered because suddenly the world was so cold and I didn't want to raise my child alone, he or she had a right to know his/her father and I deprived him/her of that, it was all my fault and I would never find him again because I fucked it up with Kenny and I could just shoot myself for that, the one golden ticket to Thomas.

She was clapping and laughing happily.

This was the best news. Words she thought I'd never say. "You're in love. You? The woman who said she'd *never* fall in love, the woman who played men like Chess and an episode of who sunk my Battleship?"

"Yes." I looked at her with so much pain on my face and she took my hands. "I am in love. But he doesn't know I'm in love with him."

She searched my face, looked deeply into my eyes as only she could do, she had it down pat, she knew when I was lying and when I was telling the truth, I hated she knew the keys to my kingdom. "You got it bad. You. Are. Gone. Chile. Wow, are you serious? Who is he?"

"Girl he's gone, gone forever, we had a passionate night, he made love to me, while he was drunk, better than any sober lover I ever had, he changed my life, made me look at myself. Oh girl I can't live without him."

She was squeezing my hands, crying with me, kissing my hands, telling me it'll be ok. "Girl in life friends come and go."

"But I wanted him to come and go with me."

"Season's change, my love. You know this. It isn't summer all year round, winter turns to spring eventually, its inevitable."

"But why does it have to be that way?" I asked angrily, jumping up and pacing the bedroom, kicking off my shoes, enjoying the comfortable feel of her plush white carpet tickling all between my toes.

Georgia's house phone rang. "Hold on, girl. Hold that thought." She went over to the caller I.D. She picked it up. "Sup, man. What do you want now, *more* money?"

I looked at her while she engaged in her phone conversation.

She looked pissed. "What? You still haven't found a job? You want money to buy food? Don't you have a food stamp card? Yes you do, I got it for you. Listen, I got you a car and I got you some money, lined you up with a job, look, cousin, I am family, yes blood is thicker than water, but god the fuck damn Niggah get off your ass and help your motherfucking self I am not the ATM machine!"

And she bammed the phone down.

"Damn, girl, that phone call was intense."

"Girl, my cousins have been living in Miami for a few months. One had a job, lost it and the other just gets on my nerves."

I couldn't keep my mind off Thomas. I covered my face and leaned against the wall, shuddering. She went on and on about her cousins, the hell with her cousins.

I didn't know what it was but some unknown force pulled me off the wall, took my hand and before I knew it I silenced Georgia when I opened her door, walked down the hallway, to the guest room, opened the door, smiling at the black carpet, the Bob Marley photos…I lay in the bed, rolling across it, rubbing my pussy until I shuddered, crying for Thomas, wanting him, I was crying so hard I came on myself just thinking about him, my body on fire, trying to find the flames of finality so I could have a fulfilling relationship, but that would never be, could *never* be. Thomas was out there, somewhere, going through a divorce, probably doing what his brother did, fuck all the girls, kiss them and make them cry.

I was crying, and he kissed me from head to toe.

"Princess! Girl, get over that man!"

I stood up, wrapping the sheets around me, like a cloak that protected me and my baby…my subconscious revealed the carefully placed memories in this room. I rushed over and closed the bathroom door, didn't want to remember Ed's memories from the toilet and beyond.

"Why did you come to this room, girl?"

Georgia was carefully observing me, not getting the big picture.

I looked at her with a sweet smile. "I *love* this room."

She studied me carefully, looking around, trying to figure it out. "I see that, girl. What's going on?"

"I made my baby in this room."

She looked me up and down, taking the sheets from me and lifting my shirt. "OH MY GOD! YOU'RE PREGNANT!"

I hugged her. *"Yes!"* Then I fell silent, because I didn't want to say the words, I didn't want to say "And I'll be raising my child alone. Another black single mother in America to get frowned down on talked about and ridiculed."

"How many months are you?" she asked, in a state of disbelief.

"A little over two months."

She pushed me on the bed, got on top of me, playfully and tried to tickle me. This was my girl; we always wrestled and had fun.

"And you didn't tell me?"

"I didn't want to make it a big deal."

She was skeptical as hell, over analyzing the entire ordeal in her head, probably, I knew her like a book.

"You didn't want me knowing you might be going on Maury to find out who is the father, *Billy you are NOT the father, Frank you are NOT the father!*"

We were laughing so hard I damn near fell out of the bed.

"Sam you are *not* the father," I said, warming to our subject with a smile. "Jarvis, you are damn sure not the father, you're too fucking fat! Larry, you're *not* the father."

"But Maury, my son has Larry's nose! Look at the screen Maury, it's a mistake it's a mistake?"

God, we were tearing our stomachs up, laughing.

She went on.

"And you don't know where the father is?" Ok. Spotlight back on me. Damn, I was damn sure trying to evade it.

"*No*, girl. No clue. And before I could get his number out of his brother's phone, he snatched it and has been AWOL ever since."

"Have you tried *calling* his brother back?"

"Yes. Repeatedly. But he blocked my number."

"Crummy men!"

"He was an asshole, really. A big one."

Her phone rings again. "Damn it," she said, waltzing over to it like a spoiled brat. "It better not be my cousin again."

She looked at it. She said. "Oh, *good*. It

isn't him." She answered with a smile. "Well, well, well. Tina. Sup, girl…yea, I know right, divorce isn't cool at all," said Georgia sadly. "What? You're trying to milk him, girl he has to live, too. I know, but did you actually see him cheat on you…I know, girl what was her name then?"

Her eyes lowered to the floor. Then she looked at me with her mouth open.

"What?" I asked her. "Is it somebody I know? Who are you talking to anyways, Georgia."

"Oh my God! Princess Webster is my best friend; you mean to tell me your husband called out Princess Webster's name in his dream?"

The room was spinning, I had to sit down.

Why was I smiling, why was I smiling.

"Oh, God, girl! Are you telling me my Thomas, the man of my dreams, my soul mate is your *cousin*?"

Georgia said, "Tina, get over to my house, now. Princess is here. And she's pregnant with Thomas's baby."

Georgia's head snapped away from the phone.

Tina had clicked in her face.

Booty-Do Part V: GHB

"Princess, this is crazy. You met him at my party?"

I tried to smile. "Yea. He was drunk. *Very* drunk. I was feeling it, dancin' and groovin', Hennessy and Coke drink pulverizing my blood stream, girl." They shared a chuckle. "He approached me. I felt the chemistry. *Strong*, girl. He could barely stand on his own two feet, Chile. So I led him to the guest room because he was not stable. I wiped his face with a wet rag, trying to nurture him. By then the drink had started to have an effect on me."

She was really having a hard time with this. She was trying to put two and two together. "I can now understand why you stayed away from my house, girl what you must have been going through, thinking you would never see him again, getting real feelings. Honestly, he didn't love Tina anyways; he only married her because everyone around him basically coerced him into doing it. It was all for show. He worked his ass off for Tina, and yea, Tina and I are cool, but she can be a bitch. Take his money, buy this and that, saw other men behind his back, I knew it, everyone knew it but we didn't want to break Thomas's heart."

Why was I upset? "She did that to him, that incredible man?"

"Yes. Then, after months of playing the field, someone robbed her in an alley in New York. She almost lost her life. She was stabbed and left for dead. Through the miracle of God she survived, she knew deep down that was her punishment for creeping around on her faithful husband. And you would think going through the darkness would make you a better person. She and Thomas got worse. She talked down to him, didn't appreciate him. She stopped the cheating, but the night Tina said he called out your name, she told me he was moaning your name, telling you how to take it, that he loved you, that he wanted to divorce her and spend his life with you."

I had to sit down, this was overwhelming. All I knew was that I wanted Thomas, I had to have him and I didn't quite know if I could have him. Maybe this was a fantasy; all this was in my head. I did screw his brother; this union with Thomas would never work. How could it? With so many factors against me?

"Girl, I need time for all this to digest. Life isn't to be played around with, girl."

She smiled easily. "I can see you and Thomas together. He's fun, loving. He's one of my favorite cousins."

I still couldn't believe it. My nerves were bad. "Why didn't you introduce him to me?"

"Because Kenny is a jerk, his older brother. I wouldn't introduce that dick head to anyone, Chile. Girl, I helped them move down here. I got Kenny a Cadillac Escalade; one of my friends at the car dealership owed me a favor. I even got one of my home girls to get him a food stamp card, in her name so he could keep his fridge stocked and he calls me every other day for more money, won't go get a job."

So much for the lie, Kenny. Your bitch got you a food stamp card, 'ey? You probably didn't even get to sniff the Cooch. I hated men who lied on their dicks. "And he's a piece of shit." I told her Kenny was one of my clients, I also told her about his cell phone, and when I saw Thomas's number I thought that was the key to being led back to my love, but it blew up in my face.

"Kenny always prided himself that he never had to pay for pussy."

I laughed with her. "Girl, first time for everything."

She fell silent, like she just remembered something. She had a very disquieting look on her pretty face. "Some man got arrested at my party."

"What does that have to do with anything?"

"Well, the bartender claimed there was something fishy about the short black man, that he was stalking your friend, I forget her name."

"*Who*, girl?"

"The Latino bitch. She's in jail, too."

"Oh, she gave me the drink." I blinked twice. "Why is she in jail?"

Georgia stared at me. "Shit, the Henny and Coke, you just said that."

"Yea girl what's up? Are you getting at something?" I was starting to feel queasy. Tina was on her way over here, and she better not come with the noise either because I will whip her ass.

"He put GHB in the Henny and Coke he

gave to your Latino friend. She saw him put it in there. She told the police when she saw him lace the drink, he came over to her and she took the drink, pretended that she had to go to the bathroom, and she gave the drink to a friend of hers…"

I was talking really slow, the room spinning. "Girl, she *gave* me that drink."

"Yep. She then befriended the bartender, bought a bottled water, had him pour the water in a cup identical to the one she gave you and had little man thinking she actually drank the drug-infested liquor."

My hands were shaking. I was having a hard time with this. My Latino friend and I were really cool, but not anymore. What real friend would do something like that? But then again the bitch has always been jealous of me. "No wonder I felt out of it, got sloppy and everything while I was dabbing a cold rag on Thomas's face. The night of your party Thomas and I made the baby I am carrying, I love him, I don't know girl, he was so drunk and I had a date rape drug in my system."

"At first we had no proof of an actual drugging taking place, but the miniature plastic bag the GHB was in was found by my bar. And the cup on Henny was in my guest room, apparently girl you didn't finish it all. The cops ran tests on it and viola, GHB was all in it, girl."

The room was spinning, faster. I moaned piteously, trying to stop the migraines from taking over my brain. "I need a minute to be alone, would you mind, girl? If I stayed in here?"

"Take all the time you need. I'll go put us some corn dogs and fries on, you hungry?"

"Girl you know I love food."

"Shit, you're eating for two, now. Goddamn it, Thomas got a baby on the way."

"You say that like he doesn't have any kids."

She kissed my lips; I loved my sister at heart. "Girl, he doesn't, you are about to give him his first biological child."

When she left I savored the moment. Yes, that's because I was his soul mate.

I waited until the door closed behind Georgia before I made my move.

I went over to the caller I.D. I saw Tina's name. Had a "305" area code by the number. Must be the house phone.

I picked up the phone and made a call.

"Yes, how are you? Me, I'm fine. Thank you…"

***

Thomas was getting out of the shower when his wife came into the bathroom and threw some bills in his face. The envelopes hit him on the forehead and snow flaked towards the wet tiled floors. Angry, he said, "What is your problem?"

"I thought you paid the light bill."

He rolled his eyes, drying off his nuts, dick, ass and lower part of his track runner legs. "Whatever, you pay it. Aren't we getting divorced?"

She put her hands on her hips. "That's why I'ma clean you out in court."

He laughed so hard she tucked her chin back. "Well let's spend some tax payer money. Because I'm not giving you shit."

"You aren't shit."

"I should have never married you."

She withheld the knowledge of another woman being pregnant with his child. She told herself *I'm not telling him. He doesn't deserve to know.* "Whatever, Man. I am so glad I didn't have your child."

He lowered his eyes to the floor. He always wanted to be a father. He loved children; they were his pride and joy. Something about a child that comforted him, allowed him to escape the real world and see things simply through the angelic eyes of a child. And now he would never experience that because Tina destroyed his will to want to father a child.

He looked up at her. He wrapped the towel around his hips. Walking past her, he said, "I don't want a slut having my child anyway."

Infuriated and getting tired of Tina, he opened the top dresser drawer, pulled out a pair of boxers, put them on and slid into a T-shirt.

When he turned to go over to the closet Tina got in his face. She wasn't happy. "Look, motherfucker. I'm going to be real with you. You don't want a slut having your child then why did you marry me?"

"Get out of my face. I'm not about to stand here and let you turn this nonsense around on me."

"Oh, you're going to stand there. Listen, Thomas. I am fertile." His face was a frown. He just stared at her. "In fact if you touch me I can get pregnant. I just didn't want to have your child." She walked over to the dresser, opened it, and then pulled out the secret compartment. She wiggled the birth control pills in his face. Her eyes sparkled while the sparkles in his eyes died. He shook with rage, his hands fists.

"So you lied to me."

She laughed playfully, tossing the pills in the trash. "Don't need those anymore, since you won't be fucking me…"

Impulsively, he grabbed her by the neck and started squeezing, as hard as he could. She grabbed his hands, but he squeezed harder, death in his eyes. They fell on the bed tussling. His anger got the best of him.

"Die, bitch!" His face was shaking; she was losing air, losing it all. She kicked her feet as hard as she could, trying to get away from him. He put all his weight on her, spit in her face, let her go, stood up and said, "Go to hell, bitch!"

"Have you lost your mind?" She was in fear, for the first time in her marriage she feared him. *What have I done*? she thought to herself. She shook her head, rubbing her neck.

Getting out of the bed she opened the closet and took out a few suit cases. He watched her, torn up inside. She sat on the edge of the bed. He kept staring at the small trash can, her words flowing through his brain. She took birth control pills. Bitch!

Taking the birth control pills from the trash, he extracted the remaining twelve, rushed over to her, she tried to run and he grabbed her feet, pulled her to him, put his hand around her sweaty neck, forced her mouth open and pushed the pills down her throat.

She spat a few of them in his face. He punched her in the jaw and she kicked him in the balls. Falling to the floor, he moaned piteously, quickly getting up to his feet. She got on his face and started punching at him. He slapped her so hard she fell to her knees. "I HATE YOU!"

His words shook the room. She stood there, blood on her lip, breathing hard, hair disheveled. She closed her eyes and covered her face, falling to her knees in shock. He hated her. This bothered her more than she thought it would.

He cried to himself, silently. He wouldn't dare sob. He reached out to her, his hands shaking, attempting to hold her, become one with her but he withdrew his hand and turned his back on her. He didn't love or trust her anymore. He didn't care if she lived or died. He was tired of being her fool.

His cell phone rang. Answering, he said, "Hello."

"How are you, sir?"

He narrowed his eyes. "Who is this?"

"I'm calling you about a position that is available at the Motel 6."

He wasn't interested. "Is this a survey?"

"No, sir. Your name was given to me by a George Harper. Said he went to school with you. We are looking for a manager."

"I like the job I have now."

"Would you like to reconsider?"

"No, thank you."

"Well we want you."

"So does everyone else."

"Stating pay is $35,000."

He sat on the edge of the bed. "When do I come in?" *And who the hell is George Harper?*

"Now, can you make it in, say, fifteen minutes?"

"I'll call you when I'm on my way."

"I'll call you. And good luck."

The line disconnected.

Tina was in a myriad of thoughts. First her husband called out another woman's name, in the bed they shared during the course of such a rocky marriage, and then he showed his ass, talking down to her, jumping on her. Where did he get off? She didn't believe in calling the police so that was out. Her jaw hurt, she made herself regurgitate the pills. That's what she got for playing with his emotions. She knew she was wrong for what she did. Thomas, deep down, was a good guy. And she was turning him into a bitter fool.

She didn't have to put up with his shit. If she wanted to she could have him thrown out of the house, but her civilly caring side didn't let her.

She had to admit that she didn't love him, she only married him because the dick was good, the money exceeded $29,000 a year, he pampered her, bought her anything she wanted, let her do what she wanted and she had become so accustomed to the "finer things in life," diamond rings and jewelry, getting credit cards in his name, that she lost touch with what really mattered in a marriage: the Union.

She dated other men behind his back. She fucked other men behind his back. She didn't think anything of it. Why should she? She had loyal friends. Her friends always covered for her. She had no desire to stop, that was until Thomas called out another woman's name in bed.

Part of her was crushed that she never got to give him the child he always wanted. She told him she was infertile, that if she carried a child she would die. Buttered him up. Got into his mental. Made him believe her bullshit, and gave him some pussy to set it in stone.

But the truth of the matter was she didn't want a baby, and she damn sure didn't feel like pushing one out of her pussy. She didn't want to deal with the needles, or appointments, shitting for two, the baby showers, the gifts, having a bunch of Hoes all up in her house, all up in her face pretending to be friendly when they all wanted to fuck her man.

But none of that mattered now. She was waiting on a delivery. A friend of hers bought her one of those organizers, and she was really looking forward to getting it, so now she could properly keep notes and schedules, and all that good shit.

Yes, Georgia was sweet to get her the organizer, such a sweet gesture.

Something good actually came out of her gravely defunct marriage: Georgia, who she was very fond of. She couldn't say the same about doggishly whorish Ed. He tried to fuck any and everything on two legs.

"Now I wanna gut the motherfucker" She was fuming, her blood running cold. "Getting another bitch pregnant? Oh, our marriage is so over. I can't believe this shit. I should go whip the Ho's ass; she's over Georgia's house right now. Damn it, I can't believe this shit!"

There was a knock on the door.

Answering it, tossing blonde weave out of her face, she cracked a smile and signed the clipboard the UPS man handed her.

He was kind of cute, shit.

He looked her over, slowly taking in her presence. She had a nice body, baby making hips. Easy on the eyes.

He had to will the penis from erection prematurely.

Didn't want to appear out of control.

Eyeing him, she took the package, kissed his cheek and closed the door, opening her package.

The organizer looked really nice.

I approached the Motel 6.

I was sort of nervous. Shaking uncontrollably, I brushed lint off my clothes and looked in my compact mirror, making sure I looked decent. Lipstick was off the chain. Make up, all right, nothing overdone. I smelled really nice.

I wanted to run, though, for what I was about to do. I was going to do something I have never done in my life. And quite frankly, I needed to get on with it. Sometimes in life you gotta go after what you want and don't let anybody stop you or stand in your way.

I worked up enough nerve to knock on the door. When Thomas answered and he saw me he frowned and said, "What do you want?"

I stared at him. My prince, my baby. So much love and respect burst deep inside me. I stood in one spot, hot tears falling down my face. He cocked his head to the right, wondering what was wrong with me.

“Are you ok, Diamond?” It hurt him to say the words. It hurt him to be nice to me, to see what was wrong with me. He had to force himself to show me compassion.

I just hugged him, threw my arms around him and started sobbing uncontrollably, I let go; I couldn’t help it. I loved him, would die for him, and looked forward to having his baby. He’d hate me, call me names because I was a prostitute; well used to be a prostitute. I didn’t want to be one anymore, I wanted to be faithful, be in love with someone who would treat my body like it was supposed to be treated. I reverted back to the little girl I was when I was teased, called all kinds of names, fat and unwanted. I vowed then to work on myself and my body to make myself look hot and sexy and I started selling my pussy to fit in and to belong and to feel special. I thought men were only here to give me good dick, give me some money and then get the hell on.

Thomas changed my life. In one night.

I felt his hands go around me. He held me close, smelling my hair, rubbing my arms. I felt the chemistry, the same chemistry we felt when we met, when he approached me at

Georgia's party.

Oh God I melted into him, kissing his lips gently, then it built to a tsunami of kisses and tongue lashes that left us breathless. He was rubbing my back, our tongues fencing for the next Olympics…I vowed to never let him go.

But I had to tell him who I was.

We slowly pulled away from each other. He shuddered, a pleased look on his face. I forgot I ordered Tina the organizer, and pretended I was Georgia. Had to distract her. I forgot I used Georgia's phone to do the ordering, after I called Tina and made sure she stayed home. I made sure she didn't come over to Georgia's. I forgot I told Georgia I had an emergency, that I would be back to her house shortly. I forgot I called Thomas's cell phone, told him Motel 6 was interested in interviewing him for a job, just to get him out of Tina's house, so I could tell him who I was.

The sparkles in his eyes arrested my attention and kept it. He smiled really big, hugging me. "You don't have to say anything. I'm glad you came back to me, Princess. Goddamn it you've been right under my nose and I didn't know it, until now."

"How did you know?"

He kissed my lips. I knew at that moment I was going to be his wife. That we would never be separated again. "The smell of your hair told me everything, smelled the same way it did the night we met. Oh, God I can't believe this."

"Well believe this. I'm pregnant with your child, a little over two months. And if you want a DNA test, I'll give it to you. The night we made love at Georgia's house was the night our baby was conceived."

He hugged me, picking me up and spinning me in a circle. He was jubilant and ecstatic, I fed off it. I had my King back.

"But what about Tina?" he asked me. "We're going through a divorce."

"Let's just leave town. Pack up and go, start over somewhere else."

He thought about it. "Yea, we can do that. How soon do you want to hit the road?"

I looked at him, hugging my future husband. "Right now."

"I thought you'd never say it."

Georgia was in her closet, taking the suit case down. Inside was all of her high school memorabilia. She cherished it. While in high school her mother loved her acting. She majored in Drama and excelled. She loved it so much she wrote a play. In it she pretended to be on the telephone while cooking dinner at the stove. She was a lonely woman who had just lost her husband. Her teacher loved her play. Pulling it out Georgia wiped some of the dust from the document, smiling bitterly. Tears fell down her face.

She opened it to the first page.

Act 1: Scene One:
The Pretend Conversation.

[Georgia was cooking black beans at the stove]

"When are you going to fix my sprinklers, John? And what is that smell, I have a really sensitive nose…"

[Georgia joked through the phone, stirring some black beans].

"I'm back. What were we saying now?"

[She held the phone to her ear with her shoulder.]

"Oh, yea you wanted the recipe for my mama's ribs. What? I'm cranky? I need a massage? Nah, my husband will do that. What does that got to do with ribs? His job is to make sure I'm ok not yours. Ok? I don't cheat on my husband and he would never cheat on me…"

Dead inside, Georgia put the papers back in the suit case, frowning. "Princess you fucked my man. I know you did. I saw you two in the shower together…"

She closed her eyes and would continue to play the game.

When my fine boss walked into his expensively-designed office he took one look at me, smiled to himself, and closed the door. He always loved looking me over, as if his eyes were scanners and my taut, voluptuous body was a carefully created document. He was 6 feet tall with an athletic body. Very sexy smile. He was sort of LA Lakers Kobe-ish. But he looked more like Michael Vick. Croppy hair. Smart chin. Thick old school the Jackson 5 nose. Had a knack for using his hands when he spoke. So that told me he'd use his hands to split the peach between my legs. He had creamy milky skin. His eyes were reminiscent of a black panther, seriously. Cat eyes, in a very masculine way. Like Tyson Beckford, but he made Tyson's eyes look like puddles of dog shit. He was well trimmed and well groomed. Everyday. And he didn't have a nappy hair line.

"*Sup*, Brandy, how are you?" he barely said above a whisper. He was having one of those long days at the office, you know, when nothing went right. Maybe it was because it was Friday the 13th. April 13, 2007.

"I'm cool. What's wrong with *you*?" I played around with the stretch bangles on my wrists I ordered out of the Victoria Secret catalogue that came in the mail last month. I was the queen of catalogues and the Home Shopping Network. I was tired, been up since 5:30 a.m. I normally got up at 6:30 a.m. but this morning I had given my car a quick wash because I was tired of the neighborhood kids writing "Wash your car!" on my windshield every other day; I vacuumed my living room, did some dusting, dancing to Patti Labelle at about 6:39 a.m., and then I cooked a small pot of grits and eggs that I never got to eat because I turned on the news and got lost in the ways of God's dying world.

"I don't know. People don't know how to follow directions."

I smiled at him, standing up and giving him a much-needed hug. We weren't lovers. God, no! But I have often thought about how good his love making might be. Especially when I go to bed at night, my "cold cocoon" I called it. I really thought about his loving then. Especially the dick. My clit was throbbing right now but I swallowed extra hard and tried not to think about it.

"Are we talking about people that work for you?"

He sat behind his desk and threw files by the computer, rubbing his temples. "*Yes*. People that work for me."

I looked at him more intently. "People that *you* hired?"

He started smiling, "I know, I wrote my *own* Scarlett Letter."

I was smiling. "Sure did."

He kissed at me. "They are messing up faxes. Coming in late. Calling out for stupid reasons…Showing poor customer service. Clarisse was taking minutes for the Builder Architect Meeting earlier today and guess what the bitch wrote?"

My brows rose. I always loved hearing about Little Slutty Clarisse. To put it bluntly, she had sex whenever/wherever she chose. She didn't care if she was stuck in traffic, she'd get her bump and grind on in broad daylight, and she didn't care about the police. If it was about a) money or b) dick oh she was so there for the taking. Realest woman you'd ever meet. Very down-to-earth, like ocean shores. "What did she write?"

He looked me over for a minute. "Well, physically, to the naked eye, she was taking notes about our merger. The building that is in production, the way they wanted the blueprints done up, zoning, permits, clearing, the whole nine. But in her mind and what she actually wrote were two different things. So I'm reading over the minutes, because I type them up myself."

This surprised me. He wasn't strong in the clerical field. I liked it, though. "You don't get the secretary, Melissa to do them?"

"Nah, I love typing, keeps my mind clear." He stood up, deep in thought. "Want some coffee?"

Hell to the no! "Sure." I hated coffee, but how could you tell this sexy, brilliant man "No?"

"Anyways." He poured the coffee in a mug with his daughter's face on it. She's about eight years old, with her snaggle-toothed ass, but she was cute. "I'm typing, *right*? And she wrote, 'So I went down on him, sucking his big ole dick, and I tasted pre-cum, tasted like a Klondike bar, I felt like a...lesbian!' and so on and so forth." He looked embarrassed. I was laughing.

He handed me the coffee with the weirdest look on his face. I laughed harder, covering my mouth, stunned. In a good way. I could see her writing that. I thought about the long talks me and Melissa had about men and their strokeless attributes. "Thank you, so what else she said?"

He smiled. "Let's just put it this way. By the time I was done reading the story I locked my door and masturbated."

"Oh, God TMI." I sipped the coffee. *Yuk*! Nasty shit! I hated black coffee, where's the cream and sugar?

"Too much info, I know, we're adults here, deal with it sweetness." He sat on his desk, holding the coffee mug as if his life depended on it.

The tone of his voice changed. "Are you ok? I'm sensing something else is bothering you."

"My baby mama." He narrowed his eyes. "She called me today."

Here we go. Making my ears bleed talking about his retarded baby mama, the bitch who hated the very ground he walked on. "Oh, God. More money?"

He stared at me. "How do you know?"

"She's a Ho, I warned you about her before you married her. She thinks her pussy is laced with gold, when I heard it smells like baby shit."

We laughed, he damn near chocked from the coffee. "Gurl, you so wrong for that."

"I hope you bought some Tic Tacs," I said, frowning. *I hate bitches that don't douche and keep their bodies clean.*

"Why do you say that?" He set the mug on the desk, by the conference phone.

"Because, if you went down on her, she shoulda tasted like...sewage."

He laughed again, an easy-on-the-ears laugh, one that made you smile, and one that soothed you. I could look in his eyes and tell an incredible weight has been lifted from his shoulders. He had a younger brother. I forget his name right now. My boss raised him because his parents died in the military, a horrible chopper accident many years ago. He was about 18 at the time, so he raised his only sibling, beat his ass, got him out of school and worked two jobs to pay for him to go to college. His brother was in school to be a lawyer and when he thought about joining the Armed Forces my boss, Daniel Lynn, kicked his ass all across the city of Miami.

"Are you *crazy*?" he had said, very hurt, very angry. "Our parents died in that shit, I don't wanna loose you, too. You're all I got." And Joseph Lynn, his brother, never thought about it again.

Daniel said, "My baby mama don't smell like sewage."

"Maybe you do, then."

"You got jokes. But back to my baby mama. She's a bitch."

"You shoulda thought of that when you were rolling all through her pussy like you were looking for the needle in a haystack."

"Good one." He stretched, and then opened his jacket.

I was trying to calcify the situation, when he got hot headed he got crazy, stubborn and I was pretty much the only person who could calm him down. He was in love with me but never actually told me. I knew because once a week he took me to dinner and he bought me roses. He sent little notes to my office. "You're beautiful. Lunch is on me." He was very thoughtful. He told me I reminded him of his mother. I told him I reminded myself of my mother Darla Way, Puerto Rican bombshell married to my ex-gangster father Johnny Way, award-winning freelance photographer. But Daniel's situation was one that was very complex.

He hated his Baby Mama. She hated him. They used to love each other, back then they had everyone fooled. Thinking they had a rare type of love, until one day he came home and saw, in his bed, another woman sucking her pussy. Every picture he was in was turned face down on the shelves, dressers and niches throughout the house. Crushed, he went postal, whipped both their asses. He did 6 months in jail. Once he was released I went to pick him up, bought him some new threads, and drove him around town to take care of his personal business. He called his lawyer a few weeks later and filed for divorce. He couldn't prove she was unfaithful, and since they co-signed everything from the bank accounts to the cars he was stuck with not only child support, but he had to pay her car notes, and she drove some thug called "Big Baby Gangsta" around (or Big Baby Gangsta flossed (showed off) in the car, always harassing Daniel) to the point Daniel wanted to kill him.

Sometimes Daniel was calculatedly stubborn, a bastard in other words. He was class-conscious, and therein the problem lied. He had his own set of morals, and always pushed his beliefs on other people. Wherever he went chaos was the end result, which was why I didn't give him any pussy yet, didn't want him going Downtown and breaking the store windows from my pussy. Hell to the no!

"I just don't understand people these days," he went on derisively, standing up and walking over to the window, that overlooked Bayside Miami, a very profitable tourist spot that charged you damn near five percent of your paycheck just to park. Then he said more fixedly, "They say, well women say, they want this and that and don't really know what they want. We've become so shallow that we look to musicians to help raise our children, to give us some type of outlook on life. You know you're fucked up when you study Old Dirty Bastard's words just to find out how you like it: raw or fake."

We shared a few giggles. But I felt him, really I did. Whenever I get my heart broken, I pop in Whitney Houston's "Saving all my Love," "It's not Right, but its Ok," "Heart break Hotel," and she's kicking crack like she kicked rocks, and maybe that was the same damn thing.

"Hell, I said, "I heard music calms the beast."

He looked over his shoulder, hands in his pocket. He had a nice ass. "It does, but it doesn't get rid of the beast, I tell ya'."

"Ain't that the truth?" I set the coffee down on the low-table, I couldn't drink this nasty shit anymore. If I kept sipping this poison I wouldn't live to see twenty-three. And I'd be hitting that magical number in three weeks.

He faced me. Studied me. Blushing, I averted my face and couldn't wipe the smile off. Damn it. My pussy was wet. So I squeezed my legs together. So tightly I thought my water broke and I wasn't pregnant.

He had dimples in his cheeks. Never noticed it before. "I like you," he said throwing me off guard.

I circled the right dimple with my index finger. "I hate you."

He gently took my hand and kissed it. "Whatever."

"I don't know what you're insinuating," I told him, the climate changing. He wouldn't let my hand go.

"You're so stuck up," he joked with a boyish grin.

I flipped the bird, looking flawless in my

black pinstriped skirt suit. My hair long and real, curly, the right side of my hair pulled away from my face to show off my Asian-like hazel eyes.

"Whatever."

"I'm tired, I'm horny, I'm mad at my baby mama, and I wanna kill her boyfriend. Driving a car with my name of it, and I can't do a thing about it. I have no time for presumptuous B.S."

He sat back behind the desk, took off his jacket and undid his lavender-colored tie. Matched his shoes. I remembered seeing his feet before. His second toe was longer than the big one. He had big feet. Pretty feet. Clear toe nails. Big hands. Clean nails. Low-cut nails. His middle finger was bigger than the index finger and the thumb was thick. Mama always told me those were signs that a man had a big, thick dick. I never believed in superstitions. But with my pussy quivering my clit was telling me to make like the center of a Tootsie Pop and "find out."

I could hear his suit rustling. It was so quiet in the office; the silence was popping in my ears. I kept crossing and uncrossing my legs. I was very uncomfortable. I kept having...visions of this man eating my sugar Puss. For real. I had to squeeze my legs together to keep my pussy from gawking like a goddamn parrot.

I looked him over while he took a quick phone call. He handled his business. My eyes handled theirs. I was eye-fucking him. I was descriptively encoding the essence of his being into my brain, since it was like an IBM computer. Ciphering something that would be gregariously deciphered later.

But the downside. He was an arrogant S.O.B. Four-dimensional and talkative. But he actually had something to say. I heard he was playah-playah. But this pussy was the playah slayah. Seriously. I was a take-it-back-ho in the bed. A straight freak-a-lic. Work it, these hips won't lie when it hypnotized the Anaconda.

"Ok, I'll call you later," he told someone on the phone, bringing me from my thoughts. Damn it, don't disturb me, I was trying to...assess the possibilities here. I smiled to myself. He picked up the remote and turned on Bob Marley. He loved Bob. Always listened to Bob once a day. The stand out track, "One/Love, People get Ready" from the 1977 *Exodus* album, his favorite of all-time. I knew he wanted me to know that information. Woman's intuition. And he told me one day last month over dinner at IHOP.

With that being said, since I was far from being some independent PMS-ridden feministic bitch, I, forsworn with a secret crush on him, amply tuned into his world with a flourish.

Leaning forward in the chair, I relaxed. I was about to head back to work. Lunch break was nearly over.

"We're both adults, right Daniel?"

He didn't get me. "Yea," he said cautiously, looking me deep in the eyes. "You haven't really touched your coffee."

I challenged him. "Can't drink it without...cream and sugar, and Lord knows I can...swallow some...coffee."

He caught my innuendos superbly. Standing up, he walked around the desk, with a strut stank of masculine charm. He was impossibly fine! Damn it! I didn't mix business with pleasure but after business, when we clocked out, it was such a pleasure to mix thoughts and world events with him over dinner. He leaned against the desk. The screen saver, on the computer monitor, turned into Janet Jackson slapping Mariah Carey in celebrity death match.

"Obviously, this conversation shouldn't be entertained in the office," he told me matter-of-factly. "Don't wanna be filed against, you know, for sexual...harassment."

I ducked his chauvinism. "I feel you." I stood up and stretched. "I gotta get back to work." He hugged me, for a long time. It felt good to be in his arms, to smell his cologne, the SMELL turned me on. My nose always found me good men with good dick in my life. I'd date a man who worked for the Garbage Company that smelled like Zest soap and Cool Water over a man in an expensive suit that smelled like dirty shit. For real.

To my complete dismay, I started for the door. Put my hand on the door knob, looked down. Had to play hard to get. I wanted to fuck. I was like Janet Jackson in Poetic Justice. Let's cut the bullshit ok. Now what do you really, really want from me.

"Stop back by after work," he told me, I heard sadness in his voice. Like he didn't want me to leave.

Fuck him, I wasn't staying. Yes, bitch, yes you are. No, I was not, I gotta clock back in, but he's the goddamn boss.

I was stuttering. "Ok, for coffee?"

"Yes. Cream and. Sugar, right?"

Hesitantly, with my mind telling me to leave, I faced him. He was in my face, our noses damn near touching. He reached past me and locked the door. Against my better judgment, risking losing my job for some goddamn dick, I kissed his lips, a peck, slowly pulling away. He was feeling on my booty. I was measuring the length of his hard dick, using my fingers like centimeters on a ruler.

…one, two…

I got greedy so I diverted the centimeters into inches...

…three, four.

I kissed him, giving him some tongue.

…five, six.

I licked his top teeth; bit his bottom lip, pulling him to me.

…seven, eight, nine...ten.

Ten inches. A ten inch dick, hell to the yea!

He gripped my face like a fine piece of crystal just super glued back together, and our faces and lips bobbed and weaved like my grandmother's needle shaping patters on an artistic quilt. I pulled myself to him, kissing, our tongues dancing. I was Ginger Rodgers, he was Fred Astaire, of course the restored with color, ghetto versions.

"I love you," he said. "I want to be with you; I can't...breathe without you."

I put my hands in his pants and held his dick. *Yea* its mine. I just claimed it. I knew the bitches in the office were going to be hating on me, because I was in the boss's pants and they didn't even get to hardly see him with them on when he was on the clock. Tough shit. "My bed is...cold without someone in it, I'm...tired of playing with my...pussy all by myself."

He backed away from me, slowly, taking his time. I loved his sense of urgency, his control. He unbuttoned his shirt, and revealed such an incredible chest. Lovely nipples, I had to place my hands flat on his chest and just look into his eyes. He handed me my coffee.

"Hold the coffee, baby." Pulling out his dick, through the unzipped hole of the pants, he started gently stroking it. I drank some coffee, held it in my mouth then, feeling adventurous, I got on my knees and took the head of his passion into the confines of my strong jaws…His eyes rolled to the back of his head, moaning silently, nothing too loud. Just right. He matched my rhythm as the warm coffee tingled the head of his dick, giving him a warm sensation. I never slept with anyone from the office, I thought about it a few times. But I never acted on it, I didn't want to go through the sexual harassment thing, I didn't want to lead anyone on. I didn't have time to teach grown ass men how to be classy, they shouldn't act like little boys. You didn't hear Boyz II Men on the damn radio that much anymore. Fellahs get a clue!

My male co-workers took bets on who was going to fuck what woman at whatever time. That's why I never went to parties or the clubs the job set up for employees to network and get to know each other. I took my black ass home and did my thing behind the four walls of my bedroom.

Now I was sucking my boss's dick, riding dirty to say the least. I played with his balls, gently cupping them like the contents of my coffee cup and basically brought him sheer ecstasy. He looked down at me with narrowed eyes, his male hardness sliding in and out of my mouth, I gripped it, jacked it hard and fast, spitting on it and using my baby soft hands to smooth my saliva all over his incredible member until is glistened.

"Jack it, baby…yea, baby, just like that."

I looked up at him, loving the way I was making him feel. He was at my beck and call, my mercy, dependant on me. "You like that, baby?"

"Yes, baby." He shuddered.

"Oooh, you taste so good in my mouth."

"Let me feel your throat."

I tried with all my might to put his entire package in my mouth, I started to gag, he had too much dick, but he smiled and gripped my head and fucked my mouth, gyrating his hips like Van Gogh paintings on canvases…he appreciated the feeling I gave him, he didn't try to make me choke.

Reaching into my panties, just under my loose skirt, I started rubbing my pussy, bringing myself pleasure. I closed my eyes, enjoying the feel of my lips and tongue on his shaft, lifting the dick up and putting his nuts in my mouth, bouncing them on my slick tongue.

"Oooh baby, yeeeees! Yes, baby, damn…"

I opened my eyes and rubbed my pussy juices all over his dick, and took him back into my mouth, tasting pussy on dick ever so gently. Tasted good. I was the master at giving head. I didn't do it much, but sucking dick was an art form to me. You took your time, you got into a Niggah's head, his soul, through conversation, you opened him up mentally then you used your tongue and lips physically.

He jerked, and his hips moved so fast his dick fell from my mouth. He instantly grabbed his dick and started jacking it, "I gotta cum." He stood over my coffee and his ass cheeks locked and his hole started pulsating as he came in my coffee, his head leaned back, sweat all over him. I watched with a smile from the chair, crossing my legs, looking like I didn't just do anything naughty.

"Damn, daaamn, damn, baby." He was trying to control his breathing. He looked at me lovingly, like I was an angel visiting earth for a little while. He put his dick in the coffee and stirred it, smiling with sparkling eyes. His lips formed an "O."

Handing me the coffee he said, "Cream and sugar."

I stood up, gripped the mug and I wolfed it down. Smacking my lips. "Ah. All gone. So, what does this mean?"

"I got court with my baby mama tomorrow, would you like to join me?"

I kissed him, wrapping my arms around him. "I wouldn't miss it for the world. But only on one condition."

He ran a shaky hand through my hair and just looked in my eyes. I could see the love dancing across his handsome face.

"What would that be?"

"Bring along Clarisse. So she can take down…minutes."

"You are a goddamn fool," he joked, hugging me so tight we would rock and dance to Bob Marley until the CD ended. Fuck work, and fuck clocking back in.

I got a new man now, and I was going to appreciate the fact that we were friends for two years before we were lovers. Which was a good thing. Because I knew all his flaws. I saw his good side and his bad side. I know what makes him happy and sad. I know all of his fears. I know what drives him and what doesn't. deep down inside I told myself that I enjoyed being alone but now that it was changing, I welcomed it because I needed a good man in my life. I tell you one thing:

If his Baby Mama comes with drama I will stomp the Hoe.

Seriously.

Red,

What's up! I want to be in your world because I really feel God put us together. I'm writing in text form, the way I do when we text with cell phones, because its easier to say what I have to say and its quicker to write. I have tried nothing like this before but I want to be happy so I'm willing to do this for the first time in my life to be in a relationship with someone I care about, which is YOU.

I want us to just accept each other for who we are. We are soul mates. We will last and finally get it right because we want to and because we are ready to start over fresh with no judgments of any kind, please.

When I come to you I will trust you and I do trust you. I have and will make sure I put all my baggage behind me. No more comparing you to my Ex. I may not hold psychic power but we just feel right when we look at each other and when we kiss oh God! When we kiss its like we just met for the first time. I love kissing you, OH YEAH! You're my girl and I want you to be there for my son...You are the aggressor! You are my life! I love when we're lying in the bed playing and my son Renaldo just burst into the room when you're tying to get my coochie!

I love that smile of yours. You're beautiful inside and out and even thought we're both strong women and have soooooooo much in common we are still sooo different in sooo many ways. Example:

I love food. You love junk! I'm a fem. You're a stud. Your mannerisms are different. I would like for you to communicate with me more about your feelings. Please, please stop taking me so seriously. I love that you know when I'm playing. I will never hurt you, Red! I love you Pooh Bear! And please no secrets! No lies! And no people who want to fuck numbers or pictures and for you to let yourself love me. Don't hate because I'm like you. Embrace me more because you wouldn't accept me as your girlfriend if you didn't think I was special.

Thanks for going to therapy with me, to help me deal with my past. This truly allowed me to open up about my life and work on myself, and that made me a better person. A better mother. And a better lover.

We are both strong 'cause we have to be. All we had is and was our moms. The difference is that you wanted to be strong like mine and what we have in common with our "strongness" is that we are raising 11 year old boys that we want to be strong. Just please take your time with me, please! And have patience with me even in games because I love you very much and I will like to show you what real love feels like. And baby my humor is only in fun and sometimes when I'm nervous and this is a part of my soul. I won't make it seem so serious, Boo! I just love playing with you. I know my part as your lady, the main parts. Who is the woman and who is the man when it comes to the boys but anything else I don't know because I'm just trying to get to know. I hope I really get to have my second child with you. However God wants it.

Sincerely yours,

Miss Fate Williams

I sealed the letter with a kiss, wondering did I just make the biggest mistake of my life. Should I have written this letter? Should I throw it away and speak from the heart? I shouldn't take her back; I shouldn't even entertain the thought. She lied to me. This *beautiful* person, this woman who looked like Gerald Levert deceived me. I loved the way she looked and how she carried herself like a classy thug. She smoked weed, drank alcohol and fought like the Niggahs. When you spoke to her you'd swear she was a man.

But she lied. About everything. Our entire relationship was a lie, orchestrated by a very insecure, selfish bitch!

Yes, I was a lesbian. I loved pussy just as much as I loved my own. I am a very feminine woman; I loved women who looked like men. Because it was like I was having my cake and eat it, too. I get to have a woman who knew how to be touched, cuddled and held, yet I kinda had a man also because she looked like one, dressed like one and acted like a straight "Butch." I remembered when I first realized I liked women. It was in high school. I had a big crush on a girl name Lianna. I was with my boyfriend at the time, my son's father, but I never stopped fantasizing about her. I used to masturbate thinking of her touch; and her lovely smile. I was too gullible to approach her. I never did. And I never would.

I could still remember how I met Red. It was at Club Goodfellahs, in Perrine, Florida on Gay Night (Sundays). It was well after 2 am, when everyone started arriving. I was dressed Gucci down to the socks, my weave long and curly, I went for the Tyra Banks look, very *America's Top Model.* I loved that show; I gotta catch the next season.

I had sat down at the bar, I went there solo, didn't need to be harassed. I smiled at the short, white female bartender, who kept giving me the once over. It was mighty dark in here, some smoke looming here and there. The green wrist band was making me feel uncomfortable because my outfit was pink and this green stuck out like a sore thumb. I had a lot on my mind that night, thinking about my past and my Daddy. Daddy couldn't get him off my mind, nor could I get my son off my mind. It was very hard to do.

"And what will you be having pretty lady?" the Bartender asked me, shuffling her long dirty-looking blonde hair from her face. I smiled and shook her hand. "Could I get a Rum and Coke, light ice?" I was Jamaican, so my accent was noticeable. A few lesbian Hoes were all on my jock so I grabbed my titties and wiggled them playfully, feeling it tonight. A bitch was out and about and loving it. My son was with my mother, and I was glad he was because Mama and I fell out today. She told me she was going to call Child Protective Services on me because I was a gay woman raising a son on my own. I looked at this cunningly stupid bitch and told her, *"Bitch, try!"* I couldn't believe after all the hell she had put me through in my life, she was trying to fuck up my adult life in the process.

She challenged me. She stood up from the Lazy Boy in my living room and said, "Oh, I will. My grandson doesn't want your lesbian lovers around him. He goes to church, he believes in God, he don't want all that damnation around him."

"This is my house, my son, I went through eleven hours of labor with him. I take care of him and feed him you don't do jack shit but claim grandmother parental rights over him, its all in goddamn name only."

"You're a pussy sucking whore and I'm ashamed to have you as my daughter."

I blew a gasket in my brain. "Get out, now!" I was slightly taller than my Mama. I was 5 feet 11. I weighed 180 pounds, chunky but a nice chunky size. I still had on my medical uniform, I was a medical assistant, making $20 an hour at Baptist Hospital, been there for three years and I was tired of being single. My son's father, well, my eyes welled up with tears thinking about it.

"I'm not leaving without my grandson." She snatched up her purse from the low table and she walked to his room. I was right on her ass.

"Leave, mother!"

"RENALDOOO! Where are you, baby." She was determined to get to my child.

She opened his room door. My son, with his handsome self, spitting image of his Daddy, was at the computer. He quickly sent a screen to the bottom of the page. I said, "Mama, good bye, time to go home. I'm not trying to be rude."

She ignored me. "Grandma is taking you home. You don't need to be living with filthy slime."

He looked scared. "Grandma," he said, lowering his head. He was holding back what he really wanted to say. "That's my Mama; please don't talk like that about her."

She dismissed his comment with the wave of her bejeweled hand. "I'm sorry, grandma don't fake it for nobody, baby. Your Mama licks pussy, simple as that now LET'S GO!"

I snatched her ass by the hair and dragged

her ass into the hallway, slapping her face, kicking her, "You bitch!" I was so hurt, so disrespected in my own home I snapped on her. I never hit her. She was clawing at my legs, my thighs…she managed to pull herself up and she scratched my face and I spit in hers. "Don't. You. Ever. DISRESPECT. ME. IN. FRONT. OF. MY. GODDAMN. SON! I'm gay because *of your* molesting ass, cunt! Tell him how you use to sneak into my room, Ho and make me do things to you!"

My Mama froze and just looked at me. We looked like two train wrecks, breathing hard. Hard-eyed, in defense mode, fight mode. Picture frames shattered on the floor. My statuettes on the floor, broken. None of it could replace what my Mama had done to me thirteen years ago, when I was a little girl.

"Yea, bitch!" I screamed at her. "Let's talk about it."

"Talk about what?" Mama stared me down evilly. "I never touched you, why are you making things up just to have your way. All you do is lie; you will always be a fucking liar!"

"I'm lying, Mama?" I intimidated her now. She remained quiet.

I said, "*Aw,* you all quiet now, tell my son how you used to sell your body…and bring those untrustworthy men into our home."

Recollection bit her eyes but she kept a straight face.

"Don't believe it, grandson. Your Mama turned those men on behind my back! She let them crawl through her windows; she even got thrown out of high school for sucking damn near every football player's dick on the team."

"You're lying! I never even slept with a man in high school," I said, defending myself. I couldn't believe this. "*Why* would you lie, Mama?"

"Mama did you do those things with men?" my child asked sadly. "Grandma told me a long time ago you were a Hoe." My mouth fell open in shock. "I just never…"

I snatched his little ass by the shirt collar and yanked him into my face. "Now you listen. For starters, watch your mouth and your tone; secondly your grandmother is a stone cold liar. We couldn't afford to pay bills, my Daddy worked three jobs. She wanted revenge on Daddy for his work ethics keeping him away from home. My Daddy slaved away to feed us, and this bitch, selfishly I might say, received money from military people passing through, to feed her sick need, and sent them into my room and they had sex with me. I had no choice. She was always in the room, coaching me. Suck it like this, fuck them like that, and learn how to take the dick. Son I am talking to you bluntly, your grandmother put me through hell."

He snatched himself out of my arms, turned on my mother and stomped her foot. He then ran into the room and slammed the door. He was screaming all kind of shit, my heart hurt, it killed me to tell him about my life, my past like this. But I had no choice.

"Get out, Mama. Get out; I don't wanna see you again."

"I am not going anywhere. You can't just turn on me, I'm your mother, and I did what I had to do to survive." She straightened her jacket and ran her hands over her hair, trying to look presentable and I snatched her wig again, slapping her ass, fucking her up and she bear hugged me and ran into my body, the both of slamming on the sofa. She got with me, Mama taught me how to fight so she gave me a run for my money but I had a change up for her funky ass that turned her dollar punches into three goddamn quarters. We fought and just held each other; we wouldn't let each other go. One of us had to give.

"Tag out, bitch!" I yelled at her, spitting in her face and she sank her teeth into my breast and I screamed so loud we both fell off the chair.

"You tag out, bitch!" She retorted.

This was ridiculous, fighting my Mama was wrong, God frowned on this but did he frown on those men destroying my innocence? Where was God? Why did he allow this to happen to me? Fuck the book of Job! Why did he let those men destroy a little girl?

I let her go and openly sobbed; we both were at the point of no return. She never accepted my lifestyle; she never accepted responsibility for molesting and sexually assaulting me. She never admitted to herself that she actually tried to sell me for crack. She never admitted that she used to dress up in my Daddy's clothes, cutting her hair like his, spraying on his cologne and trying to make love to me, her only daughter, when I was 15 years old. She was delusional, paranoid. I tried to urge her to go to a mental institution, but she blamed herself for my Daddy's death. He died in a car accident. I missed Daddy. He always protected me. I never told Daddy I was being raped by men while he worked. I never told Daddy Mama snuck a different Niggah in his house every night he worked and fucked her in the ass or pussy or mouth, in his bed, while he slaved away trying to give us a better life.

Mama wanted to hold me. My head said "No," but my heart allowed her. I needed to be held. I let her.

When she wrapped her arms around me she kissed my face and old feelings of lust awakened in me, she rubbed my arms the way she used to when she raped me, tried to kiss my lips and I pushed her on the floor and I said, "You are not going to do this to me again! I'm standing up to you. You're a sick bitch!"

Like Lucifer himself, she slowly rose to her feet, smiling maliciously. "You praise your Daddy, don't you?"

"Yes. I miss him. He would have never approved of what you did."

She laughed bitterly. "Renaldo. Let's go," my mother said. I seriously doubted if she hurt my son. I knew in my heart she would never hurt him, why, I didn't know, call it a sixth sense.

"He was a good man, your father," Mama said off-handedly.

I was silent for a moment. "That we agree on."

"With a dark heart," she snapped.

I got quiet. Then I exploded, walking in her face. "Don't even try to denounce my Daddy's good will. He was a caring man, a good man."

"So am I, I'm caring. I provided for you."

"*Yea*, by sending men to rape me, Mama?" I was shuddering, so much pain enveloped me,

I felt betrayed all over again, reliving my childhood standing in my living room as an adult, a successful, college degree earning adult. "We never talked about this, we both have lived our lives trying to pretend this didn't happen, because we try to live a lie. Worrying about the public scrutiny. Fuck the black community! All Niggahs do is hurt each other, bring each other down. Fuck that. Fuck you!"

"Your Daddy worked very hard," she said, scaring me.

"I know," I said slowly, suddenly guarded.

"He never wanted you, girl."

I was cautious. What was she talking about? Through clenched teeth, "What are you suggesting?"

"Your Daddy wanted things done a certain…way."

"I know that. Even though he worked he gave you instructions, have this and that cleaned, feed my daughter at such a such time, wash all the clothes, iron my clothes and give me my pussy when I get home. I know all about that Mama. He was a provider. And you shitted all over that."

"He controlled everything in our home. Everything was approved by him."

I narrowed my eyes. "What do you mean everything was…approved. By. Him?" I didn't like the feeling that suddenly overcame me. "Tell me."

She smiled wickedly. "Those men that came and went out of your room wasn't sent there by me. Your Daddy sent them; in fact he collected the cash before they even arrived to our home."

I had to sit down. The room was spinning…my Daddy. My sweet Daddy. I started remembering what he used to say to me when he came home. *"How are you doing, baby? Rough night? Couldn't sleep, baby? Why is that? You help Daddy around the house, don't you? You are so pretty, so smart. You g'on make Daddy rich one day."*

He was getting rich off pimping his only daughter! How could he? I can't deal with this. I gotta get out of here.

I made my mother leave. I grabbed my knife and chased her ass outside. My son appeared out of nowhere and said to me, "I'm going with grandma. I don't wanna stay here anymore, Mama I hate you!"

And I thought I was losing my son.

No time for that. All I could think about right now was Red. Maybe I was fucked up for putting thoughts of women before my son's well being. I seriously hoped he didn't need therapy. I damn sure needed it. I was dealing with a lot. I didn't know how to really handle finding out my Daddy pimped me.

I remembered Red sat next to me at Goodfellahs, paid for my drink, bought me another, looking spiffy in a suit. All the gay men tried to holla at her. She said, "I'm a butch, female, lesbian. I don't do men." They still tried to holla. She looked better than any man in the club.

I loved her instantly. She was very polite and patient. We danced and talked about life. I told her I had a son, that his father died during a drug deal gone bad. A few tears fell from my eyes. Graciously, Red wiped them away. She was from Opa Locka. She was Haitian. I cringed when she said that. I didn't date Haitians. I was so sorry. Nothing against them but that was just not my cup of tea. But she was persistent; she didn't act or look Haitian. I gave her a chance. Her biological name was Lolita Harvey. She had an eleven year old son named Jameson.

Around 4 am she asked me to go out to eat at Denny's. I loved that place. Denny's was the hang out spot after you left the club, you swapped numbers, flirted, and got your groove on. I drove in my Dodge truck behind her Dodge Intrepid. We both had Dodge vehicles. It took everything in me not to just make a U-turn and go home; I was too scared to go any further with Red.

But I did. Something pulled me towards her.

I didn't want Red in my life, in my family business. I was going through a lot. I wasn't settled emotionally. It wasn't fair to bring her in on my abusive past. So I made a vow to keep it hidden from her. I'd make shit up. Tell her my life was peachy teen.

We got the corner booth and ordered a country breakfast. Red paid for it; put it on her platinum card. I was hurting for my son, hurting for my lost innocence; I was hurt about what Daddy had done. Part of me didn't believe what Mama had said. But part of me did. I had to wear an invisible mask. Couldn't let Red in my world. We just met. It would be months, if ever before I let her in my universe to see how fucked up it was. But I wanted someone to talk to. Someone to lean on. A shoulder to cry on. Someone to stroke my hair, tell me that everything would be all right. I knew deep down that was a fantasy. But it didn't hurt to dream.

I wound up crying and Red comforted me. We kissed, gave her some tongue, not caring about public affection. Everyone in here was gay anyway, so g'on and get your swerve on

I told myself..

I wound up in Red's bed. I didn't even remember getting the doggy bag, because I couldn't finish my food. I didn't remember getting in my truck and following her to her house all the way in Opa Locka, not too far from Ali Baba Boulevard in Miami. I didn't remember how my panties wound up in her mouth and she ate my pussy with them in her mouth. I felt tongue, lips and lacy panties all at the same time. Drove me wild.

I never fucked on the first night or the first date. But getting some head was not fucking. This was the dental part of the package you got with a friend with benefits.

She spread my pussy with big hands and tongued my clit, bringing me to utter ecstasy. I shook on silk sheets. In the darkness, with just the glow of the TV beaming on our bodies. We bumped pussies, she got on top of me, one of my legs bent back, and our pussies gyrated on each other, sending me shivering and coming all over the bed.

The dildo. I sucked it then beat her pussy with it, like a belt on an ass cheek, taking my time, sucking her barely-there titties, spanking her ass, relinquishing control.

She sucked my pussy until I came again, then she got the double ended dildo and I got in the doggy position and she slid it deep in my wet cunt, then she slid the other end inside her flesh and our ass cheeks bumped and jiggled while the plastic toy, eleven inches long, brought us to Pleasure Ville.

I thought about my son.

After that night we were inseparable. We didn't become friends; we dove right into a full fledged relationship. After the months peeled away to hours wasted on sex, sex, sex, I didn't know a thing about her and she didn't know a thing about me. We then talked about it because I vowed to keep my pussy under lock and key until we got to know each other. She was all for it. So we talked and related more than we had sex. I loved it. We knew each other's favorite singers, foods and colors. We knew each other's birthdays and favorite holidays. She helped me wash my truck. I knew when she went to work and when she came home. She was a pharmacist at the local drug store. She was very loved at work. I had to drive for forty minutes to Baptist Hospital everyday from Red's house. She tried to get me to give up my apartment and fully move in with her but for some reason I declined. I wasn't ready. I changed Renaldo's school.

Over pasta at the Olive Garden a week later I told her about my mother and what she did to me, how my son felt. I couldn't lie to her. I couldn't look someone in the face and blatantly lie. I had to slay in the bed I made. I couldn't sleep at night if I lied to someone.

Red met my son and he liked her instantly. We got really close. Then she told me she had an eleven year old son, who looked just like her. I told her she had already told me about Jameson at the club the night we met months before. She just laughed.

We combined families, moved to North Miami Beach, never to see my Mama again. I changed my cell number, and my life was so fulfilled. I used to love the way my son and Jameson would come into the room, when Red and I watched TV, and disrupt her from getting my pussy. We'd play it off like we were wrestling. Our sons hit it off, they got really close really fast, they protected each other, went to the same school, did everything together. I really felt like I found my soul mate.

Jameson was a handsome young man. We

clicked instantly, just like my son and Red had. He always asked me questions, loved reading books, and loved the Cartoon Network. He liked his fried chicken cooked with Oregano and complete seasoning only, and Louisiana Hot sauce.

My son liked bar-b-que everything.

One day I was home alone. I was going through all my old stuff, trying to throw away what I didn't need anymore, that included old photos. I had too many.

I came across a picture with me, Lianna and my baby Daddy from high school. I was close to Lianna, I loved Liana but I never had her. She was in love with me, but we never did anything. And when her parents found out their daughter was a lesbian all I knew was that Lianna was withdrawn from school and no one had ever heard of her again.

I was sad and depressed, such a sweet girl. I had one other picture of Liana. She was wearing a red dress, her hair piled atop of her head. She had gained a few pounds in the picture, but her beauty was so radiant it was breathtaking.

Red came in the room and looked at me, and then she said bluntly, "I'm taking our sons to the store for ice cream. Want anything?"

She was a darling. "I'm ok; I need to throw half this shit away."

"Ok, we'll be back."

I stood up and gave her a firm hug. Gripping a hand full of my ass, she gave me some tongue. We always kissed like it was the very first time. "I wanna do something for our sons…put like a little family tree thing together."

Red said, "Ok, that's hot to death."

"Ok, I need your Mama's name, and your son's father's name and all that good shit."

"Ok, when I get back I'll get you everything you need."

"Ok, damn we're damn sure saying 'ok' an awful lot."

Red looked deep into my eyes. "I love you."

"And I love you."

Red got serious on me. "I will never hurt you, never lie to you, baby. I will die for you."

I felt appreciated. I truly missed my son's father, and he was the first and only man I ever wanted. I loved him, when we were together everyday was a holiday. I remembered rumors circulated around our high school, Miami Central Senior High, that he slept with Lianna. I didn't believe it of course.

He was too busy selling dope and talking

to me on the phone. I knew that couldn't be true. Then I got pregnant. I kept my son, and Mama tried to make me abort him. I told her to fuck off. My life was on the upswing, that was until my baby Daddy, Dunn McKinney, was murdered.

I never thought I'd love again. So I turned to women again and the rest was history.

"Ah," I said, hugging her tighter. We held each other. "For some strange reason I believe you."

And we kissed.

I was nearly done throwing shit away. Took me twenty minutes and they still weren't back. I didn't worry; she did call me and said she was stuck in traffic. Go figure.

I opened Red's closet and put my photo albums on the top shelf. One fell down.

"Shit!"

I suspected it was hers. Breathing through my nose, I picked it up and decided not to be nosey. I was gonna put it back.

When I reached up to slide it on the top shelf, some photos fell out.

I squatted on my knees and took them up but the instant I looked at them the breath caught in my throat.

I held my neck and sat down, staring at

the photos in disbelief. I opened the book and right before my eyes I found out all I needed to know.

Lolita Harvey wasn't Lolita Harvey.

And I didn't need to ask her who her baby Daddy was.

Lolita Harvey's real name was Lianna Gregory.

My long lost friend, the woman I was secretly in love with from high school.

And her son's father was the same man who fathered my son.

Dunn McKinney.

The high school rumor was true!

Oh, God! *Renaldo and Jameson were brothers!*

When Red came into the room an hour later she handed me some flowers. I just looked at her. I looked at the floor and she instantly knew something was wrong.

"Baby," she started and I turned my back on her, my heart split in two. "Baby!"

"What?"

"Talk to me."

"About what?" I was seething with rage.

"Something happened. What is it?"

I smiled bitterly. "Guilty conscious, 'ey?"

She waltzed around me and gripped my shoulders. "We can talk about anything."

I wanted to spit in her face. I hated a lying

ass bitch. If I could keep it real then damn it so could she. She was my love, my life. I opened up to this girl, told her about my abusive past. Did I tell her as a means to keep her? No. But at the same time she never really touched on topics from her past.

"Sure. Let's talk. Then I'm taking my son home."

"You are home."

"HOME!" I didn't mean to yell. She blinked several times, backing away from me. "Home, down in southwest Dade. My apartment. I should have known I couldn't trust you."

"You can."

"What high school you went to?"

"Miami Southridge. I told you that. You know that?"

"Really? And I guess you're going to tell me your name is Lolitha Harvey right? Or is it Lianna?"

She stared at me, her mouth open.

"Can't talk, Ho? You lied to me! Do you even remember me? Do you?"

"No, I don't. What are you talking about?"

I smiled graciously, taking apart the flowers and ripping them to shreds. It rained rose petals in the room, a room I didn't want to share with her anymore. This was how it always ended. Bitterly. A motherfucker couldn't be honest to save their lives. What was it with black people and honesty?

"You don't remember me, Lianna? We went to the same high school."

She stared at me, taking a few more steps back. "I don't…"

I approached her. "Your son's father, what was his name?"

"Jack Stephens."

"More lies. Your son's father I dated in high school. Rumors were flying that he fucked you. I never believed it."

She was in tears. "No, no…Are you telling me…you are…"

"Yup. Yup. Its me. You were fucking my man behind my back in high school. We were really close. And you mean to tell me you didn't recognize who I was at the club when we met?"

She got really quiet. She lowered her eyes and sat on the bed, folding her hands. Part of me wanted to hold her. But I couldn't hug a liar. "Yes, I knew who you were."

I was stunned. "So you played games with me."

She looked up. "No..I mean it looks that way."

"Why?"

"I have my reasons."

"Why? Tell me. Or I'm gone forever."

She pleaded, "Please don't leave. You have a piece of my son's father with you. Your son. I know he's the father."

I was hurt. My blood turned cold. "So everyone knew but me?"

Her eyes lowered to the floor. "Yes."

It took a while to gather my thoughts. I was rubbing my arms. "Why hide it from me? I'm going through enough shit, Red."

"I had to." She averted her face. I was getting angry.

I sat next to her and glared at her. "Tell me, everything. What *aren't* you telling me?"

She said it hastily. "It's about your mother."

I cringed inside. My Mama. She didn't *know* my mother.

My eyes wide, I breathed in deeply. "What about her."

"I can't get into it…" She turned away from me and I walked around her, getting in her face. I was on the verge of whipping her ass.

"Talk to me. What about my Mama?"

She looked scared, her teeth clicking together.

"I can't talk about it, Fate."

My eyes were slits of malice. "TALK!"

She retaliated. "Mind your business. It slipped out. Disregard what I said. I was making it up, just to get a reaction out of you."

"Why are you lying to me, woman?" I was about to lose it. "Open your goddamned mouth and talk before I snatch it out of you."

"Don't threaten me, bitch. Just because I bounce in that pussy don't mean you can whip my ass."

My brows rose. "Bounce?" I mocked, laughing. "The dildo bounces in this pussy pot, you strokeless bitch." I was getting her upset. She always spilled her heart when she was mad. She didn't realize that.

Red had an attitude. She got like that when you tried to force her to talk.

"Mind your business, Fate. Some things are better left unsaid."

Forcibly, I slapped her so hard she looked at me in shock.

I didn't give a shit. "…Talk…"

Angrily, she rushed me, grabbing in a bear hug. We slammed into the wall, pictures falling on the floor. We were going at it. Punching me in the face, I grabbed her by the afro and snatched the Ho across the room, kicking her in the lips. Blood on my shoes, she catapulted up to her feet and I Karate chopped the Ho in the face. Wincing, she fell to her knees, disoriented.

Yea, bitch. Didn't expect that One, Two Chop did you? She looked up, breathing hard and I stood there, breathing hard, my hair disheveled. The bitch fucked up my hair do. Silly, Ho!

When I looked up at the ceiling she attacked, jumping to her feet and punched me in the gut, ripping my top, my tits springing free. I rushed her and we fell over the bed, my head hitting the nightstand.

"Nobody hits me, bitch!" she was screaming and I bit her tit, jumped up to my feet and pushed the nightstand over on the bitch.

Spitting on her she pushed the nightstand like a beast and she grabbed my foot and pulled me down to her. She held me so tight I couldn't move.

"FATE!"

"I hate you, bitch!"

Red wouldn't let me go.

"Your mother is the reason my son's father is dead."

I was breathless, I was getting a headache. I had to stand up. She had to be lying. Blood on my face, I went into the bathroom and wet a wash cloth. She was behind me, tears in her eyes. I looked at her through the mirror. On her face was regret and remorse for hitting me. I didn't know how I felt about the bitch anymore. No one got saucy with me. I should grind my foot in her ass. Nah. She might like it too much. Bitch!

Mama never…wait a minute Mama did hate him. But she never really *met* him. I *never* brought him around the house. And when we did see each other I had to sneak out the window.

"My Mom don't know my baby Daddy, Red."

"Yes she did."

"Why do you say that?" I was wiping blood from my face, running warm water over the rag, wringing it out.

"He was killed during a drug deal."

"I…I know. He was the only man I ever loved."

"Same here. He was the only man I ever had. He was selling crack to someone and the person was short of money. When he asked for all his money a gun was drawn and his life was taken, like it meant nothing."

"And what does my Mama have to with this?"

"…Um…"

"Red, please. Just say it…"

She looked at me. "Your Mama pulled the trigger."

I looked at her for a long time before I did anything.

She was trying to hug me. Pushing her away I glared at her and said one thing, "I need some time alone. I'm going back to my apartment, and I will call you when I'm ready to talk or see you."

I walked past her. "If I ever wanna see you again," I went on, slamming the door behind me.

I locked myself in my apartment for days. I couldn't believe it! I just couldn't wrap my mind around it. I burned on the inside I couldn't eat or sleep. I cried so much, tears failed my eyes the way words failed my tongue. I tried reading the Bible to understand it all, but it was like I was reading empty pages. Nothing registered. I let my son stay with Red. For some reason I couldn't separate him from his brother. No, we haven't told them they were brothers yet. I didn't know how to. I didn't know what to say. Why would Mama kill my man? Why would she? Hadn't she robbed me enough in my life? Hadn't she allowed people to hurt me, shatter my soul, shit on my self-esteem? When would this shit ever end?

I couldn't live without my man. I loved

him so much. But did he love me? He slept with Red in high school. She looked dangerously different than she looked in school. I could have passed her on the street and not know she used to be sweet Lianna. That chubby sexy girl I wanted with a passion. I guess I got what I wanted.

Why would my man cheat on me? Wasn't I enough? Didn't I please him? I gave him pussy gave him the ass and gave him head when and where he wanted it. I never protested. I had his child. I thought I was the only one with bragging rights.

How could Red deceive me? What was her purpose for finding me? Leading me on? Was it all a lie? Was it really because she wanted her son to know my son? Combine my dead man's seeds? Was that it, or was there more to it? What did I do? If I was another woman in America going through this would I react the same way? I couldn't watch TV, I couldn't brush my teeth. My hair weave looked like shit. I smelled like it.

Several times over the next few days people knocked at my door. I didn't answer. My phone wailed like drunken sailors. I didn't answer. I didn't go in to work. I was probably fired by now. I didn't check the mail. I didn't get horny. I thought about Mama.

Before I knew it a few days later I was in the shower, took a long one, did my hair, got dressed and hopped in my truck and drove to Mama's house.

When she answered the door I stared at her. Dead inside. She looked radiant. A party was in progress. It took a while to realize it was her birthday. Oh, well. I wasn't here for celebrations.

I wanted to whip her ass! Shoot her the way she shot my man! I shook with rage, my blood boiled.

I got all the way in her face and told her one thing.

"I know."

She turned her back and said, "Everyone meet my daughter. Isn't she grand? Welcome to the party! Come on in!"

Otis Redding was singing. Everyone here was over 40. I felt like I was in a nursing home. They were dressed to kill. Dancing and sipping booze. Conversations ranged from Vietnam to Bush lusting over oil.

"Hey," they said. Some danced over to me and gave me a hug or shook my hand. I was very polite. I smiled at them. Then I glared at Mama. I took her hands. I spat "You look ravishing mother," so icily she shook.

She was trying to read me. I shut the radars off in my eyes, giving Houston a fucking problem.

"Thanks, baby."

"I know you killed my son's father."

She laughed nervously, snatching her hands back. "I don't know what you're talking about."

I gripped my Chanel purse under my arm. I was beautiful in a Baby Phat shirt with spaghetti straps and tight blue jeans dangerously riding my ass crack.

If I couldn't beat her, join her. "Would you like something to drink? I know I need one."

"Baby I can explain…"

"Wait here."

Dying inside, I snapped my fingers, swallowed my anger and danced across the room. Her old friend George grabbed my wrist and kissed my hand.

"Hey, George."

"Hey, sexy! Been a long time."

"I know. They make Viagra. And I'm not the supplier."

Kissing his cheek I waltzed over to Mama's bar. Years of whoring like the second coming of Jezebel got her the most fabulous two story $450,000 house in Miami-Dade

County. Foyers and a four car garage, even the guest house was an actual house in the huge back yard, complete with Olympic-sized pool and TV screens built into the walls.

Stubbornly, I looked over my shoulder. She was dancing and carrying on like I didn't just drop the bomb on her. And that was her life. Getting away with everything. She dissed felons, but she did felonious things throughout her life. She used to rob people, sell drugs and use them. Prostitute. Check. Whore. Check. Adulterer. Check. Married a man who fathered me and pimped me. Check. Check. Check.

I looked at the short, old woman with a gray stinky wig and pink dress. Her dentures reminded me of Mr. Ed. She looked lovely nonetheless.

"Hey." I just looked at her. Never saw her before in my life.

"Hi," she said. "What are you drinking?"

"Make two Rum and Cokes. Light ice in my mother's."

"Who is your mother?" she asked me, getting right to work with the skill of a well seasoned bar tender. I was impressed. She had a big ass and big titties. She still had that "Umph" that made men go "Whomp!"

"The birthday lady."

"You're her daughter? Fate? I finally meet

you?" Setting the rum bottle down, she walked hurriedly around the bar and engulfed me, kissing my cheek. "Oh ho ho hoo! Your Mom and I go way back. Back into time, Girl! We grew up together. We went to school together married together and had babies together."

Whoopee Do bitch! "Glad to meet you. And you're name?"

"Call me Janis the Pearl!"

What kinda name is that? "Aw, cute name. Glad to meet you."

She turned to dig in her purse and I grabbed the drinks.

Mama approached me and took her drink. I handed it to her with a smile.

"I met Janis the Pearl."

Her eyes were evil. Her smile, affectionate. "Aw, isn't she wonderful?"

"Does she molest her children like you? Since you two married together and had kids together."

"Listen, I will not be talked down to in my own home. Get over the past. That man was no good for you. The best thing he ever did was give you a son and got missing."

"YOU KILLED HIM, BITCH!"

People heard. The music died away. She looked around nervously, and kissed my cheek. "…And scene! You remembered your lines for your theatre class. Good job, baby."

And these dumb ass people clapped and whistled.

"Regular Angela Basset, honey!" Some lady clad in a yellow dress yelled dumbly and I rolled my eyes.

Another woman said "*And you look better than she do.*"

"Angela Basset isn't no Halle Berry," said Yellow Dress acidly.

"You're right she acts better. You brought up Angela not me."

"No she don't act better! Do Angela got an Oscar?"

"Nope and she didn't have to make her pussy feel good to get one either."

"Whatever, the Ho isn't no bigger than the Tina Turner role she played."

"Listen, damn it…"

"Hey hey hey," said George, looking silly in a tight gray suit that showed off the shape of his nuts and dick. He hugged both the flaming hot women, smelling like clouds of White Diamonds and moth balls. "Crank up the music. Turn on some James Brown. Otis is a boring muthafucker. I don't like docks sitting or bays goddamn it!" The party roared back to life.

I looked at Mama. She looked at me.

"Drop it girl! We all have pasts. I am not perfect. I did what I had to do. I know I fucked up. Call the police if you're sick in the head. You're trying to blame me because you let men rape you! You were a mistake! I hate you. In fact you don't even need to be raising your son! I'm calling the man so I can get custody." She leaned up to me and kissed my lips. I looked down, her nipples hardened. I could smell her pussy in the air. She was wet for me, yearning me, wanting me. Her breath came in short gasps. I closed my eyes and tried to will myself out of the room and wound up telling myself what I won't do.

I handed Mama her drink. I sipped mine, tears falling down my face. I couldn't compete with her. I didn't know what to do. How do you stand up to your Mama? Who made you? Molded you? Destroyed you? This family had secrets that would never get out and I was too afraid to do anything about it. But my job was to protect my son. Give him the protection I never had as a child. I was never secure.

She killed her drink, smacking her lips.

"Be a good little bitch and put the glass in the sink. And when the party is over be back here so you can massage Mama to sleep. I bet you still got some good pussy don't you. Mmmm hmmm. Don't act like you don't want it, bitch! I made you. You were put here to be my slave. Admit it. I own you. I possess you. You can't even fuck anyone else without thinking about Mama. Can you? Huh? I don't have emotions. They were killed when Mama let the white man rape me and make a baby. Those crackers stole my baby and told me it died. But in my heart I knew it was a lie! Mmm hmmm. Yup. My Mama sold me to those crackers. Yes, sir. She was afraid of losing her six penance. My Daddy was a punk. He let those people hurt us. He ran away first chance he got. Left a letter. That said, 'Fend for yourself, I got my own life.' Then I had to clean their houses and cook their food. Think she helped me? Nah. She was a scary bitch! I wasn't protected, so why should I protect you?"

I hurt for her. I knew this was true had to be. When Mama was telling the truth she gave it to you raw and uncut. She looked you in the face. She had a rough life. But I had to pay for it. I hugged her and quickly pulled back. I felt like water and she was electricity. Shocking. "Mama. I can't do this. I got to go."

Hurting deeply, I dumped the drink on her and I got in my truck, never to see her again. I actually smiled all the way to my apartment. When I got there I pulled out my pad and wrote Red a note.

Red,

What's up! I want to be in your world because I really feel God put us together. I'm writing in text form, the way I do when we text with cell phones, because its easier to say what I have to say and its quicker to write. I have tried nothing like this before but I want to be happy so I'm willing to do this for the first time in my life to be in a relationship with someone I care about, which is YOU….

Now I contemplate taking her back. Yes, she lied. But we all lie sometimes. Yes, we got in a huge fight. I still couldn't believe we fought like cats and dogs. People in love didn't fight or hit each other. But we were human before we were lesbians. I couldn't believe she would go through those lengths to have me back in her life. I had to believe her intentions were good.

I sealed the letter with a kiss. I stood up, put it in an envelope and walked into the kitchen. I grabbed my car keys, locked my front door and walked to my truck.

When I got to Red's house forty minutes later she opened the door and she looked as fine as ever, thus a little sad.

"Yes. Who is it…" When she saw it was me she became animated, grabbed me and turned in a circle. "Baby! You're here come in baby welcome home! I have been trying to call you for weeks! I tried calling you tonight! Something bad happened."

I thought about my son! MY SON!

"Where is my son?" I shut down. Fell to my knees. Please don't tell me my son…

"Mama!" I froze. I stopped crying, sucking in air. "When did you get back? I missed you, Mama. Red told me her son is my brother. She told us yesterday over cake and ice cream. We actually have the same Daddy, can you believe it?"

I slowly looked up at Red. She extended her hand. "Our family is whole."

I took it, handing her the note. "Read it later."

She kissed my lips. "Ok but seriously haven't you heard?"

"Heard…what?"

"Your mother…it's about…"

I flashed with anger. "What did she do this time?"

"She died tonight."

I just stared at her, immediately looking at my son. He looked like he could care less. He grabbed his brother's hand and they went to play the Playstation 3 game console.

I looked at Red.

"How did she die?"

"I don't know. People are saying she…dropped dead at her birthday party."

Crushed and devastatingly hurt, I hugged Red, clinging to her. It hurt to know this. To find this out seemed a dream.

Red cried with me, kissing my face, wiping away my tears; whispering sweet nothings to me…

It hurt that my Mama was dead. Part of me allowed myself to mourn. I burst open and sobbed so hard I cracked open. Mama was Mama. She wasn't perfect.

Something had to have happened to her in her life that made her hurt me.

She was acting out. She told me the story of her life. Our last moments were spent talking about her bitter and painful past.

I would never find out because.

I poisoned her Rum and Coke when Janis the Pearl turned to dig in her purse. I had blended rat poison and weed killer together at my apartment and concocted a nice little mix.

I then poured some in a small empty test tube from my son's science game.

The bitch would never hurt me again.

I had to protect me. And overall. I had to protect my son.

Plus she killed his father.

No way in hell she could ever get away with that. She got away for years.

I would see to it she was buried in an expensive casket and given the proper burial.

Sweet dreams.

Mother.

“Goddamn it, don’t drop my shelf!” I told the short, stocky white boy who worked for Hermit’s Furniture store. “I paid a thousand dollars for that case. I need my case, damn it watch my goddamn walls! I don’t care about you huffin’ and puffin’ like you’re a Backwood cigar. *Listen,* man. Set it over there by the living room sofa! What? I paid for the assembly and the delivery, and you're going to give me $75 worth of delivery service cracker boy now hop to it!"

Jesus! Good customer service was hard to come by these days, especially when you're black and a woman. And add the third strike for being a black woman.

He looked at me like he wanted to fight. "Ma'am, it doesn't look right over by your sofa."

The nerve of this creepy asshole! "Do you pay my bills?" I spat nastily.

Ugly with Coke-bottle glasses, the kind that made his eyes look like marbles, he left my shelf alone, wiping off his finger prints with a rag. And he had some big ass fingers. "Well, who would want to?"

I tucked my chin back. "Don't get smart, do you pay my bills?"

"No, Lady!"

My hands rose to my hips the same time my brows rose.

"Watch the tone of voice in my house…"

"I'm grown," he responded. What man argued with a woman?

I started shooting from the hip. "Are you *fucking* me?"

He gave me the once over, smacked his gum, rolled his beady eyes, sashayed over to his power drill by the end table and said, "I don't do fish," more sassily than Halle Berry in *Cat Woman*.

"Well *don't* tell me what looks good in my house. As a matter of fact get out, your services are terminated, thanks for bringing my shelf."

"What about my tip?"

I snatched up my huge purse, took out my wallet, turned my back to him so he couldn't see me shuffling through my cash, I was funny about my money, and when I was done scribbling with my pen I turned, smiled, walked up to him and handed him a note. He read it out loud. "Tip for the day, I need to get some Oxy pads to terminate the oily pimples all over my face, what is this? I said a tip, not a tip."

"Ok, you can leave now." I was pushing him out the door, and his body odor wasn't making things civil, either. "You sound Chinese, *same thang, same thang*," I went on, trying to sound Asian. "...Repeating the same things over and over, I asked for a *tip*, not a tip, confusing me, guy. Have a nice day!" I gave him a huge shove and slammed the door behind him. He called me a "Bitch," and left after cursing through my door for about thirty seconds.

Anyways, I didn't feel up to all that today.

White people were crazy anyways. Yea, baby.

My shelf looked magnificent. The same way it looked when I saw it at Hermit's Furniture Store a little after the orgy I had at church. I went into my room, opened my bottom drawer, pushed my panties to the side and took out the Golden Mask. Open Says Me. Images flashed in my mind. From a few weeks ago.

I had to lean against the wall because the power of the memories took my breath away, of when I defiled God's House with my own sick, selfish pleasures. That morning my flesh was so weak I couldn't think straight.

When I sashayed down the hall of my church, my heels clickety-clacked with sounding echoes towards the double doors that led to paradise.

Coming face to face with Big Daddy Good Dick, or whatever his name was. I was smiling, my body coming alive. I was to get Dicked Down Froggy Style.

I remembered being breathless, so hot and bothered I didn't want to be left alone.

I could still feel the pleasure that overcame me when I entered lustful terrains, even though, back then, I thought I was dying of Cancer, only to find out, after the orgy, that I really didn't have a sickness.

I kissed the mask, went back into the living room, opened the shelf, and set the mask inside it.

After closing the glass door and locking it, I took a few steps back, lighting a Black and Mild cigar, puffing smoke through my nostrils, bursting from my sensual lips and just admired how it sparkled.

I would cherish this mask for the rest of my life.

No one was allowed to touch it.

What did *Rollingstone* magazine know about journalism? I was reading the latest issue I just got in the mail, hoping Janet Jackson's ultra-sexy ass would be on the cover. Instead I had to settle for Led Fucking Zeppelin. Led Zeppelin? Oh, please! Janet did have an album coming out on September 26, 2006 called 20 Years Old, which was now being marketed as 20 Y.O. I had just gotten home from B.E.T's 106 and Park this morning. I was an unnoticeable part of the so-called "Livest Audience in the World" propaganda that I had heard about for so long. I knew three year olds who were graciously more audible and raunchy. I hated B.E.T. anyways. Same ole commercials, same movies old movies at that. Shit you only owned on VHS shit you never even contemplated getting on DVD. Same award shows, really who wanted to see Mo'Nique do the Beyonce booty dance fifty times a fucking week? Seriously, B.E.T. was once a step forward for black people. Now they market Justin Timberlake more than Janet Jackson. A step back.

106 and Park was definitely not as good as the Free and AJ Era, two enormously enigmatic and energetic VJ's B.E.T seriously needed to bring back to hype the fledgling music video countdown show.

I was jet-lagged, tired, and my body felt like it was beat up. I got some good dick while in New York. New York Dick. It was something extraordinary giving up some Down South Pussy in the City that Never Slept. Just constant partying, drinking, weed-smoking and a feel-good atmosphere not seen in Miami. I wanted to go to the raves, pop ecstasy pills and twirl some glowing lights all up in my face. But I was too scared to do that shit. I saw a documentary that showed more youngsters winding up statistics attending those dangerous raves and I decided against it.

I needed to clean up my house. I had bills to pay. I was already behind on my light bill. And I still owed another $40 on my water bill. I wished FP&L supplied my electricity because Homestead Lights were rip-offs. They fucked you out of your money. Seriously.

I worked at the Precision Response Corporation, known as PRC on the Direct TV account. Made nine bucks an hour. Good money, but my bills ate my good money to hell. I had to return to work later on today. It was hell getting three days off so I could go to New York. I was still marveling at the Golden Masks Orgy I attended in the back of my church.

I checked my phone messages. The box was full. This many people hadn't called me in years. I wondered why. And it wasn't because Fidel Castro might be dead. The shit was all over the news. Maybe now Cubans could stay their funky asses in Cuba!

Sliding out of my Nautica jacket (even though Nautica was so defunct from the fashion scene) and kicking off my G-Unit sneakers, I let my hair down from the loose bun and flopped on my bed. I missed home. I was hot in this jean outfit. So I stripped down to my panties and matching bra. There, I felt better.

I pressed "play" on the machine and just let her rip.

Angela. *Girl I saw you on TV! You go bitch! I can't believe you met Janet!!*

Jake. *Oh my God! Girl, you represented for Miami! And Janet was ravishing!*

Bob. *You lucky bitch! You got to hug the sexiest bitch on earth!*

Paul. *Your Grandma told me you were on TV with Janet Jackson. I didn't believe her. And when I seen you in the crowd hugging Janet oh my God! I pissed in my pants. You better have gotten my autograph! Everybody in the Hood is praising you. You're a star, Melissa!*

Sitting up I pressed "stop" on the machine. I'd had enough. I turned off the ringer on my phone. I didn't want to be bothered.

I was still in a daze. Meeting Miss Jackson. How many bitches from the Hood could say they shook hands and met Janet Jackson? No one here. I was the first and only one. I sent in my request to attend online when I heard Janet was going to be on 106 & Park Friday, July 31st. I think it was July 10th I had found out. I had gone online at Miami Dade Community College Homestead Campus and sent in the request. Being from Florida City, a ghetto-within-a-ghetto, I never thought I'd be selected, especially with Michael Jackson's little sister coming through.

How wrong was I?

I saw Janet Jackson in the flesh! Oh my God! Being a twenty-three year old mother of one, even though DCF recently took my child because my Baby Daddy lied on me and said I rarely fed my five year old son, you would think my teenage fascination with Hollywood people would apishly halt. And it did for the most part. When I was a teenage girl I had LL Cool J on my wall, and every other rapper of the moment. My girl Latonia used to masturbate to his posters. I haven't spoken to her in ages.

I met Ludacris on South Beach last year. I was happy but not excited. I met a certain slain rapper when I was a little girl when I won a contest at my elementary school, West Homestead Elementary. I never knew I'd meet him, and when I heard about the short story essay I had to write detailing who I wanted to meet and why I never knew the actual first prize would be to meet who you wrote about. Hey, I was from the Hood, the ghetto. Ghettos didn't get any love.

But when the future controversial, slain rapper, I'll leave nameless, walked into my classroom, without a camera crew and goons surrounding him, nor the media, they didn't have the slightest clue, I died! All my friends fell over in excitement, running up to him, hugging him, I died again! I was like OH MY GOD! He instantly knew who I was. My ecstatic teacher, Miss Sharps, who had a wet pussy just goo-goo eyeing him, pointed at me.

"That's Melissa Jackson right there," she said excitedly, pulling out her mirror, fixing her hair and putting on a thick coat of lipstick, ripping the bottom of her dress off so it could be shorter.

When he smiled I knew I'd be strictly dickley for the rest of my life. Even though I wasn't having sex nor thinking about it. I was only about five years old.

With the grace of a ballet dancer, he walked up to me, gave me a hug, gave me his latest CD and said, "How about posing for a picture with me. I read your essay. Very talented."

I didn't get excited. I was just happy that a star was in the Hood. My classroom door was locked but when the school heard the future slain rapper was there you suddenly heard a roar outside the door, kids kicking and screaming his name. Teachers were running from other classrooms, trying to get inside. I felt lucky.

When my teacher took our picture, and one with the class, the superstar rapper kissed my cheek and slipped out the back door in full Thug apparel, into an awaiting SUV, and disappeared as if he was never there.

I didn't get excited.

But when Janet Jackson shook my hand at

106 & Park and gave me a hug, I hyperventilated, clad in my sexy tight black pants and plain T-shirt baring her face. I lost it. I cried so hard this black girl next to me had to hug me to calm me down.

"She touched me! She touched me!" I chanted, shaking like I was the Queen of Tremors.

I watched excitedly, hanging onto her every word. I loved the ripped jeans, the colorful high heeled boots, the slanted red hat, the huge hoop earrings. She was so stunningly gorgeous, nowhere on her was a trace of the 60 extra pounds she'd shed over the last few months, when she was the butt of a thousand jokes.

Those same people were now biting dust. Janet Jackson was back.

After admiring her and drooling for the next hour and a half, she signed my T-shirt and new promo poster handed out to me when I got there. I would cherish it. I also told her I entered her Design My CD cover contest. She only smiled.

But before I was to go through all that with Janet, on the previous Thursday, I flew to New York via my grandmother, who knew how much I looked like, loved and admired Janet. When I told her I was selected to attend the live taping she told everybody. Grandma paid for me to go, my hotel for two nights, my plane ticket round trip and my food. She gave me 400 dollars.

"Go rep us Miami Bitches," she said, no teeth in her mouth, bald head (because she just beat cancer). She was just the most humorous, uplifting soul you'd meet. I did just that. Represented.

I was still on a dick high. I got my first taste of New York dick on the plane. I met a handsome man with the charisma of Billy Dee Williams. He said he was from New York. He sat by me. I wore a long dress and some red pumps, my hair long and real. No weave going on here.

I was trying to ignore him but he pulled out one of the magazines from the back of the seat and was like, "Doesn't Bill Gates look ugly?"

And I smiled, saying, "His money isn't ugly."

"And neither are you. Sup, Ma. You're traveling alone?"

I didn't appreciate him trying to get all in my business. In fact it pissed me off. "Yea, why?" He gave me a long, lingering look. I felt like the Dow Jones on Wall Street. "Because I think you look good."

Get out my face, I am not feeling you! "So do you, pimp." Why did I just lie?

He saw the lust in my eyes. "What that pussy smelling like?"

Time to pull his card. "Roses."

"Shit, can I see?"

"You can smell."

I took his hand and put it between my legs, looking around making sure no one noticed. I took out my huge blanket and covered the lower half of our bodies. He slow fucked me with those hairy, thick fingers. I grinded on them.

"Taste my pussy..."

He put his fingers in his mouth, closing his eyes, moaning softly. Hmmm. Good.

"I know," I told him.

"Sup with tasting this fat dick?"

I licked my lips, but when he unzipped his pants and I saw Pee Wee Herman waving at me I was like, "I'm straight."

"Sup, Ma?"

I was deeply offended. "I don't do little dicked men. Sorry."

He huffed and puffed and changed seats.

Oh, well.

Was I supposed to be offended?

Nah. Didn't think so.

Fuck you, too! Little dick man.

***

Then I got a nice surprise. I sucked this Juelz Santana-looking Niggah off in the small bathroom on the plane. His name was Naygee. He was sitting in front of me, gave me the eye from the Miami International Airport, to the plane and when we got 40,000 feet in the air I started really eyeing him, loving what I saw. I loved men. Men were my weakness.

When we were flying over Georgia, he turned and asked me could he use my phone because his phone died and his sister, who was knocked out sleep next to him, wouldn't come off hers.

I said sure.

He called his phone from my phone; I didn't know it until I got a text message from a number I had never seen before. I read it.

Meet me in the trap.
It's going down.
The Niggah in front of you.

I smiled. Homeboy was 6 feet tall and just handsome.

I went to the bathroom first. The plane wasn't full and almost everyone was sleeping. It was after 11 PM that night. When I got there I waited, debating. I didn't know him but my pussy *wanted* to get to know him. Seconds later the door opened and he came inside, not smiling, closed and locked the door, unzipped his pants, pulled out that huge Spanish dick, and went up in my mouth. I loved his scent, his taste. I ran my hands through his pubic hairs, sucking on them, then putting his dick back in my mouth.

"Help me get that nut, Ma. Swallow my shit, bitch."

He fucked my mouth real good.

"That's my wife out there, not my sister," he said, watching me play around with his dick, his nuts swinging back and forth. He looked so good. I was so gone. "Play with that pussy, leave your panties on, just rub that pussy and let me smell it tramping in the air."

I did what he said. After all, this was his Freaky Deaky Show.

The bathroom was small and compact, but I was so flexible I got on my knees, crawled all the way up to him and deep throated his dick, smelling my pussy mixed with his nuts and dick and cologne in the air, which brought the freak out of me. I was holding my breath half of the time so the length and thickness of his penis wouldn't make me gag or wanna vomit.

He then sat on the toilet and pumped my

wetness until he came down my throat. He was lost in my rhythm. He looked at me like he loved me. Real Thug here. Spanish Fly. With some black in his blood stream. His Nextel phone rang. Playing the "Getting Some Head" ring tone. How fittingly coy.

I put his dick back in my mouth, surprised it stayed hard. Most men dicks went limp, but his stayed rock hard. He had a pretty penis.

He answered the phone.

I slurped really loud, the saliva from my mouth and the force of my jaws creating a very noisy tune.

He smiled.

"Sup playboy. I'm getting my dick sucked by Freaky Deaky."

"Damn let me hear," said Playboy through the phone.

He put the phone down to my lips and the head of his dick. I gave them the audible, smiling like the bitch I was at heart.

"Oooh yea, she sounds like a *bad* bitch."

"Wanna video of it?"

"Hell, yea. And send it to me."

He decided against it. "Nah. Go get your own bitch." And he hung up.

"Suck that dick, Freaky Deaky. Suck it like you want it…want Daddy to take dis dick out your mouth?"

"No, Daddy Freaky Deaky," I said, sucking on it a little bit better than I had earlier. I gave him pleasure in spurts. Rule number one in Sucking Dick 101, never do your best skills first. Issue the skills out.

"Pull dem titties out and tit fuck this dick."

I was amazed. At his frankness.

I never titty fucked a man before. Shit, what pleasure was I going to get out of it? Suddenly I was selfish; I didn't want to do this weird shit!

There was a knock on the door.

"I'm taking a shit," he said aloud, and the person went away, mumbling.

His eyes sparkled, the light from the bathroom soft and sweet. He leaned forward and took my right nipple into his mouth, suckling on it hard and thuggish. I loved it. I held his head, running my tongue over his low-fade with the green Tupac-like rag tied in a knot around it. His earrings glittered.

Leaning back he took both my tits, spit on his dick, and used my tits to smooth saliva all over it. He long stroked the tits. I positioned myself where the head of his dick went in my mouth when he slid my titties down on his dick. He loved it. He said, "Damn, Ma. Be my bitch. I'ma leave my wife to have a Freaky Deaky bitch like you."

Ignoring him. I played with his balls, sticking my finger deep in my ass, finger banging myself for a few minutes, enjoying the feeling. My pussy was dripping. I then pulled my finger out, putting it under his nose, he took a whiff and was in heaven, smiling, throwing them hips at such a fast pace. Those nuts bounced, you hear me? Feeling nasty, I stuck my finger in his mouth and he sucked my asshole right on down his throat.

"Are you Freaky Deaky?" I asked him, putting my hands up his shirt and fumbling with his chest. I squeezed his chest like he squeezed my tits, watching his nuts dance.

"I'm Freaky Deaky," he responded breathlessly, his second nut creeping on the come up.

"Take off your shirt. I'm tired of crack head DMX looking me in the face."

Unhesitant, he took the shirt off.

"Now bang my tits, Niggah."

He used my titties to begin his crusade. Seconds later he moaned softly, being discreet, my tits jiggling all over the place and beautiful thick cum spurted all over them. His orgasm seemed endless. He shook and trembled, the silkiness of his pleasurable moans set me on fire with enough flames to suffocate Puff the

Magic Dragon and evaporate his sea.

When it was over he leaned over and licked up his nut. He swallowed it, and then tongue kissed me. I loved the way he kissed. "Freaky Deaky Session is over," I told him.

Then he stood up, zipped up his huge baggy jeans with the huge cowboy glittering belt, fixed his green rag on his head, put on his shirt and he went back out to plane and sat by his wife, totally ignoring me. I sat behind him and played with my pussy, hiding my lower body under my blanket. Put on my earphones and watched the Nutty Professor, and melted into an orgasm. I got a text message.

What happened in the bathroom
stays in the bathroom.
Erase my number when you read this message.

Bitch, I thought, staring at this creep from behind. I never saved your phone number to begin with.

When the plane was flying over Virginia I got another text message.

Meet me in the trap. I want some more head.

Smiling to myself, I thought.

Freaky Deaky Sessions starts again!

Freaky Deaky
Part 2:
Black Paintings

When I got to New York I put my Freaky Deaky ego on the back burner. I was ecstatic about being there. This was a place I said I would never go. When I went to Times Square I took some pictures of the buildings and passing cars. I went to the Statue of Liberty. It was so beautiful. Why couldn't Miami have something this breathtaking, besides the huge hand statue dedicated to the Holocaust victims down the street from South Beach?

I asked a few strangers to take my one-time use Kodak camera and take some solo snap shots of me in my Apple Bottom outfit.

My ass was big. Men drooled at the booty. They couldn't touch the booty. If they had a little dick and was fruity no can touch the booty. Period. Fuck you if you didn't like it. I was a real bitch and real bitches did real things.

I was all about the name brand. With my Sony CD Walkman in my pouch with my wallet, and my ear phones pumping Case, R&B singer, into my ears, I was definitely into the groove like Madonna minus the "Hung Up" bathing suit.

In contrast to Miami, New York was just too much. Too many goddamn people. Too many men. Too many cars. Too much cursing. Just fine, sexy men everywhere I looked. I like. I like.

While in Downtown Manhattan, I met a man who looked just like "ER" actor Mekhi Phiefer. He had ocean-green eyes, caramel-kissed skin that glistened from the sun radiating on the sweat trickling all over his sculpted body, deep waves soaking under a black do rag, bling bling out the ass, a bunch of dope in huge pockets stitched on low-hanging baggy jeans showing off a silk-clad ass that had my pussy feeling slutty like Britney Spears, wanting to come off that Boom Boom.

I was at the store, I forget the name of it, buying some shoes and he came up behind me, pressing his penis on my ass. He was cocky and confident. He made it seem like a natural thing.

I was pissed for one. I paused, held my breath, my attitude surfacing in record time and just dug my nails in the dress. I turned to face him. Then I said, "Get you dick off…"

When I saw him, this sexy thing, I was like, "*Damn*, baby, sup with you?"

"I knew you'd change your mind when you took a look at this."

I tucked my chin back playfully. "Arrogant Niggah."

"Naw, Ma. Confident."

I felt tremors in my legs. "I see."

He took my bejeweled-with-flea-market-gold-hand and kissed it, making my panties wet and my nipples hard. "I'm Melvin. From the Bronx."

His nipples poked against his wife beater (a tank top undershirt). Huge nipples, nice and long. Damn!

"I'm, I'm…Melissa. From Florida City."

"Down South gal." He cupped my hand.

"Yep."

My eyes dropped to the escalating lump in his pants. Damn, getting bigger by the second. Why my mouth suddenly watered beats me. Felt like I was talking with a whole bunch of spit in my mouth. I looked at the expensive gold rope chain around his thick neck, a scorpion medallion glittered. Hung just above his belly button. He had Mel's Hell tattooed on his neck, and had a huge red and black dragon tattooed on either arm.

We couldn't stop staring at each other.

Freaky.

"You're a sexy woman."

"Thanks."

"Where's Florida City?" he asked and I pat his shoulder, looking him over.

"In Florida."

"Well, duh! You buggin'!" he joked, smiling. "I mean what part of Florida?"

"Miami. The southwest region of Miami."

"Interesting."

"I see."

"I love your twang. I can damn sure hear it in your smoky voice."

"Yea. That's what my man back home says." I didn't have a man. I always told Niggahs that. They seemed to get locked nuts when I said it.

He got competitive. Most New Yorkers were that way. "So you got a man?"

"Yea."

He took both my hands, pressing his hard dick against my pussy, bringing my hands back to grip his ass while he played around with my hair. I dropped the dress on the floor. Some white woman sneered at me, whisking around the rack, picking up the dress, putting it back on the hanger and hanging it on the clothing rack with the other dresses. She had an attitude. I ignored her.

I was on fire. He kissed my forehead. We were the same height. Five feet eleven inches.

"Does he treat you the way you need to be treated? Cook for you, cut your toe nails, caters to you?"

The woman stood on the side of me, her hands on her hips. I watched her from my peripheral vision.

"He's all right."

"Ma'am," said the store employee. We ignored her and didn't break eye contact. But home girl got bold. "Ma'am! I am talking to you."

Not letting my new flame go I happily looked at her. I wouldn't let her break my funk.

"Yes?" It was getting cold in here.

My Dude lowered his head, suppressing a laugh.

"You can't drop our expensive clothing on the floor."

"I got arthritis. My fingers locked up and I dropped it."

He started laughing, chocking on his saliva. I chuckled, too. White people, so uptight.

"That's before or after you and your fling here bumped pelvises in the aisle around little children?"

My mouth falling open I turned into her face and said, "For one bitch you watch your goddamned tone! I'm not these New York bitches! I'ma Miami bitch and I'll fuck you up with my razor under my tongue, Ho! And I don't see any kids around here."

"Whatever, listen I'm gonna call security—"

"Call Ghostbusters too, bitch, I don't care."

"*Listen* you Flee Market Outfit wearing tramp…"

I stunned and excited shoppers when I, without warning, snatched the bitch by her airbrushed-looking hair and she fell on her face. Homeboy took me by the arm when I tried to dig my heel into her ear.

"Nah, Ma. I got this."

Helping the shockingly disgruntled bitch off the floor, he pulled three hundred dollars from his wallet and handed it to the woman. "That should pay for the dress. Keep the change. Gift wrap it, please."

Taking the money the white lady with "Bertha" on her tag said, "I will do. And when you want a real woman, drop this Miami Trash," and she and her blonde hair spun on her heel and waltzed to the register with the dress.

I was burning up.

"Lemme whip that Ho's ass."

He was trying to hold me. "Ma. Calm down. I definitely like your fire."

I rolled my eyes. "Whatever." He held me again, tightly, kissing my lips. "I'm not your Mama. Stop calling me that."

"Let's cut to it, Ma. When can a Niggah get that pussy?"

What's with the Ma bullshit? "Damn, and he's direct,"

"Life is too short to fuck around."

"No, some dick is too short to fuck around. You shoulda been on the plane with me."

We laughed easily. The chemistry building in us was breathtaking. I felt like a magnet. I was naturally drawn to him.

"So can we get out of here?" he asked, matter-of-factly.

"You live in the Bronx, right?" I was a little scared, I didn't know if he was a rapist, had AIDS or was a good boy next door type of man. I'd soon find out.

"I'm from the Bronx. I live here in Manhattan." I loved the way he talked, his arrogance, his confidence was refreshing. He had a lot of class, rarely seen in a thug Niggah. He had a very deep voice, like Busta Rhymes. I liked that. He looked me deep in the eyes, never wavering. I felt like the only woman in the store.

"Cool. Well, I don't just give up the pussy when I first meet somebody and I'm going back to Miami tomorrow. I'm only here to attend 106 and Park so I could see Janet."

He smiled. "Cool, that's straight. How about I buy you that dress you're holding, and wine and dine you, and make sure you get to your Janet thing. Would that be cool?"

"Yea. That's straight, gangster. But remember, you ain't getting no pussy."

"I promise to behave."

Walking towards the unprofessional Bertha, who was explaining the situation to her co-workers, who were all white, I paused in front of her when she was about to put the money in the register and I snatched his money out of her hand, spitting at her. It hit her dead in the face. I slapped her so hard store cameras caught visuals of her falling on her elite circle of friends.

"You aren't getting me or his business.

He's nice. I'm *not,* Ho!" And we left the store in silence.

"Damn, you Miami Girls are the shit," he said, taking his money back.

"Nah, we're gentle creatures. Until you piss us off."

Hugging me he led me up the crowded block, making small talk.

He wined and dined me at four o'clock in the evening. I felt special. He drove me all over New York in a Lincoln Navigator, all paid for, with the spinning Spreewell rims. He had a killer booming system. He smoked his "Hydro." Weed, with the windows down to spare me. I used to smoke weed. But I haven't touched the shit in ages. He bought me Letoya Lucket's new CD. "Torn" was one song I wouldn't be listening to because I was tired of it. Home girl definitely was positioned to give Beyonce's scream-singing ass a run for her money because "Deja Poo" wasn't hitting on shit.

When I got to his apartment, very spacious, clean, and looked more like a Bachelor Pad with all the technology to go with it, PS2, stereo with DJ speakers, Ella Fitzgerald and Fabulous on his wall, he poured me some Dom. I had never had Dom Perignon. He put on Letoya Luckett. We listened with open minds and very horny souls. Her CD was marvelously crafted, liked it a lot. But I liked my prize catch better.

Despite my better judgment I wanted him so bad. But I didn't wanna give him the impression that Miami Girls were easy. Easy to piss off but not easy to bed like sheets clinging to a mattress. Buy them a dress and drive them around like your name was Miss Daisy and viola! Instant Pussy Access.

Ain't happening.

He showed me around his place. Definitely a reflection of him. He lived on the tenth floor. I stood out on the balcony and looked at Manhattan. Gorgeous. The sounds of the horns blowing, people talking, air blowing, trees rustling created tranquility in my head. Peace.

"Melissa." I closed my eyes at the sensual sound of his heavily smoky masculine voice.

Going back into the apartment I froze when I seen him laying on his couch, naked, with whipped cream spread all over his dick and hips. His nipples were mouth watering. His feet were gorgeous. He looked like a Tyson Beckford pin-up. There was some strawberry cheesecake on the low table. Every blind and curtain was closed, keeping out the rest of the fading sunlight; and a few candles were lit. Soft jazz played. I thought it was Letoya. Winston Marsalis, I knew his material. I was nailed to the floor.

"Sup baby."

Black paintings all around him. "Hi." I couldn't speak, I couldn't find the words. I walked over to him and towered over him, just looking into his eyes, invitingly gorgeous eyes that dared me.

"No pussy, my Niggah. I don't know you like that."

He played around with his nipple. Smiling. "Get to know me like that." He made his dick jumped and I quivered.

I was getting weaker by the second. "No."

"Suck the whip cream off my dick."

"Hell, yea…I meant, no, hell no, Niggah."

"Come on, baby. Hold out your tongue."

I did. Wondering what he was up to. He rubbed his finger on his asshole, took some pre-cum from the tip of his dick and some whip cream and he stood up, pulling out my left titty and rubbed it all over my nipple. He lay back down.

He said easily, "Suck it off your nipple, baby. Damn get freaky for me."

I cupped my breast, pulling it up to my lips. I ran my tongue all over his essence and the whip cream, swallowing what exploded inside me once it touched my throat.

"Taste good, doesn't it?" he asked, looking boyishly handsome. I was on fire for real.

"Yea. But no pussy."

Reaching out, taking one of my legs, he pulled me to him, put his face under my dress and he stuck his tongue deep in my wet pussy, not moving his head, just the tongue, which was long and thick. Goddamn! I tried to force myself into a state of unwanted bliss, actually trying to go numb but I couldn't. He squeezed my ass cheeks, a little painfully, and used those thick lips to torture my clitoris, which awakened with an aching it had never experienced and sent shivers up and down my spine. He would do this for a long ass time. I stood there letting him rock the boat and work the middle with his experienced tongue like I was slow dancing with an invisible man. I had to hold the arm of the chair to keep balance. Damn he was hungry.

"Come on, Ma…" He kissed my pussy and lay his head back on the cushioned arm of his black leather sofa, like he hadn't even moved.

I went crazy.

I took off my dress, revealing a birthday suit for his ass. I was top notch, a dime who was top of the line with a big ass booty, good pussy and deep throat skills to pay the bills. Let's show this Bronx Bred Niggah some new shit.

I took the small candle from the table and told him to close his eyes.

"Oh, I finally got you, huh, baby?" he said.

"Shut up. Close your eyes," I suggested.

He did so.

I got on my knees and slowly took his whip-cream-clad-dick into my mouth, sucking on it slowly, locking my jaws, using my tongue expertly.

"*Gooooddaaammmnnn*!" was all the poor boy could say.

"I am home sick," I told him, sucking on his nuts, running my tongue across gorgeous-smelling pubic hair and skin. "I'm gonna suck Florida City out the head of your dick, spread it all over your shaft and nuts so it'll feel like I'm at home."

"Goddamn, bitch," he said admiringly, his dick jumping in my mouth. Home boy was about to lose control.

I sucked it good, swallowing the cream, playing with his balls, working the cream into his skin. He smelled good, tasted good. The air smelled like strawberries.

Running my fingers over my pussy I wrote my name with my juices on his forehead.

M-E-L-I-S-S-A.

Spelling it out soundly as I did so.

Taking the candle I stood his ten inch dick straight up and wiped hot candle wax along the shaft. He bit his lips, arching his back, his huge nuts dangling and he was like, "Oooh my God that feel so good, where in the hell did you learn that trick?"

I worked the head of his dick, letting the wax harden on the shaft. I used a delicate finger to wipe hot wax on his nuts while I punished the head with my hot mouth and tongue. He rose with my head, veins popping all over his dick from out of no where. He moaned so elegantly, turned me on. Oh Baby. Fuck that dick. Feels so Good. You're the best. I never had wax on my dick. I love you Miami Women. Marry me. Yea. Rub some wax on my asshole. Yea, baby. Hot! I feel good.

I was swallowing whip cream, pouring the rest of my warm Dom Perignon wine on him, fucking up his white rug, tasting his sweat, watching my titties bounce. I played with my pussy. Careful not to bring myself to orgasm. I moaned with him: Yea Baby you got some Good dick! Imagine this is my pussy on the head of your dick. Take it, Niggah. And you call yourself a man?

Trapped in La La Land his nuts jerked, his thighs locked, his toes bent and I felt his dick contract, then he suddenly burst with cum, spurted straight up in the air, all over his nipples, chest and abs and as quickly as I could I put his dick in my mouth, the entire dick and swallowed the nut and the hardened wax all in one gulp.

He moaned out my name, dug his fingernails into the chair, fucking my mouth slowly, tenderly, twirling his hips, tears escaping his eyes.

He opened them. He had to get a visual. Cum everywhere.

"Your Freaky Deaky, baby?" I asked him, challenging him. His manhood was compromised. He got dark.

"You fucking right, bitch!"

"Are you Freaky Deaky?"

"I'm Freaky Deaky!" His voice filled the apartment.

"Ok, watch this. You gonna do what I say?"

He was like a determined college student wanting to get the grade. "YES BITCH!"

"Then shut up while I do this."

I sucked his dick again, slurping my spit off his shaft, playing with the head with my tongue, stronger, smoother, more forcibly. He jerked, grabbed my hair in closed fists and fucked my mouth. I squeezed his inner thighs, bringing him pain while bringing the head of his nature pleasure. His toes went haywire.

"Jesus Christ."

"Ain't sucking your dick, leave him out of it," I said, with his dick in my mouth. I sucked and sucked, trying to find the golf ball in his nuts and suck it out. I moaned sensually, said "Oh, yeah Daddy you like the way Mama suck this dick don't you?"

"Yes, baby, yes, baby…damn, you suck a mean dick baby, damn!"

Seconds later, like I expected, he locked up again.

"This shit has never happened before, I'm coming again! Yea, I'm 'bout to buss again bitch!"

And he released a "Grr" sound when he started coming in my mouth and one I received it all, I got in his face and he opened his mouth and I spit cum in it and he swallowed his own shit, while I tongued him, trying to find spare babies to swallow my damn self, my skin needed nourishment. I ain't playing with cha. I was Freaky Deaky.

"Stick your finger in your ass, and fuck that asshole, Niggah," I demanded. I wasn't through with him. His eyes wide with a smile, he said, "Damn, I love you, bitch I met my match."

"Hurry up, your asshole wants to be tortured."

"You ain't said nothing but a word."

He slid his lubricated finger in his tight asshole, his tight walls sliding on it made me quiver. He fucked himself good, fast and hard. I sucked on his hole, fingers…nipples, one by one, running my tongue over them like a snake across well-cut grass.

I wiped up his excess cum and put it in his mouth. "You Freaky Deaky," I told him. "Swallow your nut, Niggah and fuck that asshole. Shit, let me help you."

When he was done swallowing his own seeds, sharing them with me, I turned him over on his stomach, got on my knees and spread his ass open, sticking my tongue all up there. He smelled so good. He was so clean. I slapped his ass, wiping some of his cum on his asshole and sucked it off, licking the ass cheeks, fingering the asshole with two fingers.

He went wild. He fucked my fingers, throwing that ass back. I saw his nuts and I sucked on them, working my fingers deep in his tunnel, grinding this New York Freaky Deaky Niggah. He was in a state of pure pleasure, never before experiencing what us down south bitches could do.

He moaned obscenities, riding my fingers. I sucked his essence off them.

Made him do the same and I used the cheesecake, put a huge glob in his asshole like moon beads, wiped cheesecake over his ass cheeks, nice ass this Niggah had.

And began my licking. Taste really good.

I sucked on his asshole until all the cheesecake melted down my throat. I smacked my lips, standing up and asking him to,

"Fuck me in my ass, baby."

"Thought you would never ask."

Wiping cheesecake on his dick he slid up in my ass, without a condom, and fucked me good and long.

He bounced up and down in my ass, the leather chair wet from our sweat. We were sliding all over it.

He pulled my face back to his and kissed me, grinding that good dick in my ass trying to recreate what my fingers did to his.

I felt sensational.

I threw that booty back, the popping and squishy sounds filling my ears. I was turned on.

I sweated so badly it got in my eyes and I couldn't see. This Niggah fucked me so good I began coming all over myself.

He felt my asshole throbbing.

He spread my ass cheeks, got up in there and just went to town.

Before long he pulled out, stood up over me and came poured down all over my hair, neck, face, lips, ass and thighs.

"Oh shit, bitch. Oh, shit."

And he lay down on the chair and fell asleep.

Holding me tightly to him.

With his dick deep in my ass.

And now I was home, reading *Rollingstone* magazine with Led Zeppelin on the cover.

I smiled, thinking about Janet, New York and the sex I had.

I got a text message. I picked up my cell phone.

I smiled.

Meet me in the trap.
It's going down.

I text him back.

Niggah I'm home.
In Miami.

He sent another one back.

I know.
I'm on the plane headed
for Miami right now.
Pick me up at the airport.

I smiled really big, dropping the phone and spent thirty minutes speed cleaning my house, washing my clothes and calling in to work.

"I won't be in today. Hold over in Georgia. Gotta wait three hours for the next flight. I know you want me at work. But I can't control the airlines. They had a bomb scare…uh yea, Boss! You didn't see the news. Oh, ok, I'll call when the plane lands in Miami."

Click. I hated lying, but Dick was on a plane coming to see me. He was in for the time of his life.

I hopped in my black Impala and hotrod up the block, signaling right onto 4th Street. A yellow cab passed me, going up my block.

I did 85 MPH to the Florida Turnpike, heading for the Miami International Airport.

The world beneath her rhinestone pumps, Bernice Sinclair entered the elegant hotel. Full of promise and her attitude in check. Her hair was luxuriously done at La Chic Hair Salon in Naranja, Florida; across the street from Popeye's Chicken, earlier today. She paid Miss

Parish a whopping $200 to get a perm. Then she got extensions. Miss Parish curled her hair and used bobby pins to keep it atop her small head and she didn't leave until every strand was in place. She had on nine inch stilettos, with rhinestones on the back. Her panty hose seemed to trap the glorious light from the baccarat crystal chandeliers looming all over the high ceilings.

She was a go-getter and she tasted the big time. A woman who'd been stomped over all her life, never getting what she deserved, she wasn't about to let that happen again.

Because I won't let it. I got a game plan, and I hope it works!

She ran her hand up and over her hips, her portfolio hanging at her right side, like a purse. She had a glass of Grey Goose in her blood stream, some weed pounding through her lungs and she could not get out her head her motto:

I'm not leaving here until I am picked for the fucking job! I'ma Dirty South Bitch from Florida City! My Mama's a crack head and my Daddy's a failed Pimp with no money, no house and no car to show for all the bitch slapping he's done over twenty years. He's a has been and still begs for change at the Citgo gas station on 127th Avenue and 268th Street. I can't wind up like that!

Fuck that! This bitch got a pussy and a brain! And I want the big time!

She passed four hundred hopefuls in the Main Lobby. The place was resilient! Dreamy! A world inside of a world unknown to the inner cities. A place only seen on TV and graced the pages of Architectural Digest! You could feel the excitement charged with the cool air. It crawled up her spine and made her nipples hard. She had to resist rubbing her titties. The anticipation made her horny and when she paused at the receptionist desk, she had to hold it because a mild orgasm shot through her like rockets. She closed her eyes, moaned to herself, squeezed her legs together as tightly as he could, and regained control.

"Are you all right, Miss?" A pimple-faced, donkey-looking white woman asked and she smiled.

"Yes, I'm fine. And the try-outs are being held where?"

She pointed down the long, chandelier-clad hallway, hung with paintings. "Follow the arrows. But they don't start up again for another hour."

That's what you think, bitch! "Why thank you for your kindness."

"Honey, you're kissing the wrong ass. I'm not the one you need to be sucking up to."

"With teeth like yours, Mr. Ed, I can certainly see why. Thank you, bitch!" And she pivoted on her heel, sauntering towards her destination. "Slut!"

The receptionist ignored me and went back to business as usual.

The Hopefuls, from all walks of life, beautiful, full-figured women, anorexic-looking broads mingled together; a few chubby bitches who hadn't a chance in hell shared champagne, listened to Sean Puffy Combs' music; got to know each other, took pictures with their digital cameras for memories and Bernice wanted none of that.

I'm going to show you bitches what I'm about to do!

Taking out her ID, she flashed it to the security guard in front of the closed ballroom doors. There was a sign on the side of him.

<u>BEAUTIFUL MAGAZINE TRY-OUTS</u>

She smiled, spreading her long, gorgeous legs. She didn't wear a bra or any panties. And the guard noticed. His hard-on was the end result.

She tossed the free curls behind her head, "FBI, I'm here to check out the validity of this try out."

The blood left his face and his hands were trembling. He stuffed them in his pockets, trying to play it off.

She went on with her prank. "I would appreciate your full cooperation."

She flipped her Toy's 'R Us bought badge closed and was granted access.

The sexy Niggah looked nervous. "Go ahead. We don't want any trouble."

She read "Donald Rolle" on his name tag. She knew a few Rolles out of Goulds. *I wonder are you related to them?* she thought.

She touched his cheek. She looked down and seen the product of her gesture. He was rock hard. "I don't want any trouble, either. Not a word the FBI is in the building. I'll have your goddamn job and your balls floating in my martini on my next fucking break. Got that, Jack?"

And she went inside, smiling to herself.

You dumb ass! How stupid can these Kindergarten Guards get? That's not even a picture of me on the badge.

Oh, well. Plan worked. I am number 300, and I just skipped every bitch out in the fucking lobby! Kudos to me!

She held in her amazement. The ballroom looked like Cinderella was preparing for a grand entrance. Candles lit here and there, oriental carpeting.

Plush leather settees. Fancy couches. Cameras set up everywhere. Amazingly crafted photo opts here and there.

Usher sang "Burn," her favorite song. *A further omen that this is for me!*

A huge banner was sprawled before her very eyes, hanging behind a sexy, breathtakingly handsome black man, seated behind an African desk.

BEAUTIFUL MAGAZINE TRY-OUTS.

He seemed untouchable. Having one of those gangster looks. All business. Tailored out the ass; impeccably barbered. Looked like he took years preparing for this moment. The suit was silk, he wore $15,000 worth of diamonds in his ears, freezing his wrists, and a gold and platinum Scorpio medallion rested in the middle of his fabulous chest. His shirt was open. He seemed frustrated.

Carefully placed memos lay before his eyes like Earth before God. Huge red X's were drawn across a few women's faces. *They failed,* Bernice thought. *Hoes I don't have to worry about.* She remembered seeing some of the faces mingling in the crowd. Her expectations rose.

"I'm here for the magazine tryouts."

"Are you the FBI woman?"

"Yes. With a fake ID to match. I am a go-getter, I go after what I want and I'm not going to bullshit you, my brother."

His eyes flashed sexily. He loved the way she talked, looked. He loved how she got inside a try-out that was closed down for lunch.

He was actually waiting on his food to arrive.

He looked back at his hired help, black men from the Hood, and snapped for them to leave.

"Take twenty. I want to talk to this one

alone, since she wants to impose like she's the FBI."

He gave them a knowing look.

Snickering, they left.

She was young. Check. Sexy. Check. 36-24-36. Check. Ambitious. Check.

"Are you going to say something, Mr…"

"Hanson."

Stars dancing in her hungry eyes, she licked her lips, clad in a black pin-stripped business suit. She had her portfolio in her hands, well manicured fingers, ghetto-looking acrylics. *Why do these hoes love acrylics,* he wondered.

She read his mind. She snapped each nail off. She had well-cut regular nails, with just clear polish.

He was impressed. He remained silent. He ignored the bulge in his slacks. He already fucked thirteen bitches in the tryouts, X-ing them all off the list. Good pussy, good head didn't equal good photo opts and sell millions of magazines, especially one trying to get off the ground. Or so he told them. He was looking for a challenge. Someone with class and wit. Some business sense.

He rubbed his small goatee, deep in thought. *Are you going to get X-ed? Or are you going to the next round?*

Yeah, Niggah, I'm reading your mind. She was prepared to do whatever it took to get to the top. She would knock any bitch, fuck anybody, male or female. She would pull a J. Lo. A Jennifer Lopez. You had tons of record labels turn you down but ten minutes in Tommy Matolla's office you walked out with not only a record deal but a full aerial assault.

Yes she gave up the pussy for that deal, probably played tennis with the cracker's nuts! And I'm going to do the same thing if I have to!

She had a baby face, was barely 18, and he had to wonder was there any truth to the rumor that chicken sold in the grocery stores had hormones in it. Judging by this girl's banging body, that had to be true. She looked like a black Pamela Anderson with Trinidadian eyes and a Jamaican accent that set him and his loins on fire.

He studied her, quiet, observing the way she talked, the way she sauntered into the posh hotel ballroom at the Doubletree Hotel, Downtown Miami, where the old Omni Mall used to be. He could hear the brakes from the Metro Mover sing into his ears. This was a by invitation-only call for *Beautiful Magazine* that was up and running and needed a fresh new model-like bitch for the cover. The first cover. This was a big deal. Every girl had to pay $500 to the organization, send in snap shots and essays on why they should be picked. You had hungry-for-fame girls there who pawned jewelry, come up off their welfare and child support checks to pay the fee, just for the chance at stardom. Mr. Hanson banked over $300,000 dollars in Miami alone, not counting the fourteen other cities they trampled through before getting to the last stop in Miami.

All together they banked over 8 million dollars.

He was prepared to pour thousands into marketing. *Beautiful Magazine* was like *XXL, Maxim* and *King* magazines poured into a blender with skillful writing, a kick ass executive team from the University of Miami, and a skillful, sexy creator, Billy Songs, from Opa Locka, Florida who was an up and coming rapper with dreams of making it big. All the dope he slung and all the money he made he poured into his passion, to have his own publication, certainly looked like it was paying off.

Mr. Hanson said, "Lock the door. Can you do that for me. And put the "do not disturb" sign on the door knob. I'll give you an interview, if you can tell me why I should pick you to be my cover girl."

She gushed with zeal, wetting her panties.

I got the spot! I GOT THE SPOT! Why else would he ask me something like that! Oh my God! Mama will be so proud! Hell yeah, this is dedicated to all the bitches from the hood, the Pine Island Projects in Naranja, who told me, while in Job Corps on the Homestead Airforce Base, that I wasn't going to amount to nothing! Suck my clit, bitches! Looks like I proved you so wrong! I can't believe this is about to happen. Ok, Ok, can't get excited. Control your breathing! Keep it grown and sexy.

"I should be picked…"

"Whoa Lil' Mama. Lock the door. As a matter of fact, go to the bathroom, practice what you're about to say. Judging from your answer, I will X your sexy ass."

"Well, goddamn, brother."

She made him laugh.

She was the first woman to make him laugh all day. Shit, all year. Plus one, he thought.

"Go on. Practice. You got two minutes to prepare." He pulled out a stop watch and started it. Keeping her cool, she turned to the right and went into the bathroom, closing and locking the door and whipping out her cell phone. She called her girl Jamilla. "Hell, yeah girl! He's going to pick me! I can feel it. He gave me two minutes to prepare. Tell all the girls! Shit, find my Mama and tell her I'm moving on up to the East side when I get a piece of this goddamn pie! And tell Daddy the beans don't burn in the goddamn kitchen anymore! To give up the pimping, his daughter is going to take him to the top! I got to go!"

She hung up, looked herself over in the mirror and went back out to Mr. Hanson.

When she paused before his desk the buzzer went off.

After Mr. Hanson took a few test shots of her with his $2,300 dollar Motorola camera with the huge lens looking like a telescope, he set the camera on his desk and said, "Ok, why should we pick you to be our first cover girl?"

This is it! Don't blow it, Bernice! "I should, fuck it; I *am* the Face of the Magazine. I am a go-getter, prize winner and I want the brass ring. I will do whatever it takes, I will do the grind work, I will promote this publication, promote myself and make *Beautiful Magazine* not only a startlingly good magazine, but a force to be reckoned with."

"Damn. Confident."

"Yes I am."

"You got the job."

"What?"

He stood up, walked around his desk and paused in her face. "You got the job. Your pay will be about $20,000." She was speechless. *Ka-*

ching! Ka-ching! "Not to mention some endorsement deals we'll set you up for. We have a press run of a million magazines, pre-ordered all over the world. We have a Myspace.com page. We'll do another featuring your test shots I took today. I'll get right on it. Move over *Suicide Girls*! We got to set the world on its ear. We're taking a chance on you."

She stood five feet eleven. He was 6 feet one. He took her into his arms, studied her. She was wet instantly. He sank to his knees, lifted up her skirt and stuck a finger in her pussy.

"Goddamn, you don't have on any draws."

"I like to let it all hang out."

"Pussy smells good."

"Always does."

"Really tight."

"Haven't been fucked in ages."

"Are you going to resist a city Niggah like me?"

"Why should I give it up to you?"

"Because I'm in it."

"Yea, your *finger*. But I can put this shit on pause at any given moment. How do I know you won't fuck me and X me out, like you did the other Hoes?"

He smiled then. *Smart bitch!* "I just gave

you the job."

"I have nothing in writing yet, Gigolo."

"You'll get it in writing."

"Do I have your word? Come on, Niggah! I have nothing, trying to get something. My parents are low-lives. I want it all. Don't bullshit me."

I see a lot of myself in her, he thought to himself, amazed by a woman so young being so direct.

"Like Scarface, you got my word."

"Then eat my pussy like it has never been eaten before."

He leaned up to her velvet box, spread her walls and licked around the surface; his hot breath teasing and pleasing. She shuddered in her pumps. He tongued her juices, let his mustache tickle the clit and he rubbed his goatee hairs all up in her twat. She held his head, leaning back against the desk.

"You want me in this pussy?" he asked rhetorically.

"Hell yes." She shuddered, her huge booty on the edge of the desk. She spread her legs open, pulling them up, her knees bent towards her. Her high heeled pumps brought the freak out of him.

"You smell so good."

"You feel so wonderful."

He tongue fucked her, her breasts shaking under her blouse. She unloosened each button, seductively, showing control under strenuous circumstances. When her tits popped free, he went wild. He stood up, unzipped his pants, his huge dick springing free and she got on her knees and took him into her wet mouth, her tongue quick and slick. He never took his eyes off her. She pulled, slurped and noisily moaned her approvals. She enjoyed her power, enjoyed bringing him satisfaction.

"Damn. You're a dirty bitch, I like that."

"You do?" She looked up at him, grabbed the rest of his liquor, poured it in her mouth, tossed the shot glass, ignoring the shattering; and she took him back in her hotness, the alcohol pleasurably stinging his entire shaft.

He screamed out in delight.

"Goddamn, pull on that shit, suck it, baby...*make it spit*, make it spit."

She pulled on it harder, increasing the suction in her jaws...He humped her mouth, unloosening her hair, it fell all around her angelic face.

"Fuck it. I want the pussy! I can't stand it! You suck on my shit I'm gonna wanna hit."

Aggressively, he pulled her up to her feet, unbuttoned her blouse and jacket, tossing it on the floor. He pulled off her skirt. Tossed it. "Leave the pumps on. You look so damn sexy. Get on my desk, on your hands and knees; let me see that pretty pussy all up in my face…damn, you shaved?"

She did what he said, getting into the position. He stuck his dick in her raw dog, slowly, sticking both thumbs in her ass. She let out this moan that set him on fire. She never had anything in her ass, but her new boss wanted it so hey, he signed the goddamn checks, he called the shots.

She was so wet and tight. She took all ten inches like a pro. She rose and fell with him, jumping on the tidal waves, surfing, traveling and skiing across pleasurable turfs…He fucked her senseless, her ass jiggling on his dick. He thumbed her asshole as hard as he could, leaning forward and spitting on his thumbs for some extra lubrication. She moaned and called out his name in sheer delight.

"Goddamn baby, yes, ahh shit…! Damn, take my shit!"

He gave her what she wanted. He crawled on top of the desk, his hired help peeping through the ballroom door, slapping palms and video taping the two, and he turned her on her back, put her legs behind both elbows, entered her slowly, expertly and banged her until the sounds of sex filled his ears. He smiled down at her, biting his bottom lip, looking her dead in the eyes, giving her the best plumbing job of her life.

She shivered and trembled, tears falling from her eyes, his amazing ass opened and closed as he entered and exited her as fast as he could. Never in her life had her pussy been stretched to such limitations. She felt him in her gut, but it felt so good.

"I'm bout to cum!" she sing-songed, feeling her toes curl in the stilettos and her muscles began contracting, her wetness increased and she sucked on his intimidating nipple as she shook from the desk to ecstasy. He pounded her harder, faster, deeper, filling her up and he hit a spot in her pussy she never knew existed and she had multiple orgasms, which she never experienced before and she cried out, "*Stop Stop Stop it feels SOOO GOOD NIGGAH!*"

Suckling on her left nipple, biting it teasingly, he released the beast, coming deep inside of her, speeding up like a runaway train, claiming the pussy, marking his territory. He moaned seductively, a soft release from the pit of his vocal cords that not only drove her crazy but set her off. He sucked on her neck forever, hard, making it hurt, putting a huge hickey on her body. Making sure Niggahs on the block took notice.

He fucked enough Hoes for the day. Exhausted, he rolled off her and lay, spent. He gazed into her eyes, his chest and stomach moving fast. Uncontrollable breathing. "I want you to be mine. You have a wonderful future with *Beautiful Magazine*. Let's get the papers signed."

"I can't believe this is happening." His minions pressed stop on the recorder. Little red lights on the other twelve cameras carefully hidden in the room suddenly went black.

Once the papers were signed the competition was over. All the other hopefuls were sent home. How disappointed they were. They cursed Bernice and screamed obscenities at Mr. Hanson. Security was called. The ladies were escorted out of the building. Bernice could picture the world bowing at her feet. She got a deal!

She was going to be somebody. She waltzed up to the ugly receptionist and said, "You're right. Your ass was the wrong ass to kiss. I'm the new face of tomorrow."

"Whatever, lady. It'll blow up in your face."

"Like it blew up in yours?"

"Whatever."

Her Big Break
Part 2
Bernice

It was three months after she and Mr. Hanson had rough sex at the Doubletree Hotel that she went townhouse hunting with Jamilla and Antoinette, her two most trusted friends.

She and Mr. Hanson had been in constant contact. They talked about everything. Became good friends. He told her he was unhappily married. That his wife didn't treat him with the respect he deserved. Considering she was now pregnant. And wanted to file for divorce and take everything he owned.

But that was his problem.

Nauseated from taking too many Tylenol

Sinus pills, Jamilla opened her black windbreaker, revealing a tight Paris Hilton halter-top and gut-stricken midriff. Kicking off her black Nikes.

"Girl, I don't know about this one," said Jamilla in disgust, looking around the amazing townhouse recently build by the brand new Publix Supermarket in Naranja, by the Waterfront housing complex. She frowned at the double glass doors, which was just thrown together haphazardly. She hated the size of the living room. Sucked. The bedrooms weren't big enough for roaches. No wonder those home makers were losing money, according to the newspapers and she read them religiously. People who bought these cheaply built, expensively priced homes were foreclosing already.

Bernice smiled, clad in a simple green pants suit. Her hair pulled back from her face. She ran her hands over the cream-colored walls.

"Why don't you know?"

Antoinette was admiring the staircase. "Girl you can hang some paintings right along this wall, leading up the stairs, Chile," Antoinette suggested. "And you can get some…dick…right about there in the middle of the stairs girl, towards the top. You have a lot of space to have sex."

"Yea, I'll consider it, Antoinette." She looked at Jamilla laughing. "What's wrong with the townhouse?"

"Well for one these glass doors. They look weird."

Bernice said, "I like them. They're unique."

Jamilla stuck her tongue at Bernice. "They're fucked up. And two, there's barely a front and back yard. Snap and you'll miss it. Shit, I would hate to break a plate in this bitch. Nine houses down up unto your neighbor will hear it soundly. And where are the black people? All you hear is salsa music and fucking Spanish!"

"You do have a point."

"Plus they want $240,000 for it," said Antoinette. "These goddamn Cubans come over here on a boat and jack all the fucking prices up on shit. Changed the Cutler Ridge Mall to the Southland Mall. That's some Castro shit. And I heard they're trying to change 'Goulds' to 'Cutler Bay.' We gonna riot on their asses! Just crazy. Why would you go to the Hood, tear down every tree, build houses on it and charge a bitch $300,000 for a house in Goulds? The ghetto? Yea, right, bitches! But outside of that I like the condo."

Jamilla snorted grotesquely. "You have no

sense of style, Antoinette. Don't influence Bernice into getting this funk box."

"Girl, whatever," said Antoinette. "She can do better. She should move to Georgia. $300,000 would get her three homes and a shit load of land. She could build a thousand staircases and get some dick then feel like Jezebel Cinderella, Chile!"

Bernice implied, "All right, women."

"I'm just saying…" Antoinette looked impishly. "She needs to look around before she signs any commitments."

Bernice smiled. "Good. Then it's a wrap. I'm going to put $15,000 down on it and then pay it off when I start getting royalty checks from *Beauty Magazine*."

"When are you getting your check?" asked Jamilla. Antoinette was on her cell phone with her man.

"Soon." Bernice's life was about to change. "Very soon."

A few days later, Bernice got a phone call.

Grim-faced, she answered her cell phone, pacing around Henrietta's living room in Liberty City, Florida. "Hello." DMX growled like the dog he was from the 60 inch plasma TV built into the wall.

"Sup, Bernice."

It was Mr. Hanson. She smiled, getting butterflies in her stomach. "Sup, man?"

"Where are you?"

"My friend Henrietta's house. Where are you?"

"I was back home in Detroit, Michigan. The wife has filed for divorce. Trying to take all I own by saying I was being unfaithful. She even got big gun lawyers. But she can't prove it because I covered my tracks with you."

"We only fucked once."

"Duh, Bernice. Unfaithful."

She laughed with him. Her heart warmed up. She knew he was a stone cold playa. She knew his type. She knew he fucked other Hoes in that competition in every city they went in. Men with big dicks swore they had the anecdote to make a bitch stupid. She needed to take the hair rollers from her hair. But she decided against it. She was staying with Henrietta for a few days. She thought she told Mr. Hanson that when they spoke three days ago.

"So what are you going to do?"

"Well, remember I asked you to give me Henrietta's address so I can send you a few recent pictures of me?" he asked jubilantly. Too jubilantly.

Her eyes narrowed. *So I did tell him I was here.* "Yes?"

"Well they should be delivered there anytime now."

"What should be delivered…"

There was a knock on Henrietta's front door. Henrietta was at work. Sliding into house slippers, closing her terrycloth robe, she, mystified, walked to the door. "What did you send, Mr. Hanson?"

"Stop calling me Mr. Hanson. I'm not your damn teacher."

"What about for Sex ED.?"

"Oh, I got you."

She answered the door and Mr. Hanson took her into his arms, sticking his tongue down her throat, picking her up, kicking the door closed. Stunned, she couldn't react, but she melted into his embrace, her heart thumping out her chest. Her pussy wet instantly, she wrapped her legs around him, her robe coming untied. Her titties pressed against the fabric of his silk shirt, which put a tingling in her nipples to the point of erection.

"I want to fuck you. Cover Girl. Can I get this pussy before it hit's the big time?"

"Hell, yeah... But what about your wife taking you to court?"

"She doesn't know I took a flight out of Detroit."

Laying her on the sofa he dove in her wet

pussy, tonguing her speechless. That quickly turned to deep moaning. His head bobbed like a ball on water. The heat from his lips and tongue set her on fire.

Spreading her legs open she held the arm of the chair, arching her back, her breasts dancing to their own tune. *Maybe I can have him when his wife leaves him. He has long money. And an even longer dick. He has everything. Plus he's my new boss. Why not?*

"Damn, baaabbbyyy! Yea, my Niggah eat that shit baby, yes."

Sitting up he unbuttoned his shirt, taking it off. Fabulous chest, goddamn! Unbuckling his pants, he pulled a Trojan condom from his wallet, setting the wallet on the low-table. He pulled out his dick and she sat up, taking it into her mouth, suckling on the head slowly, pulling on it and he humped her face for dear life, getting lost in her rhythms. Becoming one with her. He was obsessed with her, hadn't stopped thinking about her since the magazine try-outs. When he fucked his wife he imagined he fucked Bernice; he found himself calling out her name every night but she wasn't there to answer him. He accidentally called his wife "Bernice," when she had come home from the mall a few weeks ago, but thank God she didn't hear him. Because she was flapping her jaws on the phone with her sister in Reno.

He leaned his head back; his heart pumping blood through his veins at breakneck speed. Kicking off his shoes, he got nasty.

"Let me see those deep throat skills…open your mouth! Fuck this dick with that hot mouth…*yeeeaaa*! Take this dick, Ho. Get nasty for Daddy. Likes the way you slurping my shit. Suck my wife out the hole of my dick and swallow the bitch whole. Lemme see the bitch try…to…swim. Out. Of. The. Acid. In. Your. Stomach with my nut…*yea*!"

She sucked, slurped and pulled, tears running down her face. She loved his juicy dick. She wanted it in her ass. She wanted to get kinky with it, role play. She'd be the doctor and he'd be the Medical Board. Yea. That was hot.

She squeezed her nipples. Releasing his nature and playing with herself. She kept sucking on his dick with a technique called "No Hands Barred."

His orgasm beginning to bubble in the base of his nuts, he pushed her back, lifted her legs, put on the condom and went up in her asshole. She screamed out from the pain. He didn't even lube her up.

Pushing her legs as far back as they'd go, he fucked her long, hard and fast. She got lost. She fell in the dark pit. She felt his passion.

Got swamped with his heat. His technique. Fell in love with his skill. His stamina. "Play with that pussy while I get this tight ass..."

She rubbed her love, as fast as she could. Fuck the slow shit. She wasn't in the mood to play around. She started fucking herself. Her eyes tightly closed. He gave her what she wanted. Good dick. She screamed vulgarities that even had him like, "Damn, Ma. My dick feeling good like that?"

"Give me that dick!"

"I'm giving you this dick. Beg for it."

"Give me the dick give me the dick GIVE ME THE DICK PAPA!"

"I'm giving you the dick giving you the dick giving you the dick."

Farty sounds filled the house as her ass got loose. She was reaching her climax, and before she knew it she was coming, snatching his dick out her ass and shoving it in her pussy.

"Damn, Ma!"

"I'm cumin'!"

He slow grinded in her wet tunnel, bringing her to a heightened pleasure. She lay spent when it was over.

"Where's the bathroom, little Mama?"

She was in a daze. "Upstairs."

He kissed at her. "Can I go wash up?"

"What, I didn't hear you…"

They giggled. "Can I go take a bath or something? I hate feeling dirty."

She was rubbing her nookie. "Sure."

He kissed her lips. "You are a passionate woman."

"And you're a passionate man."

"I'm all right," he said, craving a cigarette.

She kissed his pretty feet. "You're the best…"

He left, forgetting his wallet.

She couldn't take her eyes off it.

They were making love in the shower. He gave it to her passionately slow. Made her come four times. This time without the Trojan condom.

After the shower she asked him, "Why is it taking so long for you guys to get me started on the cover shoot?"

He got really quiet.

She studied his face. "Baby?"

"Next week you're booked. Just a lot of minor details adding to big problems."

"Like what?"

He turned her around, and got on his knees, eating her sore asshole.

She began rising up to the clouds. "What was that I said? I forgot," she said, bracing herself for some more Married Man Dick.

A few hours later she cooked him a

burger and some fries. Henrietta wouldn't mind. She'd pay her back for eating up her food, and she'd wash the dishes she messed up. No biggie. She was fully dressed in a skirt and his silk shirt. He had on one of Henrietta's husband's shirts. He didn't care. A shirt was a fucking shirt. As long as it was clean.

"So when are you going back to Detroit?" Bernice asked, handing him a plate with steaming fries and two bacon and cheese burgers.

He smiled at her, kissing her lips. "Soon."

"Soon like when?" Her plate was bigger than his.

Jesus, bitches loved asking questions. I wasn't married to you Ho, damn. But I do love you. At least I think I do. Or is that I love the way you fuck? Oh, well. I had time to decipher this whatever it was!
"Well, damn! Do you have enough food?"

He thinks he's slick, trying to be evasive! "Yea. Anyways, when are you leaving?"

"Tonight," he lied. He had other bitches to fuck.

"Tonight?"

No. "Yes."

"When did you get to Miami?"

A week ago. And the pussy and ass I got. Phew. Should be a crime to be this slick. "Two days ago."

Her voice got dark. "And you're just showing up here today?"

He felt an argument coming on. And. He. Wasn't in the mood. "Yea, Bee."

"My name is Bernice. Not Bee. What's up with this?"

Damn it. This is what happens when you give a bitch good dick. They turned into the Exorcism of Emily Rose, took a goddamn Priest to pray the bitches off. "Are you going to start tripping?"

"Yea. How many other Hoes you fucked when you got here?"

Bertha. Simone. And a couple Niggahs, too, he thought bitterly. "Look, I got a wife. I don't need a lecture."

"You need your ass whipped."

"By *who*?" He was laughing so hard he chocked.

"This Naranja Bitch! We do it big down in the dirty south, Niggah. This isn't Detroit."

"Whatever. Just shut the fuck up before I rearrange your teeth."

"With what? Your dick?"

Too bad she was a good fuck. I had a lot of bad pussy in my lifetime but she was the best fuck I had. A rookie at heart. A man didn't let go good pussy. Not until he got bored with it, molded it. Had a Ho sick in the mind without it. In it to win it but Lil' Mama was going to lose me. "Bernice. I like being here with you. Please stop." His blood was boiling near the danger zone.

Bullshit! "Why should I?"

"Because I'm not trying to go there with you."

Lets go there Niggah. "Go there, I dare you."

"Look, I like you. I'm trying to keep it civil."

Is this a war, damn it? Civil, as in civil rights? Do I look like Coretta Scott King bitch? "Man, look. I'm getting really aggravated, and fast."

"And I guess what I feel just don't matter?" he shot icily, made her shiver. But she played it off.

"It does matter, but…"

"But, *what*? All you're trying to do is get a reaction out of me, typical little girl, elementary school shit. And how old are you?"

"Whatever. I want to show you this condo I'm getting. When you give me the $20,000 I'm going to put a down payment on it."

He was confused. "Twenty grand? From *where*?"

She laughed. "*You*, silly."

He rolled his eyes, uninterested. "You're getting $5,000. I never told you you're getting 20 grand."

The room was spinning. He couldn't be serious. "You *can't* be serious."

"I'm as serious a heart attack."

Her eyes clouded over. "But you said I was…" She was stuttering, her heart failing her.

I lied to you, bitch! You got good pussy but it isn't worth twenty grand. Maybe fifty dollars but certainly not twenty grand. Dumb bitch!

He was at the boiling point. "I never said that."

She exploded. "YOU DID!" The house shook.

Angrily, he threw the plate of food and it shattered on the wall, falling all around her.

Stunned, she stared at him. "Get out." She was scared.

He laughed. "Bitch, with pleasure. I got another bitch to go fuck before I board the plane. I shouldn't have showered, so she could suck your asshole off my dick."

And he was gone.

She eyed his wallet on the low-table, smiling through tears. How could she have been blinded by the man?

Why did she get pulled in? She was embarrassed. She felt dumb and stupid. All of her dreams were exploding in her face. The smell of food made her wrench all in the sink. She was nauseated, she hated to be betrayed.

But she had no one to blame but herself. Letting a complete stranger screw her, even without rubbers. Was she stupid? What if he gave her a STD? She could never show her face ever again. And that was her problem, thinking with her pussy instead of her brain. Hadn't that caused her enough grief in her life? Hadn't she learned from her mistakes that were gentle dress-ups for bad decisions that would follow her for the rest of her natural life? Would she ever wake up? Life was bigger than sex and money.

"But that's ok. I signed a contract. I signed for twenty grand, or did I?" She got his wallet, opening it.

Three platinum cards.

A shipload of hundred dollar bills.

"I will get my money. One way or the other"

Her Big Break
Part 3

A few weeks later, after her physical examination at the doctor's office, Bernice got a call from her home girl.

"Sup, Antoinette." She was not in the mood. In fact she felt crummy and shitty.

"Girl, when was the last time you been on the internet?"

"Last month sometime, *why*?" Her eyes were blood shot red from crying for days and days on end. Over Mr. Hanson. Over life. Was this damn *Beauty Magazine* shit even going to fly. *They got 500 dollars of my money! What if this was a fucking scam!*

"There's something you should know."

There goes my condo! My townhouse I should say. The one Jamilla hated and Antoinette loved!

"What, girl?"

"Bernice, you know I love you, right?"

She felt queasy. "Yeah, girl."

"And I'd do anything for you."

Now she felt uneasy. "What is this?" Bernice was suspicious. "Are you trying to ask can you come to Hollywood with me?" *Yeah, right! Me? Hollywood? Fat chance! Mr. Hanson stole 500 bucks of my hard-earned cash! I sold my pussy for that money.*

Silence. Then, "Well…"

Bernice smiled, playing it off. *I can't let my friends know I won't be a star!* "Yea, girl, you're coming. How about you become my PR or agent. You damn sure know what I like and what I don't."

"I'm flattered."

"You better be."

"But back to the reason I called you."

"Let me guess. Your man ate you out again on the roof of your house like he did last month. I can't believe he actually did that, girl. On the roof? In the rain? In broad daylight? That took guts." She actually cheered up a little bit, rubbing her stomach, staring at herself in the mirror from the unmade-up bed.

"He doesn't have big nuts for nothing. And this ain't about him."

"Ok, so what is it?" Bernice asked.

"Lets just say your *Beautiful Magazine* spot is the hottest thing in the world."

She got so excited she jumped off her bed at her friend Stella's house and screamed for all to hear. "I'm on my way!" Bernice said happily, jumping up and down. All her girls, eight of them, burst into the room. In pajamas, turning on some music and celebrating with her. *It wasn't a scam! It was a dream come true! Thank you Jesus!* Bernice was elated that she was actually going to be a cover girl for a national, well global magazine! She was definitely headed for the good time.

Antoinette said into the phone, not believing what she saw on the screen before her very eyes. "Bernice log onto the link I'm about to send you on your AOL account."

Bernice turned on her laptop computer, telling her other friends, "Wait, I'm 'bout to pull it up. Ya'll going to be so proud of me. I'm classy! And I'm about to launch a new magazine! One my people can be proud of."

"Did you fuck to get the job?" asked Samantha, whose mind was always on dick.

Bernice lied, "Hell no! I used my business sense, girl. Ain't that type of party?" *Hoe, stay outta mine! If I fucked or not its my pussy, can't help that your shit was ruined before you even got out of the ninth grade.*

"That's my girl," said Jamilla, pulling on her joint.

Antoinette said, "Oh, girl, what's done in the dark comes to the light."

"I know, Chile. And with my success the darkness is about to end. I am the light." *I shouldn't have treated Mr. Hanson badly when he came to Henrietta's. I should call him and get him his wallet back. I'm pretty sure he's wondering where it is. He did call me last week and ask me did I see it and I said "No."*

"Yes you are," said Antoinette, turning off the computer. Even Antoinette's mother, in a state of shock, set on her daughter's bed, speechless. She whispered to her daughter, "I need a stiff drink. Fuck it; give me the entire bottle of Grey Goose."

Antoinette buried her forehead in her open palm, shaking her head.

When Bernice opened the link in her email and paste it in the search engine, she clicked 'Go' and it came right up. Her sex tape, filmed in the ballroom. Everyone's mouths fell open in shock.

Jamilla, chocking, dropped her blunt.

There was Bernice, sucking and fucking Mr. Hanson.

"Oh my God! What is this?" asked Bernice, frozen.

The audio followed.

"Goddamn, you don't have on any panties."

"I like to let it all hang out."

"Pussy smells good."

"Always does."

"Really tight."

"Haven't been fucked in ages."

"Are you going to resist a city Niggah like me?"

"Why should I give it up to you?"

"Because I'm in it."

"Yea, your finger. But I can put this shit on pause at any given moment. How do I know you won't fuck me and X me out, like you did the other Hoes?"

"Hell nah!" said Henrietta, laughing, slapping palms with Jamilla.

"Dirty bitch!" said Coquette Bautista. "You are amazing, girl!"

"Look at that ballroom, shit, Mr. Hanson is fine as fuck! Can I make a video next, Chile?" said Germaine, the lesbian.

"Look at the bitch's hair! Can you say *Fabulous! Fabulous! Fabulous!* faster than Eddie Murphy dressed as Mama Klump?" joked Jamilla.

Devastated and embarrassed, wanting to crawl in a ball and die, she snatched the power cord from the wall. The monitor went blank. She gritted her teeth, her eyes laser beams.

All her friends stared at her.

"The bitch is about to go postal," said Germaine.

"Let me go put up my knives," said Jamilla, laughing and stomping her feet. Finding this all funny.

"Your *business* sense, 'ey?" said Coquette, laughing. "You dirty bitch! How much did he pay you to be exploited on the net? You didn't say you were doing porn!"

"No, no, I can explain…" Bernice started to cry and her girls didn't play the bushes. They fired question after question.

"Where's your money? You can sue!" said Bernadette. Miss Ghetto Fabulous with nine kids from nine different men and she was only twenty-eight years old, "You didn't sign a media release!"

"I damn sure didn't!" Bernice said. "I'm suing."

"Where are the papers you signed? Did Mr. Hanson give you a copy?" asked Jamilla. Bernice hung up on Antoinette. She didn't need to hear it from her.

"Yes he did." She pulled them from her purse and Jamilla snatched them. Reading.

She got really quiet.

"Jamilla!"

Jamilla handed her the papers. She read them.

Oh, God!

"Did you even read them before you signed?" asked Bernadette. "You should have had a lawyer present."

Jamilla said, her heart going out to her girl, "Those were media releases you signed. Meaning those are actual contracts. They will stand up in court. And there's not a damn thing you can do about it. *Beautiful Magazine* is a porn magazine. I'm pretty sure this man fucked other girls before you came in there and did the same thing. This man lied to you. Your face will be splashed on millions of porn magazines all over the world as their premiere magazine. You're right. You're on your way to the big time. And your first check will be cut in a few months, according to these documents. So while they're making millions off you, with a website already generating multiple hits world wide, in a matter of days, you got to wait to be compensated. So much for your big break. They're taking a chunk out of your ass. Looks like you've been pimped."

Her world of luxury, fame and fortune crumpling about her, Bernice lay on the bed, sobbing and screaming curse words into the pillow. Jamilla, Bernadette and the rest of the girls left her to herself, closing the door behind them.

***

When the door closed she got a burst of energy. Whipping out her cell she called Mr. Hanson.

"You have reached the rejection line," said the answering machine. "Obviously you aren't going to find who you're looking for. If he or she gave you this number to call. Then you've been royally fucked. So hang up and go wipe the shit from your face."

She turned the phone off. "Are you serious? I can't believe this is happening."

Her life was over. She just paced the room, deep in thought. Her mom would laugh at her. Her Daddy would ridicule her. They already thought she was a loser. Never been to college, and barely graduated high school. She attended the Job Corps, learning a trade. Sad. And her big break blew up in her face. Like the bitch receptionist at the hotel had told her. Dark clouds loomed overhead. Zapping her happiness. Taking her zeal for life and crushing it. Her chest burned. Acid bubbled in her stomach. Giving her heart burn. Then it hit her. *Oh my God! How could I forget!*

Opening her purse she pulled out his wallet. Looking through it she pulled out a list of numbers scribbled on a small post-it note.

She made a call, pressing a series of buttons after she dialed the number.

He answered. Good. Let the games begin. "Mr. Hanson. You sneaky son of a bitch."

"I take it you seen your porno on the web. Exciting isn't it?"

"You tricked me."

"And other bitches, too. There's nothing you can do about it."

"You are a creep! You just *ruined* my reputation!"

"You ruined it yourself. I liked you. But you got too much lip."

"Whatever. You're not going to get away with this."

"Oh yes I am. And my wife ain't going to get away with trying to take my house and cars and money."

"Oh, yeah?"

"Yea."

"I hope you rot in hell. She will find out that we fucked. I'll tell her."

He laughed sinisterly. "You sound a) naïve and b) insecure. You don't know my wife's number, my address or anything for that matter. I'm not even from Detroit."

Her heart stopped. She couldn't' breathe.

He went in for the pleasurable kill. Felt

better than her young pussy. "I'm from, well, *you* know how that goes. That's none of *your* business." She closed her eyes.

Holding in her rage.

Bernice sucked in air. She would not be made a fool of. "We'll just see about that." She fell silent.

"See about what bitch? You need to let me come get some more of that pussy and stop acting so whorishly retarded."

She opened the post-it note, smiling victoriously. "Tell me. Is your wife's name Georgia?"

He stopped smiling. "What, how do you know?"

"What, do I got your dick in a bunch? Is her cell phone number…well, *you* know how that goes? Bye, I'm 'bout to give her a call."

He had heart failure. "Wait, Bernice!"

"You get me off the fucking web. You get me off now or, well, *you* know, I *call* your wife. I got her number on a post it note I just took out your wallet, you asshole!"

Click.

A few hours later her website was down temporarily.

"Ok. Good. He listened."

But that wasn't enough.

She wanted revenge. All she could think of was her friends ridiculing her and laughing at her. She'd be the butt of a thousand jokes. People would laugh at her.

Angry, she called Georgia.

She answered.

Her voice was shaky. "Is this Georgia?" Bernice asked.

Georgia poured a cup of coffee, sitting at her dining room table in Portland, Maine. "Yes, who is this? I don't know anyone named Bernice from a 305 area code. Isn't that Miami?"

"Yes. I'm calling because your husband used and abused me."

Georgia chocked on her coffee, smiling, a trembling hand finding her neck, as she toyed with her pearls. "Speak, go on. You can tell me."

"Ok. He got me to pay him 500 dollars for some *Beauty Magazine* try-out. And he tricked me into thinking it was a classy publication when in fact it's a porn venture."

Her eyes were wide with anger. "What? He is using Beauty Magazine for porn?"

"And he fucked me on the day of the try-outs. And not too long ago he claimed he flew from Detroit to come see me when I was staying at a friend's house. We fucked then, too."

"Can you prove this? You know I'm filing for divorce, and I'm trying to prove he cheated on me so I can clean his ass out. I'm a scorned white woman. I know I'll win."

"*Yes*. I can prove it."

"How?"

"I found out at the doctor's office that I'm pregnant with his child. Two months pregnant, to be exact." And she smiled dangerously, smoking a cigarette. "I'm keeping the baby."

"Well, Bernice is it? How about helping me clean his ass out. How would you like to own *Beauty Magazine* and you can turn it into something more classy?"

She smiled through her tears. "Most *definitely*. But, wait? He doesn't own it. Doesn't a man from Opa Locka own it, some so-called used-to-sell-dope rapper?"

"No, my dear. *He* owns it, I funded him the money to get it started. I didn't know it was really a porn venture. I tell you what, prove to me you're carrying his child, and I'll make sure *Beauty Magazine* is yours. Deal?"

"Yes, ma'am. Deal. And I got something even better."

"Oh, yea? Credible?"

"Yes. My cell phone records conversations. And I got our conversation lock, stock and barrel. Would that help?"

"Girl where in the fuck did you come from? You're a goddamn angel."

"With devil's horns."

OK BITCHES! BERNICE IS BACK!

"That's fucked up, Girl," said Bernadette, running into the other room, tuning on the computer, setting up her DVD burner.

"How much are we going to sell it for?" asked Germaine, her hands itching. "I got about four hundred blank CD's. I can go to Liberty City by the USA Flee market on 79th Street and sell some there. I know Niggahs will eat it up. We can call it Her Big Break!"

"Ten dollars a pop," said Jamilla. "She's our dog, but hey, I got rent to pay. And she has been living here for free for too goddamn long, eating my damn food and using my water and shit…"

"Hey!" said the girls.

"Let's set up shop. But we can't tell her," suggested Bernadette.

Coquette had a change of heart. "She's our girl. We can't do this to her. She needs us."

"Yes. She needs us to make her some money," said Jamilla.

She went on. "I'm going to set up an Ebay account. Lord hot damn we all going to make some money. Let's beat *Beautiful Magazine* at their own game."

"Amen to that!" said Bernadette. "We gotta give Bernice a cut."

"She gets twenty percent," said Jamilla. "I swear to God. We'll get her some loot."

Everyone pinky swore. "Let's put our girl on the market."

"Her Big Break! *He-eey!*" They all singed together, turning up Jay-Z.

Jamilla clicked on the website. It wouldn't load.

"Girl, don't you have DSL?" asked Bernadette.

"No, I have dial-up," said Jamilla, aggravated.

"No you don't," said Henrietta. "You got DSL! I went with you when you ordered it from Bellsouth."

Jamilla sneered. "Then why isn't the page loading?"

"Because Mr. Hanson took that shit off the site." Bernice had a packed bag in her hand. She looked good, hair done up, the Gucci outfit slamming. The make-up knocking Halle Berry right off the commercials.

"What?" said Jamilla, looking guilty.

Henrietta kicked the DVD's under the bed and Bernadette picked imaginary dirt from her nails.

"Yes. You guys were supposed to be my friends. And you were actually going to sell my porno all over Dade County."

"And the Palm Beaches," said Germaine, quickly regretting her words.

"Shut up, Girl!" said Henrietta and Jamilla slapped her in the back of the head.

"Don't worry about it. I'm moving out."

"Why?" asked Jamilla.

"Because you bitches betrayed me."

"Aw you just mad because you sucked dick to get a deal that was bogus."

"Jamilla, that's your opinion."

"That's a fact!" said Germaine. "And I have been trying to eat that pussy for years. And you meet that man and he tasted the passion fruit in an hour flat. World record time."

"*Whatever.*" She pivoted on her heel and was gone.

"The hell with her," said Jamilla.

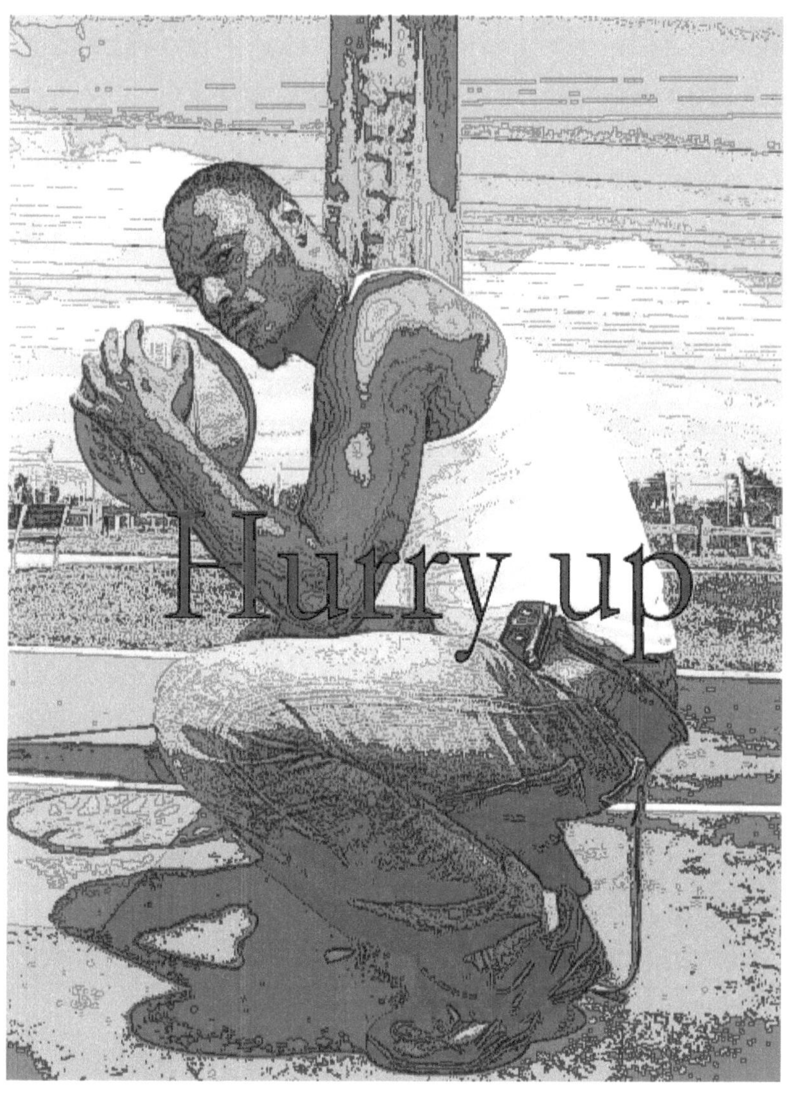

Hornier than two toads, Crucial Williams, a gorgeous vamp, rushed into the law offices of Gregg, Gregory and Craig's on South Beach around 8 a.m. this glorious Miami morning. March 25, 2006. She turned on all the lights, killed the alarm, sent the security guard's fat ass home after giving him the rest of her Dunkin Donuts and she flipped on her laptop.

Dressed to kill in a snap-and-you'll-miss-it black pinstriped skirt suit with African bangles, she looked over the paintings hanging around the fancy office. All black art. She loved it. Tapping her foot to some Lyfe Jennings booming softly from her radio, she stuck a number 2 pencil in her curly hair and smiled to herself.

Sighing and still a little tired, she wanted to go home. She partied hard the night before. You didn't turn down her best friend Etta's parties, which she seemed to throw once a week. She quickly checked the lavish bathroom with the fancy Jacuzzi and bathtub, sprayed some air freshener to get the smells of yesterday out of there, opened the blinds by remote control, keeping the vertical blinds a little angled so not to get too much sunlight and she whipped out her huge vibrator.

"Shit, I'ma get me a quick cum up before the boss gets in. He always call before getting here, probably getting used to his fancy Razr phone."

She left the panties home. Who needed the hassle? Panties were just indiscreet cock blockers and she didn't feel like being bothered by any barrier between fingers and pussy. Not today. Especially after last night. She didn't have the sex-sational night of passionate lovemaking like she'd grown used to. Her lover seemed preoccupied and thoughtless, her movement like sharp razors on concrete, just wasn't getting anywhere. And she went to bed, angry and frustrated, having to suck her thumb through the night to keep from throwing her lover out on her ass!

Sitting behind her desk, she pushed her skirt up past her hips with a flourish, and what voluptuous hips. She damn near pissed on herself from the anticipation. She turned on the vibrator, which lubricated itself, some new fancy shit her cousin bought her from Tokyo and sent to her Federal Express. His whorish-ass was in the United States Airforce over there, fucking anything with two feet, trying to convince her to pay him a visit. Chinese men with narrowed eyes and an even narrower dick never got her past the thinking stages.

Time to get to work! She rubbed her pussy with long black nails, careful not to cut herself…sucked the wetness from her fingers, tasted like salt, the smell sent her haywire, and spread her velvet box with mountains of pubic hair in the V-shape, sliding the dildo so deep into her body she had to arch her back.

What a wonderful feeling!

Feeling adventurous she opened the vertical blinds so people in the other buildings could get a sneak peek and she got a burst of excitement, putting her stiletto-clad feet on her desk, spreading her legs as far as they'd go, and working the vibrating plastic toy, angling it so it hummed against her achingly sensitive clitoris. She bit her lip, grinding on her seat. The leather felt like the hands of a man…the grooves pressed against her back; felt like those massaging balls.

She could feel orgasms about to make their gentle but explosive debut already.

Not yet! Can't cum yet! Plenty time for that.

She had to admit that she'd never done this before, masturbate in the office. Hell, if she had half a brain, she'd realize her pension was in jeopardy, her 401 (k), the welfare of her only daughter Jessica, age 15, who was getting more and more into boys, and she was risking the best career of her life. Hell, if caught there would be news reports. Newspaper headlines. Public scrutiny, though she really didn't give a fuck about public opinion. They were freaks anyway, half of which were probably fucking themselves with dildos right this instant.

Before this very life-changing, challenging job as a paralegal, she worked at Winn-Dixie Supermarket in Naranja, Florida, thirty minutes south of where she was now. But she got fired after fucking the boss, his son, and everybody in the stock department when she was married, which prompted her divorce from a very bitter and angry black man who tried to shoot her, but to no avail. He wound up with full custody of his daughter, and when she rebelled, Jessica, by running away, going back to her mother, they arranged another court date and he signed over custody back to the mother, Miss Crucial Williams, from the Bronx, raised in Miami, graduated from Miami Edison High School.

Seemed like yesterday!

Staring at the janitor across the way, in the opposite breathtaking building, who stopped mopping the floor when he saw this sexy vixen going to town, she licked her lips at him. Pulling the dildo from her pussy, sucking the depths of her womb from the damned thing, she moaned again. Sliding it back up inside of her, she squeezed her legs together, bringing her feet up and over to the side so the rest of the business men and women, who gawked at her in surprise, shock, disgust and excitement could get a good look at the huge dildo spreading her pussy to kingdom come. She caused quite a stir in her body.

Her loins were on fire! Her ass was pretty, clean and tempting. Her feet ached monstrously. Trying to maintain control, her chair was rolling back from the desk.

Standing up, pulling her little friend from her body, she placed it on the desk in the upright position, climbed on it, lowered her body onto it and rode it like a cowboy, her knees two inches from the desk. Her weave fell from the bun and framed her beautifully made-up face.

"Fuck me, Daddy!" she screamed out in delight, smiling like a Cheshire cat. She closed her eyes and suddenly it was actor Mekhi Phiefer under her, beating that chocolate stick into her Candy Shop, tasting the Jolly Ranchers of her walls, the Snickers of her clitoris…and the Willy Wonka of her sweat.

About to lose his mind, the janitor quickly closed the door to the office across from her, unzipped his pants, pulled a chair up to the window so she could get a good look at his juicy dick, and he started masturbating, not even lubing his hand.

His legs shook.

His eyes wide and congratulatory. He didn't even realize people from Crucial's building were forming at the window, mainly women and a few gay men, pointing, admiring, about to have information overload in the eyes. He focused all his attention on the slut across from him who was trying to drive him up the wall.

He pulled his pants down to his ankles, as he kissed at her, winked, smiled boyishly, how handsome he was, and the bouncing of his nuts between such chiseled thighs sent her over the edge.

She slammed her pussy on the dildo, her hands pressed firmly flat on the desk. It was a feat to keep balance, but she loved things that were hard to attain. She was sweating all over, her heart racing, feeling her salty walls slide up and down on such a fantastic creation.

She licked her lips, flipping the button on the toy to "very fast," and she lost control.

"Oh shit, baby, fuck me, *Mekhi*…MEKHI! Yea," she went on breathlessly, opening her eyes and being enraptured by her friend across the way, "…jack that dick, Mr. Janitor! Fuck me FUCK ME! Yes, fuck me long, hard and good! I know you can read my lips, you sexy bitch! Yes, fuck me fuck me, oh shit, yea…"

The toy hummed and hummed until the battery died, but she didn't lose a beat. She leaned forward; the toy angling and she continued to ride it, her titties falling free from the white lacey bra, bouncing all over her chest. She sat up, riding her toy, taking her left breast into her hand, thankful for the "wardrobe malfunction," and suckling on her swollen nipple, sending electricity up and down her spine, exploding in her toes. "Shit, my God this, this shit right here feels…so….good!"

She had enough of the desk. Back in the

chair she went, opening her legs, sticking the toy up her tight, virgin ass. The pain was great but the pleasure that swarmed her like bees on honey more than made up for it. She went crazy. She grinded on the dildo, sending it deeper and deeper inside her.

She felt uncomfortable. “Ain’t lubed enough.” *That’s it!*

Taking it out she sucked on it, tasting her ass, thankful she was a clean bitch. She spat on it repeatedly, taking the mushroom head of the toy and running it back and forth on the opening of her rectum, careful not to push it inside.

Then into softness she went, playing with her pussy while she banged her hole.

Her skin tingled. “YES!”

She rode it, cowgirl style. She felt powerful, invincible. She smiled when the police showed up to arrest Mr. Janitor. She had a gut instinct to stop, but she kept going. They were arguing, unfortunately she didn’t hear when was being said. Mr. Janitor pointed at her, she laughed, using her left hand to spread her ass, and she rammed the toy deeper, deeper…sending an earthquake though her sweaty, tired body.

The cops were uninterested, the white female handcuffed him, leading him, kicking and screaming, out of the office. The other cop, white male, early twenties, slid the chair back behind the desk and when he turned to face Crucial. She smiled at him, fucking herself harder and smoother with her toy. He paused, wide-eyed, his dick getting hard instantly.

Whipping out his walkie-talkie, he attempted to push the button and she winked and kissed at him. He thought about it. Locking the door, he said something into his radio, smiling lustfully at her, and then his blue eyes sparkled. He hurriedly got the chair, unzipped his pants, and he started pulling on his little weenie roast of a dick.

How pathetic, she thought happily. *Serve and protect, 'ey? Yea, right!*

Ok, it was time to signal Mt. Saint Helen.

Spread-eagled now, she rammed her toy deeper in her ass. Her fingers were soaked; she played with herself faster, more passionately, biting her lips.

Replaced was a pleasure she'd never felt. She'd never been fucked in her ass before. Never even thought about it really. She was a black woman; she didn't think black girls got kinky like that. She thought that was a white woman's trademark, their thing to do, their way to hook a black man, by letting him fuck her into remission with their Donkey Kong dicks.

And now she was doing it, and it felt WONDEFUL! GREAT!

Shit, what have I been missing?

Mr. Police unbuttoned his shirt, his walkie-talkie and gun holster falling on the floor, and he fingered his nipple, spitting on his hand, jacking his dick. He spread those legs. He didn't notice more and more people crowding the windows, all of them laughing at him. They wondered what he was looking at, what was he so focused on.

He smiled, licking his lips, his legs trembling. He exploded with a ball-busting jolt! He squirmed in his seat as his torso moved up and down faster and faster and faster.

She ran her tongue across her full lips, tasting the candy-flavored red lipstick her lesbian lover California bought her for their third anniversary last week. She had on this lipstick when she ate her woman out just after dinner the same night, smearing red lipstick all over her pink, sweet smelling pussy. She could damn near smell it now. Conventionally pretty, she pushed those thoughts from her head, and she stifled an imposing orgasm. The phone rang. Damn it!

Putting up her toy she answered. "Boss, that's you?"

"Yes it is. Today is interview day. Got the

files ready?"

"I know, boss," Crucial said through the speaker phone on her cluttered but organized desk.

She loved interview day.

"You know what that means?"

"Yes. Hold all your calls, unless its one of the interviewers calling to cancel."

"This would be career suicide because no one turns me down."

"I know, boss. I know all too well."

"I bet you do. How's your mother?"

"She's in L.A. shooting a commercial for dentures. She's pretty as hell, but I can't say the same for her teeth."

"So she got the gig? $1,200 for the spot. Extra cash she could use for her knitting class."

"She loves the commercial, but I doubt if she spend it on knitting. Hell she got a closet full of goddamn quilts, now."

"I need another assistant," said James, cruising the Macarthur Causeway, which linked Miami to South Beach. Beautifully constructed buildings were on either side of him, across a huge stretch of glittering water under the Miami sun. The top was down, his dick was hard, his nuts pulsated with vibrancy because he was on the verge of getting blue balls. No pussy action in a matter of months, too busy with work, paying bills, battling his Baby Mama in custody battle court (she didn't stand a chance), and warding off bill collectors, the same people he paid off days ago.

"Well, hopefully today you'll get one, James. Like you got me"

"Well, let's hope you're right."

An hour later, James Stewart entered his lavishly-expensive office on South Beach and sat behind his desk, silent. His glittering watch rented for show, he dusted the lint off his silk suit and smiled at his reflection in the mirror before him. Mr. Narcissistic. Knowing he had a shit load of emails, he leaned back in his high backed, cushioned chair, fixed his silk red tie and sighed.

Another day of interviews.

He had to admit that he'd been too lenient on potential prospects. Yes, he was a cut-throat lawyer, but he needed cut-throat employees. This was how it was going to go. There were twelve interviews scheduled for today. He was going to test each and every applicant. He didn't care if they had felonies or not. To tell you the truth, the more checkered the past, the more he had to work with.

Bianca Samuels. Ted Franks. Stephanie Johnson. Donald La'Shay. Fanny Daniels.

Archie Bunker. Henry Jameson. Sampson Burkes.

He smiled. He wondered how many he could fuck before the day was over.

Being the boss worked wonders.

I met him on Myspace. I was checking out the men in Atlanta, Georgia, just *hoping* one was cute enough to spark my interest or at least get my fingers dancing across the keyboard by telling him the most sensual things about myself. I never knew that the very first black man I saw would do the trick. I just hoped he wasn't gay. Seemed like every man in Atlanta was either gay, bisexual or fucked men on the low and having chronic denial about it. They act like a sister didn't know.

I went to "Advanced Search" first. I went through the Process of Elimination. I didn't want a smoker, breath would be funky, and I didn't care how many Tic Tacs he sucked on or how much Scope he gargled. Smoke was smoke, and it would be in everything from his car to the clothes he wore. I didn't want a bisexual man, or a gay man. Double strike, mind you. I wanted my man to be just that: my man, I didn't want to leave for work and have to worry about him throwing on some Madonna and prancing around my bedroom clad in my thongs and bras. I didn't want an alcoholic, they didn't know how to act, and I knew where most of their paychecks would go: on goddamn liquor and the only liquor I wanted them drinking was my liquor, pronounced "lick her" from here to Kingdom Come when we're between the sheets.

I didn't want Hispanic men. They laughed too much for my taste. I liked my men to be serious, with a hint of humor, kind of like Oregano in my fried chicken. You can't really taste it, but it heightens the taste, feel me? Asians and anything that wasn't black didn't have a chance with me. He had to be at least 6 feet tall. I was a petite woman, five feet 2 inches with the most gloriously worked-on body. I took pleasure in how I looked and how I dressed. But the main reason why I loved tall men was because I liked to feel protected when we went out in public. What was a small, leprechaun-looking man going to do for me if trouble arose? Defend my ankles? Please!

After a minute of searching, I found him. Mr. Right. Well, I should say Mr. Right At this Moment. He was 6 feet 3 inches, Jamaican and Haitian, and he dressed immaculately nice. Who knew Haitians and Jamaicans mixed this elegantly well? I might have to send my home girl Danielle his profile and let her check it out. Nah. Couldn't do that. When women wanted something they spared no expense to get it, and Danielle was a jealous woman. She'd take any and every man I wanted, and I'd fuck her up today if he told me she got at him with a message, so I would keep him my guarded little secret.

Intrigued and turned on by him, I checked out all of his profile pictures, carefully combing my eyes across his beautiful face and chocolate skin… they were very classy, nothing to showy or promiscuous, his nipples and chest were covered up, he smiled in every one of them, he didn't smoke nor drink. He was straight as an arrow. His profile was very tasteful. I liked it a lot.

Since I didn't like adding friends cold turkey on my profile, I shot him a very brief, to the point message. Hoping it would do the trick without the use of fireworks and explosions. Hell, I didn't need a man that badly.

Or maybe I *did* need one. I missed the company.

Of a good man.

And good men didn't exist.

Hello, beautiful Stranger;

Hey, how are you. Hope I'm not a bother. I find you interesting, I'm 40 years old and I find men on Myspace interesting, go figure, lol (laugh out loud). Check out my profile, if you like what you see I would greatly appreciate it if you hit me up and let me know what the deal is.

Much Love,

Stacie Mender.

After sending it, I then sent the friend invite. I felt like I was sending off for a job interview. The letter seemed so formal. So, you know, in your face. Did it sound desperate? I didn't want to come off seeming like I couldn't find a man in person. But he was 10 miles away from my zip code in Marietta County. He was single, so why not go for the juggler?

Before I could log off, my heart pounded just waiting for his response, I looked at his pictures one more time. Fanning myself. Phew. *Hot*!

Quicker than Bounty paper towels soaking up spilt milk, he sent a response. This was the Cash 3 winning numbers. The jack pot! I damn near fell on the floor. Covering my mouth in shock, my hands begin trembling. Why was I in shock? He was just a black man, probably a dead beat, with three kids, Baby Mama drama and a few diseases. He probably didn't have a bank account, lived with his Mama and never met his Daddy. Probably been to jail, or even worse, prison. Maybe I should just erase his reply, he probably found me to be desperate or one of those fire-in-the-pussy Hoes that probably hit him up every day.

"Oh, *God*, I shouldn't have disturbed this man," I whispered nervously, my throat constricted…standing up in my sexy black lingerie and pulled out a Benson and Hedges cigarette, lighting up and by the time I took a puff I realized I had a Nicoderm patch on my upper arm, been wearing them for about six months, haven't touched a cigarette in that long, and I was taking the back slide, all over a man. I stubbed it out in the ash tray on the nightstand and looked at the picture of my son Billy, framed in silver. He died last month, car jacking in Portland, Oregon. I was still distraught over that, because we were on bad terms when he was gunned down over those pricey rims I warned him not to buy. In fact the last few weeks of his 23 year old life I begged him to come back home, but I was hardly there for him because I worked all the time to keep a roof over his head, and being that he was well-fed and well taken care of, he needed his mother and I wasn't there. I did it all on my own. I never married his father, because he was too busy chasing Hoes all over the place, and had eight other children from eight other women who all hated me with a passion, and I hated them, well, maybe hate was too strong a word.

Tears wet my face as I sit at the computer, pick up the remote and turn on some Al Green *Good or Bad, Happy or Sad,* and I sing along, *I, I, I*...rhythmically snapping my fingers, bobbing my head, moving the cursor to the "inbox" link and clicking it. I saw his beautiful picture. I smiled, tasting some tears and opened his response.

Beautiful Stranger,

Hello, pretty lady. You seem like a real genuine woman. I read your profile. You like Al Green. I love him, but I've been getting deeper into Gerald Levert, since the brother just passed away. I don't respond to women on here, all they want is sex, sex, sex, and never bother to ask how a brother's day went.

But your message struck me as odd, because you are a very sensual woman and your message was very refreshingly different, but it's all good because you have become the first woman I've responded to.

I know it's a bit presumptuous, but I'm free this evening, I don't do Myspace all the time, I come on here to promote my spoken word CD "Fire in my Eyes." So if you would do me the honor of going to dinner I would be flattered. I know we just met, sort of, and freaks are on Myspace. So if you want to meet me at a discreet public place then that's fine as well.

My phone number I will include after this

message so you can call me with your answer. Much love, and once again you are a very pretty woman. Is your personality an identical twin?

Hope to find out soon.
Thad Johnson.

Thad. *Thad* was his name. I *loved* the name, damn near original, different. I racked my brain, trying to see if I met any Thads…*Chad*, yes. But *Thad*? Very original. Thad, Mr. Thad Johnson. Mrs. Thad Johnson, Mrs. Stacie Mender-Johnson! Sounded like a *ding ding ding* winning situation to me, sh…it! I damn near fell over in my chair, smiling. I hoped he wasn't a player, but he didn't seem that way. Yet since when did words someone typed online packed emotion? Why was I thinking of churches, wedding bells, expensive-Pawn-ready-engagement rings, champagne, dick, honeymoons and thresholds? Maybe I was losing my mind! How did one find out his true intention? He said women hit him up all the time tying to fuck him. I wasn't trying to "fuck," I needed a friend, a good friend, a man I could talk to, be down with, and be there for. Be his companion if it came to that. Slowly grow old with. My wet mid-section wasn't the issue. I didn't need sex for validation or to get in fit in then get out. Nah. Those years were gone. And what animatedly-colorful years, *Ow*, baby! I had good pussy. So I sat on it like gold. Dick was the fire to test the gold lining in my vagina; I was talking about the type of good dick that didn't come with Nutrition Facts, a stench or side effects that landed a bitch like me on the doctor's cold-ass iron tables, dreading STD's.

But my dildo has done the honors for the past year. Of testing the gold trim in my pussy…and really done the honor when my son died. I swore. My dildo pulled me through. Yea, I had the Bible, read the Bible and dissected the Bible; I could even open the Good book and remind myself of the tear-stained pages that attempted to get me through my ordeal. Yet failed miserably. But my dildo was here with me. Kept me sane. Rocked me into a deep sleep, so deep alarm clocks and buzzers failed to wake me up on time for work.

As much as I didn't want to think about that dark time in my life, I remembered his funeral, I was a wreck. Thank God my friends helped plan the funeral, I was indecisive. I cursed the workers from the funeral home out because they kept harassing me about what color suit my son was going to wear, since half of his pictures (when he was living) were taken with a purple, feather-clad fedora, should he wear it while being lowered 6 feet into God's Ice Box of an Earth. Should his friends be allowed to give testimony? Who was going to write the poem? I didn't have the mentality to deal with all that.

On a muggy, rainy Saturday, his funeral day had arrived. I wanted to stay home. I couldn't go to his funeral. I didn't want to feel the sunlight on my skin, and I didn't want to breathe. I felt like I was being robbed and had been robbed every time I drew in God's resilient air and my son couldn't do the same anymore. I remembered our last conversation. We argued big time. I wanted him home, because he wrote me a letter stating that he joined the ridiculously formed Blood Gang. I was in an outrage. My son was never abused, never talked down to, never ashamed by me. I gave him the world; I just couldn't give him all my time.

I was a nervous wreck, scared for my child. "What do you mean you joined the Blood Gang?" I wanted to throw the lamp across the room and dance in the solace of glass shattering. "Have you fallen and bumped your damn head, boy?"

He sucked his teeth, pure bitch fashion. "I'm 23 years old! I don't fall and I bump my head in pussy, I'ma grown man."

"Stating that you're grown is supposed to be the Kryptonite to Superman's S on his chest, right?"

"In English, please."

"How about in Japanese?"

"I don't know what that Kryptonite shit meant."

Wide-eyed, "Watch your mouth."

"I *am*, standing in the mirror, holding the phone, smoking my joint, listening to you babble."

"Babble? I'm your mother, and I never raised you to do drugs."

"All the kids are doing it."

"At least I know you're a hypocrite."

"Meaning, Mama?"

"I thought you were a grown man, yet you are following little kids."

"Stop playing your mind games on me, it doesn't work anymore."

I said "Whatever."

"Hold on, the AC is too cold, let me turn it down."

I was brutally defiant. "Where are you living up there? And I don't want to hold on."

"What?" he screamed; his voice an echo. I heard some soft banging noises, like he was opening some closet doors. "I didn't hear you."

"Am I on speaker phone?"

"Yes, Mama, I need both my hands."

"TMI, Niggah!"

"Too much information, now you sound like Sting and the Police."

"This is getting us nowhere."

He took me off speaker. "Mama, deal with it, I live once in my life, I don't want my Mama trying to embarrass me before the world because she can't let go of her son and let him try to grow into a man."

I was infuriated. I couldn't believe he would talk to me in this fashion! My *sweater* didn't even itch across my ample breasts in that fashion so I would be *damned* if a Niggah that came kicking and screaming out of my pussy, putting me through ten hours of the most painful labor of my life was going to talk down to me like red carpets all over Hollywood! "Watch your mouth. You aren't too grown for me to kick your ass."

He laughed bitterly, made my skin crawl. Angrily, I rubbed the Nicoderm patch, hoping it released enough nicotine to keep my eyes off the cigarette pack on the dresser, by my perfume bottles. I kept eyeing it, trying to keep myself calm. OK, gurl, he was a hurt young man lashing out. I had to deal with it, good or bad he was my son.

"I am too grown, and I will call 5-0 if you put your hands on me."

I was hurt. "You'd call the white man on me?"

He was silent. "No, Ma, I am not a snitch, but damn you got to cut the umbilical cord at some point in my life."

"The way your Daddy cut yours then left me to go make other babies with other women to cut their cords?"

Suffice it to say, he became less bitter and more sympathetic, yet he still had an attitude imprisoned in the soul of his voice. He was a very intelligent, handsome young man, just like his Romeo-and-Juliet-looking Daddy, no good piece of shit. "I'm sorry, Ma. He shouldn't have left you out to dry. I know you love me, you did keep a roof over my head."

Ha! "You remembered, goddamn shocked that you do, thought you had selective amnesia for a second…"

"I respect you, Ma."

"Then why are you making me suffer?" I spat without thinking, trying not to sound venomous.

He went in for the kill. "Because you were never there for me. You always worked, never spoke to me, and were too tired to speak to me. When I was 14 I lost my virginity. I tried to talk to you, because I didn't know I was not supposed to fall in love and marry the first piece of pussy, I meant cunt, I meant coochie that I got. But you told me you were *too* sleepy. You'd just gotten home from work. I was deeply hurt. When I was jumped on after graduation I called you at your job, and *yea* I understand you're a police dispatcher, but I needed you, yet you were too busy. But you always found time to go to Christmas parties and outings with your co-workers, yet I'm your only child and I was at home, crying myself to sleep because my Daddy abandoned me, cut the cord early, and you abandoned me, and still haven't cut the cord yet."

"I did what I had to do; do you want a druggie mother? An alcoholic mother? A mother who is an abuser, stripper?"

"I respect you, Ma. I'm glad you're strong. But I joined the gang to fit in. I love it on the West Coast."

"Son, *please*, I *beg* of you, get out of that gang, don't they kill you if you try you demolish ties with them? Kill up your whole family?"

"I don't know, this *isn't* the mafia."

"I got to go, don't have time for all this."

"Ma, I love…"

"I'm mad at you!" And I hung up in his face. My son was murdered not too long after that.

Maybe that was why I was having such a hard time dealing with his death. I couldn't accept it because of the unresolved feelings he had towards my never being there for him. Because of the things I told him. Because I gave him such a hard time. Because I was actually mad at him when he died.

Maybe that made it easier for him to die, thinking I was mad at him, which probably made him think his own mother didn't love him anymore. This tore me up, I began shedding tears the way snakes shed skin…shaking with fear and trembling…I needed those cigarettes. I picked up the pack, extracted one and quickly threw it on the dresser.

I looked at Thad's easy-on-my-itchy-red-eyes picture. Calmed down some, sat down and I checked my inbox again.

He'd sent his phone number.

I snatched up my cell phone and called him. I let it ring once, goddamn it I shoulda pressed the "blocked number" feature so his caller I.D. wouldn't register my name and phone number.

It'd show up as Private Number.

Before I could hang up he answered, speaking with the smokiest, most ghetto-flavored voice I'd ever heard, packed with the ingredients that electrified my favorite strawberry ice cream.

My mouth agape, I started stuttering, a duh a duh a duh I got the wrong number.

Click.

Before I could turn off my phone he called back, damn it I hope he wasn't a stalker, I hoped I didn't make a mistake, calling him. And why did he call me right back? Wasn't that too soon to call me back, shouldn't he wait for me to call *him* back? Wow, what did I get myself into?

I answered, lighting a cigarette, puffing it so strongly I snatched off the patch, fuck the goddamn patch, the hell with all the goddamn patches!

"Yes, yes, yes, hello." I strained to sound like a white bitch. All airy and shit, air-headed. I had "As if," "Not even," and *"Like, totally!"* on stand by in the dusty chambers of my lips.

"Hello, how are you, ma'am?"

Oh, God! And he got manners! He spoke *before* he asked for Stacie. Phenomenal, and emphasis on the word "men" in phenomenal.

"I'm fine, like, totally fine." Oh, God, shoot me, I was making a complete fool of myself.

"May I ask with whom I'm speaking?"

"Donjanabi."

He chuckled. "Donjanabi? Unique name."

Flirt!

"Thank you, it's African for good punani!"

He chocked through the phone, laughing. "May I speak with Stacie, please?"

"As if, not even, like totally not cool, dude!" I wanted to laugh; I stuck my fist in my mouth, about to run out of the room. A forty year old woman acting like a kid. I never thought I'd see the day. I know the stock in the gold trim of my pussy just took a nosedive by 23 points on the Dow Jones.

"Why you say that pretty lady?" he asked.

God! He's. Saying. All. The. Right. Things! "I don't know," I went on, tossing my hair all girly, looking silly.

I stomped my toe on the bed post and I was hopping up and down in grave pain.

Damn, that shit hurt. I couldn't help but laugh when the pain subsided.

He said, "Are you ok?"

I said, "Yes."

"So I want to just forget all the

preliminaries. Let's grab a bite to eat. Hell, let's go now, what do you say?"

Hell nah! Are you serious? You can be a stalker, a rapist. You can try to kill me; I don't just meet men and go out with them! Hell no!

You must have fell and bumped your head, like I said I don't need men that desperately and you're trying to call me a damn liar! if I say "yes" it would confirm everything I just said.

"Sure, let's do it."

"Where do you live?"

I gave him my address.

I heard the doorbell an hour later.

I was looking myself over in the mirror, loving what I saw. A very sexy woman, yay! I closed the magazine *Black Confessions* and I tossed it on the low-table. Thankful I went for my Pap Smear test on time this month. Now I didn't have to worry about it.

I was wearing a boat neck sweater I ordered from the Victoria's Secret catalogue and black pants. High heels, and a bunch of accessories. I looked flawless. No make-up, didn't feel like being carbon copies. Tonight. Let's set the tone. Let's be real and original.

I was walking towards the front door when the thought of my son hit me like bricks. I rested my hand on the door knob, twisted and the man stood before me, a sight for sore eyes. He looked better than his photos. He wore a thin leather jacket, nice sweater, and loose jeans with black leather boots. He was meticulously groomed; I loved the way he smelled.

"Come in."

"Thank you." He handed me a box of Vera Wang perfume and a dozen white roses. I was wet instantly, yet I tried to keep my mind off the bedroom, I didn't want to play ring around the sheets and matters with him just yet.

He followed me into the high tech kitchen.

"You have a lovely home."

I put the roses in a vase, turned on the tap water, opened the Tylenol and put two in the water, and in went the stem of the roses. Mama always taught me that roses would live longer if you gave them Tylenol. I never believed her, but I've become superstitious and now I do it.

"Thanks. I do what I can."

"You do it well." He gave me the once over, without seeming perverted. "You are absolutely amazing."

I tucked my chin back with a smile. "Damn, it's like that?"

"Yea, Ma, it's like that!" Thad sat at the dining table, looking over the ceramic bowls, the non-stick pots hanging on hooks, dangling over the three island counters, the fake plants. The tiled floors. Everything in my kitchen was where it was supposed to be.

"Stacie, so are you ready?"

"Yes. Let me grab my purse, wait here."

I went up the stairs, to my room, grabbed my purse and pivoting, I froze. I could not get my son off my mind. I missed him, truly felt guilty. I needed him, he was my baby. This burned me inside. A mother losing her son. I didn't want my son thinking or dying thinking that I hated him. I loved him so much and before I knew it I dropped the purse on the floor, fell to my knees, snatched out my wallet, pulled out a picture of my son and I held it to my heart.

"I love you, my son Mama loves you. I miss you; I can't believe you died on me, baby why did you leave?"

I was whisked off my knees and pulled into Thad's embrace. I fought him, this was my pain, not his, he just met me but he wouldn't let me go. "Beat me, Stacie, I don't care, beat me, scratch my eyes out, fight me and I'll still hold you, get out all of your anger, and properly mourn your son…"

I punched him repeatedly in the chest, he didn't wince because he was a real man, and real men were wired differently from immature so-called thug men.

He held me, rubbing my shoulders. He

rocked with me, back and forth, our groins pressed together. He looked into my sore, red eyes, our lips finding the metal for the magnets on our tongues and before we knew it we were kissing, while he hummed a Sam Cooke Cut. Only you send you. Darling you send you. Thrill me.

Our tongues danced in complete harmony; as I tried to turn every romance novel I ever read into a reality, I took off his jacket, wanting to feel his skin. Off came his shirt. He took his time, he didn't show a sign that he wanted to rush. We kissed and kissed, trapped in a lip lock, my nipples erect, my desire wet and willing, throbbing and pulsating. I felt him pressed against me, the urgency breath taking, we kissed and we kissed, until I couldn't breathe.

I backed away, squatting down and picking up my purse. He snatched it, threw it across the room, pulled me to him and said, "First, I'm going in your fridge and cooking you a meal. Two, we are going to sit at your dining table, and enjoy it. Three, we're going to watch an old school movie, I'll pick it. Four, I am going to run you a hot bath. Five, I will turn on jazz on your stereo and watch the TV in your room while you spend quality time with Stacie, you need it. Six. When you're done with your bath I will dry you off, carry you to the bed, and give you a deep body massage for an hour, with lotions and oils. Then I will strip naked, hold you and we will sleep the night away. I don't want to have sex with you. I want to pamper you, spend the night with you for your companionship, your company."

By the time he was done I looked at him and said, "So when you want to get started, since you invading my space, lol."

"LOL, laugh out loud, 'ey? We can get started now."

"Well, follow me to the kitchen. I got a feeling you won't be going home for a long time."

"Do you want spaghetti or lamb chops, I know you got some lamb chops."

"Guess we'll find out, Thad."

He made do on everything he promised.

All *that*, and *no* sex.

Guess there are some good men in the world.

Saxophone Jenkins
Special Day 2006

Hello, baby! How are you doing today? I hope this little "note" found you in the best of health and good spirits. I know you're fed up with the fact that you haven't boned your wife yet. Bitter pill to swallow, I know. But this is only temporary. I compiled a little list, which I'm typing right now. You have to do everything on the list so lie back in the tub, relax, smile and be to yourself and your thoughts. Forget about church today, even though it's Sunday. We need alone time. Please don't fight me on this. While you relax, I want you to think about your past. Do you remember how we first me? Do you remember the first words we said to each other? I can remember when you first smiled. I nearly fell down the stairs at the Convocation Building on the University of Miami College campus. Do you remember that? Do you remember our bond? Reflect. The glow and the warmth of the candles should dig silence in your head, allowing you to open-mindedly engulf everything you feel for me. The incense and the gentle smell should open the deepest part of you, a part you thought was forever sealed, and you should let what comes out walk out so you can examine it and hope it makes you a better person. It should allow you to flow with what I'm doing for you. The bubbles in the tub and the warmth of the water, mixed with some edible oil should make your skin soft and collaborate with your being able to allow yourself to let your special Day engross you. I went all out for this day, pulled out all the stops. I know you work 6 days a week and you come home drained and tired. Today is your day, baby.

Let go your inhibitions. Let go of your problems. Forget that people exist in the world. When you hear my voice let the universe cease to exist. The only two people that exist are you and I. The bathroom is the Meditation, Release Room. Utilize it. Let go of imposing bills. I'm cutting your phones off. The special request goes as listed below:

1) *Open the envelope titled: Mr. Jenkins, leaning against the wall on the front of the tub. You should be facing it.*
2) *Secondly, listen the Zhane songs "La La La," and "Off my Mind." Listen to the words. That's how I feel about you.*
3) *Then listen to Mary J Blige's "Beautiful Ones." And "All I have to Say." "Beautiful Ones" embody everything I feel for you. When I hear this song I think about you.*
4) *Then put in the PM Dawn CD and listen to "Die Without you" from the* Boomerang *soundtrack. This used to be my "cry" song. When I was depressed I'd play this to cry to.*

I know in my heart you are my soul mate. Life is too short for all the fighting and arguing and fussing and alienation.

By now you should know you have a beautiful best friend who thinks the world of you and would do anything for you.

Sincerely,

Jadish Houston. Your wife.

***

Feelings of ecstasy surging through me like out of control waves, I smiled, pressing print and watching the paper spit from the printer. Neatly folding it, I went into the bedroom, sprayed some perfume on it and sealed the stationary inside a scented envelope.

Yes, it was set.

When my husband comes home, everything will be perfect.

Tossing my short, croppy hair behind my head, I stood up from the chair and tugged on my tennis skirt. My tits were bare.

Quite the little slut today, I frowned because I never really felt this way about my husband. Considering we haven't made love yet, I know he had a lot of anger towards me. But like most wives, I wanted to believe that he loved me enough to get over that anger. After a couple years of marriage, I was exhausted from fighting with him. I was tired of putting off the inevitability of sex with your mate.

I knew I was to blame. What man wanted to be married to a woman he couldn't fuck?

I unscrupulously ran my hands over my dripping kitty cat and wiped it all over the envelope.

Thank God I wasn't wearing any panties.

My man would love me tonight, but first I had someone to go and see.

There was something that I wanted to know, and I couldn't put it off a moment sooner.

I grabbed my car keys and hit the door.

When I turned my car onto the turnpike, I huffed and puffed because I immediately saw two major traffic accidents, all involving these non-driving Cubans. Damn it! I couldn't turn around.

Damn it!

I brought my car to a halt and put it in park, turning off the ignition, saving gas. I was getting mad really fast.

On the radio was the weather report. Partly cloudy. *Yea, I know. I'm looking at the sky right now, dumb announcer. Chance of rain, got that. I do see rain drops on my windshield, damn who paid your payroll?*

My cell phone rang, startling me. My heart hammering, it took a minute to calm down. It was Daddy. *What the hell does he want?*

Exhaling audibly. "Hey, Pop," I said excitedly. He knew I was faking the funk.

Cautiously, he said, "I'm doing good. Where are you?"

I narrowed my eyes. "I'm trapped in

traffic on the turnpike."

He grunted. "Damn, baby. I needed a ride home."

Call Mama! Isn't she your wife? "Dad, I can't control the traffic."

"I know, baby. I didn't mean to sound like I was coming down on you."

Oh, yes the hell you did! "No problem."

"I guess I got to find another way home."

The guilt trip starts. "Call my husband, Daddy."

"Well I'll be damned. Why didn't I think of that?"

We kissed each other through the phone, something we always did.

"Call me later, Pa."

"Love you, baby."

"I love you, too."

"And be careful…"

I flipped my cell phone closed, staring at a cement truck.

I thought about my God Daddy.

Tommy.

Tommy

I have photos of all my lovers. I either took the pictures with my own camera or they gave them to me. I have four photo albums filled with them. Sexy, beautiful black women.

With huge red X's over their faces.

Those were my Ex Files.

There were Ex Files in my year books. From junior high to high school. I still have them, put up somewhere in the storage closet. People smiling, laughing, and frowning in their pictures.

With big red X's over their faces. Meaning they got the Mark of the Freak. I fucked them and left them. They were forever branded with the big red X.

Ten ladies from the cheerleading team with small red X's on their magnificently gorgeous faces.

We didn't speak or know each other during school hours. But during the freak-comes-out-at-night hours, from 8 PM until 2 AM, we got it on fiercely, like two dogs. I had an orgy with four of the cheerleaders, and two women from the track team also stopped by and got busy with me. Being that I was the only man, I tried like hell to handle all that pussy. I did a superb job. That's how my father raised me. Being from Alabama, he raised me to fuck 'em and leave 'em. He did my mother that way. She didn't seem to mind being dogged. And even though she was my mother, if she didn't help herself why should I waste my time? Growing up, I didn't understand it, but I did what Dad said. He used to bring grown woman over to the house when I was twelve and he pushed them on me. So I had a crash course in Fucking 101. The best of the best taught me what I know now.

Dad and I hardly spent time together, because when he wasn't working he was fucking bitches from here to California. Getting them pregnant and leaving them. At last count Dad has twenty-three children. And he did nothing for them. Presently, Dad and I occasionally speak. But I felt nothing for him. When I thought about him I thought of pussy. And that's bad.

Now that I was a man I had a problem with commitment. I was more committed to taking bitches to the telly (Hotel) than making them happy. I loved fogging up those mirrors. Once my Grade A beef knocked 'em out with one shot for the rest of the night I'd write "The freak was here" on the mirror, put on my clothes and drive my ass to my crib.

But the high school days were on my mind right now. The Ex Files. The female softball team. Eight of them. We were hungry and searching for the next nut before the squirrels came out to play with the roosters every morning. So full of testosterone I was. So full of emptiness when the bitches drained my nuts dry.

Two females on the cross country track team. Big red X's. Three from the water polo team. Big red X's. Women's basketball team. Nine of them. Big red X's. Male basketball team. Eleven red X's. All one-night stands. Fuck now, forget me later.

Prison: four big red X's. I only took photos with the ones I did something with. Had to survive in jail. No way was I going to get killed or stabbed. So I did what I had to do, slinging this dick for food, protection and continued coverage. I kept it discreet, even had a few corrections' officers, and got out with no bumps and scrapes.

Throughout my twenties, before I got locked up, and even after that, I only dated people for one reason: to see how many I could actually date and get away with it. The only thing that separated me from my low-life father was the fact that I didn't father kids. I didn't want kids. Seemed women these days only wanted to have your babies so they could get a certified check to go spend on their new men and I'd kill the bitch. So why put myself in that position?

Once I fucked females I crossed their faces out with a red marker. They ceased to exist in my world. If I got it in one hour, one minute, one second or one week, I crossed them out. Too quickly. No respect for themselves. No hesitation. If they could fuck me at the drop of a dime then how many other people did they drop dimes for?

Biggie Smalls said "It was all a dream," for me it was all a game. I used my strong sex appeal to get my lovers in the sack. I set records for myself. I never had to pay for it. Never had to really beg for it. My body alone and my handsome face and brown eyes did that for me.

I sometimes fell in love with a few lovers. But the love wasn't what you thought it was. It was a love for sex. A love for having powerful orgasms. A love for the chase. A love for the thrill. When I cut them loose, I didn't weep, shed a tear or ask for them back.

Almost everyone have Ex Files. One night stands thrive on this. Meaningless sex has gone public. If meaningless sex was on the stock market, this would be a wicked world, more wicked then it was now.

But there was one photo I didn't put in my photo album. I couldn't do it because I felt bad enough as it was now. How could I betray a woman that was my best friend's daughter? I had to get the pussy, she was banging. The sexiest woman I'd ever seen. It wasn't about my homeboy, who I respected with everything in me. This was about testing the pussy before anyone else did. Yea. I was a grimy Niggah! If he found out he should kill my ass. But getting the panties was worth it. I fell in love with her the day I hit it. I couldn't get her off my mind. Day in and day out I thought of her and what she may be doing. I was proud of her when she graduated college. I'm in the college photos with her, sometimes the red marker beckoning me to X out her face. But how do you X out love?

Back then, she was so stuck up. She saved the pussy like it was gold. And knowing that I was the first to beat the pussy up fulfilled me in ways I couldn't explain. Her husband, Sax, hadn't even tapped the pussy yet and he's married to her. I felt so sorry for him, knowing I was the reason he wasn't getting any. I couldn't stand the Niggah anyways, talking shit to me. Insulting me in public. I will never forget he dumped Sprite soda on my head at the Red Lobster. I wanted to shoot his Ho ass!

I thought about this when there was a knock at my door. I wondered who it was. People didn't really visit me. I put on a baseball cap and answered the door.

I blinked once. She blinked back. Jadish Houston hugged me, "Hey, how are you, God Daddy?"

I cringed inside. Have to save face. I could hardly breathe.

"Come on in, girl."

She walked past me like a good dream. She was fine as all outdoors. I had to will my dick not to get hard. When good pussy was around you, your dick had a mind of its own. I had to act like a grown man right now, and not a little boy. I closed the door, tugged on my NY Yankees sweater and said, "Want something to drink?"

She gave the sweetest smile, standing in my need-to-clean-it-living room, trying to look innocent. "Yes. You got a Coke?" She sat on my sofa, crossing her legs. She leaned back, eyeing me suspiciously. I didn't quite understand why she was sizing me up, but I liked it. I loved attention.

I went into the kitchen and opened the refrigerator. I needed to go grocery shopping. Pulling out a bottle of soda, I closed my eyes and breathed in deeply. I could smell her on the air. I had to stand at the sink to keep it together. My nature stood at attention. I wanted Jadish, God I wanted to fuck her again. I couldn't get my mind off…

"Are you ok, Tommy?" she asked me, walking up behind me. Her hands were on my shoulders, softly massaging them. "Where's the soda?"

Please don't touch me, girl! I won't be responsible for what I do. I squeezed my eyes closed tightly, feeling like I was being taunted.

I turned around and gave her the soda. She unscrewed the top and took a hefty swig. Smacked her lips. Looked me deep in the eyes.

"How was your day, haven't heard from you in a long time, Tommy." She drinks from the bottle again, rolling her tongue across the top, making me shiver. Wide-eyed, my mouth open, I pulled my sweater over my hard on. She looked down at it, smacking her lips again. "Something wrong with your dick or something?"

I couldn't believe she was being this direct. She hardly ever *used* that word. She was a good girl and I liked her being a good girl.

"My day was good, and I'm just fine."

She looked at the junk on my dining table, the lotion bottle, the empty beer cans, and the cigarette butts overflowing in three ash trays, the uneaten KFC (Kentucky Fried Chicken).

She softly bit her index finger. "I have a question, and I want you to be honest."

I was stuttering. "Yes, Jadish, I have never lied to you."

"…You look tense. Have a seat at the dining table."

I didn't move. I was a block of cement.

"Come on," she went on, setting the soda on the table, and pulling out the chair. "Sit." I stood there, staring at her. She pushed me in the chair, I just looked at her. "You love me, right, like a daughter?" she asked, and the question threw me through a loop. My head was ringing, my ears doing the same thing.

"Yes. You're my god daughter." She straddled my leg, gripping the Coke, taking it to the head. Her small Adam's apple bobbed with each satisfying gulp. She smacked her lips, got on her knees, unzipped my pants, pulled out my dick and began chopping me up. Oh my Lord. I went wild. Her lips felt so good, so right. I *knew* she would eventually come back to the dick that popped her cherry. She was wiggling her head, tossing her hair, running her tongue along the incredible inches.

She took the lotion bottle, lathered up her hands and began jacking my dick. She stroked it just right, the way I loved. She didn't rush, she took her time. Her soft hands drove me crazy. I pulled my pants down to my ankles so my nuts and legs had fighting room. My toes curled in my Nike Airs. She sucked my balls, jacking just the head of my passion, looking me deep in my narrowed eyes. Sensations tempting me to bend her over the sofa, my mouth hung open from the pleasure.

She said, "I remember when we fucked on my graduation night, baby…You had some good dick, Daddy..."

I empathized with her, knowing I was a scum bag. "Baby, I didn't mean to. I wanted you. Yea, baby, suck them nuts, goddamn baby." I held her head, guiding her lips up and down on my dick.

"You were…" Slurp, slurp. "Good,

Daddy, the way you beat my tight pussy, the way you fucked me in the ass. It felt so right and so good."

I was stunned. I thought I doped her up good. I was a little nervous. What if she told her father? He'd shoot my ass, and I was scared of that Niggah. What if her husband found out? Now that I think about it, I think Sax does know.

I was in love, I wanted her, I needed her. "I can do a repeat right now."

"Let me get your first nut out of the way." She sucked me really good; she upped the ante, pulled out all the tricks. Damn. She sucked my dick like she loved it, like the world was about to explode. She tasted my nuts, spat on my dick, made it super wet, the way I loved and she gave me that hot mouth. I had my hands over my face, my hat falling on the floor. My hips were out of control. I felt the heat rising, mixing with the cold air, creating in the base of my testicles a tornado, spewing my seeds into a rage. I was about to come and I said it amidst a plethora of moaning, my loins locked up, she sucked harder and faster, making my nuts bounce on her open palm. Damn! I loved being a man! I loved pussy! Damn I was addicted! Come spurted from the hole of my dick and I started screaming when she bit my dick like it was a Vienna sausage, sank her teeth deep in my skin, she punched me in the nuts and I was trapped amongst the worst pain in my life. Blood was everywhere as a terrible stinging sensation shot through my body, why was she doing this? Why did she attack me?

She felt betrayed; I could see the hurt on her face. "You *drugged* me, bitch! *And* you raped me! I didn't *remember* that shit, I lied, leading you on! You're the reason why I haven't even fucked my own husband yet, why I caused him so much grief, because I tried to understand why I woke up a day after my graduation with my asshole and pussy throbbing and hurting!" She slapped me so hard my head slammed into the edge of the sink. I held my head, moaning piteously.

"You will pay, motherfucker!"

She took the frying pan from the dish rack and all I remembered was blacking out on the floor when she brutally beat me in the head with it, screaming in a fit of rage.

X'ed out in my own Ex Files.

Jadish walked out to her car, running her hands up and over her skirt. She felt like a huge burden, a huge weight, was lifted off her shoulders. She felt she could breathe, the chains of the unknown snapping free, releasing her from bondage. She felt whole, like a real woman, and not a zombie, coming and going throughout her life because she didn't understand why she felt the way she felt after her graduation. She knew something wasn't right with her body, she knew it then, but couldn't prove it. And now she knew the truth.

Tommy lost her trust forever.

She called her father.

"Hey, Dad. Where are you?"

"With your husband. He says hi."

"Tell him I love him."

"She said she loves you, Sax," her Dad said, his voice a little distant.

She heard her baby say, "I love you, sweetheart. See you when I get home."

"Dad, give Sax the phone."

"Damn it, why can't you call him on his own fucking phone?"

"Because I pay your cell phone bill."

"Low blow."

"And I pay Mama's bills."

"She's your Mama, you're supposed to."

"No," said Jadish, getting in her car and leaving Tommy's house forever. "You're supposed to be paying her bills."

He avoided the imposing argument. "Here's Sax."

"Hey, baby," he said, faking.

"Hello, Sax. When are you coming home?"

Does it matter? Am I gonna get to fuck? "In about an hour."

"Make sure you do."

He sucked his teeth. "Whatever, and do the same thing, hug, kiss, maybe a little rubbing, cuddle, watch TV, and go to sleep. Wow, I'm really looking forward to that."

She smiled, turning up R. Kelly's old school cut "Your Body's Calling," from the 12 Play album (his best album) on the radio. She snapped her fingers, bobbed her head and said, "I'm looking forward to it, too, baby."

And she hung up.

I, Baxter Douglass, immediately jumped in the shower when I got home. Sharon, a fine ass dime piece, called me on my cell phone and told me those life changing words.

"When you're coming to get this pussy?"

"Shit, you don't gotta tell me twice."

I've been waiting on this pussy for fifteen days. I was the type of Niggah who got the panties within seconds of meeting women. I wasn't trying to be serious. Hell, I had fourteen baby Mamas from here to Beaumont, Texas. I beat all their asses, too. I used to pimp nine of them, had those bitches slangin' pussy like the shot put at the Olympics. One of my Baby Mama's worked at Target Superstores in Beaumont. She put me on child support. Called my phone, talking all kinda crap. "My new man called your son his own and your son called him Daddy!"

"Don't get homeboy fucked up!"

"Die, Niggah! You *better* have the money in the mail or that's your ass, faggot!"

"Watch your mouth!"

"You are tutti-frutti! All the threesomes we had with Niggahs, to please your appetite! What about when I spanked your ass with a dildo! Talk about *that*!"

I was steaming. "All right, Ho! You're *pushing* me!

The truth hurt, but my sex life and what I do in the bedroom and inside cars in the bushes was on the low. I never discussed this and she pulled my card.

What she said had me upset. Ate away at me. I hated lippy bitches.

I had to do something about it.

No one stepped on my manhood.

No one!

Angrily quiet, I booked a flight online, cheaptickets.com. I paid out the ass. I didn't care. I had money to burn. I packed a small bag and printed out the confirmation page. Folding it, I stuffed it in my wallet and locked my crib. Hopping in my car, I headed for the freeway.

An hour later, I was in the air via Continental Airlines.

When I got to Dallas/Ft. Worth Airport, I had a rental on standby. Took me thirty minutes to find her crib. I smoked two blunts and intoxicated myself with a few natural Ice beers. I stopped by a liquor store and bought a pint of vodka and killed it before I made it back to the rental car.

I called her and she answered with an attitude. I could remember when she used to be the sweetest girl in the world. I told her I wasn't sending her any money. By now I was plastered and zonked. She talked shit; I was parked under a huge tree in front of her house, watching her pace back and forth around her living room. Her man was in the background running his jaws. I saw him now, barking over her shoulder. Some thug dude. Rag on his head, pants sagging. Unlaced Timberland boots. Smoking a blunt.

"We getting' dat money, Niggah!" he kept rapping. "I need some new threads, Punk!"

My eyes clouded over.

Showtime.

I knocked on the door.

"Tammy. I give you enough money!" I said into the phone.

"The police gonna put your sorry ass in jail! Hold on, lemme see who at the door."

I pounded on her door.

"Who is it? Stop bamming on my door like you the muthafuckin' police—"

The door swings open and my fists slams into her face. She falls back into the wall, her ponytail flying from her head, landing in the fish tank and her cordless phone hitting ole boy in the head. I had on black gloves, Goose Down jacket and unlaced Timberland boots. I tied her ass pussy ass up. Ole boy jumped in my face and I bitch slapped him, and brutally punched him in his stomach.

"My son called you Daddy, Niggah? No, I can't have that." I was standing over him, with a boot-clad foot pressed on his face, bending his nose. "You want to buy some threads with my cash, Niggah?" He tried to plea bargain. I reminded him I wasn't a judge, I didn't look like a Prosecutor and I wasn't on parole.

I tied a sock around her mouth, dragged ole boy in the room, closed and locked the door and showed him how RuPaul got fucked in the ass. When I was done I pissed on his punk ass, and went out into the living room and beat her so bad she dropped child support on me real fast. I grew up being emotionally abused; my Daddy beat me so badly I couldn't walk. He always told me to get revenge on anyone who screwed you over, and if it came down to it get revenge on bitches before they get it on you. I was raised tough. Had to fight everyday of my life.

I told her, "I will send you some loot. If you spend my hard earned money on your boyfriend, the fish g'on order a Happy Meal on the house and get chicken, you feelin' me, bitch?"

She was a good little girl. She followed my directions. I should know: I paid two Niggahs to keep tabs on her at all times. I was gangster like that. I heard she left her boyfriend; he was now turning tricks, dressing in drag. I always said I had the type of dick that turned men into bitches.

Pushing all that to the back of my mind, I had to get to Sharon today. Unfortunately, I didn't have that much time. My apartment in Kendall no one knew about. I sold dope from here. Everyone thought I lived in rundown, pissy Perrine, not too far from Bell Short Stop, a convenient store that had seen better days. I had one couch, a pit-bull roaming around inside, and my drugs stashed in the walls.

I met Sharon a few weeks ago at the Super Wal-Mart in Florida City. I had just gotten off work, as a Pharmaceutical employee at a drug store, South Beach. My lesbian co-worker, a woman named Red, had been on my mind lately. She actually fell in love with a chick named Fate Williams, rumored to have been abused by her own mother. That night I drove to Southwest Dade to see my mother, Veronica, because she said she needed some cash. Her social security check was late, and she only had fifty dollars left on her American Flag-clad food stamp card. I loved Mama; I had to look out for her, since I was her only son. She tried her best to help me release the anger I have on the inside. She didn't understand how I could go from being a good kid to being a rebellious man with a gun-toting problem. Blame that on Daddy not really spending time with me. Blame that on watching Mama struggle when my Dad…I couldn't think about it now.

I did have an education. Thug by day, schoolbooks at night. I always made good grades, but I loved fast cash and ass. When I was eight years old I knew I'd have the profession I have now. I used to watch my uncles cook crack on the stove. They used baking soda to confuse drug consumers. My uncles were straight gangsters, would shoot you dead without losing any sleep. The number of people they snubbed would leave one in awe, in a bad way.

They drank liquor 'til the sun came up. That's how we do down in these parts and they smoked weed.

Once I gave Mama three hundred dollars, which I already knew she was going to blow away at the BINGO in Naranja, across from McDonald's, I grabbed my keys from her dining table. Kissing her cheek, I fondly squeezed her aging hands, giving her a loving look. My head lowered, I slowly walked through her moth-ball-smelling living room I was raised in with my late father, Earl, who died at the hands of my Mama's oldest brother. Dad cheated him out of a thousand bucks during a crap game.

Driving in my Cadillac Escalade was uneventful. I shed tears for my father, who was a good man. Unfortunately, bad things befell him. I felt guilty about his death. I blamed myself. I was fifteen years old. Just lost my virginity and was on my way to tell my Daddy about it. Mama always told me to save my dick for marriage, but I wanted to fuck like my peers were doing. School wasn't about work, it was about pussy, football games and having a good time, or so I thought. I wore nice clothes, had big money, by robbing motherfuckers left and right. I also did my crimes solo, never told a soul. But one robbery left someone dead, and I kept quiet about it.

With all these unwanted thoughts swirling around in my head like clockwork, nakedly I get in the tub, the hot water washing over my tired, sore body. I rest my palms flat on the light blue tile, the last of the Miami sunlight fading to hints of a half-moon affair. I felt elated, about this girl, Sharon. When I met her she was shopping at Wal-mart. She wore the tightest pink sweatpants I'd even seen. She had big titties elegantly hiding behind a ruffled top, with a huge medallion dead center. She had rosy cheeks, a friendly smile, soft skin trapping the flare of store lights and perfect white teeth. She walked like poetry, and I was straight hip-hop.

I just had to approach her. Soft as all outdoors. "Excuse me, Miss. May I get your name, I'm Baxter, but you can call me Bax."

"Nice name." She shook my hand. Then I kissed it, my protruding, luscious lips falling on soft skin with the aplomb of honey bees on petals. She seemed to get wet between the legs. They shook a little, I pretended not to notice.

She said "I'm Sharon."

You are so gorgeous. She looked like Meagan Goode, the actress. I couldn't breathe. "Are you single?"

"Nope. Gotta man."

"Damn he's lucky. He lets you shop solo?"

"No. He's in here, he just went to get some grapes, and things for the salad we're having tonight."

"Well damn, can I come over for dinner?"

"Sure, why not."

I gazed deep into her eyes. She licked her lips. The sign I needed. I slid my hands in my pockets. "Seriously?"

"Yea, just as long as you don't come up in my house all rowdy, Niggah."

We laughed like old friends.

"So, I'ma be straight. I just wanna have sex."

"You gotta work for this lovin', baby," she informed me.

She looked me dead in the eyes. The chemistry would shatter test tubes the world over. I wanted to fuck. She wanted to fuck. My dick was rock hard; I had on brown Dickies pant and my white pharmacy coat, opened to reveal a Bob Marley shirt. My hair was a Caesar's cut, nicely trimmed along the edges, leading into a very thin, geometrically daring mustache, beard and goatee.

"So when can a Niggah hit?"

She brushed off my coat. "Give me your number. I'll call you.

Now it was going to happen. I was in a pair of jeans, T-shirt and Jordan sneakers in twenty minutes. I dabbed cologne on my nuts, wrists and neck. I didn't put on briefs or socks. Elated, I turned off my cell phone, locked up my crib and took the turnpike to her house.

She lived in the Redlands, way out in the boonies. When I pulled up to her house I saw her fixing food, setting plates on the table. I smiled easily.

Cutting the engine, I popped a few Tic Tacs into my mouth, and walked up to the door. She had an amazing spread. Six bedroom four bath home. Well-tended lawns. I knocked on the door and she answered, clad in a robe. We stood there staring at each other. I was on fire. I just wanted to fuck. I wasn't trying to wreck her happy home. No promises. No woman, no cry type shit. Bend over, give me a shot of pussy, let me get my nut and I was out.

Licking her sensual lips, she opened the robe and bare tits stared me in the face. I was rock hard. She had on ruffled panties. Looked real cute on her. Grabbing her ass, I pulled her up to me and gave her some tongue. She sucked it tenderly; I opened my mouth wide so she could do so.

I picked her up, kicked the door closed, ignoring the little shiatsu dog. He barked so much I kicked him across the room, laying Sharon on the couch. The dog runs upstairs whimpering. Little bitch, stay up there. Zebra skinned rugs. Matching throw pillows. A breathtakingly gorgeous bar by the back door, soft classical music playing.

She runs her hands across my waves.

"The Atlantic Ocean up there, 'ey?" I asked her, kissing her breasts. My tongue sensually circling her nipple. I used my fingertips to trail her arms, her thighs, her stomach, her legs and her inner thighs. She cooed playfully, arching her back. I squeezed the titties together and run my tongue over both nipples, my head going side to side. I was straddled over her on the table. I gave her an eternity of pleasure this way. I pulled out my dick, and put it in her mouth. My pants barely covered my ass, but I didn't care. She squeezed her titties on my pulsating member and she tit fucked me. Felt so good, I humped her breasts, never did this before. But I liked trying new things.

I decided I had enough after I came all over her mouth, face and breasts with a ball busting jolt that had my toes on lock. I massaged my juices into her skin, giving it that rich texture. She told me to eat her pussy. I said why not.

I started licking around the Panty Region, hair was all over the place. I liked pubic hair, so I ran my tongue all over her panties. Every so often I had to keep pulling hair from my damn teeth. I wanted to eat pussy, not floss!

"Baby, oooh wee, tassstee me, babbyy!"

"Want Daddy to taste this pussy?"

"Yes!"

With one hand, I slowly pulled off her wet panties, trailing fingertips over her skin, giving her butterflies in her stomach, like the magician I was. When the panties come off her legs are closed, she's teasing me so I opened her legs, put my face between them and I froze. She had so much goddamn hair I thought it was Groundhog's Day. She had hair all over the goddamn place. I was mad! I couldn't even *see* the pussy. How could this fine ass woman have jacked pussy hairs like this? I got some choice words for her: Hygiene, bitch! I was fuming. I went through all that hell, of getting ready and shunning much needed sleep. I drove out half my gas tank coming to the Redlands, thinking I was getting some quality pussy and I wound up with a ferret with too much hair! Were you fucking serious, woman?

Wanting to puke, I inserted a finger inside her warm flesh anyway, determined to get this hairy pussy and my hand fell in like a penny inside a wishing well, nothing gripping the sides. Her pussy was ruined! God! I hated ruined pussy!

My eyes were laser beams. "Baby," I told her, mad as fuck. "I forgot my rubbers in the car, I'll go get them."

"My brother has some in the room."

"Your brother?"

"The one who was at Wal-Mart with me, I told you he was my man. He's really my brother, he's mentally challenged."

So is your pussy! I wanted to say but I refrained."

I got my own, give me a second." I gave her some tongue, keeping the act up. She smiled so sweetly, damn she was beautiful! But her pussy was sloppy, slaughtered as we say down south.

I buckled my pants, grabbed my wallet and keys and went outside, looking back at her.

"Give me a second." Closing the door I ran to my ride, hopped inside, and turned the key in the ignition and hot-rod out of there. I was more disappointed than I was angry.

I wasn't about to handle all that hair.

I'll leave it to beaver.

The Legendary Necklace

Love. Tell me something about it that I didn't know. Love was patient. Well. Sometimes. It was understanding. Well, that was until you put sex in the mix, then you loved fucking and not the *nature* of love anymore. Love didn't boast…well, that was until you found a helluva sexy black man to show off. Then he became your trophy. You polished his good dick. Kept him satisfied. Put him on the shelf until the sun rose. Took him out in public. Dressed him up like Ken dolls. Let him drive your Nissan Maxima all over Dade County with a killer stereo system that you could hear blocks away. Took him to all the parties. Bitches were jealous that you had him and *they* didn't. Then when the moon got off the recliner and trekked her sexy ass across starry skies, back on the shelf your "Trophy" went.

Which brought me to my boyfriend of three years? Legendary Bridgewater.

I've loved this man from day one. He was attentive and inspiring. He had goals outside of the ghetto, where we lived at the time. He had passion, and we all knew that without it you truly didn't have the desire to live. He loved my mind; he loved the way I thought. He appreciated the black woman that lived deep inside me. Taught me how to talk as opposed to cursing. This was a first. Because the black men I was used to dating, fucking and yea, "raising like little boys," completely lost my trust. They tried to run game on me. Tell me our relationship was one way and it turned out to be another way with other women thrown in the mix to make Jerry Springer rethink his defunct career. He showed me true love. Cooked for me. Gave me expensive things without trying to "buy" my love. He never tried to change me, if anything, he tried to do a Beyonce: "Upgrade" me to living a better life.

He had a quiet sex appeal about himself. He didn't make trouble. He had no idea how sexy he was. But let me paint the picture for you. He had the creamiest skin of chocolate with almonds. In fact I loved his...nuts. Hazel eyes that trapped everything from the sunlight to bedroom candles with such aplomb it left me breathless. He was 6 feet 8 inches, two diamond earrings, eleven tats (of Nefertiti, Ramses the III, Akhenaton, Queen Hatshepsut and a few other Egyptian pharaohs, he loved Africa); his huge booty made even the homosexuals swoon when he walked by with a swagger stank of the type of aura the dope boys truly appreciated; and he wore a size 17 shoe, and yes, his dick was over half of that, thick, long and full.

He was the sole reason I stopped thinking all men were dawgs. Not "Dogs," but D-A-W-G-S! Straight up mutts! He called me whenever he stepped out; I always knew where he was. When he wasn't working he was home, being with me, or working out at the gym, or cooking, reading, studying, since he was trying to get his major in, shit, I forget, couldn't think of it right now. He opened doors for me. If men stepped to me in public, trying to flirt, he remained quiet. He didn't get mad. He wasn't outspoken about it. He didn't disrespect me, himself or embarrass us. He left the dialogue up to me. And of course I always said, "Look, this is my man right here, so I appreciate the love, but please don't disrespect my dude."

I always got a "No problem, Ma." And they still tried to get at me when he turned his back looking at shirts or admiring the scene around him. That's when I got stupid, and it took Legendary to pull me off the Niggahs.

And vice-versa. If women stepped to him, I left the talking to him. He never got upset, embarrassed me, or tried to hug me and slip another woman's phone number in his pocket; I knew all the little tricks. I felt totally comfortable and safe around my man. It has gotten to the point where I would do anything for him, give him anything he wanted, just to keep him home with me. I trusted him and I trusted his judgment, something most young girls couldn't and wouldn't understand. We spent so many days and nights getting to know each other. I knew him inside and out. I knew what made him happy and what made him sad.

We moved out of the ghetto about eight months after we started dating. We lived together, learned each other's habits, what we could and couldn't live with. He was neat and easy going. Very organized. He cooked and cleaned better than I did, which I truly appreciated 'cause a bitch wasn't about to play Martha Stewart Living anytime soon. We went through so many channels to get our first home on Campbell Drive, in a newly built community, fresh with a brand new elementary school and all, by Malibu Bay. I loved it, despite the $1,200 a month mortgage tag, but we made it work.

He was a church-going man. A little shy; he didn't take too kindly to people calling him "sexy" or "fine." In fact the more people told him that the more inferior he became. Which was all gravy to me because I was a dime piece myself, 19-24-36, little tits in other words, but enough junk in my trunk to stop the garbage men twice a week, when they collected my trash. I even told them I had a man, and like the old school cut went, "What your man got to do with me?" they would ask me, meaning every word.

I would have answered the lingering question, but one day, when Legendary came home early from work—he worked at the Fort Lauderdale Airport, made good money—and stepped out of his Chrysler with the Bentley front frame, the men suddenly got really quiet. He offered them cold Zephyrhills waters, shook their hands and didn't show an ounce of jealousy. I admired that about him. Quite frankly, his nonchalant attitude scared the garbage men so badly they never stopped by my house again.

And the sex! God, the sex! It took us a month to finally fuck. And it was really driving me crazy, because, *yes*, I fucked on the first date. I was a grown woman, and real women didn't put time and restraints on the inevitable. I jumped in the hay and popped my pussy until I came. Had to test drive the stick shift before I committed to buy. Had to ride the clutch. Simple as that. I didn't want to be committed to a strokeless, dickless man. Size was everything to me. Yes I was a Size Queen. The motion in the ocean was for simple bitches. Not me. As long as I could ride it then damn it the rest was history. I didn't do dicks that were 7 or below. Just not my cup of tea. But in my case. It wasn't my cup of dick.

He said that he had his share of wham, bam, thank you madams. That he didn't want to rush with me. That every time he started a relationship with sex, that's what it became: a *relationsex*, not a relationship and that always concluded into being a relation*shit*. And he didn't want that with me. I didn't want it either.

So he spent time talking to me, taking me

out, spending quality time and asking me about my goals. He wanted to know my dreams and what I was going to do to achieve them. That was high on his priority list. I told him I wanted to be a published author like my favorite author Teresa D. Patterson, who wrote a too fabulous book called *It's your World Black Girl*, which I absolutely, positively loved! I liked her better than raunchy ass Zane. Now don't get me wrong, I loved Zane, thought she was amazingly talented, but Teresa was it for me.

So he bought me the priciest computer from Best Buy electronics store, a Gateway, with laser printer and he persuaded me to write. So I have been doing that everyday. Writing on my computer, and he has been my best and worst critic. Since he was an avid reader, currently reading Eric Jerome Dickey's *Liar's Game* (his favorite author), he couldn't wait to read my stuff.

I remembered when we did finally bump and grind. It was after my mother's 50th birthday party. I was helping Mama clean the dishes, everyone had gone home. Mama loved Legendary, she said she might even adopt him, I was like "Mama you can't adopt a grown man."

Curtly, she looked at me with love in her eyes. She was cute in her pink apron. She was battling osteoporosis and social security was fucking her over so I had to look out for Mama. She put the left-over Mac and cheese in the fridge. "Yes I can. Plus he's very loving. He's certainly better than any man *you* ever had."

"I know, right?" I was wiping the counters, clad in black coveralls. I had changed out of my slamming Gucci dress, because I didn't want to mess it up. I was Miss Prixy when I wanted to be— too cute for my own goddamn good.

She eyed me, sipping some wine. Looking ghetto fabulous for her age, Mama had a body that would make Halle Berry turn gay. "And God knows I wondered when you were going to get it right."

I rolled my eyes, and my heels clicked across the fake marble floors. I sat at the dining table, using my fingers to dig up some icing from the cake. Yummy. "Mama. Don't start."

Exhaling audibly, Mama sat across from me, handing me a cold beer. I loved beer, just like I loved my man. "Seriously, you had two yeast infections, an HIV scare, three miscarriages, four abortions and one delusional ass Niggah trying to shoot you before you found Legendary."

Now see, I was upset. Why did she go there like that? That hurt for Mama to say, but Mama represented the truth and she was one way everyday. She wasn't some-timing like most of my friends and family.

Before I could start an argument, despite my respect for her, Legendary entered the kitchen from one of the bedrooms, leaned to kiss Mama's cheek, and then he kissed me. He said, "Baby can I talk to you, alone please?"

Mama stood up. "Ya'll can talk in here, I gotta go shower. Lock my front door when ya'll leave, I do stay alone."

"Got you, Mama." She hugged me and kissed my lips. I was still mad at her. After squeezing my hand fondly, she vanished upstairs and a few minutes later I heard her blasting Tyrone Davis and the shower came on after that. Mama showered for an hour or so.

He made me stand up. I studied his face, he looked bothered. I asked, "What is wrong, baby?"

"I'm just pissed."

"Why?"

"My ex girlfriend, Kizzy Lyons, called me, threatening to take me court for child support, and I don't have any kids by her," he said discerningly. "I really don't have time for this type of discomfiture."

I wasn't that bothered by it. Women always tried this tactless shit on men. "Then why would she threaten you? You dealing with her is disconcerting enough."

He was steaming. "Because my dumb ass put down I was the child's father on the birth certificate. Back then I guess I was being fanciful, instead of being realistic. Caught up in the idea of being a good father to someone's child and trying to do the right thing."

I always loved his honesty. He held nothing back, no matter how much it may hurt. "Baby, just take a DNA test. The answers lie in the results. Then we could forefend the bitch forever."

He was deeply depressed. Heartbreakingly, I kept quiet. I hated to see him in any type of pain. "I told her that, but she refused. Then I had to go through the hysterics."

I'll stomp the bitch! "You can set up a court date." I thought about it. "Want me to shoot the Ho?"

We laughed playfully, but I was deadly serious. Either that or I'll cut the Ho with my rusty razor. "Nah. I don't need my woman fighting my battles. I feel clabbered enough."

I was uncomfortable. "This seems so laissez-faire."

"Unfair is more like it…" He smiled faintly. "…You can kiss me."

I softened up; suddenly Kizzy Lyons was

a distant memory. The chemistry built dramatically. I saw longing in his eyes. "But that might lead to teasing and temptation and we haven't fucked yet."

He gave me some tongue. Leaned back and looked at me. Eyes glowing. His dick rock hard. I squeezed it, then quickly pulled my hands away. Damn it I needed him in that sexual way, it's been a month. I kissed him again, this time we kissed long and hard, rubbing and feeling. He pulled off my coveralls, ass naked in Mama's kitchen.

I could hardly breathe. "What about Mama?" I asked breathlessly.

He kissed my left breast. "She had her Dick Fun over the years, time to give you some Dick Fun."

I was nervous. Mama was a nut case when you did freaky shit in her house and you weren't helping pay bills. "Wow, baby. Are you *serious*? Not in Mama's kitchen."

"I love your Mama but fuck her kitchen. Give me my pussy right here, right now or wait another goddamn month—"

He didn't have to tell me twice. He lay me on the dining table, took a huge piece of Mama's birthday cake and smeared it on my pussy, asshole and titties, diving in and having a bite of the good stuff. Yea, he tasted good pussy. I damn near died, he was incredibly breathtaking, and never did I dream he was this sensual and poignant with his tongue.

"Your…cake taste good," he said softly, moaning as his tongue divided thy pink walls and conquered thy clitoris with the zeal of Shakespeare and that untalented fuck was dead. Shakespeare stole his plays, but my man inherited good pussy eating skills from the sands of time, which separated him from the rest.

He ate forever. I was shuddering, shaking, going through a cornucopia of feelings, a plethora of emotions. I didn't know if I wanted to die or cry. My feelings were a bit inconspicuous at the moment.

He pushed my legs back, ran his slick tongue from the pussy to the asshole, tongue fucking my rectum until I shuddered with pure bliss. I was moaning as quietly as I could. All I seen was his head bobbing.

He got bored easily, so he turned me on my stomach and spread my ass cheeks and put his face all up in my hole again, running his tongue across my chocolate like he was auditioning for the Charmin Toilet Paper commercials. He felt so good, so right. He sucked my pussy, spreading my legs, lifting me to my knees, pushing my face down. He leaned back and admire the eighth, ninth and tenth Wonder of the World. He spanked my ass repeatedly, in a way that enhanced his performance, my ass jiggling like Jell-o.

Without further ado he got his big ass up on my Mama's table and slowly slid his hardened nature deeply inside me, pausing, letting it sit there for a few minutes, so my tight pussy could get used to the feeling of a tomb raider trying to unearth the Nefertiti in my freak bone. He kissed the "Akhenaton" tat, and he tongue kissed me passionately, his amazingly experienced hips coming alive. He felt SO WONDERFUL! His long strokes took my breath away. He was very good at what he did. My rainfalls wet him all up. He moaned softly, his lips by my ear, sucking the back of my neck, pulling me up to him as he tapped that ass from the back, I was gyrating myself all over him, wanting him, needing his energy, feeding from his urgency, he was touching my pussy in ways my soul appreciated.

I felt the rise of smoke in my loins, the feel of elation stunned me. I was jubilant and beautiful, sultry and demanding. I felt myself drifting as I began exploding all over him. He laughed in my ear, "Yea baby, let's get it together," and he began coming deeply inside me. Together we moaned and exploded. I was hoping we were going half on a baby. Shit, I wasn't going to lie. A man with dick this good deserved a baby.

When we subsided, moaning and sweaty, Mama said, "Now get ya'll asses off my goddamn table, go rent a hotel room and Legendary, take my girl's hand in marriage. You aren't gonna be giving her *yeast* infection number three, you hear me?" she asked with a satisfied smile on her face.

My heart dropped, Mama caught us, but she winked at me in a way that told me that everything was all right.

He helped me get off the table, my pussy sore, maybe because I haven't had any activity in my tomb in a long time. Once I put on my cargo jumpsuit and he put on his Sean John attire, I kissed Ma goodbye, and when he tried to she said, "Now I watched you eat pussy and cake, don't think you g'on give me a pussy kiss. Just don't flow like that, Jack. And I saw you licking her all in the ass." Oh, no! He covered his face, I covered my ears. Jesus strike me dead, NOW! "Didn't I tell you she was a shitty baby when she was little. All she did was shit, shit, shit!"

Oh my God! He was so embarrassed; I couldn't stop laughing with Mama. He tried to laugh it off, but we both could tell by the look on his face that his stomach was in knots.

"Now ya'll go home. And before you leave, I need a hundred dollars each, because ya'll fucked in my goddamn kitchen. I will never eat my cake quite the same. And Legendary, do your new Mama-n-law a favor, write on a scrap piece of paper how you did the hurricane tongue with the cake so I can pass it to my man on the side, I gotta try that shit!"

She was slapping her knees, laughing so hard. I tried to hold it in, and when he looked me in the face, I burst open, slob falling from my mouth, I couldn't breathe. Now he was mad. After he broke her off proper, we had never run so fast in our lives, laughing like school kids all the way to his Chrysler.

We would spend the next ten months love making. He was gentle, very loving, he loved foreplay, loved giving me head before I sucked him off. He made it interesting, fun and exciting every time. When he kissed my clit and sucked the walls of my pussy I felt beautiful, like I could conquer the world. He never stopped until I came. He was smooth. He spoke to you without seemingly trying to prove himself. He always told you that you tasted sweet, and he described it. Like last night, when he ate me out, he told me I tasted like watermelon. That was because he had dumped diced watermelon all over my enticing body parts and he gave a new name to the word "foreplay" that led to floor-play.

I wasn't a fan of the Sucking Dick Club. But when I gave him head, he truly *loved* it. He'd rub my face; look at me like I was the most beautiful woman in the world. He was creative, sometimes leaving on his Timberland boots. Sometimes he turned on some old school music and sung to me while I polished him up. He was nasty and freaky without coming off as predictable and tacky. When he slid up in me, he did it with zeal, taking his time, studying what worked for me and always asking me questions.

"Baby does that feel good to you...how do you like it when I stroke the Kat like that? You love my dick, baby? Take this shit, pretty lady..." Drove me crazy!

I was happy when he decided to take his ex girlfriend to court and demanded a DNA test. I hated the fact that her five year old, cute little boy had to be pulled in the middle. He looked nothing like Legendary. The court, over a couple weeks, ordered the paternity test. Shockingly, she listened and obeyed the judge's orders. When the test came back the following week, it turned out he was *not* the father, totally freeing him from her clutches forever. She bitched and moaned in court, saying that Legendary was the only father her son, Legendary Bridgewater, Jr, had ever known. That he had his "father's name." How could he just walk away? I felt so bad. The child shouldn't *have* to suffer, so he offered to adopt his "son at heart," and I supported him. Because it was what he wanted. Another court date was made, and a few months later Legendary, Jr. legally had a father.

I would grow close to him. He'd come every weekend and spend with us. We built an amazing relationship. He liked me, and I thought he was a sweet little black boy, full of promise and life. He loved Bugs Bunny and Disney movies, I would constantly be at it with his mother, who thought she could come in my crib, because Legendary was her son, and tell me how to run my shit. My man had to pull me off this Ho a number of times.

That was two years ago.

I was going through his wallet this morning, while he was in the shower, and I was going to take forty dollars because I didn't feel like going to the ATM. His money was mine and mine was his, everything was jointly owned. When I took out two crisp twenty dollar bills I noticed his wallet-sized photos. I looked really pretty in my pink dress in one pose, so I flipped to another of me with a black leopard-print pants suit. I remembered that pose; I took it last year at the Dade County Youth Fair, by F.I.U., the college. But the third picture made me freeze up with rage. He had a photo of his ex girlfriend, the bitch who cheated on him and gave birth to another man's baby.

"What the *fuck*?" I asked myself, and I heard him turning the shower off, humming an Aretha Franklin cut. I was fuming. I stood in the door way, just waiting for the door to open. I had never heard of him speak of his ex. In fact he told me he hated her, that he never wanted to see her again, yet he had her photo all up in his wallet, how did you explain that? Did he forget to take it out? Before I jumped to conclusions I would ask him.

The only contact he had with Kizzy was talking to her about his son. And once the subject ended, he hung up. He never went to see her, and the faith I had in him was tugging at my heart, telling me not to flip out.

I didn't know what to do, really. I never really had to question him. When he went to see her concerning his son he always called or offered that I come along, but I trusted him, so I let him deal with the clueless bitch. He was a good father. I loved that about him.

I heard him going through the cabinets in the bathroom. I put my hand on the door knob and slowly opened the door. Steam erupted into the bedroom; I fanned steam away, and looked at him. Dripping wet, his sexy body made my pussy wet. I wasn't even going to question him anymore. He would never hurt me, how could he hurt me, he was faithful to me, catered to me and his child. His co-workers loved him. I adored him.

Just when I was about to close the door he opened the medicine cabinet, took out a few bottles of Tylenol pills, and opened a secret compartment. He took out a folded piece of paper. My mouth fell open in shock, I didn't know he had a secret compartment in the medicine cabinet; guess Niggahs really did have secrets, no matter how Mr. Rodgers they seemed.

Sitting on the toilet he read silently, hot tears running down his face. He was wiping them away.

My heart bled, what had my baby in tears? What was going on?

Was it the letter from his Dad? His Dad did die a long time ago.

Maybe he was reminiscing about the old days, wishing his Dad was here to share in the joy of raising an adopted son.

That had to be it; he always talked about his Dad.

I closed the door and let him be to himself.

I put his wallet up and decided to drive to the ATM machine and withdraw $40 of my own money.

And give my man his time.

When I got home his car was gone. I looked at my watch. It was well after 9 a.m. Yup. My baby was at work.

I couldn't get my mind off my man. His secret pain. The way he always put on a brave face, yet never really talked about his dead father. Most black men I knew were so bravado about their secret pain, because they thought society would frown down on them for showing even a hint of emotion. So faux paw in my opinion, yet I didn't want to push myself on him. Legendary was the type that would come to you when and if he wanted to talk or vent. He did have a stubborn streak in him that I hated, but for the most part, I could tolerate his flaws to the T.

His Mama was in the Airforce for twenty-eight years, retired in Germany a Master Sergeant. She never came back to the states. He said she had no desire to come back to such a repressed country that would bash Janet Jackson, a successful black woman, over a white boy yanking our her titty at the Superbowl Halftime Show a couple years back; yet praise Bush for cheating to get into office, and praise Madonna for tongue kissing Britney Spears in front of children at the MTV Awards some time ago. He said her beliefs meant a lot to her considering she didn't like Janet Jackson or her music. But the way the world bashed the "black woman," and was now praising the slut Anna Nicole Smith, former Playgirl Playmate who was found dead in Fort Lauderdale, Florida further told her that America was no longer for her.

His father had been dead five years at the time she retired, and she found a new man shortly after that. One with money, status in the Marines and treated her well. He was always close to her, but when she married the Marines Fluky, he lost that connection with her. She changed her address and phone number, and he never really cared about it, really, said he wasn't a little boy anymore, that as long as she was happy and was being treated like a Queen she could live her life, considering she gave birth to him when she was 13 years old and lost her life trying to raise him, and a good job she did.

All wasn't lost; he did have her email address. Once a week they sent each other emails. He used to show me all the emails his Mom sent about Anna Nicole. That's how he found out his mother detested her. We were all sick of hearing about the bitch, to tell you the truth. This chick had problems that even dead-ass Marilyn Monroe wouldn't want any part of.

In a myriad of thoughts, I went in my bedroom, tossing my purse on the unmade up bed. I was tired. I had to go to work at 2 p.m.; I worked at Publix supermarket as the lead Customer Service representative at the service desk. Been there for about four years.

My baby must have really been pissed because he always made up the bed before he left for work. I couldn't get over the letter he was reading, I wanted to be nosey, yet I didn't wanna go snooping around his shit. That was his secret pain, all his own. Who was I to jeopardize that?

Yet I was a black woman more than a human being so I went into the bathroom, opened the cabinet, took out the bottles of pills, opened the secret compartment, which was cleverly camouflaged to look like the rest of the cabinet and I pulled out the letter.

I closed my eyes and sighed, I shouldn't be invading his space, which was wrong of me.

Yea. My heard pounded, my blood turning cold at the though of betraying such a good man.

I attempted to put it back, and when my eyes locked on "I will always love you, Legendary, you're my life, my strength…" I froze like a block of ice.

The letter wasn't from his father.

It was from Kizzy Lyons.

His ex.

"What. The. Fuck. Is. Going. On?"

The Legendary Necklace Part 2: The Letter

I had to lean against the sink to keep from falling on the floor. All sorts of anger surged through my body, I felt like a hot air balloon about to drift through cloudy skies, blocking my sunshine. Incomputable, I was thinking. Inconsequently, I couldn't reason. My eyes hurt; in fact the more I looked at this letter, the more animosity filled my lungs, killing off my air.

When I worked up enough nerve, I sat on the toilet and read the note, dated December

12, 2004, way before we met. Thank God for that. It was on scented Strawberry Shortcake stationary. What grown bitch wrote notes with Strawberry Shortcake? Grow up, bitch! I thought to myself. The strawberry aroma now smelled like a faint hint of peach. Dying with time, or just fading every time my secretive man locked himself in the bathroom, reading this shit every goddamn night.

When I did open the note I couldn't look at it. I was about to crack open. I was hurting myself. Was I right for snooping, going through my man's shit? Was this truly invading his private space, regardless of the situation? Mama always said when you look for something bad enough you'll find it. But I have already gone to the point of no return, so I might as well finish what I started and read the goddamn note.

Ok. Breathe. Girl. Breathe. It couldn't be. That. Bad. Damn *shame* I had to pump myself up to read something that may or may not end my three plus year relationship with my knight in tarnished armor—tarnished because the motherfucker lied to me. If he lied over the author of this letter then what else did he truly lie about?

That's what I was afraid of finding out.

God shoot me now.

Without further ado, my heart pounding out of my chest, I opened the note.

And began reading…

Dear Legendary,

I love you more than words can express. You are a good man with a good heart. I understand you don't trust me right now, because you think my cousin Harold is actually a man I'm seeing behind your back. But this couldn't be the furthest from the truth. You are the only man I have ever loved. The only man I care to love. I am so thankful you have been a father to my son. I really appreciate that, as a single black woman in such a racist country most women gotta lay on their back just to make ends meet, but you help me so much, you give me money to pay bills, you sometimes cook and clean for me so when I do get home from work all I really have to do is relax. You're selfless and compassionate; you make love like a tyrant. I'm glad we waited about a month or so before we fucked, it was definitely worth it. I won't make this letter too long, because I hate writing, but every night before I go to bed I'm gonna write you a letter, telling you how I feel. I love you.

I seal this with a kiss.

Kizzy Lyons,
Your Baby Mama and your Soul Mate.

I was in tears, quietly crying to myself. The letter was an old one, and definitely confirmed what kind of man he was. Yes, he was selfless, yes he was compassionate and caring, yes, and even with Kizzy he didn't just jump into sex. I smiled, actually smiled. But that was short lived.

I stood up, intending to put his letter back, and I paused. Trying to keep it together I looked into the man made cubby hole in the medicine cabinet and I saw more letters, neatly folded. I also saw photographs. I was simmering now.

Taking out the pictures I looked at them. Of Legendary and Kizzy at the Dade County Youth Fair. Of them out at the Red Lobster having dinner, looking snappily jazzy in church clothes, to tell you the truth. Of them at Disney World, with their son. My heart ripped in two, they looked like one big happy goddamn family! I understood he had a past and he was with other people, but goddamn did that mean you keep this memorabilia under the roof I shared with you? I paid bills here not that dizzy Ho! I felt threatened now, what didn't matter to me months ago now mattered to me at this moment. Had he truly moved on beyond Kizzy? Did he still love her or was he in love with her?

Depressingly sad, I slowly thumbed through the rest of the color photos, in a rut. What do I do? He obviously was holding on to the past; trying to cling to a woman who was trying to ruin his ass and put him on child support. Despite the court's ruling, he did adopt Little Legendary, so the financial burden was still on him, he self-inflicted this on himself and I had to go along with it because I loved him.

I started to put the pictures away when I heard a noise down in the kitchen. Shit, he was home. I didn't care, I wasn't going to act like a scared bitch in my own home, and after all I split the mortgage once a month. Feelings of autonomy eating me alive, I looked at the picture of Kizzy handing Legendary a gift, another picture of him opening it, and another picture of him admiring his gift, which totally pissed me off. My man had lied to me. What did he lie about? *Hmmm.* Putting the photos and the letters up as neatly as I could, I closed the cubby hole, replaced the Tylenol bottles, closed the medicine cabinet and went out into my bedroom. Trying to breathe in and breathe out, I was counting to ten like I was taught in Anger Management class when I was 14 years old, after bashing my ex boyfriend's head in with a bottle when he took my virginity and spread rumors around high school that I was an "easy bitch!"

As cute as a puppy dog, he walked up the hallway, humming happily, a huge smile on his face. He was carrying the most beautiful bundle of red roses. I wasn't a rosy bitch right now.

When he got up to me he gave me a huge hug, the cackle of his leather jacket popping in my ears, he smelled so good, I loved his scent, and I looked forward to smelling my good-looking Niggah everyday. But today I didn't want to smell him; I didn't want him touching me. I was hexed about Kizzy's picture in his wallet. The letters. The photographs. The "special" gift she bought him.

His face beaming. "Hey, baby," he said, kissing my lips. I didn't move mine. They were blocks of ice. I forced a fake smile.

Wrinkles on my forehead. "Sup with you, baby?" I asked him, eyeing the roses. I wanted to slap him with them. "Those for *me*?" *Or for Kizzy, you lying motherfucker?*

"Yes." A huge smile. Like he won the lottery. "These are for my beautiful, *lovely* girlfriend."

He handed them to me. I took them and tossed them on the bed. He just looked at me, really studied me.

"Baby, what's wrong?"

I faked a yawn. "I'm just tired; my period came on early this month." I was lying, was I any better than him?

"Poor baby, anything I can do?"

I eyed the necklace around his neck, I loved that necklace, and it was very valuable to him. His father had given it to him when he was younger and when his Dad died he didn't even let his mother touch it.

A smile. "Yes." Then more contently. "Can I wear your necklace, to ward off the evil spirits in here trying to get me sick? I don't feel too good."

Anger washed over him, but he did a good job of hiding it.

"Now you know I don't let anyone hold this necklace, I don't even take off, even when I shower."

I didn't understand his attitude. Over a necklace? "*Please*, baby? Once upon a time you said you'd do *anything* for me."

Catch-22 dancing in his beautiful eyes, he

closed them, sucking back his anger. "I *did* say that."

I tested him. "And you are a man of your word, right?"

He opened his eyes, a little sad. "Yes."

"So by you telling me I can't wear the necklace basically shows me that you are actually a goddamn liar."

He hated being called a liar, especially when he was a man that claimed to never lie about anything. Well, I knew that was a lie.

"Baby, I didn't lie to you."

He is lying with a straight face! Liar! Fucking asshole! Just tell me the truth goddamn you! "Well," I went on, walking up to him and snatching off the necklace, "you shouldn't mind if I wear this piece of shit necklace!" I spat more angrily than I intended. He was shocked, his mouth hanging open, wide-eyed. I was just getting started. "*What?* Say something, goddamn it! Say something! SAY SOMETHING!"

He was upset, deeply. He grabbed both my arms and shook me. "You just broke the only connection I had to my Daddy—"

I rolled my eyes. "—the only connection—?"

"—how could you do a Niggah like that?"

The guilt trip speech. Shove it up your ass, I am so freaking mad at you! "I'll tell you why," I responded with an attitude, slapping him across the face, wide-eyed myself. Niggah didn't scare me! When were these Niggahs going to realize that just because dick beat pussy didn't mean we were pussies? "Let me read that letter your Dad wrote you, the one you read in the bathroom all the time."

He got quiet. Really cautious, measuring his words. His hands were shaking, so he put them in his pocket. "I can't let you read that, I am very private when it comes to things related to my father."

I was shaking my head. "*Why* is that? If I'm the woman of your dreams, the woman you wanted to one day marry, why all the secrets? *Why* all the lies?"

"I have never lied to you." He didn't even convince himself with that one.

My brows rose so fast I got a migraine in one second flat.

"Really?" I was twirling the necklace, with the little heart-through-another-heart medallion. "*Never* lied." I was twirling it faster. "About nothing?"

"Can I have my Dad's necklace back?"

I challenged him. "Take it from me."

He didn't want to fight with me I could see it on his face.

"Baby, please! Just give it to me."

I was toying with it and he winced trying to keep it together. What was it about this necklace?

"No."

"Baby." He was getting angry.

I wanted to slap him. "What?"

He breathed in. Then breathed out. "Give it to me."

I was defiant. "No, man."

He reached for it and I pivoted. "This is ridiculous."

"Ha. You *lied* to me and *I'm* being ridiculous?"

He felt violated. "I don't have to take this."

"Then don't because, baby I don't have to take this either."

I threw it at him, hitting him on the chest. It fell to the floor faster than a leaf. I calmed my nerves a little bit. "You're sleeping on the couch tonight; you will not get, look at or sniff my pussy until I feel comfortable around you."

I walked over to the nightstand, snatched up my purse and walked towards the bedroom door. "I got someone to go see, I'll be back around 8 p.m., don't wait up for me because I damn sure won't be up thinking about you." I leaned down and picked up the necklace. "I'll take it to get it fixed."

He tried to hug me and I kicked him in the balls, walking around him, angry as hell, and I slammed the room door behind me, keeping to myself the small black velvet box on my bed, next to the roses.

He was going to ask me to marry him today, and I couldn't stop the tears from falling as I hoped into his Chrysler, and burned his gas to hell, speeding up the block.

Headed for my Mama's house.

Disoriented, I got out of my car and killed the engine.

Didn't look like anybody was home. I walked up to the front door, a little cold because the air was chilly. I could hear the leaves of the palm trees rustling, a quiet sound that relaxed me. I put his necklace in my pocket and rang the door bell.

No answer. I lowered my head, sucking in air, ringing the door bell again.

How could he lie to me? Keeping all those old photos of him and Kizzy, in my house. The nerve of him! All the pictures of my old boyfriends he made me put in a safety deposit box at the post office, he raised a stinker just at the thought of me going back in time and reminiscing over the photos, yet he locked himself in the bathroom reading notes from his baby mama?

Chile, please. Make my booty squeeze!

What did I look like?

Punk bitch of the Year?

"Yes," came the soft voice. I held my breath.

Gathering my nerve, I then looked Kizzy deep in her pretty eyes.

Despite my anger, I managed to smile.

She smiled in return.

Easily, I said, "Are you busy? I *need* to talk to you."

Kizzy said, "Sure. Come on in, I know you're cold, girl."

Not as cold as his Daddy's necklace in my pocket.

The necklace with the untold story attached to it, a necklace that was in one of his photos, with "LIE" written all over it.

The Legendary Necklace Part 3: Souls Connected

She offered me some hot tea, which seemed to do the trick. I get cold very fast; the slightest hint of wind would break me out in Goosebumps.

I was sitting on the sofa, looking around her magnificent house. It was a very articulately-decorated house. Furniture with clawed feet. Soft reds and pinks flowing into breathtaking purples. Soft purples, more like lavender. Lavender was Legendary's favorite color.

"What brings you by?" she asked, clad in an African Kimono. Her hair up in rollers. She didn't have on a hint of jewelry. She sipped her tea and said, "Want me to turn on some music or anything?"

I said "No," rather quickly. She blinked a

few times and lit a cigarette. She smoked Kools. I was trying to keep my cool as well.

Setting the huge coffee mug on the low table, next to a picture of Legendary and her son clad in a breathtaking black suit, I never saw the picture before, I said, "So how have you been doing? For some reason you been on my heart."

She smiled easily, searching my face for any sign of flaw. She listened to my words, trying to see if any betrayed me. I was very guardedly cautious.

"I've been good."

"That's good to hear." I leaned back, crossing my legs. I was rubbing my right foot, showing the sign of relief all over my misconstrued face. "How's your son?"

"He's your step son, so its ok to refer to him as 'step-son,' I have no problem with it."

Now I smiled. "Really?" Eyes sparkling. "That means a lot. I am very fond of Legendary, Jr."

"And he's very fond of you." A beat. "He told me you spanked him last week."

OK, I got quiet. This was the part all the fake Kodak moments went out the window and the Ho turned "Cindy Lauper," meaning her true colors was about to shine through brighter than her chandelier lights. "Yea. Nothing abusive or anything…"

She held up her hands, tucking her chin back. "No, its ok. He's a hard headed ass child sometimes. I firmly believe in a village raising a child, like in the old days, before the government stepped in and fucked up American Families."

I inhaled, and then exhaled appreciatively. I thought I had to get Kung Fu on this classy bitch.

"I don't know about American Families, but on Black Families, we are suffering the brut of prejudiced rage."

"Tell me about it, girl. My friend Estelle lost her two boys years ago. Both 14 at the time." She got really quiet, and the silence weighed on my ears like comedian Bruce Bruce was running on my back in a tutu.

I sat up, and said, "Anything happen to…them?"

Her eyes were filled with tears. "Yes. They were identical twins, forced to split up. They were from right here in Miami, girl."

"What part of Miami?" I found myself asking.

"Richmond Heights."

"Really, I am very familiar with the Heights."

"As a matter of fact, they lived in a little

house across the street from Bethel Church."

I frowned at the mention of Bethel Church. Whore Fest U.S.A. Hated to say it, but it was.

"I know a few people who live in that area."

"Girl, you ok with me." She stood up, stretching. "I think I'll turn on some music, how about some old school James Brown."

"Fine with me." I was lightening up. She was acting like a woman with class, so I would reciprocate it. I reached over and took one of her Kools. "Do you mind?"

She dismissed my comment with a wave of her hand. "Girl. Go ahead, I can't smoke all those damn things." She sat next to me, looking me in the face. "But about the two brothers. No one in their immediate family wanted to take them in. They were very responsible young black men, good in English. Were on the verge from graduating high school two years earlier because of their I.Q."

I actually smiled. "I loved English in school. Hell, now I'm thinking back to high school, when I thought I had it all figured out."

"School was a blast. But for the two brothers they wouldn't get the chance to finish…Through some sheer luck the boys were reunited. The judge ordered that they remain together. So once they were reunited, in Chicago, they started going through grief. Don't ask me how they wound up in Chicago's system, still a mystery to me, Chile. One of the boys, Trevor, was found dead in the kitchen's pantry a few months later."

She was getting chocked up, I was covering my mouth in shock. Oh my God! I didn't come here to hear this, I had a chip to get off my shoulder, but suddenly I just realized that there were people in the world with bigger problems than me.

"Who found him?" I asked and she looked at me, shaking her head.

She sipped the tea, sitting on her legs like a little girl. "His brother found him a few days later. They both worked in the kitchen, dish washers. That particular orphanage is notorious for kids getting abused. He went to the kitchen's pantry, because the main cook asked for thirteen cans of creamed corn. And when he opened the door, walking inside—it was one of those huge, organized closets—he turned on the light and the cook, who would be on the news telling the world what happened, dropped a huge hot pot of chicken when James, Trevor's brother, started screaming, a piercing wail that made every kid in the Chow Hall stop and stare, without moving. His brother's throat was slit from ear to ear. With a letter next to him, in his handwriting, stating that he couldn't live without his mother, that he wanted his family back, that he didn't want to live, that he loved his brother but he loved his mother more than himself or his brother."

"God, girl, suicide?"

"Yes."

"What did James do?"

"James didn't want to go on living, he became rebellious, cold-hearted. He blamed his mother, since her drug use was what got the boys taken in the first place. He abandoned education, and the last I heard he's finishing a five year prison sentence. He stabbed one of the line cooks. He said the cook tried to rape him, so he stabbed him in defense."

"Poor boy. Whatever happened to the letter his brother wrote? His suicide letter."

"Well before the authorities got there, he took the note and photo copied it, keeping the original, and putting the photocopy by his brother. He was distraught; the letter was the one connection he would forever have with his brother. Even when he went to prison, the state allowed him to keep the note. They sympathized with him. He didn't have a mother or a brother. He would read this note over and over, the note pulled him through. Made him want to get better."

"But he was in prison." Like my man, holding on to notes of the past. The images from the photos went through my brain: of the two of them at Red Lobster. He was *so* in love with her.

"Yes. He was reduced to a state number, but present day he is about to get a degree in criminal justice."

"Wow, girl. That's great."

"Yea. He attended school in prison. And now that he is about to get out, he is coming back home, to Miami. He remembered his address and wrote his mother from prison. She kept in close communication with her son. Being that he's the only living, healthy and breathing child she has. He plans on reuniting with her, since he's a grown adult male now."

"Does she still live in Richmond heights?"

"Yes."

"I would love to meet him."

"That could be arranged."

I stood up, taking the necklace from my pocket. I held it up, looking her deep in the eyes. "Keep it real with me. Because my man has been lying to me. *Why* didn't Legendary let me wear a necklace his father gave him? The necklace he has been holding onto ever since his father died is plaguing this relationship. Yet in *one* of the photos he has of you, from years ago, you have the very same necklace on *your* neck."

She was quiet. Her eyes bouncing all over the objects in her living room. She stood up and faced me, real classy about her shit. She smiled, shaking her head. "Legendary's father didn't give him that necklace."

It felt like Zeus, the God of War, was sucking the air from my body. "What? He told me the only reason he didn't let me wear it was because he didn't want it getting messed up, that he wanted to honor his father's memory."

"Wait right here." She walked over to the entertainment shelf, bad ass shelf. Top of the line everything, thousands of DVD movies lining eleven different polished red cherry wooden shelves. She got on her knees and opened the bottom counter, pulling out a velvet box. She said, "Come here, girl." I walked over to her, slowly, my heart torn into pieces. His father didn't give him the necklace. Then who gave it to him? Where did it come from? I should have known better. If he'd lie about the letter then he'd lie about the necklace.

I helped her stand up. She nearly fell on the shelf. Slowly, she opened the box. I saw a series of receipts.

"I keep all of my receipts," she told me,

pulling out one in particular. There was a photograph taped to it. She handed it to me, lowering her eyes to the floor. I saw the tears fall. Oh my God, why was she crying?

I looked at the receipt, from Kay's Jewelers. For $780. A necklace. The heart charm was $345. I looked at the photograph.

It was of Legendary. Kizzy. And their son.

At the Red Lobster.

I was pissed. "So you bought him the necklace?" I asked her.

"Yes. I had just had a miscarriage. I lost my baby. I was in the hospital for about a week, girl. Devastating affect this had on me because I was finally going to have his child."

I hugged her, gripping the necklace. "I am so sorry, girl."

"I bought him the necklace, said that the necklace would be our bond, that we would have shared a beautiful baby girl together. I was in my sixth month of pregnancy. I really wanted to make him a father. He wanted that very much, more than life itself."

In grave pain, Kizzy shook in my arms. Maybe I shouldn't have come here. No *wonder* he read the old letters and kept the pictures. No wonder he got antsy when anyone touched the necklace. This was a gift from her to him, when they lost their baby.

He never disclosed this information to me, and I could certainly understand why. It was probably all too painful for him, a man had his pride, a man hated to cry in front of his woman. He did tell me there was something about him and Kizzy's relationship he wanted to tell me about, but it was all together too painful.

I held Kizzy, I let her vent. "Girl, it hurts *so* bad!" Her nose was stopped up, her arms dangling at her sides. "I wanted my baby. She would have been so pretty, so…beautiful…she would have. Been. A. Ballerina. She would…have had a room filled with dolls, girl! But one night… I was drinking. I got so drunk I couldn't *think* straight. Legendary and I had a huge fight. I was saying things I didn't mean, girl. I punched at him, and my fist missed his face. I spun around and fell down concrete stairs. That's the night I lost my child. And he blamed *me*! *Oh, God…!*"

I was an emotional wreck. "Kizzy, girl." My heart beat for her, become one with her. I knew at that moment we would be great friends for life. I hurt for her; I certainly knew what it was like to lose your child. I had a miscarriage a few years ago, with Hank, my ex. I lost my baby after the first two months; my womb wasn't strong enough to carry it to term.

I didn't eat or sleep. I stand here now, crying about the death of my child, my innocent little baby. A baby I was looking forward to meeting. I loved my unborn child with everything in me, and when I lost it, I wasn't right for months! I hated life, dreaded going out into the sunshine. I couldn't do it. My family helped me through. I lost forty pounds, looked like I was Nicole Richie, I was throwing up the food I tried to eat. I wanted to die, die for my child.

I now understood, it all made sense.

Legendary wasn't mourning his father's death.

He was mourning the death of his child.

A child that would have made him a father.

Officially.

At that moment I had an entire new respect for my man. I would never doubt him or his judgment, again.

When I got home Legendary was sitting on the sofa. Naked. Soft lighting. He looked withdrawn into himself. I sat by him, looked into his eyes. I said, "I'm sorry. I shouldn't have doubted you."

I handed him the necklace. He cupped it, kissed it and said, "Would you put it on my neck, baby? Then I'll tell you about it. Why I lied and said my father gave it to me."

He turned his back to me and I put it on, kissing the back of his neck. My hot tears fell down his back. He faced me, hugging me. "The necklace…"

"I know. I know about your daughter. Kizzy and I had a heart to heart. I'm sorry about everything."

He hugged me, and we rocked with each other until we fell asleep.

Man in Uniform

What was it with women these days? They said they wanted a decent man. A man who wasn't full of himself. Someone who could tie his own shoes, break down a car and fix his toilet while dancing through flaming hoola hoops. They wanted a caring man; a man who never had a run in with the Law; a man who wasn't a whore. Someone who knew his shit around the bedroom as well as the boardroom. They said they wanted a strong black man who knew how to treat a lady; someone with a Lesbian's Heart, meaning he could be as sensual and elegant as a woman, yet he could be rough and tough in the sack. They wanted a man who drove a BMW or a Lexus coup, had his own house, a 401 (k), medical and dental, and a wallet the size of the Great Wall of China. They wanted a swell guy who had people skills, public relations experience—meaning knew how to carry himself in public. Females wanted a fellah that bought his auntie, sister, daughter and Mama roses twice a week. A man who knew how to cook, clean and quite possibly sow the buttons back on his dress shirts when they popped off.

I was all of those things, Super-Goddamn-Man, and I was still autonomously alone. Nursing Paul Masson brandy, a broken heart—broken three times over from the same woman—and a body that wanted to be held, consoled, and appreciated.

Decidedly withdrawn, the phone breaks the silence. Answering, I knew it was Mama. Funny how men professed to being men, yet when the rip tides your ass through hell you had Mama on speed dial.

Mama was her usual want to-be Oprah Winfrey meets Dr. Phil self. She thought she knew everything because she had a little money and dined with white folks. She must have forgotten that her life waqs crazier than mine.

"Baby, not all women are bad," she told me with so much love and understanding in her voice. I wasn't trying to hear it.

I leaned forward on the sofa in my living room. Picking up the remote I turned on some sad music. When you're heartbroken you only listened to sad, love music.

"Yes they are."

She was defiant. She said, "So what are you saying about your mother?"

Trick questions. Sure, Mama. Make this all about you.

I puffed a cigarette, knowing I hated smoking, but the cig calmed my nerves.

"Mom, this *isn't* about you!"

She guffawed. "You coulda fooled me. I raised you better than that."

The candles flickered silently, giving off scents of strawberries. Always soothed me, yet the shit wasn't working tonight.

I sipped the brandy. Good bourbon.

"Mama, please…"

"You get on my goddamn nerves…"

"Whatever." My voice was tired and strained from cursing out my co-worker, Officer James, down at the Metro-Dade Precinct. Because I gave him forty dollars to play the Florida Lottery for me. He not only forgot to play the lottery, he spent my money on a bitch at the Samurai Chinese Restaurant, somewhere around the Falls area.

"Don't whatever me, Son."

I was getting saucy. "I'm grown."

"Then act like you are. Crying over a bitch."

My eyes laser beams. "She was my *wife*, damn it!"

I was a cop, mind you. I was supposed to protect the cruelly cold Miami, Florida streets with professionalism and zeal. But I couldn't protect my wife's pussy from being violated by a willing participant, her lover Sean. He used to be my best-friend and my partner on the force.

Mama said, "Get another wife! I swear, I know I raised you better than this…"

Woman, please! Not tonight, I am not in the mood to be lectured by you. I narrowed my eyes, clad in a tank top T, socks, and brown police pants barely covering my ass. They were unzipped, and I could see the glow of the candles reflecting from my black silky boxers. "*You* raised me?"

She was a little hesitant, as she should be. "Yes. I raised you. Worked three jobs to take care of you. You were my only son."

"True. I am your only son; your only child for that matter; but I hardly consider hooking, cooking *and* tricking three refutable jobs. In fact you couldn't even file income tax off hooking."

"That's a low blow; I did what I had to do.

We're not going through this again, are we? I'm done explaining myself to you, you came out of my pussy not the other way around!"“

"You could have got a *responsible* job." I was getting heated. "But you didn't. And while we're on the subject, do you know how hard it was to go to elementary, junior and senior high school, knowing half of my homeboys' fathers *paid* to sleep with you?"

"Oh, God! Lennox, *how* old are you?" my mother spat icily, sending chills up my spine. I knew I was out of pocket for talking to her this way. But I didn't want a woman who barely had a decent relationship outside of Prostitution 101 giving me advice. That was my own fault. I shouldn't have answered my phone.

I was guarded. "I'm 28 years old."

She laughed pleasantly! Could you believe this? "Grow up, let go of that little boy shit! Your problem is that you want your way when you want it and *how* you want it. Your no-good ass father couldn't stay out of jail and stop pimping women; your father wasn't as responsible as I was. He ran the streets, trying to be Scarface Noriega the Third! *Yea* I stripped and did what I had to do to keep food in your mouth and cool, crisp sheets on your body. That's more than what I can say about your Sperm Donor, you little arrogant asshole!"

It tore me apart to hear her sniffling. She was trying to hide it and a huge part of me wanted to hold and console her. I loved my mother and I respected her regardless of her past. I shouldn't be doing this to her. Good or bad she was my Mama.

Bitterly, she went on. "You weren't saying that when you had shrimp and lobster for dinner while everyone else in the Poke-N-Bean Projects had Top Ramen noodles, praying to God every night it turned into shrimp pasta!"

"*Mama*!"

"*Lennox*!"

We were very quiet, my heart beating rapidly. I felt really low for doing this. Trying to blame her for my problems. I didn't want to admit that I was actually 28, would be turning 29 in a few days, March 15, 2007, and I hadn't gotten my life together.

I couldn't keep friends. I kept chasing them away. I couldn't keep a healthy working relationship with other cops. Being that Mama was Cuban and my father was African-American and Trinidadian, my temper flared when it wanted to. I had cold cuts in my blood, so in all actuality I didn't even know who the hell I was.

"Son, talk to me."

I ignored her.

To my complete dismay, I eyed the pistol on the low-table, next to Cedrick the Entertainer's *Jet* magazine cover from some time ago. Wedding photos of my wife and me hanging in pricey frames all over the place.

I looked at the picture of me and Mom; I was wearing a cream-colored tux with lavender silk tie.

Smiling so big I couldn't see straight. Thinking that marrying Danielle was the best moment of my life. Mama hugged me, smiling bigger than I was.

She was happy to be a part of my Big Day.

Mama said, "Son…this is breaking my heart…"

Whatever. All of the pictures made a sudden drop on the Dow Jones of my soul. The biggest drop of my entire existence. I was embarrassed and ashamed; I could barely show my face around the neighborhood. People knew and people talked. They were in my business like my business belonged to them. They speculated and dissected every aspect of what happened. The fellahs talked about my ordeal in all the barber shops from here in Liberty City to the Greenroom Barber Shop in Goulds.

Putting the phone down on the couch,

leaving mama to talk to herself, I realized that I needed to get away. Leave town for a few weeks and not tell anyone where I was going. Surround myself with people who didn't know me. Perhaps go to Istanbul, fuck it. I never have been there. Plus I didn't have to worry about people being in my business. But I couldn't as of yet; I had a ton of bills, mortgage needed to be paid. I had a decent job and I didn't feel like putting in for leave. I didn't feel like dealing with the paperwork. Not today. Leaning back on the sofa, I closed my eyes, rubbing my temples. In a couple hours I had to be leaving out of here for work. I couldn't stop daydreaming about walking in on my beautiful wife—a woman I would lay my life on the line for—SERVICING MY BESTFRIEND SEAN IN MY BEDROOM!

I needed some alone time. I was retarded for calling Mama about my problems anyway. What grown man did that?

Picking up the phone I uttered, "Mama, I got to go."

"...Lennox."

With an attitude that rendered me speechless, I hung up. Anger exploding inside me, I jumped to my bare feet and threw the liquor bottle through the living room window. Glass shattering, the liquor rained down on everything from my mahogany-colored entertainment shelf, my plasma TV, and the carpet. Material possessions meant nothing to me right now.

Like a zombie, I walked over to the small mirror hanging by the start of the hallway. Nefertiti was on a pedestal next to me, along with my wedding picture. I breathed in so deeply my lungs and chest seemed like hot air balloons with no sign of landing. I ran my hands over my wavy hair, perplexedly sad. I could remember my wife bought that Nefertiti statuette for me. There was an Egyptian Festival that came through Miami, Florida, and she knew how much I loved Akhenaton and Nefertiti, his wife in Egyptian Literature. I was fascinated with Kings and Queens, even though these days white people were trying to say they had olive-colored skin and were white. Yea, right, bitches! Didn't think so!

The images of my wife's infidelity bit at my skull. Danielle gripping Sean's organ; slurping, sucking and pulling. Intricately rolling her tongue across the head of his passion. Their heat rising and cool air falling, creating tornadoes all over my satin sheets. Neither one of them, two people I left alone countless times, saw me standing in the doorway, my hand on my pistol, my heart broken. I had feelings of nausea, but I swallowed it, backed into the shadows of the hallway and watched her perform.

I had just gotten home, thankful for the comfort of my own crib, thinking about my bed, my dogs (feet) were killing me. I had run a hot bath in the guest bedroom, wondering where my wife was. She'd normally have dinner cooked, I had sniffed the air, and it smelled of perfume and other things, but not food, so I was a little disappointed. But I didn't trip; she was probably in the bedroom, watching the Lifetime Channel, television for Women with absolutely NO GODDAMN LIFE!

When I reached the top of the stairs, I started down the hallway, passing framed pictures of my Mama as a little girl, my daddy and Mama when they married, even though it lasted two years. I was smiling, longing my wife, wanting to find her, massage her and eat a little pussy. After all, my lips needed their daily supplements.

When I got to my room I froze in shock, not believing my eyes. My mouth agape, I covered it to stop myself from screaming. The curvaceous breasts shook when she crawled on top of him and he, gripping her amazing ass, lowered her wet opening down onto the rod that would comfort her. He became her Pslams

23, rejecting her wedding vows, vows I thought she made whole-heartedly (or was it for show, since half the bitches in attendance she couldn't stand?) with the flick of his experienced tongue across very erect nipples. Her face turned into green pastures every time she and Sean locked lips, her hair framing her angelic face, forever disguising the women I sought out for eight months from the love contained in my heart.

Holding the headboard, she tossed her weave from her face, held her breasts like doves with broken wings and I saw all the explicit details, his huge organ playing the flute of her vagina, the wonderfully created music deafening me every time she said,

"You fuck *better* than my husband."

His eyes sparkled. "...Oh, yeah, baby?"

"Hell yeah, and you got...some good dick, baby. Goddamn, baby, shit feels so good deep inside me."

"Yea, baby, praise daddy."

She laughed coyly. "Oh, yea I'm praising Daddy! Lennox will never be big daddy!"

My heart burst, the wind knocked from my gut.

"The hell with him," Sean, a man I loved with all my heart, my brother in name, a man I knew for twenty years, had said, with no emotion for me in his voice. He actually betrayed me for some pussy, a twenty year friendship gone down the tubes. Like it never existed. Words couldn't describe how I was feeling at that moment.

I closed my eyes, taking out my cell phone. Quietly, I slipped into the hall closet, leaving the door ajar, my eyes clapping on two bodies, sweaty and taut, loving, teasing and admiring. Rising and falling, becoming the Pacific and Atlantic Ocean, intertwining two gloriously seasoned shores into one breathtakingly sinister picture only Lucifer could imagine.

I called Sean's cell phone. It rang, sitting on my nightstand, the photo of me and my wife laying face down by the telephone. He looked at it, smiled, put a finger over his lips and answered with a belligerent, "*Hey*, buddy, where are you?"

I wanted to cuss him, spit obscenities at him. "Close by, thinking about coming home early tonight. I'm hungry, where are you?"

"Busy at the precinct?" He kissed my wife's lips, and then she crawled, like a pussy cat, down to his penis and took his member into her mouth trying to pleasure him orally. He locked a huge glob of her hair in closed fists and started humping her mouth. The pleasure dancing across his face made my stomach hurt.

It took everything in me not to just jump out the closet and shoot them both, but timing was everything.

"Well I could swing by Checkers and get you something to eat," he said, a moan escaping his lips. Holding the phone to his ear with his shoulder, the muscles in his amazing abs contracted every time he flinched. He cleaned it up by saying, "Damn, I'm tired, can't stop...yawning."

"Oh yea. Working out?"

"*Trying* to. Gotta get a few bicep workout in before tomorrow, you know Spring Break is right around the corner."

I wanted to just die. This was my homeboy; I would do anything for him. The men I shot over him, the people I locked up because I wanted to protect him. His Mama was raped and murdered when he was ten years old and his father was booked and charged with her death. I was there for him, brought him into my Mama's home and always supported him. We went through high school together, graduated from the Police Academy together. He was the best man in my wedding, and now the Niggah turned out to be flaw, camouflaging-ass Niggah.

Working up enough nerve, I said, "Well, I'll holla before I get home. Much love."

"Love you, brothah." He hung up and

started laughing. Tossing the phone he said, "*Suck that stupid Niggah from the head of my dick...yea, baby, umm hmm just...like. That. Yes!*"

I was shaking my head. Then it dawned on me, he never loved me, never respected me. Our entire friendship was a big lie.

A little plan forming in my head, I called my house phone. My wife froze, looking at it. Sean said, "Don't answer it."

"I got to; I always answer when he calls."

They smiled discreetly. "Well get it, just don't stop blowing me off." He sat up straight, putting a pillow behind his back. "In fact, it's turning me on, my so-called best friend's wife, giving me some head while he's on the phone."

She answered, gripping his dick, studying it, and then kissed the head. "Hey, baby."

"I miss you." Tears were falling down my face. I tried to will the pain away but I couldn't. I never cheated on her, and I wasn't about to start.

"I miss you too, Lennox."

"Oh, I'm not *baby* tonight?" I asked. She never called me Lennox.

"I'm just tired."

"Where are you?"

"Over my Mama's house." How she could lie so easily? I had to wonder, how long had she been cheating on me? Did it just happen? Or had this been an ongoing thing?

I smiled. "I'm at your mom's now, I don't see you." She stopped sucking Sean's dick and stared deeply into his eyes.

"You're at my Mom's house now?" Sean was alarmed. He mouthed, "Make up something," and she nodded her head. He was getting out of the bed, putting on his police uniform, his athletic body shimmying from the dim lights.

"Yea, where are you? In the back yard or in one of the bedrooms, I'll find you. I'm hanging up now, makes no sense to talk to you when you're here at Mom's house. What is she doing?"

"Oh, she's cooking a pot roast."

I opened the closet door slowly, my gun aimed, holding the cell to my ear with my shoulder, walking heel to toe towards my bedroom. "Sounds delicious."

"It is." She covered the receiver and whispered to Sean, "I don't know what to say. He's at Mom's house."

Sean seemed nervous. "I'm going to buy him something to eat. I'll somehow distract him. Probably call the precinct and have one of the fellahs radio him for backup."

"But he's off duty," my wife said, about to pull her hair from her scalp. I was in the doorway, aimed at Sean's back. My room was huge, so they still didn't notice me. They scrambled, putting on clothes, tidying up the place, setting up my wedding picture. Sean stuffed the condom and opened Magnum condom wrapper into his pocket, snatching up his badge, putting it on, and slid his pistol into the holster.

"Baby, are you there?" I asked, my eyes red.

"Yes. I had to leave really quickly; I left through mom's back gate. Gotta run to the store. Need feminine products."

Fucking liar! You just went to the store last week and raked up on $120 worth of feminine shit! "Ok, I'll see you when I get home."

"I love you, Lennox."

I hate you, bitch! "I love you too, Danielle." I hung up, stuffed the phone in my back pocket and when they turned to face me, both of them had heart failure.

"Dawg," said Sean, pleading, his hands raised. He was walking towards me. "I can explain."

Not wanting to hear excuses, I shot out the lamp and he froze, dropping to his knees. I had a heart of stone. "Famous last words. How do you explain fucking my wife?"

She was crying, sitting on the edge of the

bed. Looking like the victim, trying to be the victim. "Baby, this isn't what you think it is."

She screamed when I shot the ceiling fan from the ceiling. I was an expert marksman. Shooting targets came second fiddle to me.

"Oh, *now* I'm baby. You called me 'Lennox' twice on the phone a few minutes ago. I was watching you two from the closet for the past thirty or so minutes."

They just stared at me. Sean reached out to me, his hand grazing my pants leg and I kicked him so hard in the face blood splattered this way and he flew that way, crashing into the foot of my bed. Moaning piteously, he lay there, holding his face, shuddering with fear.

"You know what? You two deserve each other; you're not worth my time. You're not worth my freedom. Sean, get the fuck out of my house. And Danielle. You get out, too! The clothes on your back, since I bought them, stay here. To the left—to the left out of my goddamn room, bitch!"

She stood up, running up to me. Embracing me, she showered my face with kisses and my lips automatically danced with hers, urgent and probing, wanting and needing. I was tasting Ted from her tongue. I held her, gripping the gun with my right hand, slowly gyrating our pelvises together. I didn't know if

I should kick her ass or love her. I sucked on her neck and she begin rambling, "Oh, baby...you don't want to do this. I'm so sorry I shouldn't. Have. Done. This. To. You. It's not your fault. You *work* too much. You're never home..."

I looked deeply into her eyes, smiling, the sadness washing over me. I loved her with all my soul. I took vows. For better or for worse, 'til death do us part, yet I didn't remember the vows reading, 'til you suck my best friend's dick.

"I love you," I told her.

She relaxed. "I love you."

Impulsively, I slapped her so hard with the butt of my pistol she fell on her back, painfully falling on the floor. She was whimpering, crawled into the fetal position. I never hit a woman before, but I always told myself, hey, my Mama was a pricey Ho when I was growing up, when I found the woman of my dreams, she must a) be classy, b) respected and c) far from promiscuous with other men if it wasn't me, and she just failed all the choices.

Unzipping my pants, I pissed all over her, draining the rest of my urine on Sean's cut. It burned him. I started kicking him in the torso, the face, the chest. My rage boiled over. I snatched my wife by her hair and dragged her outside, throwing her into the grass. The sprinkler system was on, soaking her clothes. I snatched off her silk blouse, I paid for this, $590 from Bloomingdale's, because I wanted her to have the best; off came her silk skirt, $389 dollars, the matching pumps...I used my shirt to wipe the make-up from her face. I bought that shit from the Dadeland Mall with my hard-earned money.

My friends were filing out of their houses. A couple of my homeboys ran over and grabbed me. I spat at the bitch, becoming a savage. All my pain and hurt boiling over, I couldn't talk straight, sounded like I was speaking gibberish.

In a fit of rage I said, "You bitch! How could you...cheat on me, Ho! Get that bitch out of my front yard before I defile that slut!"

One of my friends, Jay, 5 feet 4, took her by the arm, and told Danielle, "Come with me and my wife. You can stay the night with us, until you find out where you're going."

His wife, Valletta, was at his side. She tried to calm everyone down. She said, sinisterly, "And you're sleeping with me, Jay. I don't trust this bitch around my husband!" She looked at Danielle, handing her a coat to cover her naked body. "If you so much as look at my man, Ho I'll fuck you up! I'm only doing this because I care about you!"

A couple hours later, I zipped up my pants, put on my police shirt with "Sergeant Pale" on the tag and grabbed my keys. I was due in to work at 5 a.m. I was late. Fuck it. Who cared? I had nothing to work for.

I needed to engross myself with work so I didn't think about Danielle. Sean was still in the hospital recovering. Of course the police questioned him. I was present.

But I knew Sean. Despite it all he wasn't a cowardly snitch, like most men I knew. He said he was robbed and when he came to my house for help, because the robbers took his wallet and cell phone, he sought out my wife for help. The robbers followed him to my house, and hoped to get more cash.

When they didn't have cash, they jumped on him and my wife. Miraculously, my wife confirmed the story and no one in my neighborhood spoke against it.

They better not; I had enough dirt on half the people in this neighborhood to get them locked up for life without the possibility of parole. A few weeks later Danielle called me. It took everything in me to be civil. The more days that separated the actual act of infidelity, the better I felt. At work I totally avoided Sean.

He had called me and wrote me countless emails and letters. Fuck him. Fuck him to hell.

"Will you sit with me?" she asked.

"Nope. Look Danielle. Didn't my lawyer call you yet?"

"Yes." A few beats of silence. I loved her. But she disrespected me. And there was no turning back. "I don't want a divorce."

"I do."

"I called a marriage counselor."

I laughed. "Dr. Ruth?"

"Funny. We should go and work on our marriage."

"You are unbelievable. Did you only cheat on me once, Danielle?"

It took her a minute. "No. For two years."

I was silent, my heart splitting in two. "With Sean?"

"With Sean."

I was angry. "*Why* Sean?"

"He was…convenient. Plus your mother…she caused all this…"

I blinked twice. "She *what*?"

"Your Mama doesn't want nothing and no one around you. She paid Sean and I handsomely to have a threesome with her. She sucked and fucked him and I to her heart's content." I had to close my eyes. "…I knew it was wrong but you worked day and night and no one comforted me. She played on that. So we *did* it. Don't blame me for the marriage falling apart. Blame your controlling mother…Sean sold you out for your mother's money…"

I worked all the time. I had a wife and a home to support. Nothing else in this world meant more to me then breaking my back for a woman who was my Queen. My wallet, bank account and house were hers. I put my all into my marriage.

Now I had nothing.

Marriage was challenging, considering I was a white man married to a black woman. I went through all the "Oh, no you didn't marry a black woman!" stares at work and in public. But that didn't deter me from loving her and showing her public affection. Black men sneered at me in disgust and every time I turned my back they pounced on her as if she was a water buffalo and they needed nourishment. She remained loyal. She was a startling beauty: big ample breasts, perky nipples, Apple Bottom derriere, and chiseled Janet Jackson abs. She was a work out buff. She had short, croppy hair, loved poetry, loved eating the best foods and danced to the best music.

When I met her at the Muvico Movie Theater in Fort Lauderdale, Florida, just off of Sheridan West (traveling North on I-75), a couple months ago, she looked very vulnerable attending the *Mission Impossible 3* premiere by herself. I could tell she loved Tom Cruise. The stallion of black men trying to get her attention was amazing. The way certain black men grabbed her hand and she seemed to cringe. She told one of them, a tall basketball player type, "Look, *don't* touch me. I don't *know* you and I'm *not* your goddamn Mama!" He retreated without hesitation. I was laughing to myself, finding it all amusing. She lusted after a white man on a poster, so out of touch with reality because he was in Hollywood—still being ridiculed for the stunt he pulled on the Oprah Winfrey show—and she was in Florida. She knew he existed, but hadn't one iota that she existed.

Home girl looked good in tight snake-print pants, long leather boots with spiked heels with the cowboy golden spinners behind the backs. Her chandelier earrings sparkled with abandon. The long-sleeved gold blouse with a huge oval button holding her breasts in place for dear life was something I had never seen on a woman. Pretty classy, if you asked me. She definitely had junk in her trunk. I told myself: *Maybe tonight is my lucky night.* I was thirty-five, single, very handsome. My drinking buddies said I looked like a young Brad Pitt. I took that as a compliment. I actually won a Brad Pitt look alike contest three months ago up in Aspen when I went skiing with some old college buddies.

Clad in nice blue Dockers pants, a pink IZOD shirt, and pink Banana Republic shoes, I made my way over to her.

I made small talk. Why not? The only thing she could possibly do was a) dismiss me—like most black women seemed to do, despite hearing, "Damn, you're cute, but I don't do snowballs…"—or b) give me a little tongue tag.

Here goes. "Movie seems like it'll be better than the first two installments."

She smiled at me, eyes sparkling. Hotdamn. She was a beauty. Definitely caused a ruckus in my briefs. My veins seemed to tighten when she smiled. She extended her hand.

"I'm Bianca. And *your* name is?"

I was salivating something terrible. "I'm Ted Oxford."

She grinned. "Like Ted Bundy from *Married with Children*," she joked, patting my shoulder. "Just kidding."

"Nah, I am not married and I don't have children."

She didn't believe me. "Good looking man such as yourself? Not Married? What about kids you don't know about?"

"Sister, I'm 35 years old. I can count on one hand how many women I slept with in my life time."

She was definitely interested. "Wow. White men own the world and the blondes with it and you can count on one hand how many you *slept* with?"

Now I was grinning. "Yes. Don't forget HIV runs rampant like the winter Olympics."

"Amen, Dustin Hoffman. No. No. *You* look like Brad Pitt."

"*Phew.* Dustin Hoffman over Brad *Pitt*? You had me about to search for Oceans Fourteen to get the hell away from you," I joked, smiling.

She touched my hand. "I'm a direct woman."

I gripped it. "Like wise."

She rubbed her thumb over my hand. "I take it your favorite color is pink."

I felt the chemistry building. "Yea. *Unusual* for a man, I know, but I don't live by the rules."

Her eyes drank me like Scotch. "I like that. Your zodiac sign is?"

My heart raced. "Pisces."

"So your birthday passed," she said, forgetting we were in a theatre.

"Yes. March 15th."

"I'm a Scorpio," she informed me.

I was enjoying her already. "Nice. Powerful and manipulative. I better stand guard."

We laughed easily. "Down, Buster. Favorite food?"

"Shrimp scampi."

She nodded her head. "Same here. No hotdogs and pork and beans for this bitch."

I was impressed. "Articulate, are we?"

She hugged me. "Very. Favorite singer?"

I felt good in her arms. "Well, Garth

Brooks and a little bit of Janet Jackson, Tim McGraw and Faith Hill."

She pushed away from me playfully. "Garth is straight. Faith is cool. Janet is ok. You're a man so you like Janet because of…"

"Her tits. I can't lie. I'm straight forward."

"At least you're honest. My favorite artists are Nelly and The Dixie Chicks."

"Favorite song by the Chicks?"

"Wide Open Spaces. And I commend them for speaking out on cheating ass George Bush. They spoke for legions of black people in this country."

"Believe me I regret voting for a lying, oil driven man myself."

She snapped her fingers. I was confused. I figured it was some college thing. "Amen! I like you. You're not half bad."

"You're a hot cookie yourself."

"And your breath smells good. I can tell you don't do tobacco."

"Hell no. I do Tic Tacs and Jolly Ranchers. I can't *stand* women who smoke."

"I hear ya'!"

Here it goes. I went in for the kill. I was about to get shot down. I breathed in deeply, closing my eyes. "Are you here with anybody, sexy woman such as yourself?"

This is the part when I cringed. Go

ahead. Give it to me. No. Because you're white. Your ass is flat. Black men have dicks. I do dicks. Not cocks. You smell nice but I heard crackers smell like dogs when they get wet.

"I'm flying solo, like Amelia Earhart."

"Care to join me for a movie. My treat."

"Sure. I would love to. Thought you'd never ask."

"Great." I extended my arm and she put her hand through, not at all embarrassed to be out with a sexy white man with blue eyes.

"Lead the way," she said, her nipples hardening. I couldn't help but look. She didn't strike me as a tough-talking, gum-snapping, head popping black chick that got rough and tough. She seemed really down to earth. I didn't smell a hint of cigarette smoke in her clothing, didn't see a hint of nicotine on her pearly white teeth. No caps and no fillings. Definitely two pluses. We might just get along great.

I wanted to spend some time with her. I suddenly didn't want to be alone. "Do you want something to eat?"

Her eyes sparkled brighter. "Yea, I am famished. But the cost of food here is sky high."

"No problem. I make $90,000 a year and

I do a small gig as a security guard five nights a week. No kids and no wife. So why not?"

I studied her reaction when I mentioned my income. *Kaching* didn't register in her brown eyes. Thank God she wasn't a gold digger. I'd *never* tell her I was engaged before; that my fiancé died in a small charter plane cash three weeks after the singer Aaliyah perished. It took me three years to get over it. I turned to drugs to escape. Lost my friends who tried to help me and damn near lost my career as a carpenter and subcontractor. It took God to pull me through.

After paying eighteen dollars for tickets and another thirty bucks for two nachos, two large sodas and popcorn, she helped me carry the food into the theater. She led the way.

I couldn't keep my eyes off her magnificent ass. My little friend was hard as hell. Her ass bounced. She led me up the stairs and I tripped four times. I played it off. I wanted to tell her booty to stop staring at my eyes, but it seemed silly and childish.

She led us to the back of the theater. It was kind of empty anyways. Most of the people, white, sat in the front. Hardly anyone sat in the back.

I tripped again.

She looked back at me, smiling, her earrings dangling. "Are you ok, Ted?"

Had to find a quick lie. "Yea, I'm chipper."

She didn't believe me. Her eyes peered through me. "Are you sure?"

I looked guilty. "I'm positive."

We talked through half of the movie, didn't really pay it attention. We found it easy to have a decent conversation. She didn't curse once. Good sign, because when I was mad I got furious and I cursed. I had a temper out of this world.

She told me, "I wasn't raised in the projects. I wouldn't know what one looked like. I was adopted when I was three months old by an Australian family. I was a crack baby, can you believe that?"

I chocked on my Coke. "What? A *crack* baby?" People shushed me. "…Are you serious?"

She was stern. "Yes. I was raised in the suburbs of Miami. Went to the best catholic and private schools. I graduated from Palmetto Senior High, though, a public school, with honors. I did four years in the Airforce. I did a tour in Tokyo and another in China. I got my Montgomery G.I. Bill and attended college. I went to USC off and on. I did another three years reserve. Once I got tired of wearing blue I finished law school, gave up on that dream, attending TV Production. I wanted to be a reporter. That dream failed, so now I work at Channel 7 news in Miami, as a sound editor. Hey, I get the best concert seats. I know I'm boring you."

"No, not at all. I'm impressed."

She kept looking at my crotch. My dick had been hard the entire time. I tried to ignore it, but it had a mind of its own.

She sipped the soda suggestively.

"Your thing is alive and kicking."

"Never mind my penis. Just *pretend* its not there."

She stuck out her breasts. "Girls like dick, that is so hard to do."

Wow! Like, totally wow! Did she say what I think she just said? Do I bite or do I deter? "I *love* pussy." We couldn't stop staring at each other. I felt the electricity. It was strong, the current licking at my eyes and face.

She licked her lips, setting the soda down. She massaged my phallus, sending shivers up my spine. I loved her touch, she was fire. Unzipping my pants, she went down on me. Pulled an Alanis Morrisette. Well, shit, did she speak eloquently also? She didn't even look around to see if the coast was clear. I loved it.

She ran her tongue up and down my shaft, finding my balls with ease. She sucked one ball, and then the other…expertly. I went crazy, holding in my moans. I was thrusting my hips, my toes causing damage on the inside of my shoes.

Sucking me with the power of her strong jaws, she could suck a golf ball through a straw. She damn sure knew what she was doing. No one had ever gone down on me in a theater. Especially not a black woman.

She sucked my dick long and hard, taking my near ten inches as if they were five. I felt her tonsils, she played with the head, looking up into my eyes and working that tongue. I leaned my head back, savoring the moment.

After an eternity she felt me tense up and I told her I had to come and I burst deep down her throat and she swallowed every salty drop. I looked at her with love in my eyes.

Sitting up, she fixed her blouse, sipped some soda and said, as calmly as she could, "Let's get out of here. Let's do the town."

I was in love. I couldn't let her get away. "I thought you'd never ask."

And do the town we did. She drove a Benz. I drove a pick up truck. She followed me back to my house in Homestead. Waterfront condos. And we sat and talked before going to South Beach. I played some Frank Sinatra.

We talked some more, on our drive to the

beach. I took my truck. We got close really fast. We were both loners, hopeless romantics. I found myself looking at her at the oddest moments.

When we got out to the beach, crowded as hell, I paid twenty bucks to park in the garage by Ocean Drive. We walked all over the place. I bought her some clothes and a fancy straw hat. She bought me a Gucci outfit.

We ate, drank wine, danced at Club Deep and found ourselves wrestling in my bed hours later, pumping myself in and out of soft pussy. We were both tipsy and I became one with her nipples. She rode my dick wearing a straw hat, taking all of me. She rode me backwards, the Reverse Cowgirl, yelling into the darkness, her titties bouncing. I came inside her all night long. Not once did I think of condoms.

A month later, after baring our souls to each other (I shared photos of my dead fiancé with her) I knew I wanted to be her husband, but I never said anything. My pride got in the way. I didn't want to live without her. I wanted to share my life with her. She already had keys to my place. When she got off work she always came over. I sent flowers four times a week to her job. She introduced me to all her friends and her adoptive parents. They loved me.

I took her around the fellahs and they

were so jealous of me, that I pulled a Queen.

I proposed to her in front of her parents over dinner at my house a few days later. I caught her off guard. She sat there at the dining table clad in white. Just as sexy as she wanted to be. She gushed and accepted my proposal. We set a date.

A few weeks later after planning our big day we married at my house. A small gathering with family and friends. Sixty people all together. This was truly the happiest day of my life. She sold her house and we pocketed the money. I put her name on everything I owned.

Then it happened. My demanding job pulled me away from my wife. People wanted this fixed and this contracted. I did a lot of roofs and my overnight job became a hazard. Everyone was quitting and I was the only one left so they asked me to work more nights, seven nights a week, from 8 PM until 2 AM. I said sure.

My wife didn't like it.

"Baby, why are you working so much?"

She needed things done around the house. I couldn't do it. I had to make the money. So she quit her job so she could always be at home. She came to my job cursing me out.

"You need to let the second job go! I need you *home*! You can't neglect your new wife, what the fuck, Ted!"

She was right, but I couldn't abandon my boss. I told my wife, "Just hold down the fort until I get home."

When I got home I fell asleep in the doorway. When I made love to her I fell asleep before the tip of my dick could touch her urgent walls. I was unintentionally neglecting my wife. She'd have breakfast cooked, but I was in a hurry after my shower. I grabbed the toast and was out the door and by the time I came home, dinner was colder than ice. I just trashed it, showered and jumped in the bed.

Before I knew it, it was July 15, 2006. And things hit the fan. I cursed her out. I had to work. I had to pay the bills. I loved her.

I got off work early Sunday night. My stomach was in knots. I almost fell asleep at the wheel.

When I pulled up in the drive way I turned off the ignition and I nearly crawled in the house. Up the stairs I went, walking to my room to hug my wife, who tolerated my shit.

When I got to the room door I froze. I saw her tits bouncing and my friend Dexter tagging the ass from the back. I felt bile rise in my throat. She was riding him, and he had her ass cheeks spread apart and his dick, way bigger than mine, filled her up. Her come, thick and white, was all over his nature.

"You like it, Bianca?"

"I love it, Dexter!" She got off him, sucked her cum off his dick, watching his nuts bounce. He covered his face, pumping himself inside her hot mouth. I guess she got bored because she took him out of her mouth and squeezed her tits on his hardened member. She tit fucked him. My heart died. He stood up in the bed, turned her back to him and entered her asshole, pushing her forward and tearing her hole to hell. She screamed out his name, saying she loved when he fucked her senseless, that she looked forward to him always sneaking in my house when I worked late nights and he take her to town.

She threw the ass back on his dick. Her ass jiggling. Dexter had a basketball player's build. He always got the bitches. He was my best friend.

When he came she turned and sucked shit and nut off his dick, swallowing, not even seeing me in the door way.

Seething with rage I went to the kitchen and put on a pot of grits. The minute it started boiling I snatched up the pot, ran up the stairs, burst in the door and was surprised they were gone. I heard giggling from the shower.

"I'm divorcing Ted. We can build a life

together. What was I thinking marrying that punk! I mean, I don't listen to the Dixie Chicks. I just told his ass that so I could get in his wallet. I was never adopted. Can you believe he fell for that shit. My parents still live in the ghetto. I was never a suburban bitch…"

"I never him anyways," said Dexter. "Now get on your knees and suck on my dick, bitch."

"Ooh I love it when you talk dirty!"

I was betrayed. All her lies washed over me and created boulders in my heart. Opening the bathroom door, I snatched open the shower curtain and, startled, Bianca could only say, "Oops."

Fucking Oops? Dexter, trying to plead, said, "I can explain." Bianca looked frightened. She should be. The devil jumping out of my eyes I dumped hot grits on both of them. Shocked, Bianca screamed from the pain. Grits tore away at her pretty face. Fuck the bitch. I slapped her so hard across the face with the pot she flipped in the tub and fell on her knees, moaning piteously. Bet you they didn't teach her that flip in the Airforce!

I stomped Dexter, who had grits on his face, dick and chest. I beat his ass with the pot and left him there bleeding.

I trusted him! He was my best friend and

my best man and he fucked my wife? I got my revenge. Disoriented and my life blown up before my very eyes, I packed a bag, grabbed my keys and wallet and before I left I paid Dexter a visit.

"You go to the cops I tell your wife and son you fucked my wife. I tell her you been cheating on her for months and I lied for you. I'll help her take half the shit you own and custody of your child. I would advice you to not fuck with me."

And I was gone, back in my pick up truck, thinking about my dead fiancé, never to fuck with a black bitch ever again.

The next day I called my lawyer. "I want to file an annulment."

"Already, Ted?" Maybe you should consider a marriage counselor."

I was a beast. "*I want a fucking divorce!* She cheated on me. Infidelity. I want the *black* bitch gone out my life forever."

"Sure, Ted. I'll get right on it." When I hung up the phone I called Dexter's wife, Karen. She was a lively woman, always looked for the best in people. Her dumb ass just didn't know Dexter cheated on her for three years.

My heart bled. "Hey, sexy. Where's Dexter?"

"He's been gone all night. I'm tired of it.

Where is he?"

Should I tell her? "Can I come over? I have to talk to you."

"You're always welcome here."

I was about to destroy a happy home. Mine was toppled Legos. "Your son there?"

"No. He's out of town."

"Good. By the way I can tell you where your husband is."

"Where?"

"I caught him fucking my wife last night. And it's been going on for weeks now."

She was silent. I heard crying. "Come over, Ted. I'm so sorry. I never liked the bitch."

"I'm alone, Karen. When my divorce is final I'm leaving town."

"Come over. Let me show you the trick I can do with my tonsils. He hasn't fucked me in months. Its time I put my pussy back in the habit. I know its wrong, but please, Ted, I want some dick. Please come comfort me. I'll even change the locks so Dexter's keys fail him."

"Is that right?"

"Please come before I change my mind."

"I'll be right over."

Oops that, bitch!

PH Balance

Believe me I wanted to scream. Scream as loud as I possibly could! For one, I lived in Keys Gate, behind Homestead Senior High School, paying $1,200 a month for a condo that was barely big enough for my pussy. Secondly, I wanted to scream because I was in love with a man who was gay! Yes, I said it. *G-A-Y, you ain't got no alibi you GAY!*

But the sad part was that he didn't know I loved him because we were best friends.

It was odd that I had these big brown eyes and the vulnerability that made guys want to protect me but I gave off auras of insecurity because of the walls I had up, that said "Stay away bitch!" at 20 paces a minute—they didn't know how to approach me and very rarely did they proceed with caution…and when they did finally get in they fucked it up. And that's my biggest problem. Because I was so picky.

I was very fond of saying "When it comes to me, what you see is what you get." But very few bother to look beyond my titties.

I had issues with my weight. I wanted to lose 20 pounds. Like Beyonce did in *Dreamgirls*, yet after seeing plus-sized Jennifer Hudson tear it up, I couldn't lie, I had the sudden urge to stay thick. Men didn't think I was fat. They loved my huge ass, huge titties, small waist and pretty feet. One of my friends, well the man I was in love with, Mr. Y.M.C.A., brought me Janet's *US Weekly* magazine, HOW I LOST 60 POUNDS the headlines rang all in my face like a fat woman with carrot cake on cheat day. I got a little flustered.

He tried to make me laugh and it wasn't

working. "Why are you upset?" he asked, sitting down on my sofa, throwing his Jordan sneaker-clad feet up on my low-table, knocking a few of my *Time* magazines on the floor and he didn't even bother to pick them up. See, that's why I never invited people to my house. People didn't treat your shit the way they wanted their shit to be treated. "Hell if Janet Jackson can drop 60 pounds in four months and look the way she looked on the B.E.T. Awards last night then we all got hope. Well, not me. I'm not fat, mind you. Plus I'm a man."

I rolled my eyes and sucked my teeth, putting my hands on my hips. "...Nothing against Janet, 'cause I *looove* some Miss Nasty—but that woman got a hell of a lot of money, a *personal* gym, *swimming* pool, a *personalized* meal plan where a trainer created all her meals right on down to the *calorie* and a personal trainer and let's not forget plastic surgery is also an option so yeah I don't use that as a reference point."

He just shook his head. "Just focus on changing your diet, sweetness." He was always understanding, when he wanted something.

"I can't leave Popeye's chicken alone, and my cheese and spinach, and my candied yams, *Chile* are you *kidding* me?"

I sat next to him and threw Janet across

the room.

"I *feel* you, girl. I feel you, believe me. But if you want to drop the pounds you *gotta* do the work."

Ok, Dr. Phil. And I can't stand his ass, either! "I *tried*. When I ballooned last year I was so depressed. My tummy was Knots Landing all of a sudden. But I am down to about 125 pounds now and at 5'5 that's not too shabby—now if I could just completely flatten the tummy—hell a 6 pack would be lovely but I don't see it happening."

He smiled, pulling out a joint. I was trying to quit, he was making it very hard to do that. I loved weed just as much as I loved money, which was why my favorite color was green: money and weed!

The thug in him was coming out. I loved his thuggish side. He worked at Jackson Memorial Hospital. He was attending the University of Miami, trying to be a doctor, and the Niggah was doing a helluva good job.

He faced me. "Hit this weed with me," he said knowingly. Hard to believe this man never had pussy a day in his life, never even *thought* about it. Now don't get me wrong, he didn't act or look gay. He was so deep in the closet I think a pile of clothes were on top of him. He was very secretive, very private. He never put anyone in his private affairs, except for me. He had the world thinking he was going with Kamala, some clueless bitch, but they hadn't even so much as smelled each other's shit yet. Smokescreens always kept stinging sensations in the public's eye.

He was always there for me. Whenever I needed him he'd drop any and everything. When a booty call kicked me out of his car last year, fifty miles away from my home, my best friend got up out of a deep sleep, picked me up, told me to drive back to Miami (from Fort Lauderdale, Florida) because he was tired, and never asked me for gas. He has slept in my bed with me countless times and never touched me, never thought about it. But I damn sure wanted his dick because one day I walked in on him taking a piss and his dick was so huge I nearly fainted.

I was horny for this man, always have been. I looked him over, FUBU this and that. Caesar's waves in his hair. He was always meticulously trimmed and barbered. He always dressed in nice clothing without being too dressy. I loved his skin tone. He used Ambi and Oil of Olay. Pretty feet. I wanted to see them so I said, "Kick off your shoes, homeboy. Make yourself at home."

He kicked them off, lighting his joint,

taking a puff. Puff, puff then he passed it to me. "Here you go, Jenna."

"I'm straight," I told him, turning my face. I didn't want weed. I wanted him! I wanted to be the first woman to give him some pussy and show him that "boy pussy" was fake and phony. God made Adam and Eve, not Adam and Steve...wait a minute, God did make Adam and Steve, my bad. He didn't condone what Adam and Steve did, I should say.

"Turn on some music, let's jam to some cuts."

Good idea. Plus I was in an upbeat mood. So I got up and turned on some music, clad in army attire, nothing overrated. Hat pulled low over my eyes. Some Brandy "Full Moon" came on.

"Nah," I said, turning her off. "I don't do Brandy."

"I hope you don't," he joked. "Put on some Tupac."

"Nah, I want to put on some Otis."

"Redding?" He looked at me with a shit-eating grin.

"Yea." I put it on. I danced around some, acting silly, girly. Holding his joint he joined me, snapping and shaking his ass. I told him, laughing out loud, "...Cute very cute—I'm not much of a dancer—I can fake it pretty well but I'll never be able to drop it like it's hot like one of those video girls—not that I think I'd want to."

He was grinning. "I like the way they drop it like it's hot. I want to drop it like it's hot!"

And he started dropping it like the video Hoes and I started clapping. He was doing a good job.

We looked at each other and I felt the electricity, and I wasn't trying to circumvent it, nor fight it. He turned away and went over to my bar, opening the top counter and pulling out some liquor. He poured some E&J into a small red plastic cup with a few ice cubes added for bonus. Then he poured in some orange juice. I thought it tasted nasty with OJ. Maybe with Coke, yea it would taste good but OJ? But he liked what he liked.

He stunned me when he took it to the head with one hefty swig. Something was bothering him. Trying to play it off, he danced back out to me, taking me into his arms, smiling, puffing the joint, red-eyed. "So you want me to show you how to drop it like its hot, lil Mama?" he asked, with a sexy voice. Was he coming on to me? Nah, he was gay, how could he? He hated fish; he loved sausages in his bread.

"IT DONT HURT TO TRY. I CAN BE YOUR SAFETY NET!" I screamed out in happiness, just feeling some of the effects of inhaling all this weed. I kissed his cheek, my pussy on fire.

He gave me the most sensual look, that made my panties recoil. "You keep talking like that and see where that lands you..."

I wouldn't give in. "I know where it'll land me, in a chair after I pull out yours when I take you out to eat."

He smiled. "A female, pulling out my chair. I thought it was the other way around?"

"It is, but hey sometimes it's good to think outside the box."

"You sound like a Taco Bell commercial."

"Shit, let's go get some."

"Hell no. I don't think so," he blurted. He kissed my forehead, pulling me closer to him. I felt the heat rise, and I wasn't wearing Degree deodorant, either. I felt hot, unnaturally so. My hips tingled, my breasts felt like being fondled by his smooth hands. Yea, my pussy and those hands would make such good dancing partners. "Tell me about your love life. We never really talked about it."

Ok. Now I knew what was going on. He was probing for information. But watch how I flipped the script on his funky ass.

"Are you gay, for real man? Because you got me hot."

He didn't flinch. "Yes, *very* gay. *Never* been with a woman. Always wondered what it was like. But never made the plunge."

"...You know I've only been on like 2 official dates in my 22 years of living. My first was to the movies when I was 14 years old. We fucked and I found out I should have kept my virginity, but the more we fucked the more I wanted some dick in my life, hey I'm being real. My second relationship was about 2 years ago. Dinner and dancing—yeah I'm pathetic—and we wound up fucking at his Mama's crib. She came home early, caught us, and threw me out. That's when I stopped dating Niggahs who were live-in sons with their parents. Some day I want to get married. Yeah, ok. I should also warn whoever seriously asks me to marry him in the future there is a strong possibility for multiple births in my family. Yeah I so go off topic."

"No problem with going off..." He was leaning towards my lips. "...topic." He was closer to my lips. "You're a sexy bitch." The sparkles in his eyes, that man-for-a-woman sparkle, that I-want-some-pussy-for-the-first-time sparkle. "I want to *fuck* you. Let's be real. Never had pussy and I'm 27 year old. But I got a lot of dick, and I want it knee-deep in your pussy. Sup, Ma, show a Niggah how to be a man." The lips connected. He gave me some good tongue. He was a bit uncomfortable, but he tried his best not to show it. But one thing was undeniable: his DICK WAS ROCK HARD!

I felt so good, like I had a high school crush. I couldn't believe this was happening to me, finally getting to fuck a man every woman in Little Haiti, my neighborhood in Miami, wanted to fuck but couldn't fuck because he fucked men in the ass, even though females didn't know it. Since he was the "pitcher" I wanted to show him how to pitch for the Pussy Leagues.

I was an open book. "I want you, Niggah. Take me, *please*."

He was very gentle. "I am gay because of what I went through as a kid, my brother used to touch all on me and make me do things. He was older and I always hated it, but I was so young and by the time he stopped it was too late, I had anger, I slept with men out of anger, I never asked to go through this, I tried to stop."

I held him, resting my head on his fabulous chest. He shook a little, hot tears falling from his eyes. Maybe it was the weed and alcohol, but I had a feeling he really wanted to confide in me and I was about to let him. "It's not your fault."

"Yes it is. I could have stopped him. But it got to the point where I started liking it; I wanted it to happen after a while. I hated it, I actually had feelings for my own brother, but I had to end it and when he went away to the military and never came back I was both happy and sad. Happy because he couldn't abuse me anymore but sad because I didn't get to feel the pleasure."

I was so glad he came over. "All I can say is wow—you've over come a lot—you are a good man and more importantly a strong black man and this world is sorely lacking those sad to say. I won't say I'm sorry for your struggles because everything you've gone through has helped shape the man you are today."

He looked at me with a smile. "It felt good to finally get that out; I never thought I'd ever talk about it. Yea. I don't feel so incredible, though. I'm not perfect. Plus I was a kid, roughly about 5 years old when this happened. But the one thing I'm glad I achieved is keeping my sanity through it all. Thanks for being so understanding and hearing me babbling on about this and that. Appreciate it."

I kissed his lips. "Babbling is defined as

an utter meaningless sound—you are doing anything but babbling. Sanity is kinda nice—I can appreciate anyone with a working knowledge of sanity because mine is forever slipping; don't let the pretty face fool ya! I like that we're already trusting friends...and the fact that you look like a lost member of Jodeci is just a bonus—although you have gotten better with age. Yes that's the beauty of black men (and woman) they age very well."

"I can't take it," he admitted, taking off my hat, running his fingers through my hair. "I love your hair. I love women with real hair. I hate weave."

I had a weave! Oh, God! My hair wasn't real! I didn't want to lose this potential dick so I said, "My hair is real, got to be real, you feel me?"

He was rubbing my ass, kissing my neck, taking his time, pressing his huge dick against my stomach....I loved it, I wanted him to take me higher, take me to lands unknown...I couldn't believe this

Desperate for my affection, he got on his knees, hooked both his index fingers behind my panties and slacks and pulled them down to my ankles. He buried his tongue in my pussy, his FIRST TASTE of pussy, hell yea, Adam and Eve, Adam and Eve! He was hungry, like he had just discovered the fountain of youth, but this was the Fountain of Good Pussy and Fortune, his tongue probing and plucking. I damn near fell on my face.

I came so fast I leaned back and smiled. I was shivering, holding his head, tears falling down my face. *"I'm coming, baby!"*

"Lemme taste that shit."

Back in the hole he went with his experienced tongue. He sucked my pink walls and clitoris so fluidly I had multiple orgasms, he swallowed every salty drop.

I was already spent, didn't take much to please me.

But Daddy was hungry.

Standing up he slid that big, thick dick up into my wet pussy and we both had mouths agape.

He was stunned.

"I can't believe it feels like this!" he said excitedly. "Oh my God what have I been missing?"

We moved together, danced to some Otis Redding. Sitting on the Dock of his bay, watching his nuts bounce away, spending time! He was all that and then some;

I was so out of touch with reality that I couldn't believe this was happening. His dick filled me like a hand in a glove.

He held me close, showered my face with kisses, bumped groins...long dicked the pussy. Pushed it all the way in and paused, wiggling his hips. I was punching his chest.

We fucked through four songs.

All over the table, floor, washer and dryer.

I sucked his dick, slobbing all over it, taking it to the nuts….

I made him cum down my throat and when his dick started to get limp I sucked it some more, brought it back to life and told him, "Ready for round 2?"

"Hell yea!" was his eager response.

We were now in my bed, and he pushed my legs all the way back, grinding himself deeply inside me. Damn, Niggah!

Mirrors all around us. Images bouncing in our eyes. Performing for an audience of two, getting creative with it.

After an eternity he tensed up, come build up from his toes and he started grunting and stuttering and his eyes rolled to the back of his head and he came deep inside me.

I felt the spurt on my walls.

I loved the sound of his voice, that I could make him feel this way for the first time in his life. *"Shit shit shit this feels so good baby goddamn pussy feels so good I want dis shit everyday this is my shiiiiit!"*

When it was over he lay on top of me. A few days later, when he was gone I was on cloud nine. A few weeks later we fucked all over Dade County. He never touched another man again. A few months later I called him and told him he had a baby on the way. He came right over to my house with a bundle of roses, looking and smelling like a new man. Once I put the flowers in a vase, I turned to face him and he was on one knee. I was stunned, happy, and quiet. I started to cry. Marriage? I didn't think so, but he was a good man, went through a hard life. So what he fucked men in his past? Everyone had room to change, and he truly wanted to change. We were open and honest with each other, talked about everything under the sun, and trusted each other, his Mama and family adored me. His Mama took me out, and she told me, over pasta at the Olive Garden, "Thanks for making my son a man."

"No problem," I told her.

Now he was in my face, making me want to pull my hair from my scalp. "Will you marry me?" he asked. "I want to be your husband, and I want to be a father to our child."

No I wouldn't marry him! Fuck no! I couldn't! There was dick I wanted to get from a few other men. Yet HIV was out there and I didn't love this man, wanted to grow old with this man so I said "Yes, baby. I would love to!"

I had never been so sure about anything in my life, but I knew I would be his wife.

And that's how strong the Pussy is, *Strong enough for a woman, but PH Balanced for...a man.*

Purple Panties 2

Who would have thought that I, Rosaline Cowart "Roz" would get caught up in a love triangle by an intelligent man who knew more about me than I knew about him or myself combined?

Depressed beyond my wildest dreams, I stood in the spacious bathroom, cautiously trying to get it together. I didn't really want to stay in this home with my man, well my ex man, but I knew I had to go, trying to keep the stinging tears from tired eyes. I turned on the tap water, let it run as cold as it could get and I splashed it on the little face I had left because the rest of my face was out on the living room floor by the couch. Little droplets raced down my face, spilled onto my breasts. I shook with pain. I didn't want to hurt my ex boyfriend. I really didn't intend on him finding out that I was sleeping with his god brother's wife. But I was, because I craved pussy like I craved dick. I was bisexual, shackled inside a lesbian lifestyle so many people disapprove of, but fuck people! The hell with society, who were they to tell me what to do with my body?

This was mine!

Turning off the water I turned on the radio in the bedroom and started taking my clothes out of the drawers while Brandy asked the listening audience "What About Us?" When she needed to be worried about that fifty million dollar lawsuit slapped in her face by the family of the very person she killed, or so I heard. You couldn't always believe what you heard on the news, especially when you're black. The media always made blacks look like sex freaks and incompetent hags, and make white sluts like Anna Nicole look like an angel when she was one of the biggest sluts in Hollywood.

Putting Hollywood entertainment out of my mind, I looked zombie-fied. I kept going over in my brain the fact that I called Tay—my ex boyfriend—another man's name—Pierre—and hadn't even realized it. And now that I was thinking about it, he did wince when I called him "Pierre." When it came down to the nitty gritty, of him finding out I slept with Pierre's wife, part of him *knew* that I had also cheated on him with his God brother Pierre, a man he loved and respected. Yea, I could admit that I fucked 'em both. But with Pierre it was more of a thrill. I was trying to understand why a stone cold lesbian would marry a man as opposed to being in love and truly happy with a woman.

So I gave him some trim and tried to assess the situation and wound up being dick whipped, tongue lashed and came all night long. I could certainly see why she married him, because Pierre was the Justin Slayer of the Hood. Now it was all out in the open, and he wouldn't even talk to me about it. I tried calling him on his cell when he stormed out of here to work. He declined my calls. I left him a recorded message. I assumed he erased them because they went unanswered. I felt guilty; it was eating away at me, consuming me. Because of the silence he was giving me. And Blowing Kisses in the Wind, Waiting for Him like Paula Abdul and her sappy ass song wasn't going to cut it with me because she released the song for money; I just wanted an understanding from my ex.

He said he hated me. And he was moving out. I sacrificed a three year relationship with a caring and sensitive man for what? Thirty second pussy? Trashy dick from his God brother? Well, *trashy* wasn't the word to use, because Pierre had it going on.

I couldn't get over the fact that he said he followed me the other night to his friend's house and personally saw me and his friend's wife rolling around on the couch, bumping pussy; sucking and licking, finger banging and appreciating. I felt so embarrassed right now. I wondered what was going through his head at that particular moment. Did he want to shoot us both? Did he feel betrayed? Did he get off when he watched two sexy women get off 'til the break of dawn? A million and one questions that may never get answered in this life time went through my mind because he wanted to leave, but this was his house, I should be the one leaving. Not him, he didn't deserve this kind of treatment.

My hair all over the place, I needed to

take off this huge trench coat, which was open and showing off my bare breasts and purple panties. I loved those panties. The very satin panties me and Mya, Pierre's sensual wife, played in. I thought of her now, her sweet, sweet lips. Her red, red wine, and every time I drank from her wet opening I felt so, so fine. She was warm and fun, fiery and had the soul of a lioness in battle. She knew how to touch and tease me. She'd drove me crazy, draw me near orgasm every time she went down on me trying to shoot *Pearl Harbor Part II* with the film crew trapped in succulent lips and a slick tongue. But before I could send off the heat seeking missiles from the bubbling lava in the depths of my volcano, she'd stop cold turkey, sit back and watch me shiver, plead with her and beg. My orgasm fizzled into nothing, no BOOM Artillery as they say in the Army, no fireworks. I'd cry myself to sleep, wanting to touch myself and finish myself off but she wouldn't allow me.

The next day she'd do it again, get me bodied, hot and bothered, taste my love with the urgency of Diana Ross in need of a much needed number one hit and once her tongue found the *Da Vinci Code* in my clitoris and the code became the Force Being With me, I'd start climbing the mountain, soaring past the clouds, being wet by the moisture and she'd stop cold turkey before nature could yank out my orgasms. And again I would be mad, curse her, bitch at her and she'd tongue kiss me, hug me, rubbing my titties, my ass, stroking my Kitty Kat and she'd tell me, "Just hold out, I promise this will all be worth it."

Then the third day, we were at it again, kissing, tasting and bumping pelvises. She always looked me in the eyes, concerned about my pleasure. She always asked me questions. Did it feel good to you? Was there anything she needed for me to do? Did I need improvement in any areas? She was a pro; I always gave her the control.

Yet this time, when she spread thy pink walls of the flaming pussy and saw the Pink Panther dancing around chasing spots I started to shake with glee, I was about to pull my hair out, my toes curling to the point of cracking. My eyes rolled to the back of my head while I held her bobbing head. When I came, an explosion rocked me so speechless I couldn't even moan. The pleasure that washed over me was reminiscent of ocean waves across the sandy feet of two lovers running in the glow of the moonlight in search of finding their souls to open the haven so they could mate, becoming soul mates. And when it subsided and my body was no longer in an arch, reminding me of the *Exorcism of Emily Rose*, I would just hug her, tightly, and tell her how much I loved her. She said she loved me too, yet we had committed men in our lives, which prevented us from truly being together. She loved Pierre. I some-what loved Tay.

And now she still had Pierre. And I didn't have Tay.

Crying my ass off, I opened a suit case and threw in my folded clothes when the house phone rang. I froze, just staring at it. Complete silence. I didn't even flinch. I looked at it more fixedly, just waiting for the answering machine to pick up. But I couldn't wait, it could be Tay. So I rushed over to the nightstand, yanked it up and said, as calmly as I possibly could, "Hello."

Silence.

"Hello, damn it I'm *not* in the mood."

Sobbing. Heavy sobbing.

I was alarmed. "Tay, is that you?" My eyes bounced all over the objects in this room. "I'm sorry, baby, I didn't mean for you to get hurt."

Tears welled in my eyes, which kept surprising me because it took a lot for me to cry, yet I know what it felt like to be cheated on. I went through that years ago. Which was why I had conditioned myself to harden my heart against men?

Now my heart bled for Tay.

"It's not Tay," she said and I just blinked once, gripping the phone.

I couldn't keep the smile from my face.

"Mya?"

"Yes, baby. It's me. Can we talk?"

"Sure. You *know* we can talk. Where do you want to meet?"

"Downtown. Bayside. Bubba Gump Shrimp, we can talk there."

"When do you want me to meet you there?"

"*Now.* It's important."

I hung up. A tad bit disoriented, I put on a "Monika" kimono top with bold orange and black printed designs, six snake-print bangles on either wrist, I loved being...accessorized. A necklace with a huge diamond medallion that rested between my breasts, put my hair up in a bun, slid into some tight blue jeans. Quickly rushed into the bathroom and made up my face with Elizabeth Arden. Lorreal, Maybelline and Dark and Lovely would never grace my face.

I grabbed my beaded cornhusk bag, threw in a bottle of perfume, which I'd spray on me in the car, slid on some clogs, though they were played out but since when did I play by the rules and I put on huge chandelier earrings that dangled and tinkled.

I was a very beautiful 40 year old woman. In love with a woman who was younger than me—20 years younger.

I was out the door, headed for my Durango ten minutes later, after turning on the house alarm.

And yes.

I still had on the purple panties.

My heart hurting for Tay and the lives I helped destroy, I entered Bubba Gump Shrimp, a bustling restaurant, with a smile, looking around for Mya. She must not be here yet so I asked the waiter to get me a table for two, preferably in the back of the restaurant. Best to keep it discreet.

"Right this way, ma'am. You're looking rather dashing today," said the handsome young white male. I shook his hand, then he kissed mine.

"Thank you," I told him, glowing like the huge ball of fire above Bayside, one of the hugest tourist attractions in Miami.

A few men were checking me out, mumbling to themselves with secret smiles.

"I look ok?" I asked them, turning in a circle, running my hands over my attire.

"…Yes, you look good…"

"...You're wearing that kimono, pretty lady..."

"...Your husband is a lucky man..."

I shook their hands, feeling a bit festive and made my way to the table. Such the gentleman, the waiter pulled out my chair and I sat down, thanking him silently. He said, "Would you like a drink?"

"Why yes, a Sprite would do."

"Do you know what you want to order?"

"Grilled shrimp. Two orders. And bring the receipt ahead of time so I can pay it and get it over with."

"Coming right up, would you like anything else?"

"No, I'm ok. And thanks."

"I'll be right back with your drink, ma'am." When he pivoted, to go take care of my order Mya's eyes looked down at me. She smiled, leaning over and kissed my cheek.

"Hey, Roz. Have you been here long?"

I stood up and pulled out her chair. She looked ravishing. I loved the red cassimere sweater and the flowing skirt, which dangled into a split along her right leg. Her make-up, flawless. Every finger had jewelry. Her necklace, thin and glittering.

I got right down to business; I was a direct woman, in and out of the bedroom. "So what did you want to see me about?"

She was quiet for a few minutes. She nodded her head to a country song that I never heard before. "I left Pierre."

I was quiet. "Why?"

"I don't *love* him." She looked away from me, which told me she was lying. "It's not good to stay in a marriage when you don't love the person."

"Tell me the truth." I kept my voice warm and affectionate, just the way she liked. She looked at me, nervous. I held her hand.

"Anyways, how is your day going, Roz?" Her voice was strained, like she was holding something back.

"My day is…tolerable. I lost my man, of course."

She licked her top lip, averting her eyes again. She would not look at me. "That was inevitable, Roz."

"I didn't mean for Tay to get hurt."

"We all got hurt, girl. We all played a dangerous game and we lost. Tay lost everything he had in you."

"He'd get over it." My throat was stinging at the thought of such a good man going through all that heartache.

"You don't just deal with heartbreak over night, Girl." She looked at me, going in her purse and pulling out a stick of gum.

"Girl, let me get one."

She gave me a nasty look. "Go and buy your goddamn own, you took enough from me."

I didn't understand. "What did I take from you?"

"My life. You know we can't be together, even if we wanted too."

"But what about the plans we made."

"What plans?" She had selective amnesia.

"You know, leave our men and move to Polynesia."

"What black bitch you know lives in Polynesia? And you know what they say about plans."

"Plenty black people go to Polynesia."

"Name one."

She had me. "Girl, let's stop this game. I need you."

"Tay needed you, girl. I was in it for the sex; I am not going to toy around with you. It was fun while it lasted."

"It can still last, Mya."

"You sound desperate." Mya couldn't keep the contempt from her voice. "And you're getting older. You're twenty years older than me, I'm still young and I don't want to grow old with you."

Those words cut like a knife, tore through

me like an ax.

"Where is all this coming from? Why would you come in public and hurt my feelings this way, maybe I don't know you as well as I thought."

"Look, Roz. Shit just hit the fan. Tay came over and told Pierre what was going on. There was a huge fight."

My mouth fell open in shock. "*No*, girl."

"*Yes*. Pierre told him that you slept with him as well, told him everything, girl. That you two fucked for months. Tay was in a fit of rage, he said he hated you and he would hate you forever, that he'd never forgive you."

I couldn't stop the tears from falling. I shuddered with pain. I never meant to hurt such a good man. It was probably women like me that turned good men into dogs, into the disrespectful beings they would eventually become, growing hearts of stone.

Tay was good with me, knew everything about me, from my favorite color to how I liked my food. He helped me out with my parents, always took my Mama food. He never asked for money. He never asked for anything. He was the most selfless man I knew. And now he was hurt.

I didn't know what to do. "I got to call him, girl."

She squeezed my hand. "You may not have the opportunity." Her voice and eyes trailed off.

I was guarded. "What are you talking about?"

"Well I left them fighting. I grabbed my keys and went to my neighbor's house and called the police. They were breaking dishes, cursing each other, screaming I hate you back and forth. A chair flew out the living room window; Tay took bricks and broke his windshield and shattered every window on our house. He was a monster; he said he loved you more than life itself.

Pierre said something and Tay rushed into the house, closed the door and two gunshots made me and the neighbors blink in stone silence. I was so scared, girl."

Her hands were trembling.

I didn't like the picture she was painting. She had to be lying. I was in serious denial. Tay would *never* shoot anyone. He *hated* guns. Well maybe Pierre shot him. I didn't know. I was about to explode so I said, frantically, "Girl what happened?"

She didn't waste any time. "Tay shot Pierre in the head. Then turned the gun on himself."

While I went through withdrawal of my own, a terrible ringing in my ears giving me headaches, Mya slid to the floor, covering her face, sobbing so hard everyone started to notice. She was screaming, saying over and over she was sorry, that she should have never allowed herself to get involved, she should have never betrayed herself, her marriage and Tay, who had always been good to her. "I warned you about wearing those panties, I told you not too but you were so…"

Some guy helped her off the floor, and showed genuine concern for her and she snatched her arm back, got in my face and pointed a bony finger.

She had fire in her eyes, made me shudder. "I *told* you not to wear those panties but *no*, you just *had* to wear them. Those purple panties created all this. I can't believe Pierre and Tay are dead. I got two funerals to attend, how will I explain this to his family, to my family, to Pierre's family? That us licking pussy brought about this hell!" She tossed her hair behind her head and stood erectly, gazing me in the eyes, forcing herself to hate me. No one uttered a word. Even the cops over at the opposite table lowered their heads. She laughed bitterly, crossing her arms across her chest.

She said, matter-of-factly, "Don't call, write or stalk me. I got a restraining order against you. If you come within a hundred feet of me bitch you will be arrested. The love I had for you died the instant the gun went off and I lost my husband and my friend Tay. In life we pay for mistakes and bad decisions. Sometimes we can get over it, move on and try to forget it happened. But I *can't* forget I helped create this massacre. Go to hell, because I damn sure don't want to burn with you."

She snatched up her purse and I, dying inside, my world spinning, jumped up to my feet and grabbed her, pleading with her, begging her not to leave me. The cops looked sternly, but didn't move from the table.

I grabbed her in a bear hug. All the love I had in my heart for her snowballed me. I wound up kissing her luscious lips. They still felt warm and soft. I had to resist the urge to rub her pussy. I wanted it bouncing on my tongue while her clit slid against it. I wanted to watch her shiver when she came and moaned my name, telling me I was the most gorgeous woman in the world. I wanted us to slap asses with a dildo linking us together. I wanted to lick the sweat from her tight asshole and finger fuck her into a fierce orgasm. I wanted the old days back, when Tay didn't know I slept with another woman. I wanted to be her one and only, take her away from all this hell. I wanted Tay to be alive and well so he could find another woman, fall n love and forget I existed…

Now we gave each other some tongue, hugging and rubbing, our hearts mending and fencing…in front of everyone. I didn't care. I rubbed her ass, told her we'd get through this, that I couldn't live without her, shouldn't live without her and her lips didn't move anymore. Her arms dangled at her sides.

Biting my bottom lip, she slapped me and ran out of the restaurant, in tears. I, my hair disheveled, sank to my knees, my shoulders shaking, the tears ripping my soul apart and I couldn't contain the guilt and the shame that turned me to flames.

I wish to God I would have never worn those purple panties.

Clever felt elated today. Her game of mastery and trickery in the sheets filled her with a certain glee that was only found inside the cavities of the greedy and the rich. The thought of the chase engulfed her like flames on hay. Today, of course, another challenge beckoned her. Looking over the framed photograph on the nightstand, she picked it up and kissed the woman clad in the floral dress. Her misty eyes clouding over, she set it down and turned to face him. With a secret grin, she said, "Honey, I want to live out my dreams."

Clad in a top hat of velvet and a smoke-colored suit, he responded, "Then *live* it."

She looked amused. "Edgar, is she *coming*?"

He blinked a few times, sighing. "Today, my name is Edgar? I like the name, Clever. Truly, you know what my real name is…

"Yes, I do. Edgar is so…fitting. This is girl number four. All in a week's time period!"

Edgar was amused. "Yes."

She looked at herself in the mirror. "But what about the photographs," she asked nonchalantly.

Sheepishly, he said, "They can stay. She just wants to be paid…"

She smiled—a reflection of her man. "Let the fantasy begin!"

"Begin, it shall, my lady."

"I can't wait!" she gushed.

Ah, the British accent worked wonders.

The new scapegoat sauntered into fabulous bedroom like a summer's breeze— sassy, classy and she wore those chandelier earrings that almost brushed her shoulders like old slaves back in the day with their brooms. Her face made up just right. Ah, he liked! She commanded attention from every piece of expensive Picasso, Da Vinci, and Van Gogh painting on the red walls. She especially loved the oriental carpet. *So divine*, she thought meaningfully.

I'm going to break this man for his money. I'm 19 years old and I'm feisty. I went to the doctors and had my physical. I have to take my daily shot, which I forgot to do. And my throat is a little parched. Maybe I should ask for a tall glass of water.

Mystified, Edgar asked, "And *your* name

is?" The British accent did a number on the willing prostitute. She absolutely *loved* the Voice. They *all* loved the voice.

This Hollywood-type beauty rubbed her gorgeous breasts seductively, licking her lips like Audrey Hepburn back in the early 19th century. She had long, black curly hair, full, sensual lips; her nipples were at least a half inch long, poking against the expensive satin fabric crafting the rest of her magnificent dress.

"I'm Desire!"

Edgar was jubilantly pleased. *"You're mad! You're gorgeous!"* He was rubbing his penis.

Desire looked down at the shape of his penis.

It's too small to be classified as a dick. And he wants to fuck me with that little ole thing. Maybe I should inquire about it; hell my mind wants to know. And my ass and hands do, too. I'm just being real. I want my money and then I'm acting funny.

With breathless adoration, Desire brushed lint off the smoke-colored suit. "Love the choice of dress," Desire said enviously, calculatedly kissing his lips. With the skill of a seasoned veteran, his tongue danced in sync with hers. It wasn't one of those sloppy kisses, thank heavens. She could taste remnants of red wine and pistachios.

Desire was on fire, she wanted to ignite

his flames and hoped infernos turned the sheets to ashes and her horniness to dust so she could lay, spent and then spend her hard earned money. *I must not forget the real reason why I'm here, though. And money isn't the* only *reason!*

She had to pay off her student loans. She attended City College in South Miami, Florida. It used to be located just across the street from the South Miami Metro Rail station. Now Baptist Hospital took over the glass and concrete building. She used to love the smallness of the inside floor. The college was one level with small classrooms. No more than ten people; the library was small, intimate, sweet and to the point, about three computers, tops. The Computer Lab itself had about forty computers.

Now my financial advisor is always at my classroom door, calling me out into the hall. I think he likes me, and that's why he's forcing me to pay these loans! How could I? I work at Denny's at night, busting tables, taking tips and sometimes assholes come in there and they don't even leave *tips. Or they slip out without paying and it comes out of* my *check. I live in a section 8 house. I don't have any kids because I can't have any, for a reason. I want a better life.*

Pushing all that to the back of her mind, Edgar took the time to turn on Barbra Streisand's "*Wet*" album. It was hard to break away from Desire's kisses. Such passion she had.

"You never told me your name," said Desire, walking over to him and kissing him again. The way he felt, the slickness of his tongue, the smell of his fragrance pushing her up and over her limitations dethroned thoughts of unease. He was holding her face like a fine piece of crystal, pressing his warm body up against hers. Her eyes danced over the Van Gogh painting of huge sunflowers, the Tiffany lamps, the Gucci watches and belt buckles and cologne on the dressers.

Barbra Streisand and Donna Summer were singing "No More Tears." She loved the song, never heard it before. She had all of Donna's albums so she knew her distinct voice. Her eyes fell on a few 5x7 photos of a lovely woman with green eyes sitting like Queens on the nightstand. She had on a summer dress, or did they call it floral dresses?

"Are you married?"

He pulled away from her, softly pushing her to the bed. Seduction danced in his eyes. He was rubbing himself.

"Checking the package, 'ey?" asked Desire, licking her lips.

She gave a grin that made Desire melt. "Yes."

She smiled. "Is that your wife in the photograph? You never said you were married."

Hesitated a bit. "Yes, that's my wife."

She wanted to initiate some freaky shit. "Turn her pictures to the bed, so she can see what I do to your dick."

"Fire, aren't you…And for the record my name is Edgar."

"Nice name…."

Edgar said, "Why thank you, madam."

Desire turned the photos so they were facing her. She undid her bra with one hand, the red Victoria let out the Secrets that bounced with a sudden joy. Edgar nearly came on himself. He pulled her dress down to the start of her belly button. He rolled his tongue around her soft, creamy black skin. She tasted like sugar.

"You taste sweet, like sugar…"

"I put real sugar in my edible lotion everyday so that I'm *always* sweet."

Edgar wanted this one to be his! "You're *mad*! I have a question for you."

"Shoot."

Edgar went in for the kill. "Have you ever slept with a woman?"

Desire's mouth fell open. "No. I'm *not* that way. I'm a woman, I don't *suck* pussy."

Edgar's eyes beamed. "Ok, I got you."

Desire grabbed her right tit and shook it. "Now let's get it on."

"Sure." He sucked on her breast like his tongue was dying of thirst, like a fish out of water just dying for a gentle drop of the ocean. Desire melted, reaching behind the nape of his neck, rubbing it. She wanted to take the hat off, but she didn't. He looked good with it on. He moved his hand over her breasts, his lips and tongue dancing with mound of flesh. Desire rolled her groin, lust tearing her up. She ran her hand behind her soft hair, smelled of strawberry Suave, and held it atop her head; strands falling into her face as she leaned her head back.

"Take your pants off, Edgar," she cooed.

"No can do. This is *your* moment; I just want to eat your pussy."

Desire was unnaturally quiet. She didn't *want* head. She wanted to get tagged from the back. She was an *anal* bitch. *Stick it in, fuck me hard, long and good. Make those nuts slap my ass like Kobe Bryant taking basketballs from Michael Jordan while Derek Jeter looks on with his bat.*

Desire told him how she wanted it. "I want to be fucked in the ass, baby. I want to swallow your cum; let your cream play tic tac toe on thy ole tongue. I hope your come doesn't taste funky! And I hope you washed your dick.

You men have a habit of jacking off and letting your seeds dry up on your shaft because you're arrogant, territorial and cocky!"

Edgar was slowly losing interest. Prostitutes weren't supposed to be demanding or talkative. "I can do that. Mind if I use toys?"

Desire was unperturbed and appalled. "*No*! I want the real thing. Skin versus skin. I want your dick in my ass! Fuck the bullshit. And then I want my 500 bucks."

Edgar stood up. "Such a raunchy mouth you have! Online, when we met last night, before we set up this meeting, you told me you were a woman of impeccable taste. Judging from your raunchy word choice maybe that was a lie."

Desire was taken aback. *"A lie?"*

Edgar couldn't take it anymore. The slut had to go! "Yes, a lie. A fib, story telling, liar, are those *enough* words for you?"

Desire's eyes widened with shock. "Your British Accent…it's gone. Like…it…was. Never there."

He smiled. "Well, if that's the case, then game over. My fantasy is *ruined*."

Desire needed the money. She had to get him back in the habit. Suddenly the financial advisor popped in her head, taunting her about paying for her loans. "Your voice sounds somewhat feminine now. What's going on? Are you a feminine fag or something? Getting off on your sick games?"

Edgar's eyes widened. He was insulted. *This bitch has got to go!*

Desire covered her breasts with the satin sheet. "What?" She looked over and saw his Salem Lights cigarettes and a lighter. She took a cig, lit up and pulled on it, sucking the smoke into her lungs. She was stressed.

I drove south on US1 from Kendall to this jerk's house. Traffic was crazy and half my hair do was messed up because it was raining. I had to study for midterms, and he says game over? That means no money! I can't *pay on my loans. They are going to vault. I got to pay for my doctor's examination, and now I can't. Plus I owe forty bucks on my light bill, twenty more on my water and my Brinks security Alarm bill is due. Ninety dollars! And this man is playing with me.*

Desire apologized. "I'm sorry. You don't have to sex me; I'll do what you want." She blew smoke in the air. "I need the money, please understand. I'm just a little pressed for time."

"Light me a cig, Desire," he said, the accent returning, the eyes gleaming again.

Spoiled freak! "Sure." Desire held a cig up to his lips, then the flame under it. He puffed and appreciated.

"What do you want to do?" Desire asked.

Edgar didn't waste any time. "Eat you out, my lady."

She was hesitant. "Take your hat off, first," said Desire.

"Ok." He stood up, took a few steps back and took off the hat. Desire saw the hair net.

She was suddenly guarded. "That's a lot of hair," she said. He took off the net; the hair fell around his face.

"Oh my God," said Desire. "A man with hair. You look like a girl. Men aren't *supposed* to look like girls."

Off came the shirt. Desire chocked on smoke seeing two tits duck taped, making them look compressed. Snatching off the tape, Edgar winced painfully.

Desire was embarrassed. "*OH MY GOD YOU'RE THE WOMAN FROM THE PHOTOGRAPHS!* You were watching yourself," said Desire with shock.

Edgar took off the pants; the sock fell to the floor. Desire thought, *No wonder his dick looked small, he didn't have one. He was a female!* She took off her panties. Tossed them in Desire's face. Repulsed, she threw them across the room. Angry, Desire picked up some pillows and threw them at Edgar, or whoever this freak was. Cologne and perfume bottles crashed and broke open on the tile, the liquid spilling everywhere.

Clever smiled. "Hi, my lady. And you said you didn't want any lesbian action."

Desire smiled. "For a reason." She took off the covers. So sexy she was. Clever was wet all over. She started rubbing her velvet softness; she cooed and moaned to herself.

"Go on, play with your pussy," said Clever, trying to seduce Desire.

"Such raunchy words. And you came down on me for cursing…But I got a surprise for you. Come, my lady, you can eat my pussy now!"

"I knew you'd see things my way." Clever opened the nightstand, took out five crisp one hundred dollar bills and gave to Desire. She held the money. On her knees she was, between Desire's beautiful legs. Her nose was two inches from Desire's private area.

Desire pulled out her nine inch dick, which was tucked between her legs, said, "FREEZE!" and Clever jumped out of the bed as if it was on fire.

Desire smiled sweetly, watching Clever tremble with anger.

Desire said, "*I got a secret.* I got to pay for my next dosage of hormone shots, actually. I forgot to take one before I left. Causes my voice to be feminine. It's no walk in the park intravenously shooting estrogen into your body. I was born a man. Fortunately, for me of course, I *knew* you were a woman. I just played the fantasy, isn't *that* what *you* paid for?"

Clever's world destroyed, devastated, she fell to her knees, screaming into her hands. Someone tapped her shoulder. Looking up, Desire was putting on her clothes. "I'm a woman, but I never said a *complete* woman. Now you understand why I'm so…anal retentive in the ole rectum region."

Clever felt sick. The room spun. *"Fuck you! Get out! Get out now!"*

Another tap on her shoulder. She froze. She slowly turned to face Rayne, who was filming the entire thing. Bringing her face from behind the small Sony digital camera. "Stop your games, or the Internet gets the tape. Oh, by the way, my son wants that Playstation 3. I think it cost about $500. How about buying it for him when it comes out. Better yet, give me a cool thousand bucks, for pain and suffering and you won't wind up in court."

Clever paid them, and Rayne, slapping palms with Desire/Steven, left out the room.

Clever closed her eyes…

***

Clad in her male disguise, Clever said, "Honey, I want to live out my dreams!"

Staring at her reflection, she said "Then live it," using the male British accent.

Clever asked, "Is she coming?"

"*No*," he said emptily. Something died in him.

Clever forced herself to grin. "This would be girl number five. All in a week's time period!"

Edgar shouted, "No." She looked at herself in the mirror. Intently. Smiling evilly. "Desire wasn't a girl. She was a man in drag."

Clever looked blankly. "But what about the photographs," she asked nonchalantly.

He said coolly. "They can stay. Rayne just wants to be paid…paid a visit"

She smiled. "Let the fantasy begin!"

"But what fantasy will this be? Desire destroyed it."

Acid in her eyes. Clever said, "Rayne, Rayne go away, when I kill you; you will never come back another day."

Ah, the British accent worked wonders.

Smoke and Mirrors

When I first met my wife, Gladys, she was the sexiest woman in the world! She had a voluptuous body and an even hotter pussy. Back then I thought I was a player, running game on all the bitches. In fact I never thought I'd fall in love let alone stop calling women a name they call themselves. Everyone wanted

Frank Sinclair, which would be me. As much as I hated it, I was named after my dad, a real asshole who was drugged out, currently sleeping on a Downtown Miami bus stop bench by the courthouse.

My wife and I had a different type of relationship now. Depressingly sad, I lay in my bed, clad in silk boxers and a wife beater tank top T. The news of a few murders flashing in my face, I was waiting for my divorce to be final within the next few months. Where did I go wrong? Did I *not* love her enough? Did I not try hard enough? Yet all those questions I pulled from a bucket of oranges when the situation was a bag of spoiled apples. Unusual circumstances willed the divorce. Unfortunately, I didn't have a choice. And despite how I felt about her, no matter how much I *still* love her, love was the *only* thing I could possibly save from this union.

A union that shouldn't have even taken place.

I drove a recently-restored '67 Chevy rolling on deep dished chromed rims. I couldn't live without my booming stereo system that made my trunk rattle like a few screws were loose. I sold cocaine and weed on the side, while holding down college and a full-time job. And during all this my wife turned on me, and became someone else. A stranger. She had the face of a super model and a body that would turn J. Lo into a lesbian. She had everyone from the crack heads to white-collar business men begging to fuck her. Her ass was so big, when she crossed the street Niggahs would hold up traffic just to watch her walk by. She loved it, thrived on it. I used to be *proud* to be her man; I never thought a woman could capture my heart. My father was a rolling stone; my grandfather was a rolling stone. So I was a goddamn boulder.

I fucked any and every bitch and I didn't care if she was married. I didn't care if my friend dated her. If my cousin went with her I didn't give a shit. Pussy was pussy and if the bitch gave it up to me then quite frankly the pussy was never his to begin with, so why get mad at me? I was a grimy Niggah when it came to money and pussy. I was feared by a lot of Niggahs in Miami-Dade, especially in Leisure and Liberty City. I'd walk into the USA Flee Market on NW 79th Street and even the big time dope boys gave me respect. I have shot at so many Niggahs that it just didn't make any sense.

I had a rough life, bad upbringing. I didn't have the opportunities the kids in the suburbs had. After begging God for a few months to open the door of opportunity for me, and going to church to set it stone it never happened so I haven't gotten my knees dirty in years. I used to watch my Mama, Verona Sinclair, get dicked down every day by a different man with a different reputation. I was a little kid, watching her slang weed and snort coke just to make ends meet the rent and the light bill. I mentally took notes because she once told me this was how you got by in life. Hustling. For a few months on end she disappeared and I had to cook, clean and take care of myself. I took myself to the doctor, sometimes getting one of the older dope boys to pretend he was my father so my shots and immunizations were up to par. She always made sure the rent was paid and food was in the ice box. *That* I didn't have to worry about. I didn't take school seriously at all. I talked back to teachers and started letting the environment shape me. I duly listened to Elder black men in my neighborhood who told me that Niggahs were only good for three things: getting some pussy, playing a sport and staying out of jail.

We drink booze and we sold drugs, they continued to say. We whipped bitches asses to keep them in line and we protected our word and balls like they were an endangered species. I took all that to heart. I became it, slept on it, fucked and ate it. Even though Mama was a Ho, I loved and respected her no matter what. I *never* back talked her; never let her see me cry. She never talked down to me. When she saw me her eyes lit up. Mama sold her pussy up until she was found dead behind a restaurant on South Beach a few years ago, before I turned twenty. I was still bitter about that. Daddy had killed her because he got tired of her whoring around Dade County. But he never brought up the fact that he was an even bigger Ho than she was.

At her funeral I was distraught; I tore up every flower. I fought my Daddy and accused him of murder. Family pulled him from the church. I was in a blinding rage. I couldn't control myself. The police came and I denied the allegations. I wasn't a snitch. I didn't like crackers in my business. They didn't care about a prostitute anyways. The look on their pale faces told me that.

Rumors circulated that Daddy had another kid somewhere. But he denied it and without any proof, what could I say? He was a prick. I hated him with a passion and he never showed me fatherly things. We never spoke. He never looked out for me. Funny, we lived in the same house and we didn't have any type of a relationship. I stopped giving a damn after I turned eleven years old. I gave up on a Daddy/Son relationship. I even asked God to erase his existence from my memory.

Some girl hugged me at Mama's funeral. In tears of her own she held me tight. She was clad in a floral dress and big red ribbons in her hair. Her name was Paula Jakes, a year younger than me. I didn't know *who* she was, pretty little thing. But all I could do think about my mother. How she suffered when she was alive; I wanted to know what drove her to prostitution, why she never told me about my grandparents. I had so much contempt. Yea, she vanished for months but I always knew she would come home. Now she never would. I could never see the sparkles in her eyes when she saw me. Angrily, I pushed Paula off me. She shook with fear. "Fuck you! I want my mother!" I spat icily. The preacher told me to stop cursing and I pushed the podium over and threw the Bible at him. "Tell God to stop cursing my goddamn life!" One of my dope boy friends embraced me and I cried on his shoulder until my nose burned.

Little Paula ran off and hugged an old-looking man, who sat by a female police officer with the name Officer Brown on her name tag. I would *never* forget the woman because she stared at me with a wicked look on her face. I *knew* she was mad I was acting a complete fool at the funeral, but I didn't care. I didn't know how to process that type of pain, being the young age I was. It was too much for me to bear.

Years later, when I got married my wife Gladys helped me deal with my mother's death. I cursed her and called her outlandish names. She never got offended. She never turned her back on me. She let me vent and throw things. She always replaced the items when she got paid without asking me for anything. She never wanted my money. She had her own job, her own crib and her own car. She treated her pussy like it was a priceless antique; she made me work for her panties.

When I cheated on her she stopped calling me and she talked down to me. When I tried to slap her lippy ass she kicked me in my nuts, pulled my own gun on me and said, "Niggah, I'll shoot your sperm cells in the head just to make sure they die off like your no good ass if you try me." Goddamn it, I fell in love right there. She was a Gangster Bitch, without coming off looking like one. Suddenly, right then and there, what the Elder black men once taught me—that men were supposed to whip a woman's ass to keep her in line—went right out the window.

I became faithful. For the sake of our relationship I deleted all the booty call phone numbers. In fact I gave the phone away and got another phone. I didn't give out the number to anyone.

I totally reformed myself; against my will, I met her Mama, Janis Jakes, an oversized heart of gold. She looked real familiar, but we were from the same neighborhood so I probably saw her around in the grocery store or some place like that. She treated a Niggah like a black man and not like an environmentally-shaped inept asshole. She treated me like a person, told me she detested the N-word. I told her to fuck off, but she told me, "Real men don't use that word, especially after learning the history of it."

You know me. I had to debate. So I told her, "Well, I *heard* you call another friend of yours a bitch. Hey, bitch. How are you, Ho? But I can't use the N-word? Please, Mama. *Save* it."

I won.

She cooked for me. I could come and go as I pleased. She shared her daughter's baby pictures with me. She even showed me pictures of herself when she was young. The pictures look very nice. I appreciated her sharing them with me. I didn't *have* baby pictures. My parents never cared for photos.

She gave me black books to read.

Honestly, I hated reading, but her Mama was so laid back, so real and so down for being black. She represented what true black beauty was. Shockingly, I fell in love with books. They opened up a whole new world I never knew existed. When the fellahs on the dope corners saw me walking up the block reading they were stunned. "Niggah, you read books?" my good friend Harold asked, grabbing his dick and trying to stand in those loose, baggy jeans.

"Yea, man. This Sistah Souljah book the Coldest Winter Ever is the freshest thing I have ever read."

All seven dope boys looked at each other, and burst out laughing. "Stop playing," said Little Bishop, the youngest in the crew. A scar lining his face, he said, "Put that Sister Hoax shit down and let's sell a few birds. And make this money…"

I kept walking towards my crib, totally engrossed in the book. Sadly, I lost them as friends. They wanted a hustler, not a book worm. I didn't give a shit. What I acquired meant more than drugs, pussy and the block. I read Eric Jerome Dickey novels and E. Lynn Harris. I expanded my mind. I read *Call Her Miss Ross*, the unauthorized autobiography on evil, slutty ass Diana Ross. I read Sidney Sheldon and Terry McMillan. I actually hated

Waiting to Exhale, the movie but I *loved* the book. My girl and her mother became my world.

I was raised in Brownsville. I went to school there, and fought there. I had a lot of bitterness about life. I used to hate the law. I used to hate the president. I used to hate black people. I used to hate the Cubans. And I used to hate myself.

My girl taught me how to love; I dropped out of high school, never finished. My girl talked me into going back.

"I got faith in you, baby, I'll help you. You can do it."

And she did help me. I got my G.E.D. I was so happy. If only my Mom could be here to see that.

I proposed to her when I turned 20 years old. I knew in my heart she would be the woman I'd grow old with. My wife never judged me. She taught me how to have empathy. After a year I left drugs alone, because her Mama worked for the police department. I also changed my friends. Gone were the dope boys and I enrolled in school and tried to become a better man. I had to learn how to deal with the past, how to let go of it and move on. My wife helped me with that. We actually saw a therapist and we went to group sessions twice a week. I discovered growth on a grand scale. I didn't bring a cloud of disrespect around my wife's mother's expensive bungalow in Earlington Heights, Florida (Miami).

But she started changing a few months after we tied the knot. She talked down to me and started cheating. Even though I could never prove it. She harbored a secret I had found out about one day when she left her Diary on the dresser. She never finished the journal entry, and on the top of the page were the words "funeral," "flowers," "stranger." I threw the shit on the floor. Initially, it didn't interest me, and I never thought about it again. Well, that was until she came home a few days later, crying her ass off. And as her faithful husband, going through the ups and downs of marriage, I had sat her down, comforted her, let her cry on my shoulders, and I asked her what was wrong.

"Did somebody do something to you?"

She remained quiet. She wouldn't open up to me.

I said, "Talk to me," rubbing her back, fondly.

With a burst of anguish, she pushed me. "You can't help, Frank! *You're* the problem!"

I was dumb-founded, shaking my head. "What did *I* do?"

She exploded. "EVERYTHING!" Leaving me confused, she ran off, slamming the front door behind her. She wouldn't come home for days. I would worry, sit up late and every time the phone rang I'd quickly answer. It was the bill collectors, family and friends. But *never* my wife. I was reverted back to the little child I was when Mama used to disappear. My world was suddenly cold and cruel. I used to cry in the dark, too afraid to turn on the light and see my own tears. My blood ran colder than ice. It got to the point where I stopped caring and *stopped* losing sleep. If she wanted to come home she knew where we lived. She had a key. I was a man, and I started worrying about myself.

Then the shock of a lifetime took my breath away. Her Mama tried luring me to bed. I fought with her all the time. She wanted me. I didn't understand her sudden interest. It took a few weeks to realize that maybe she always wanted to have sex with me. She groomed me very well, giving me books, and cooking for me. The signs were there but I guess I ignored them back then. Now I thought of them all the time. I eventually broke down and fucked her Mama in the ass a few months later, and then I got the pussy a week after. We had a regular affair. We met up to fuck and I left to go try to be a husband. Since my wife wasn't taking care of home her Mama took care of mine. I needed the love and the attention, even though once I came in the bitch's face my love ran down her chin like tears. Janis Jakes loved the dick. She had some bomb pussy and some smoking head.

I lost respect for Gladys. I lost respect for myself. She started smoking weed and snorting coke. Every Friday night she got intoxicated with her no-good, fire-in-the-pussy friends. She was bringing them into our home. She never listened to me when I said I didn't want them there. She disrespected me in front of them. And since I didn't want to break her fucking face I just packed a bag and got a hotel room, so I could get some sleep. I had to work in the mornings. I slowly started reverting to my old ways, threw my G.E.D. away, started selling dope again, sought out the familiar bitches, and treated my wife like shit. She was losing weight, big time, but I denied it. I tried not to think about it.

I tried moving out of the house, but she caught me on video tape fucking some bitch in the ass on South Beach. I loved fucking Hoes in the ass. It was tighter than the pussy. No homosexual shit with me. I actually *thought* about my late mother when it came to ass. I remembered the day I walked in on some stranger pounding her in the ass. She was earning rent money. Mama loved dick inside of her, from the looks of it. She had a huge smile on her face, spreading her cheeks apart so homeboy could admire the sight from behind. I fell in love with it then, but of course I was only eight years old, and I didn't utter a sound. I tip-toed to Mama's closet, leaving the door slightly ajar and I watched her take dick for hours. I knew I was going to do girls like that myself. All that went through my mind when my wife threatened to bootleg the tape of me screwing the bitch on South Beach and sell DVD's and use it against me in court if I didn't become a faithful man. So I did. Reluctantly, she started controlling me. She controlled the relationship. I felt like the bitch.

Then one day I saw something that made me lose all respect for her forever. I was leaving the CITGO gas station on S.W. 268th Street—about thirty minutes away from my house—when I saw her arguing with a man across the street in the Pine Island Projects. I had slowly turned my Chevy up into the projects, turning down my music. What was my wife doing thirty minutes away from home? I had a valid excuse. My job sent me down there to drop off an employee.

I parked in front of an abandoned duplex and cut the engine. I rolled down the window and listened.

"You aren't shit, Niggah! Where's my money?" she asked, slapping him.

He punched at her but she pivoted on her heel and slapped him again. "Fuck you, Ho!" He got in her face; they were about the same size—skinny, toothpick-built people. They were on drugs.

"I am not giving you shit!" he stammered.

A crowd was gathering. I was heartbroken. Yea, I cheated on my wife, but I didn't expect to see all this. It was hard to believe this was the same woman I fell in love with. A woman who helped better myself and now she couldn't help better herself. She started smoking weed and snorting coke even more. Like my Mama, her beauty was going to hell. She was starting to look like a cracked out Grace Jones, the actress. Her ass was flat; her cheekbones looked sunken.

She was stubborn. "*I want my money!* I have been selling pussy for a year. I lie to my own husband, making him think I still work at Bellsouth when I got fired for having sex with half the company. I want my money."

He slapped her so hard she flipped on the ground. I bit my bottom lip, fire in my eyes. I wanted him to whip her ass. I couldn't lie! I didn't know what to think. But the more I sat in the car thinking about this entire so-called marriage, I realized something— that made something on the inside of me die: I only married her because she made me feel good. Because she had a banging body. Because I hit the pussy and it was good pussy. And because her Mama had money.

I turned on the car, rolled up the windows, crank up my music and got on the Turnpike North, heading for my house.

I smoked three blunts and drank some Paul Masson liquor when I got home. Depressed, stressed, and listening to Tupac Shakur. Wallowing in my sadness, I asked myself: What was I going to do with my life? Was this it? Was *this* what life was all about? Money, hoes, pussy, clubs and cars? At about 2 a.m. my wife came home. I pretended to be asleep. She waltzed in the bedroom and shook me until I opened my eyes. She turned on the light and I damn near went blind. She was naked, her sagging tits making my stomach turn. My eyes danced across the track marks on her arms. She was a druggie. I was pissed. I had actually known she started doing drugs, but I was in denial. I didn't want to believe it. I didn't want to think about it. So I worked harder, sold dope from here to West Palm Beach and involved myself in other people's business just so I wouldn't think about it.

I had put the sheet over my face. "I'm trying to sleep. Turn off the lights."

"I want to fuck," she said flatly. No emotion in her voice.

I was angry. "Hell no, Ho! I got to work in the morning."

She was defiant. She refused to back down. "I want some dick…give me some or else." She snatched the sheet from my face.

"Look, bitch." I jumped out the bed and punched the bitch in the face. She flew into the wall. I was naked, dick hanging. I had enough! I had to get out. I was drowning. Thank God we didn't have any kids together. She walked up to me and said, "You don't love me?"

I was in a Catch 22. I cared for her. I seriously had some type of connection with her, that went beyond thought and understanding…but I *wasn't* in love her. I cared about the illusion of a marriage—the *image*. I cared for her because she once believed in me.

"I'm fucked up," she went on. "I can't control my drug habit. I don't love myself. But I *can't* live without you," she said. "I got to tell you something," she went on, and I sat on the bed, burying my face in my hands. I was torn. I hated seeing her suffer. She reminded me of my Mama. In fact she looked like her, the way she looked when she was strung out, when the drugs talked for her, when she gave her sob stories. But this Ho was butt-booty ugly. She wasn't pretty anymore. People picked at her now. Kids thought Halloween kept coming early every time she went outside. How could I make love to her when she didn't turn me on?

I fed into her bullshit. "What do you have to tell me?"

"It's something I should have told you a long time ago. It's the source of my downfall. Why I can't stand myself—why I am so ashamed..."

Damn, she'll do anything to get some money! "What."

Indifferent, she stood up. "Gimme some money! I want to buy some weed and coke. My Niggah Stan sells heroine. I need a fix."

I knew it! Money to support her habit! "That's what you need to tell me?"

Her hands were twitching uncontrollably. "If you give me a hundred dollars—"

I was perplexedly thrown. "—A what?" I glared at her, my hands tight fists. She was insulting my intelligence.

"A hundred." She smacked her lips. It really repulsed me beyond understanding. "Look. My Mama isn't the bitch you were fucking behind my back."

I blinked once. "What? I *didn't* fuck your

Mama!"

She glared at me with a satisfied smirk on her face. "Yes you did. I saw you through the window one time, fucking her in the ass."

Damn it! I remained quiet. Busted. Fuck it, I was a man, stand your damn ground. That was all I could do. "Gladys…"

She spat icily, "Janis is not my mother!"

Smoke and Mirrors Part 2:

I narrowed my eyes. *Damn, what* wouldn't *she say for money? This was all a game and I have to realize that.* "What are you talking about?"

She was laughing bitterly. "…My *real* Mama sold me!" Sparkles lit her sunken-looking eyes. My heart skipped a beat; I wanted to run out of the room. She intimidated me. "Yes, Sir! She needed money for crack; she was on it badly when she was pregnant with me."

She was lying. "What? Your Mama works in law enforcement, Miss Janis Jakes don't even look like she touched drugs a day in her natural life."

She challenged me. "It's true!" I could see

her rib cage and her veins. She looked sick. She walked up to me and hugged me. I couldn't push her off. I sat on the edge of the bed and she was clinging to me. I cringed inside, like I turned to stone. I felt for her. Deep down I wanted to help her. After all she taught me empathy and she taught me how to love people enough to pray for them. I wanted to see her get well, even though I didn't want to remain her husband. She kissed my lips. I didn't move mine.

She sat in my lap and my dick got hard. I couldn't help it. I was so used to her pussy my dick was like a dog—it got excited for the master every time. She slid on my dick. My mouth agape, the warmth engulfed me. Her desire pulsating with the same fire it had when I first got it a long time ago. She rode me, slowly, looking into my face. I closed my eyes tightly, about to throw up, but her drugged-out pussy was good.

She tried to persuade me. "Give...me some...money; you *know* you can't escape this pussy."

She was right! I couldn't. I grabbed her bony ass and fucked her long and hard, squeezing my torso muscles together and made myself nut in about three minutes. Sensation rocking me senseless, I stood up with haste, grabbed her hair in a closed fist and pulled her face to my dick. I wiped come all over her forehead, lips and chin. She licked it up, swallowing every drop. The nut felt good, I couldn't lie. Spent, she lay on the floor, looking up at me, twirling a curl of hair with a bony index finger. She was lost in thought. Fed up, I started emptying out my drawers, throwing my clothes on the floor.

"You're not gonna give me the money?"

I glared at her, disappointed in myself for falling in this sick game. Did I even *know* this woman? Who was she? What happened to my loving wife, that sweet woman who talked me into getting baptized and giving my life to God, the woman with the mother who introduced me to books?

"Hell no! And I'm leaving. It's *over*; I can't see you like this. We both fucked up, doing fucked up shit. I *don't* love you." *Yes I do, love you but not in love with you.*

She was hurt. "Ask me who my Mom was…"

Time to end this game. *"Fuck your Mama!"*

My wife stood up and snatched her purse from the dresser. She pulled out her wallet and opened it. There was a slit on the side. I saw her Driver's License. It read: Gladys Jakes-Sinclair. She pulled out another I.D. She gripped it, looking down at it.

"…People take secrets to the grave everyday."

Suddenly, I was guarded. Backing up from her, I was silent.

"All this for a hundred bucks?" Something was not right.

She said, "I have been lying to your for years."

I swallowed hard. "About."

"My name isn't Gladys."

The breath caught in my throat. "Stay off those drugs!"

She smiled bitterly, fresh tears falling down her face. "I once hugged you so tightly, wanting to *love* you."

"We just had sex, damn. What *more* do you want? Money? Here!" I snatched opened the top nightstand drawer, took out a hundred dollar bill and threw it at her.

She took it and ripped it in two, tossing the bills over her head.

"BITCH! What kinda game are you playing?" I was on my feet, chocking her. I had laser beams in my eyes, sweat popped out of my pores, my dick swinging. She dug her nails in my face and I backed up, blood running down my cheek, dripping from my chin.

"I got on drugs because I couldn't do it! I

couldn't let my Mama do it to me anymore."

I was a monster. "Do *what*? BITCH SPEAK ENGLISH!"

"My Mama isn't a goddamn cop!"

God! The LIES! "I *knew* I shouldn't have fucked your Mama. I *swear*, Gladys..."

"MY NAME AIN'T GLADYS!"

"She came on to *me*. Is *that* why you turned to drugs? Because I slept with your Mama?" My heart bled for her. I was dead ass wrong. I *shouldn't* have done that to her. I could just imagine how she felt when she looked in her Mama's window and saw me freaking Janis Jakes. Her Mama may have been overweight but she had good ass.

"Frank Sinclair, I was at your Mama's funeral…."

I fell into a deep silence, falling into a dark abyss so fast I nearly went blind. The room spun. I couldn't breathe. I had to hold the dresser.

"You're lying."

"Remember. The flowers on my dress. I tried to show you so much love. All I wanted to say was that I knew what you were going through. That I felt your pain. But you angrily pushed me. I was so embarrassed. I ran over and stood by an old man. He sat next to the woman who bought me from my real mother."

Images exploded in my head. The funeral. Of the little girl hugging me. Oh, God! My WIFE WAS THE LITTLE GIRL! I remember pushing her. The red ribbons in her long, resilient hair brought out her amazing eyes. The woman with the police uniform evilly stared at me. "Officer Brown" was on her name tag. What was going on here?

Then my wife's unfinished Diary entry on the dresser came to mind. The words "funeral," "flowers," "stranger." Now made it sense.

I slowly walked up to her. "Tell me everything. How could you have understood my pain? Your Mom is alive!"

She handed me the I.D. On it she was about 14 years old, and the name, "Paula Jakes."

She said, "I couldn't live with myself. My so-called adoptive mother *never* went to court to officially adopt me. She bought me for five hundred dollars. I was a newborn. I wasn't breathing on God's green earth for fifteen minutes before my Mama hawked me off. Janis Jakes raised me. *Janis* is an alias. That's *not* her real name. Her real name is Florida Brown. She worked for the police department for twenty years. She falsified documents…changed her identity and changed mine. My birth name was not Paula Jakes. My father I never met, but I saw him before. He lives right here in town."

"Who is your mother?"

"...Verona Sinclair. Frank, you're my oldest and only brother. You've been married to your sister."

My world exploding, I didn't believe her; I punched her so hard she flew into the wall. I started vomiting all over the floor. My stomach was coming up through my throat. I started punching holes in the walls. I couldn't believe this! Incest? Was she *crazy*? Was *this* why she turned to drugs? Because she was forced to keep this secret? Did Janis or Florida, whatever the bitch's name was, orchestrate this entire thing? Was my father also her father? Oh God! *It made sense!* The rumors of my father having another child were fucking true!

Gladys, Paula, whatever her name was tried to hug me. Suddenly the connection between us made sense, like the final notch latched into place, locking our bloodline and our souls together, forever. I've been fucking my sister? MY GODDAMN SISTER?

She shook with fear. The pain tore through us like fire. I embraced her, kissing her forehead. It wasn't *her* fault my mother sold her for crack. My mother, a woman I respected, despite her downfalls, used to disappear for months on end. She had a baby girl while she was gone; sold her to keep it hidden. My sister being raised by Florida did a number on me. The horror of the entire ordeal weakened me. All the times I prayed for a sibling, a brother or a sister, and I thought God didn't hear me. I looked at her and I was so sorry for hitting her, having sex with her and loving her. This wasn't fair. Why did people do this to human beings? She and I deserved to know the truth.

I made up my mind. "We're leaving town."

She was defiant. "I'm not going anywhere."

Against her will, I picked her up; kicking and screaming, I threw her on the bed, opened my closet and took out duct tape. I sealed her mouth closed; I duct taped her wrists together then her ankles. I picked her up and threw a blanket over her, running out to my car and throwing her in the back seat. It was now 4 a.m. I wasn't worried about work; I would never work there again. I would never see Miami again; my sister would never see Florida the bitch or the state ever again.

I hoped inside and I didn't bother locking my front door. I had lots of money in three bank accounts and about fifteen thousand under the spare tire in my trunk. I owned my house. I'd hire a moving company to ship my things to the state I would live in. North Carolina. I drove for hours, never going to sleep. My sister squirmed the entire time. I left her ass tied up. Fuck it! I was her guardian now. About fourteen hours later I arrived in North Carolina. About to fall asleep at the wheel, I then checked into a hotel. I carried my weak sister, who has pissed and shitted all over herself, into the room. I took out the yellow pages and called a drug rehab center. I told them I found my sister drugged up. They told me to bring her by. I took her. She was suffering from malnutrition. She had to be hospitalized. They put IV drips in her wrist, and she would be there for two months. While she was being nursed back to health I told doctors do not let her out of their sight. I paid them under the table with drug money for their loyalty. Battling feelings of guilt, and being ashamed that I didn't know I was married to my sister, I called a lawyer, told him the situation and I paid him a hefty retainer to discreetly have our marriage annulled. He did it quickly. In a few months we'd be divorced. I then called a moving company and had my things packed and shipped to my new home in Winston Salem, North Carolina. I also called a realtor and had my house put up for sale. A Cuban college student by the name of Hector bought it. $240,000 put into my bank account. I would provide for my sister.

I would be right by her side. She was well rested and after a few weeks she started gaining her weight back. I would stare at her for a long time. As each day passed and she got stronger and the drugs were pushed out of her body, she would start to look more and more like my mother. She had Mama's eyes, nose and chin; she had my Daddy's forehead and beautiful smile. I cried for a long time I silently prayed to God and got my faith back. The mustard seed was growing every day. We would talk and talk, now that the truth about us was out amongst ourselves we got really close. It was hard not to have romantic feelings for each other but we practiced it, and every day it got easier and easier to let those feelings go. After another two months I no longer had sexual feelings for my blood sister.

I was her big brother. For now what I said, went. I had to be her protector. She'd been hurt so much, back when I didn't know she was my sibling, back when she was a "*stranger*" at my, I meant our mother's "*funeral*," with "*flowers*" on her dress. I told the Director of the Rehab Center that she would be there for at least two years.

"I'll be here every day to visit her, to see her progress," I said.

"We went through illegal channels to admit her, Frank," said Dave, the Director. He also did her paperwork. He used "Verona Sinclair" on her papers. I got her a fake I.D. and I knew a man who worked for the Social Security office back in Miami. It was costly, but I was a thug, a hustler, I made moves. He some kind of way got her a new social security card made. With that in mind, never to reveal this to anyone, I closed Dave's office door and handed him an envelope with three grand inside.

I stared into the Director's eyes, with a no-nonsense attitude.

"Silence is golden."

"Why are you doing this to her?" He took the money.

"I never had the chance to save my mother." I smiled, tears falling down my face, having empathy for my sister. After all, she taught it to me. "But I have the chance to *save* my sister. And save her I will." My face got dark, thinking about Florida Brown. "Even if I have to kill for it. I will protect my sister at all costs."

The Director looked at me, with a grin.

He said, "Kill for it?"

I sat down in the chair, lowering my eyes to the desk. "I won't actually do that, but, you feel me, she's my blood."

"Yea, family is important."

We understood each other.

Now I was flipping through the TV channels, sitting in my room, boxes all around me. I needed to unpack, but I didn't have time for that. I was still trying to get used to the beautiful sights of Winston Salem, North Carolina.

A few murders flashed in my face from the TV. An image caught my attention. A police badge had black tape around the center.

"...Miami-Dade Police officer Janis Jakes-Brown was gunned down early this morning as she was leaving her Earlington Heights home...witnesses say a masked gunman ran up to her, just as she got in her Yukon Suburban, and opened fire. He shot her three times in the chest. And once in the head. No suspects in this heart-breaking crime have been found..."

Clad in black silk boxers and a wife beater tank top, I smiled to myself.

"Damn, who did her ass in? Karma, I tell you."

I let a Salem Light cig. I puffed on it, blowing smoke towards the ceiling fan.

"Karma is a bad bitch!"

"And in related news, drug dealer Frank Sinclair, Sr., notorious in the drug world, was also found shot to death in a local Denny's restaurant on Biscayne Boulevard…The F.B.I. have been probing him for months are startled at his murder. Witnesses say a ski masked gun man, clad in a black cargo uniform, rushed inside, and shot him in the head. He allegedly threw a picture of Officer Brown on his table and fled the scene in an unmarked van…"

I was really laughing. *Goddam!* My dad got killed, too? Evil danced in my eyes as I sat in the darkness, with the glow of the tube illuminating me like a vampire.

Driving back to Miami to kill those sick bitches, for hurting me and my sister, was well worth it! I was stubbing out the cigarette. I was in so much pain. Janis watched me marry my only sister, and didn't stop it and she didn't tell us. My Dad didn't stop it and didn't tell us. They kept the secret, hoping it would never get out. I cried for my mother. I forgave her. I also forgave myself. The drugs had her mind gone, she was a victim. It was my Dad that got her hooked on drugs and introduced her to selling pussy. I cried for her being naïve. She was a fool in love. Willing to do anything to keep that man in her life, she put his needs above her own. I wished I could have saved my mother, which is why I was saving my sister.

My sister was right. People die everyday taking *secrets* to the grave. Janis was the prime example of that. Now I was another example. Because this was *one* secret even I was taking to my grave.

Sometimes murderers did get away, what do you think about that, Mr. John Walsh? I continued to ponder as *America's Most Wanted* came on, profiling serial killers. I had to look forward to my divorce.

I was losing a wife but I gained a sister, something irreplaceable. I had to get over loving her, though I would always love and care for her. I would always make sure she was ok.

I was her blood brother.

I laughed myself into a deep sleep.

I was my Sister's Keeper.

He didn't *want* me anymore. Me or my sweet Kitty. It was going to be hard putting this man out of my mind. After all, my Kitty has a mind of her own.

I remembered just last week. Tommy, my husband—well, my soon-to-be-ex husband—

picked me up from work. I left my car parked in the garage at my job. It'd be safe for the night. He took me to the Ramada Inn. When I walked in the Suite there were rose petals everywhere. Sade sung the "Sweetest Taboo" from the radio, the volume turned down low…the lights dimmed, candles flickering everywhere. Those smell good candles. My pussy was in heat and wanted the dick in the kitchen to *stand* it. My titties wanted to get right on down to business. Urgently, my husband picked me up and carried me to the sofa. He lay me down gently and took off my skirt with a hunger I'd never seen before…then my blouse slid past my breasts and navels locked under his teeth. He undid my bra. I lay there. Craving him. Wanting the Big Bang and then Quit It so I could sleep. I thought that's what *he* wanted. All we did was Bam Bam Bam Boom then its over. Never the slow stuff. Yet here we were, doing the slow stuff. How I loved this man! He finally listened to me. Thank, God!

He slowly munched on my velvet room, rolling his tongue across my pulsating, sensitive clitoris. He tongue kissed it for nearly a minute. I went wild, holding his head, my legs spread eagled. My hair in my face, I shivered with delight. He took his time, carefully sucking my work day from my body. Tiny nibbles on my nipples, tongue rolled on my belly button…he gently kissed my thighs, then sucking on my toes…I was self-conscious about the corn on my pinky toe but fuck it, he sucked it like corn on the cob. My stomach was in knots as I squirmed here and there. He was kissing my calves. He then rolled his tongue back to my pussy and ate and ate until I heard a burp.

"There, Daddy is full," he said, taking out his dick, jacking it slowly, making sure it was nice and hard. From the looks of it...Hmm, it was *ready* for Mama…

He did the unthinkable. He rubbed the head of his dick on my pussy like a painter swirling his brush in paint before the brush-to-canvas connection. Felt so good. He was looking down into my tired eyes. My face was a bit sweaty, a bit humid in here. I asked him to turn on the AC.

He said, "I kept it off for a reason…about to get hot in here."

Yes, sir. He continued playing with my pussy. Tommy was a good man from a good family. No, he *wasn't* rich but he was rich in character, treated his women like queens, and loved feminine acting women, women who loved being women. He was so unlike my first husband.

My first husband left me for the...streets.

It took forever to get over him. After months of blaming other people and lashing out at the very one's who I loved, I met my new husband. I used to compare him to my ex husband, and he hated me for it. It took a few months for me to stop. When I saw that he was there for me, I let down my guard. And when he tore this pussy up I let everything down.

Now my new husband left me and my Kitty. He packed his shit and left before I got off work. He changed his cell number and moved with his sister in Alabama. He called my phone from a restricted number and told me he couldn't take not meeting my children, that I had *too* many secrets. I found this odd because I never hid *anything* from him. And I wasn't *comfortable* enough to introduce him to my family. I loved my family more than anything, and I just wanted to make sure that he was Mr. Right before I took such a big step. When I married him my grown kids didn't come to the wedding. They sent me *Get Well* cards and not a *Congratulations* Card. I read one Get Well card and one of my sons wrote, "Get Well soon because you marrying that man will never replace our father!" They thought I was a bitch for replacing their father but they were grown! They had to grow the fuck up and let go that Al Bundy *Married With Children* Dream go and find another dream because Mama would NEVER marry their father again. I had a right to be happy in my life.

Unfortunately, I already knew the *real* reason why he left. I happened to find out when I went to the hair salon to get my hair done yesterday, and it was still burning me up inside. You know how bitches talked. Well, let's just say I found out my soon-to-be-ex-husband cheated on me with a woman I would hate for the rest of my life. It was funny because, as I sat under the hair dryer, looking prim and proper, the bitches talked about me in the second person, making it seem like they were talking about someone else.

I lived in Miami, Florida—congested-ass Kendall, to be exact. This was an upgrade from the Rainbow City Projects I lived for ten years. Back *then*, I had to wash my clothes in the bathtub with my neighbor's water hose pulled through the bathroom window because I didn't have enough to keep my water bill paid. *Then*, roaches were my third and fourth cousins. *Then,* I had to ask people to take me here and there or catch the bus with tons of grocery bags in tow, while trying to rear four sons. *Then,* I used to cry myself to sleep because I was on welfare, couldn't afford to buy my kids anything, and I used my pussy to make ends meet in ways heads and tails on flipping quarters could never fathom. *Now,* I was rolling high. *Now,* I had a 9-5 job with a 401 (k) and benefits. *Now,* I could afford for my kids to live productive lives. *Now,* I drove a Mercedes Benz, paid for. Yet all of that couldn't bring my man back, a man who had been there for me left and right, but he couldn't truly open up and love me because he had too many walls surrounding the soul of his very existence.

I was actually smoking my eighth cigarette, drinking the fourth cup of coffee, marveling over the nineteenth hour in the day because I couldn't sleep, nibbling on the same piece of garlic bread. The spaghetti had gone cold, the meatballs and the sauce looked like hot lava frozen over after the volcanic eruption. My smoothie was watery. The Billie Dee Williams' poster taped to my wall—a poster that has been up for nearly eleven years—irked me. Because, goddamn it, God didn't *make* men like him anymore. The poster was the only memory I brought with me when I moved into this $350,000 condo I got with my military voucher. I had a doctor's appointment at 0900 hours. I missed my Pap smear test last week and with my hectic work schedule I may have to cancel my doctor appointment and call the damn lawyer so I can file for divorce. I had to send some paperwork to Washington D.C. pertaining to my Army discharge. I did six years. And called it a quits. I used the service to elevate myself from the slums. I had to sign the rights to my kids over to my gregarious, too-sweet mother and she reared them while I slaved away making a living for my kids and at the same time doing a public service for a society that didn't give a rat's ass about me or my black children. I did a tour in Japan. I hated it. But it was better than living in Rainbow City!

Yes I was an adult woman, well into my forties when I was supposed to have my shit together. Hell, I didn't. Let's be real. I couldn't even keep a goddamn man! I needed a man to grow old with, someone I could love and nurture. Yet when I found Jimmy, who I dated for a month before I met my soon-to-be-ex husband, I couldn't stop trying to be his a) mother b) Mommie c) Mama and d) Provider. All of the above spelled I. A-M. A-L-O-N-E! And my kids! *Damn it!* My oldest son was a faggot. I didn't give a fuck about GLAAD—The Gay & Lesbian Alliance Against Defamation. If they come to my damn door I'ma shoot each and every one of the crummy assholes; my youngest son was an alleged rapist (now cleared of all charges, thank God). My third oldest son was a woman beater—he had a big problem with taking orders from women. This was *my* fault, he said, because I cursed and beat him so much. Now, any woman he dated that even looked like or *resembled* me he beat their asses—like he was getting back at me and the shit didn't hurt me at all. Just cost his ass a free trip to jail without a Get out of Jail Free Card. This wasn't Monopoly, but you couldn't tell his dumb ass anything. My knee baby was just so fucked up the psych ward didn't even want him. Strapping him to the bed was enough to make the hired help go insane. He actually sat on his ass all day counting tile— one, twooo, *three*, fo', five, six, se-ven, *eight*: NINE, ten blue tiles Mama!

My oldest son, Kendrick, got on my nerves! Always something with this bozo! Seriously. I wished I woulda followed my gut and aborted his ass, or swallowed him when I sucked his daddy's dick back in the day. I would have loved to feel his seed burning from my stomach acid, but I could never have that relief. I was stuck with his ass until the day I died. I knew he was gay ever since he was eight years old.

Out of all the goddamn Smurfs on the old school popular cartoon, he loved VANITY SMURF, with his little scarf and

SMURFETTE! He was Smurfette for Halloween. And he wondered why all the neighborhood niggahs around his age started throwing rocks at his dumb ass. Then out of the blue he started loving Bugs Bunny.

Bugs wore more drag queen shit then the homosexual transvestites tramping all up and down NW 79th Street in Liberty City, not too far from Club Boi, a gay club.

Just when you though he couldn't get any worse, he idolized the Snaggle Puss cartoon. Running around my house chanting, "*To the moon, even!*" drove me crazy. I threw my curling iron at him one morning and it hit him in the head. He looked at me like he lost his mind. I glared at him like I wanted the punk dead! Then He-Man burst onto the TV, with all his...muscles. His...Battle cat and his...Sword. "Mama, He-Man is cute," he once said and his brother threw a Tonka toy at him.

Then it was on to *Jem* is truly outrageous, a rock-n-roll Barbie looking cartoon that focused around music. I shook my head. By then I was at the boiling point. I was getting fed up. As a mother I couldn't explain how I felt to see my son acting like a woman. His brothers hated it. When he started walking around singing, "She-ra She-ra....*I am Sheeee-raaaaa!*" from the popular cartoon—He Man's cousin—I jumped off the sofa and slapped him across the face with the force of a Tech 9. Startled, he ran to his room and I was right on his ass. I kicked down the door, Karate-kicked him on the floor, pounced on my sweet ass son and snatched his ass to his feet.

I couldn't breathe. "Now you listen here goddamn it! I gave birth to a son with a goddamn dick! Not a weak-pussy punk!" I was steamed, embarrassed to even go in public with my son. I was so upset.

He was frightened. Being that he was a kid during the time, I could certainly understand that. I lightened up on him when he started to cry, covering his face, his fragile body shaking. What was a mother to do?

I took my son into my arms and I held him, in tears of my own. Because his father was also a drag queen, selling his body for money.

My ex-husband left me for the streets and the horny men it catered too. All for the love of money. I never understood *what* happened to the man I loved. The man I woulda died for. The man I sometimes sold my Kitty Kat for. Somewhere along the line he went from praising me and my body to wanting to BE ME and *have* my body. He started wearing my panties, then my bras, then my socks. I had tried to work with him, because I was in some serious denial. We even went to counseling. But some things were better left alone. Some shit couldn't be counseled. You had to actually give it to Jesus and hoped he passed it on to God.

Now my oldest son was headed in the same path as his fruity-pebbles-eating Daddy. All my boys had the same father. I always wondered *why* my oldest son turned out to be such a fruit cake. Hell his favorite cereal was fruity pebbles and his favorite drink was anything with fuckin' fruit! It got so bad I stopped buying fruit for my kids. Hell I even went as far as not buying anything with the word FRUIT OF A LOOM on it. I was so serious.

Yet I couldn't think of my oldest son right now. He betrayed me in the worst way possible.

My second oldest son, Man Man, allegedly raped some ghetto trashy girl who teased him about the pussy. She led my son on for months. Had him thinking he was gonna get it. Wore those shorts up her ass, shook her ass at the local DJ's, tramping all up and down the block, dancing suggestively. Her fast ass would suck his dick and stop just before he came and told him, "Your orgasm will be stronger....just do it my way."

Mind you she was only 16. So was my son. The average 16 year old didn't talk or think like this, so I knew deep down in my heart adults in her environment told her about it. She taught my boy how to eat pussy. While I was thinking he was in school getting an education he was skipping school and beating me home before the school called me to tell me he didn't sign in.

So when the rape thing came up I was furious! I tried to tear him a whole new asshole! I beat him with an extension cord until I saw blood. Then I beat him with a broom. Every time I thought I failed as a mother I'd beat his ass some more. I woke up out of a deep sleep, grabbed the cordless phone, went into his room while he slept and beat his muthafucking ass! Dumb bitch! How the fuck could you rape someone? I knew I raised you better than that! I felt helpless. I needed his father to help me, but he was too busy trying to be a woman with titties perkier than my own.

He always told me he didn't rape her. "She's lying on me!" he stammered helplessly, looking at me to save him. Sorry. When the crackers came for you a Niggah hadn't a fucking chance in AmeriKKKa.

I tried to do right by him. I tried to put him on the right path. But he chose to do something else, hanging around those losers he called friends and they abandoned his ass when his face flashed on the TV. I didn't believe him because that was so cliché: I didn't do it. It wasn't me.

Man Man said he hated me, that he would never forgive me for not trusting him, for not believing in him. They had my son in the papers. They didn't give a damn about him being a minor; all they cared about was defaming another black child and destroying his life. I stood behind him, despite it all. He was my bad seed.

Then the bomb dropped. She showed up at my house while I was filming my knee son, Lenox, 14, making his Science project. We say "Knee son" down in these parts, meaning he's the third oldest. When Keonna, the one who my son raped, waltzed in my house without knocking, I set the camcorder down on the dining table, snapped to attention and told the girl, "I don't remember you knocking." She had some nerve!

She was a feisty lil' bitch. "Your son got me pregnant! And I will be putting him on child support. Shit, I'm set! Now I don't even gotta work if I don't want to."

I couldn't believe my ears. "What? You're *set*? My son ain't rich, bitch!"

She wagged her tongue at me. "So what! I can be like my Mama. She got nine kids, and she sits on her ass and collects about $800 a month from the government. I wanna do that. Fuck school. Your son better pay up. Or I will have Uncle Sam and his brother Uncle Cracker at this damn door to collect."

I wanted to shoot this bitch! "Have you *lost* your mind? Is that what you think life is about? Having babies at a young age and collecting checks?"

"*News fa-lasshhh, Lady!* Look around Rainbow City! Poverty! We can't even afford food to eat! My Mama gotta sell her body. Do you think that's fun? Watching all those crackers on TV with those perfect little lives and the Niggahs who did make it out forget where they come from yet want our ghetto dollars brandishing fake ass we-give-back-to-the-hood smiles. Fuck that!"

I was getting real tired of this. Lenox kept tending to his Science project, listening to every word. "Don't cuss in my house."

She laughed real really loud, waving her hands. Her huge Salt-N-Peppa earrings dangled. "House? Chile, please! This is a housing project. The lowest on the totem pole. White people got houses!"

I'm sick of hearing about this white shit. "Don't matter." I was deeply offended. I didn't have much but I loved what God did bless me with." "Don't cuss in my presence."

"Where is your…rapist son? Tell him I'm gonna call the Man and tell them he raped me again he don't start paying me for this baby in my womb."

"You haven't even had the baby yet."

She sassed me. "Don't matter honey! I want money. I got things to buy and niggahs to spend it on. I got the hottest piece of pussy in town! I gotta reputation to withhold."

I had enough. "Withhold? Or uphold?"

"Fuck you." She walked past me, trying to walk up the stairs. "Man Man WHERE ARE YOU RAPIST BOY!"

Rage flashing in my eyes, I grabbed her by the arm and snatched her into my face. I was silent for a moment. I wanted to double T this Ho right in the face! Double T or DDT, shit it was one of them. Old wrestling moves. I was old school.

Defiantly, she snatched her arm back and pushed me on the floor. My head hit the dining table. My son's mouth fell open in shock. Yea, she's real big and bad now. Miss Bad Bitch. Ok, I got you. I saw where you were coming from.

Keeping my wits in check, I staggered to stand up but once I did, I brushed cookie crumbs off my pants suit, put my wig back on my nappy-need-a-perm head and got in her face. Now I was a little woman, about 5 feet 3. This Ho was about 5-9. She looked down at me, with pussy-puller shorts clinging to her ass. Her titties were barely covered by her Ice Cube halter top that looked ghetto made. Her feet were so black I nearly puked and she smelled like hard labor, and I wasn't talkin' about bean picking smells either. She smelled like ass and dick, like she just got through being fucked.

I said this one time. "That ain't my son baby."

She challenged me. "Your son *raped* me, Ho!"

Calmly, taking a deep breath, I looked at Lenox. With a smile. "Go in your room. Mommie about to have grown woman discussions out here."

He left with a humph! When he closed the door I slapped the bitch in the face and she fell to her knees. I snatched her by the little hair she did have and I slapped her again. "Look, bitch! Don't come in my house! You got a case against my son. He raped you; you aren't supposed to be here! But let me tell you one goddamn thing, I'll beat you and your crack head Mama's ass! Don't come in my crib with the bullshit, Ho now get the fuck out! My nerves are bad, I don't need this shit, and I can't even have peace in my life because ya'll keep bullshit at my damn door!"

I let her go. I wanted to kill the bitch with my bare hands!

She jumped up, snappily said, "I'm calling the cops," and waltzed to the door. She paused and looked back at me, some blood on her teeth. She smiled. "Your son really didn't rape me. I told him to stay away from other Hoes. But *no* he cheated on me so I put a rape charge on the dumb bitch! He will never see this baby; I don't want my child knowing this fucked up family!"

And she slammed the door behind her. I just smiled, because I had the Ho on video tape. I couldn't believe the audacity of these black bitches these days. You didn't get what you wanted so that meant you put bogus charges on other people's children, like I didn't love my son as much as her mother loved her.

I took the tape down the prosecutor's office a few days later. I had to actually prepare myself. I really didn't want to talk to a man who thought he knew my son was guilty. Spent the last couple weeks defaming his character, making him out to be villainous monster. I actually believed that was it for my child, that his life would be ruined, that he wouldn't be able to get a job anymore, that doors would close in his face.

But the sun was beaming a little differently today.

The elevator released me on the third floor of a building in Downtown, Miami. I didn't know exactly where I was, but me and my huge K-mart knock-off purse got there with style. After going through the metal detector three times (too much jewelry and my clitoris piercing), I entered the prosecutor's office and walked up to his ditzy secretary, a pretty blonde-haired bitch with pricey clothes and her damn stilettos were killer, damn it I wanted those shoes. I should whip her ass and take them. Bitch couldn't beat me.

"Is Mr. Rodgers expecting you?" she asked me.

"Yes, he is. I have a 1 o'clock appointment."

She looked through the list before her. Damn it gotta do something.

I doubled over, holding her desk, moaning piteously.

She was alarmed, "Ma'am, are you ok?" She rushed over to help me.

I held up my hands. "I'm. Fine. Where's your bathroom, feels like I gotta vomit, oh God I don't feel. So. Hot."

"Right this way…" She told me to go

down the hall and make the first left. I just shook my head. "And when you get back we'll get you in to see Mr. Rodgers."

"Thanks..." I walked down the hall and made the first right, walking past the bathroom and pausing at Mr. Rodger's office door. It was closed. I knocked on it with a smile, more than one way to skin a cat.

He answered. He was tall and handsome, even at 56 years old. Real butt munch. He frowned down at me, not even offering to shake my hand.

He smiled boyishly, brushing hair from his face. "Oh, its you."

I kissed at him and he wanted to puke. "Yes, it is."

"I hope you're not here to save your son. He's going down! The City of Miami wants a conviction."

I yawned, offending him. "Really? The white part of Miami or the ghetto part?"

He held up his hand and let me into his office. "Really."

I entered, taking into account the fancy certificates, the law degrees and the photos. He met a few famous people. There was an aristocratic vibe in the huge office. Overlooking the bums and the beggars below. He looked like the type who frowned down on the less fortunate and wouldn't even give a bum change.

I helped myself to some coffee.

"I have just enough for me to get through the day."

I sipped it. I liked it black, no cream and no sugar either.

Who gives a shit?

"You won't make it through the rest of the day."

He sat on his desk, fiddling with his tie.

"Yes I will. I'm preparing to take your son to court."

My brows rose. "I should make the tax payers spend money."

He smiled again, taunting me. "Well, its money well spent."

I paused before him, pulling out a video tape and handing it to him.

"I find you will watch this. I made a duplicate."

He used a napkin to pick it up, like I had a disease. "What is this?"

"Your ticket to a half work day."

I set the coffee mug on his desk. "On second thought, fuck this nasty motherfucking coffee. Watch the video tape." I sashayed towards the office door. "My son and I will be expecting a phone call from you."

"With the court date, you surely will."

I looked back. “Yes, with a court date, Prosecutor.”

“I’m looking forward to it.”

“So am I.” I slammed the door behind me.

***

Over the next few days my phone didn’t ring at all. In fact the only communication I got from the Prosecutor was a letter sent to my house by messenger informing me that the charges against my son were dropped.

I showed my son the letter, and he was thankful he had his life back. I just hoped he learned from his ordeal.

Because I was his Mama.

I had my own problems.

But that was all in the past. Pushing all of yesterday’s memories to the side, and trying to forget my son was ever allegedly linked to anything. I couldn’t get my ex boyfriend out of my mind. I drove to my doctor’s appointment in complete silence, the Miami scenery zooming by like a huge blurry picture. Tears fell down my face; it took a lot for me to cry. But I couldn’t understand why my man would cheat on me with a bitch I couldn’t stand. I smoked cigarette after cigarette, trying to calm my nerves. They didn't help. I was just in a deep depressed state.

When I got to the doctor's office in Cutler Ridge, by the Southland Mall, I parked in the handicap spot, with no handicap sign on my rear view window, mind you, got out and locked the door. I was walking towards the building when my cell rung. It was Kendrick. Asking me where I was.

I got an attitude. "Why?"

The feminine voice tore me up.

"Mommie, we need to talk."

"About?"

"I'm in jail; I need you to bail me out."

I laughed so hard I had to hold my stomach. "All the tricking you do up and down 79th Street and you want me to bail you out?"

"Yes, Mommie."

"You're a grown man."

"A grown woman, I haven't been a man in fifteen years."

I was deeply hurt when he said that. "Did you go through with your sex change?"

"Yes I did, successfully. Now I'm one of you."

"You will never be one of me; you see I'm a real woman. And check this, bail yourself out of jail."

He began sniffling, in a way that always

got to me. "So you're gonna leave me in here?"

Suddenly I didn't wanna go see the doctor, not in this frame of mind, this is why I needed to move out of Florida, leave my grown kids here by themselves because I had a life and my life was forever surrounded around doing shit for my inept, incompetent children.

"Why are you in jail anyways? Kendrick?"

"It's Keisha, and I'm in jail because an undercover cop said I was soliciting services."

"Good for him."

"We fucked, Mama and when he found out I was really a man he arrested me and denied everything."

"I'll be down to bail you out of jail."

"Are you bringing your boyfriend?"

Unlocking my car I thought about it. "Yes, I will bring him, now that I am thinking about it."

He was in Alabama with his sister; there was no way I could do that.

My son waltzed out of the Dade County Jail House like he was RuPaul. He looked flawless wearing a big pretty wig and his make-up was on point. Shit. He looked better than me, put my old ass to shame. His dress and high heels were to die for. He looked like a complete woman; everything on his svelte, voluptuous frame had been cosmetically altered. He took hormone shots so his voice sounded more feminine than Jennifer Love Hewitt. He had a huge ass, enormous tits and one look at him you would never guess he wasn't really a woman.

"Hey, Mommie, I knew you'd come through for me."

"Yea, good or bad you're my son."

He rolled his eyes, hugging me. "Oh, Mom! *You're* in denial. You'll get over it. I'm in the process of going to court to get my status here in the U.S. changed to 'female,' and have my name changed to 'Keisha James.'"

This burned me up but what could I do? He was a grown man, I meant woman, he had a legal right to do with his life what he wanted, but I was dead set against it.

"Whatever."

He got in my car and closed the door, snapping on the seat belt, turning my stereo to some house music. I turned the shit off.

"This is my car; don't switch my shit like you pay my car note."

"Mommie, quit it, can't we just get along like two girls?"

"Why won't you accept the fact that you are hurting me every time you say that to me, Kendrick?"

"Mommie, I'm not trying to hurt you." I could see the hurt on his face, he wasn't trying to hurt me, that much I did know but my son always wanted to fit in, which was why he turned out the way he did.

"But you did hurt me. And are we leaving the jail house today?"

I smiled at him, squeezing his hand. "Yea, we are. After you clarify something."

His eyes sparkled. "Yes, Mommie, anything."

I showed him a photograph I took from my purse and he smiled really big.

"That's Paul, such a handsome man, how do you know him Mommie?"

"Are you two seeing each other?"

"Yea, for the past eight months we were in a relationship."

My stomach did flips. "Did you tell him you were really a man?"

"Yea and it's like he fucked me that much more when I revealed it to him. He's my heart, my lover man. He hasn't called me in about two days." He looked at me. "I heard about this Tommy man you're seeing, so when are you gonna introduce him to the family?"

"Never. He dumped me a few days ago, moved to Alabama with his sister."

My son hugged me tight and I cried to

myself, I missed Tommy. I really was hoping it worked out with him because I was getting older; I wanted someone I could grow old with, spoil and languish happily. And all of that blew up in my face.

He leaned back and held my hands. "How did you get a picture of my boyfriend?"

"Because his name wasn't Paul. His name was Tommy. You were dating my boyfriend the same time he was fucking me."

My son was so angry he punched my passenger side window from my car, glass shattering, blood everywhere. "I'll kill that Niggah!"

"No sense in getting mad, he moved out of town. I don't have his number or an address."

"Get me to the nearest drug store so I can clean myself up, then I wanna take you somewhere."

"Where are we going?"

"To Alabama."

The End

I want to thank you all for purchasing this book. I gave a few books away free of charge, for promotion and the love already washing back over me feels so good inside. If you wish to get in touch with me or to drop a kind word, or even feed back I can be reached at:

Bacardi_raz305@yahoo.com

Thanks for all the support. And the King of Erotica III: The Sword and Superstars will be finished soon. Much love.

I promise you.
This is only the beginning.

Dapharoah69: Larry Wilson…

http://www.shanibooks.com

The Moon Rises over Deceit

Jadish Houston prepared a fabulous meal for her husband, a man she has never had sex with. After attacking the man who abused her on her graduation night, will she have a night of passion with Sax, or will it disintegrate into him leaving and falling in the arms of another woman? Or potentially, another man?

Miss Freaky Deaky met Naygee on the plane, 40,000 feet above land. With a Golden Mask glittering in her glass cabinet beckoning for another orgy and her foot firmly pressed on the accelerator of her black Impala, once she picks him up from the airport and brings him home, a surprise awaits her. Will she be Freaky Deaky enough to handle it?

Princess finally found the man of her dreams, a man with enough love and sex appeal to get her to abandon her previous profession:

prostitution. With a baby on the way and a best friend, Georgia, growing suspicious of her, will she deliver her baby and happily build her life? Or will a sudden paternity test threaten it all and she potentially lose everything?

Bernice was mauled over by a certain black man with a thirst for deception, porn and being unfaithful to his wife. She is threatening to take him to court and take it all. Will Georgia walk away with everything and give *Beautiful Magazine* to Bernice, or will the estranged Porn Star get sweet, sweet revenge and both women wind up with nothing?

Clever just wanted to live out her dreams; she has been tricking women into lesbian action for years. Until Rayne taught her a lesson. Now her fantasy is ruined. Will she move on with her life and find another obsession, or will she pay Rayne a visit, that could be sexual and deadly?

Kendrick never liked his mother, and he, clad as a Drag Queen, wants to go to court to have his name changed. Will he go through with what his heart desires, or will he and his mother go to Alabama to confront a man, Tommy who once fucked them both for sexual gratification?

Fate Williams and Red share love, life and certain past involving the same man. With news of their sons bring blood brothers, and Fate Williams feeling deceived, will she remain with her lesbian lover, or will her evil, cunning mother, who is in love with her own daughter threaten it all?

Ted Oxford married for all the wrong reasons, his wife turning into the nightmare of the century. Driven by his anger and being betrayed and devastated that his best friend screwed his wife, will he get revenge by going over to a dear friend's house? Or will he come face to face with a set up so startling that even he fights to keep his sanity?

All the answers and more coming soon in *The King of Erotica 3: The Sword.*

The King of

I represent

Goulds & the Rolle Family

I am a writer

Deal With It

The King of Erotica

www.ingramcontent.com/pod-product-compliance
Lightning Source LLC
Chambersburg PA
CBHW030813310726
48980CB00006B/484/J

* 9 7 8 0 6 1 5 1 5 3 0 8 7 *